Believe in Me

A Rosewood Novel

Believe in Me

A Rosewood Novel

LAURA MOORE

BALLANTINE BOOKS • NEW YORK

A Ballantine Books Mass Market Original

Published in the United States by Ballantine Books, an imprint of The Random House Publishing Group, a division of Random House, Inc., New York.

BALLANTINE and colophon are registered trademarks of Random House, Inc.

This book contains an excerpt from the forthcoming book *Trouble Me* by Laura Moore. This excerpt has been set for this edition only and may not reflect the final content of the forthcoming edition.

ISBN 978-1-61129-365-4

Cover design: Lynn Adreozzi
Cover illustration: Franco Accornero

Printed in the United States of America

To all the women; you know who you are

Prologue ❧

"AND HOW DO YOU FEEL, Jordan? Do you believe Richard's been doing everything he can to prove his commitment to making your marriage work?" Abby Walsh asked in a voice that conveyed just the right blend of sympathy, compassion, and reserve.

Indeed, everything about Dr. Abby Walsh, her smooth, lineless face, sleek silver bob, her wardrobe consisting of muted silk and jersey knits, was designed to soothe. As was her office's light sand and dove gray palette, with its requisite black leather sofa and matching armchairs, Joan Mitchell–like paintings and Tang dynasty ceramics—reproductions, Jordan assumed, but maybe not, considering Abby's hourly rate for couples therapy—and the dried arrangement of star flowers and corkscrew and pussy willow in a tall, raku vase positioned in the corner of Abby's T Street office in Washington, D.C. Even the boxes of Kleenex were positioned just so on the amoeba-shaped coffee table to mop up untidy tears.

For the past ten months, she and Richard had been coming once a week to this office to discuss with Abby Walsh their feelings and their progress in rebuilding their marriage, ever since Jordan had discovered that Richard was cheating on her with an associate from his lobbying firm when she was pregnant with their third child. She had come to despise this room as much as she now loathed being asked how something "made her feel."

As Jordan had discovered in the months following his

betrayal, her feelings were pretty much like the floral arrangement in the raku vase sitting in the corner: dry and brittle. Every time she was asked to bring them out in the open for Richard and Abby to poke at, they crumbled into sorry bits of dust.

"Jordan?" Abby prompted.

"Hmm? I'm sorry." She shifted on the couch and tucked a stray lock of hair behind her ear. "Olivia had a bad night. What was the question?"

"You see," Richard said, leaning forward on the sofa, intent on Abby. "Every time *I* talk about us, she brings up the children. It's like she wants to remind me of what a failure I am."

"I'm not saying that you're a failure, Richard. I know you love the children and that you want to be a good father. I'm simply saying I'm tired because Olivia's colicky. She didn't fall asleep until two this morning." And then five-year-old Kate and three-year-old Max were up at six, raring to go, and Richard had already left for the gym to get a workout in before a breakfast meeting with his team of associates.

"Right, sure," he huffed, crossing his arms. He was wearing one of his charcoal gray pinstriped suits.

Was it in this jacket's pocket that she'd discovered the condoms that exposed his infidelity? Try as she might, Jordan couldn't suppress the memory that flashed in her mind, of her in the bedroom of their townhouse, clutching the jacket she was taking to the dry cleaners, staring stupidly at the foil squares she'd found in the inner breast pocket. They'd practically glowed, sizzling hot with their bright alarm-red packaging. The shock of finding them was so great, she'd had to read and reread the word *Love* printed in big, bold letters across the packaging, underneath the promise of extra lubrication, before she actually understood what she was looking at. They'd been so absurd-looking. How funny that they'd managed to shatter a marriage of nine years.

"I get it," Richard continued. "You want to drive home

the point that I didn't do my share last night and rock
Olivia to sleep? Well, I'm *sorry* that I have to work sixteen
hours a day to provide for our family and pay the mortgage
on our house. I'm *sorry* nothing I do satisfies you. Do you
see what I have to deal with here, Abby? I'm constantly being judged and found lacking in everything I do."

Jordan massaged her forehead. "That's not true. I don't
blame you for your job or its demanding hours. I've never
complained about the long workdays you have to put in at
Hudson and White. It's that you chose to pad those hours
sleeping with Cynthia Delaroux—"

"I can't believe it. I feel like I'm on a merry-go-round.
How many times do I have to say it? Cynthia and I are
over. I'm fully committed to you and the kids. I love you.
What more do you want from me?"

Richard wasn't the only one who was tired of saying the
same thing over and over again. "I want to be able to trust
you again. I want to believe that when you kiss me it's because you really love me." Because these days even his most
casual caress struck her as calculated.

"Why in hell would I kiss you or touch you if I didn't
want to?"

"I don't know," she said for the millionth time since last
November. It was true. Jordan felt like she didn't know anything anymore. When Richard broke her heart, her sense of
trust—her sense of everything—was destroyed. She doubted
herself as much as him. She hated that. Even more she hated
that these sessions had become a weekly competition between them, where she reminded him of the myriad ways
he'd hurt her, and he accused her of being cold and unfor-
giving. She hated that every week she walked out of Abby
Walsh's office half-convinced Richard was right. She hadn't
always been like this. They hadn't been like this.

"I think what Jordan's saying, Richard, is that she wants
the kind of relationship you two enjoyed before, and I can
tell how hard you're trying to make that happen for her."

On his side of the sofa, Richard nodded his sandy blond head energetically as if he were at a meeting with one of his clients.

"And while you two may not perceive it, I do feel real progress is being made here." Abby paused to uncross and recross her legs. Jordan noticed she was wearing Fendi gray suede pumps this week. She had really good legs. Richard had once said in passing that Abby was one very hot sixty-year-old shrink.

He hadn't mentioned *she* was hot in God knows how long. But then he'd never been turned on by her breast-feeding the babies, and Olivia was only two and a half months old, so Jordan would be wearing her nursing bra for a few more months. At least she'd lost most of the baby weight. Nothing like major stress to melt away those unwanted pounds. Given the choice, however, Jordan would have much preferred being fifteen pounds heavier and knowing her husband loved her.

She sighed, shifting again on her square of the sofa only to realize with dismay that Abby had been talking the whole time and she didn't have the foggiest idea what she had said. She really would have to take a nap before heading to Rosewood later.

"I know how hard it's been with Olivia, with her feeding and her erratic sleeping schedule. What are your plans for the coming weekend? It's supposed to be beautiful. Getting away might provide a nice break from the daily routine," Abby said.

"Actually, we're going away," she replied as Richard simultaneously answered loudly, perhaps hoping his comment would get into Abby's notes for the day, "Some break, going to Rosewood and being surrounded by your sisters and their constant disapproval."

Jordan stiffened. "The only reason they disapprove is because you hurt me. And they've been making every effort to forgive you. They're pleased you're coming." Okay, that was an exaggeration. Her sisters, Margot and Jade, were willing to tolerate Richard's presence for her and the children's sake. As for Travis, Margot's husband, Jordan still remembered how, after learning of Richard's infidelity, he'd taken her aside and offered to "fix" him for her. He'd been as fiercely protective as any brother and she would always love him for that.

"How magnanimous of them." He drummed his fingers on the arm of the sofa. "I love that my morals are being judged by a fashion model, her redneck husband, and a surly, delinquent teenager."

"Richard, I don't think that's a productive attitude. Surely you can—"

Jordan cut off Abby's gentle admonition. "My sisters are pretty damned fantastic," she snapped. "Margot has almost single-handedly gotten my family's home and farm out of debt with her modeling and Jade has had to deal with the tragedy of losing both her parents in a horrific accident. I would hope you'd understand how a scared and confused teenager can behave stupidly. And Travis is one of the most talented horsemen in Virginia."

"He acts like he'd enjoy castrating me," he said defensively. Though he would die before admitting it, Jordan knew her brother-in-law intimidated him.

But she wasn't going to let him attack her family after all they'd done for her. "You know, Richard, you might find your own family a bit judgmental if you ever told them about your affair with Cynthia. Instead you've kept them in the dark. You don't even want me to talk to our friends about what's going on, so how can you blame me that I turn to my sisters for support when I'm about to explode from all this stuff churning inside me? Or do you want me to have no one?"

"Easy there, settle down," he said, holding his hands up as if to halt her outburst. "You know I like your sisters, babe. I'm just sick of dealing with their negativity. And the reason I haven't told my family about what we've been going through is simple. I don't want to worry my folks when I know that you and I are going to work this thing out and that our marriage will be stronger than ever for it. In the same vein, what possible advantage could there be in airing our dirty laundry to our friends? Why would I want you hurt more by the inevitable speculation?"

It was hard to stay angry when he sounded so reasonable. His hand, which only seconds ago had warded her off, dropped to the middle cushion of the sofa and slid across the leather to cover her clenched one. "I was a stupid idiot last year. I don't ever want to hurt you again. I love you." His warm hand squeezed hers.

Jordan looked at him, searching for any hint of insincerity. But Richard's hazel gaze was level, and when he smiled, his expression was warm and open. In that moment Jordan glimpsed the man she'd promised to love and cherish, for better or for worse. Hope flickered and caught. *God, please let us find a way back to loving each other.*

"Well, I think it's easy enough to understand Richard's point of view here," Abby said approvingly. "I can't stress how important it is during this period of rebuilding your relationship that you be aware of each other's needs."

"Yes, I guess it is," Jordan agreed softly.

Richard's mouth twitched and then spread into an inviting grin. For a moment it was as if they were newly wed again. She gave a small answering smile.

Abby spoke. "Our time's nearly up for today. As I said before, I think you two are making some real progress. Now, let's go back to your weekend plans. It's great you're getting away. Your family home, Rosewood, is in Warburg, Virginia, isn't that right, Jordan?"

She nodded. "Yes, near Upperville."

"Are you driving there tomorrow or on Saturday?"

"Jordan and the kids are going this afternoon. I'll drive

up tomorrow after work. I wish I could take the day off but I'm swamped with projects."

"Well, you'll be there for the weekend," Abby said easily. "So here's what I'd like the two of you to concentrate on while you're at Rosewood. Jordan, as you'll be arriving first, it's going to be your job to lay the groundwork. I'd like you to take shameless advantage of your sisters and ask them to watch the kids so that you and Richard can steal away and spend some time together. Go out and take a walk, shop, have a candlelit dinner at a nice restaurant—whatever strikes your fancy. And when you're alone together, don't talk about the children or what you've been going through these past months. I want you instead to pretend that you're two people on a first date, just learning about each other. Use this time to *relearn* what attracts and excites you about this person you're with." She smiled. "I think you're both going to be surprised at what you find. We'll talk about it next week."

Jordan loved Rosewood. In the spring the stately Greek Revival mansion and its three-hundred-acre horse farm, set in the rolling hills of Loudon County, Virginia, were especially glorious. The fields were colored bright green, the towering chestnut trees of the allée that led up to the house were in full bloom, the heady scent of lilacs and viburnum sweetened the air. In the nearby pastures the newborn foals with their spindly legs frolicked while their mothers nibbled on the tender grass.

With the birth of her own baby girl, Jordan had missed the foaling season, a magical time. On the drive to Warburg, their first trip since Olivia's birth, Kate and Max were unable to contain their excitement at the prospect of seeing the new crop of Rosewood Farm's babies.

When Jordan pulled up in the minivan, her sisters, Margot and Jade, and Travis came out of the main barn to greet them. For several minutes a happy confusion reigned, punctuated by hugs and exclamations. They were a horse family; no one was the least surprised to hear Kate and Max clamoring for the top two items on their wish list: a visit to the pasture to see the newborn foals, and a riding lesson on Doc Holliday, their aunt Jade's old pony.

Ned Connolly, who had begun working with Rosewood's horses back when Jordan's grandfather was alive, came out of the broodmares' barn to say hi. Hearing their excited pleas, he offered to take them and Jordan down to the pasture to see the foals with their dams and then afterward to "help" Kate and Max groom and tack Doc. By the time they'd finished brushing and saddling him, Jade would have finished riding Mistral and would be ready to give them a lesson.

Ned had been wonderful about introducing Kate and Max to the foals that afternoon. When they'd gone to bed that evening, they'd wanted to forgo reading a story in order to talk about the new additions to Rosewood Farm.

And now he'd made their morning as special as Christmas by coming to the house at breakfast and inviting Kate and Max to walk the broodmares and their foals out to their pasture with him. The old man's generosity, and his willingness to slow his day's schedule so they could watch the fuzzy-coated foals as they and their dams were led from the broodmares' barn to the pasture's gate, moved Jordan beyond words.

"You are very kind to us, Ned. Thank you." The grateful kiss she gave his weathered cheek left him blushing.

"I remember doing the same for you, Miss Jordan, when you were no bigger than little Kate here," he said, his voice gruff. Then, as if afraid she might thank him again, he'd hustled them all down to the broodmares' barn.

"Ned, what's this mommy's name again?" Kate asked, tugging on his sleeve as he walked the jet black mare and her foal out into the morning sunshine.

"This here's Night Wing and her colt's name is Night Watch," he answered. "He's a fine-looking one, don't you think, Max?"

Max nodded enthusiastically. "I like the white on his nose."

"That's what we call a blaze. I've seen a picture of his sire, his daddy. He had the same one . . ." Endlessly patient, Ned talked to them about each mare and foal they led down to the pasture, explaining about the colors of the foals' coats and how they'd change as the horses matured. By the time they'd made the final trip down to the pasture, Kate and Max were chattering like magpies about how Ventura's colt, Turner, would turn into a gray whereas Night Wing's colt, Night Watch, would end up the same shiny black as his mother. And Sava's filly, Valentine, would remain chestnut.

While Olivia napped in the Snugli Jordan had strapped on, Jordan and the kids spent the morning watching the foals cavort, racing over the fields on their tiny hooves and long, matchstick legs, bucking and squealing while their dams grazed. Now and then one of the mares would wander over to the fence to have her head and neck scratched, prompting her curious foal to come over, too. Kate and Max held their breath in delight to see it poke its nose through the wooden rails and sniff at their tummies.

Though Jordan was careful to remind them of Ned's instruction to remain quiet around the foals so as not to spook them, the warning was unnecessary. Even three-year-old Max had taken the lessons to heart.

Tearing the children away from their prime spot by the pasture was no easy feat. Only the reminder that they needed to eat a good lunch if they wanted another lesson aboard Doc Holliday could get them to loosen their hold of the fence's bottom rail. Still, their feet remained rooted. Seeing their obvious reluctance to leave, Jordan didn't hesitate to play her trump card. If they were extra well behaved and went back up to the house with Mommy and Olivia now, she'd ask Ned if they could help him bring the foals in from the pasture later in the afternoon. Like magic, their short legs began moving in the direction of the house.

Back inside, she nursed Olivia, changed her diaper, and then hustled the kids downstairs to help Ellie Banner, the housekeeper, prepare a lunch of sandwiches and soup, and a green salad for Margot, who was still modeling. Margot and Travis, and Jade, who had the day off from high school, would be coming in from working with the horses.

The kitchen was buzzing with activity when the others joined them. The children were putting napkins on the long kitchen table, Ellie was settling Olivia into her Kangarocka-roo baby seat, and Jordan was at the kitchen's granite island, chopping onions and celery to make a stuffing for the turkey she was roasting for that night's dinner.

"Hey, guys," Margot said, peeling off a sweater she'd been wearing and draping it over the back of her chair. "That soup smells delicious. And you smell pretty great, too," she said to Olivia as she kneeled down to kiss her.

"Would you mind watching her, Margot? I just heard the timer go off. I need to go and put the wash in the dryer," Ellie said.

"Of course. Here, let's put Olivia up on the table so we can all enjoy her."

"She is kind of cute when she gets those legs and arms going," Jade said. "I'm starved. Wow, that is a major turkey," she added as she eyed the bird resting on the kitchen island. "You going to eat all that, Max?"

He shook his head violently. "No, it's for Daddy."

"Daddy loves turkey," Kate pronounced, saving the grown-ups from having to comment on Richard's arrival. "And Mommy's going to bake brownies and peanut butter cookies 'cause everybody likes them."

"We sure do, don't we, Travis?"

"Yeah, pretty much, though I really like Margot's frozen

yogurt and granola desserts, too." He grinned at Jade's instant exclamation of disgust.

"Thank you, Travis." Smiling, Margot walked around to his chair to kiss him lightly. "Can I get you a cup of coffee with your sandwich and soup?"

"Yes, please," he said, looping an arm about her waist and snagging another, longer kiss before letting her move off to the counter.

It was great to see Margot and Travis's love for each other. Maybe the day would come when she and Richard would be that close again, Jordan thought, as she turned around to the sink to wash her hands. The memory of the warm, teasing light in Richard's eyes when he'd held her hand during their session at Abby Walsh's office filled her with optimism. Maybe she and Richard *had* turned a corner. And while a part of her might never understand how Richard could have cheated, she loved him. Lord knows she was tired of being angry at him. She was ready to forgive him and put the past ten months behind them.

It was spring, the season of rebirth. Maybe being here in the beautiful house that had been in her family for generations would serve as the spark to rekindle their relationship.

"So where are you planning on going with Richard tomorrow night?" Margot asked as she filled the coffee cups and carried them to the table. "No, you stay with Olivia, Jade. I'll bring your food over," she said when Jade made to rise.

"I was thinking of the Coach House."

"Mmm, good choice. Travis took me there a couple of weeks ago. It was delicious. And the dining room is lovely." Margot ladled soup into three mugs and then carried them over to the table. After setting down a plate of sandwiches for Jade and Travis, she went to the fridge and retrieved a salad to eat with her soup.

Having finished chopping the chestnuts and vegetables, Jordan mixed them into a bowlful of breadcrumbs and added a small amount of boiling water and melted butter. Setting the stuffing aside, she lifted the turkey onto the cutting board and patted it dry. "So you're sure you don't mind watching the kids tomorrow night?"

"Of course we don't. And you don't have to bribe Travis and Jade with brownies, either."

"Yeah, you do," Jade said, her cheeks bulging with her ham and cheese sandwich. "You've got Ellie trained never to make brownies, which is grossly unfair. Besides, Jordan's are the best in the world. Aren't they, kids?"

From her workstation at the granite island, Jordan listened to her children enthusiastically second and third the excellence of her brownies and cookies. After this hellish year, which began with the deaths of their father, RJ, and Jade's mother, Nicole, it was wonderful to see her sisters and her children gathered around the table. While Margot and Travis simultaneously confirmed Max and Kate's judgment that yes, their mom could bake yummy treats like nobody else, Jade, who was munching on her second ham and cheese sandwich with one hand, rocked Olivia in the Kangarockeroo with the other. Olivia liked it, kicking and squirming with the contented serenity of a third child.

This was good. And somehow she just knew the entire weekend would be good, too. Smiling, she looked down at the large turkey before her. Richard would be tired and hungry when he arrived that evening. She really had to get this sucker in the oven or it wouldn't be ready in time.

She pulled the bowl of stuffing closer to the turkey and gave it one last toss to make sure the chestnuts were evenly distributed.

Carrying two refilled mugs of coffee back to the table, Margot resumed their conversation. "You should think of what you and Richard might like to do in addition to dinner over the weekend. We're completely free—" She was interrupted by the ring of the telephone. "Hey, Travis, can you answer—"

"It's okay. I've got it." Jordan turned and crossed over to the other counter where the telephone sat in the corner. "Hello?"

"Hey, babe, it's me. You weren't picking up on your cell."

"Richard, hi! Sorry, I must have left my phone upstairs when I was changing Olivia. It's Daddy," she said to the kids, then held out the receiver so he could hear their happy cries of "Hi, Daddy!"

Putting the phone back to her ear, she said, "Kate and Max had a terrific morning. I'll pass the phone so they can tell you all about it. I'm stuffing a turkey for tonight's dinner to celebrate our first weekend away since Olivia's birth. When do you think you'll get here?"

"Oh, babe. You're roasting a turkey for me?"

She smiled. "Well, not *just* for you, but mainly—"

"Thing is, I can't make it to Rosewood for dinner tonight."

"Oh, Richard!" She couldn't hide her disappointment.

"I know and I'm really sorry. But we're drafting this proposal for a new client—a huge account, babe—and the company just called and said they want to move our meeting up to Monday, so the you-know-what's really hit the fan. I'm pretty sure if I work late, I can get this thing in decent shape. Then I'll grab a few hours of sleep and set out for Rosewood tomorrow bright and early. That'll still give us time together and I won't be preoccupied by office work hanging over me. I'll be able to focus on you, Jordan. On us."

She drew a deep breath. She wasn't going to make him feel worse by complaining. She knew how important his work was. "Of course, I understand. But make sure you get some sleep before you drive."

"I will. Maybe you and I can take a nap once I reach Rosewood."

She felt her cheeks warm. Richard and she used to steal away for "naps" in the beginning of their marriage. Very little sleeping had been involved. "I talked to Margot.

They're fine with watching the kids by the way. I thought we might go to dinner at the Coach House."

"Great idea. We haven't been there in years. Listen, babe, I gotta get back to this leviathan."

"Oh, sure. You want to say hi to the kids?"

"Definitely."

She passed the phone first to Kate and then Max, listening as they told him about the baby horses they'd seen. After they'd said, "Bye, Daddy," she took the receiver back. "As you can see, they're having a great time. But we all miss you."

"Same goes for me. I'll see you tomorrow. Bright and early, I promise."

"Okay. Bye, Richard."

Placing the receiver back in its cradle, she turned back to the turkey. Oh well, she thought with a small sigh, Richard liked cold turkey, too, and she could always reheat the stuffing. She grabbed a drumstick to hold the turkey steady, scooped up a generous handful of stuffing and inserted her hand into the turkey's cavity. At her elbow the phone rang again.

Damn it! "Hey, could one of you get that?" she asked, unwilling to pick up the receiver with raw turkey on her hands.

But her request went unheeded as chaos erupted around the kitchen table: Max knocked over his cup of milk; Olivia, deciding the baby seat was hell on earth, started wailing in outrage; and Kate suddenly realized she needed to go peepee. The refrain of "Mommy, Mommy!" echoed around the kitchen.

The heck with it, she decided. The kitchen phone had an answering machine they routinely used to screen calls.

Hurrying to the sink to wash her hands she called out, "Just coming, sweeties," but stopped as Richard's amplified voice came over the answering machine's speaker device. Why was he calling again? Had he forgotten to tell her something? "Shh, guys, be quiet for just a sec. It's Daddy. I need to hear what he's saying." She walked over to pick up the phone.

"There. It looks like you and I have another night together, Cyn."

She froze, her hand mere inches away from the receiver. What was going on? Richard wasn't talking to her. Had he pressed the redial button on his phone by mistake?

"So she believed the story about your needing to work late?" The voice was a woman's. *Cyn . . . Cynthia.*

"Yeah. I only wish I could fix it so I could have an excuse to spend the entire weekend with you. Damn, I can't wait to make partner. I am literally counting the days when I can tell her it's over for good. Until then I'm just going to have to make Jordan believe I'm shooting for Hudson and White's MVP award."

Richard's laugh, joined by a second, higher one, filled the kitchen. Then came his husky command of "Come here, Cyn baby. That wraparound dress has me hungry for lunch. Yeah, that's it. Sit yourself right down. Oh God, baby, you have the finest tits." A muffled, suckling sound followed.

A new noise crowded out the ones coming over the answering machine. Jordan couldn't figure out where it was coming from. Everything was so strange all of a sudden, so difficult to process.

She saw the shock stamped on Margot, Travis, and Jade's faces but it only vaguely registered. And she couldn't comprehend why they were suddenly springing into action, why Travis was scooping Max out of his booster chair and racing out of the kitchen with the toddler, or why Margot was bending over the baby seat, fighting with the straps to free Olivia. Cradling the baby, she grabbed hold of Kate's hand and rushed out, too, shouting something to Jade as she went that Jordan couldn't make out. That awful noise, like an agonized keening had grown intolerably loud. It ricocheted off the walls.

Then Jade was running over and wrapping her arms

about her, holding her tight, which was just as well, as the bones in Jordan's legs seemed to have liquefied. Together they crumpled to the kitchen floor.

The kitchen was empty save for her and Jade. She wanted to leave, too. The noise was unbearable. The high, rending wail rocked the walls, pummeled her brain.

Make it stop. Jordan rocked, clutching her ears to block out the sound. But it kept coming, on and on and on.

And even after her throat was raw, her vocal chords lacerated, the cry continued mercilessly inside her.

Chapter
ONE

Eleven months later . . .

JORDAN RECHECKED HER MAKEUP. Thanks to Kristin, a stylist friend of Margot's, she had become an expert in the uses of concealer. She'd learned not only how to erase the violet smudges beneath her eyes, but also how to use blush and the right hues of lipstick to emphasize her cheekbones and mouth. By employing a subtle mix of tones around her eyes, she'd discovered that she could fool people into thinking that the shadows lurking in them were exotic, mysterious, rather than a darkness that threatened her soul.

She raised her ringless hands to smooth her hair, which she'd decided to wear loose today. Better to look feminine than professional: in Nonie Harrison's world not too many women actually worked.

Rising from the small bench in front of her vanity table, she checked the floral print crepe de chine skirt and ivory sleeveless silk knit top in the mirror and wondered what was missing. Jewelry, of course. She bent down and opened a square leather case and found a pair of antique gold earrings that had belonged to her mother and a delicate diamond pendant that Margot and Travis had given her for Christmas.

There, she looked understatedly elegant, exactly how Nonie would expect Jordan Radcliffe to appear. Meet people's expectations and they rarely bothered to look deeper.

No need to take a sweater or a light jacket, she thought,

as she picked up her purse off the white bedspread. It was a glorious spring day . . . wasn't that funny, how the days had slipped by? The Virginia air was mild, sweetened with the perfume of sunshine-kissed flowers. This year's crop of foals was frolicking in the pastures with their dams. The breeding season was upon them. Nocturne, the stallion they had standing at stud, was eager to meet his mares in the breeding shed. All around her Rosewood was bursting with life. How sadly out of step with the farm she was, so blighted and dead inside. But that, too, Jordan had learned to conceal from the world.

She left her room on the third floor and went into the adjacent attic bedroom shared by Kate and Olivia, a smile lighting her face. Olivia and Miriam Banner, their housekeeper Ellie's niece, were sprawled on the pale blue and pink hooked rug building a tower with Olivia's cardboard nesting blocks. As soon as Miriam placed the last block atop the slender pyramid, Olivia lurched to her feet and kicked the tower with a happy cry.

"Hi, there, Olivia," she said.

At the sound of her voice, Olivia's face lit up and she tottered over on stubby legs, her short arms held out—a blond, mini-Frankenstein with a cherub's smile.

Jordan scooped her up and kissed the sweet hollow of her neck. "Let's get you changed so you'll be nice and clean when you and Miriam go and pick up Kate and Max at school, okeydokey?"

Miriam rose to her feet. "I can do that—"

"That's okay. I've got her," she replied, already setting down her purse. She laid Olivia upon the changing table, pulled down the elastic waistband of her blue-and-cream-striped leggings, and undid the tabs on the diaper. Moving with the precision of a pit stop mechanic at the Indy 500, Jordan shucked the diaper, dropped it into the garbage pail by her feet, cleaned Olivia with a baby wipe, sprinkled her bottom and thighs with baby powder and, for good measure, her rounded tummy, too, and then fastened a fresh diaper. Up went the leggings, down went the dancing dog printed T-shirt, and Olivia was good to go.

"All done," she announced, hefting her powder-fresh baby in her arms. "Now, Miriam, are you sure you're okay with picking up Kate and Max?"

"Absolutely."

"Okay. I left the minivan's keys on the tray in the front hall. For lunch there's mac and cheese. It's in the fridge, wrapped in foil. For dessert you can—" she stopped in mid-sentence at Miriam's grin.

"It's cool, Jordan, I've got the routine down. We'll be fine. Remember, you're only going out to lunch. It's not like you'll be away for a week."

The thought of being separated from her children for an entire week made her slightly faint. "I'll be back by three. If you could get Max to nap when Olivia goes down, that would be great. Tell him if he does, he'll have a better riding lesson with Jade. And I have my cell in case you need me."

"Of course you do," Miriam nodded gravely. "And in case all the satellites get taken out by an asteroid, Aunt Ellie might be able to give me a hand. Don't know whether I can count on Margot coming to the rescue, though, since after lunch she'll be all the way down at the main barn."

Jordan managed a weak laugh. "Right. Thanks for the reality check."

"Have a good time at lunch. You'll knock Mrs. Harrison off her feet, I'm sure. Now, give Mommy a kiss bye-bye, 'Liv, and then you and I are going to build the biggest tower ever."

"Bye, bye," Olivia said.

Bless her for being a happy, carefree baby and not a neurotic mess like her mother, Jordan thought, squeezing her daughter tight and kissing her cheek.

"Okay, all I have to do is grab my tote with the fabric swatches I picked out for Nonie, and I'm gone, really."

"Good. So go already." Miriam shooed her off with a grin before dropping down to the rug to play with Olivia.

She took the back staircase down to the kitchen. As she'd hoped, Margot was there, fixing an overstuffed sandwich for Travis and a salad for herself.

Margot looked up. "Hey," she said, smiling. "You look great. Too bad you're wasting such a pretty skirt on Nonie Harrison."

"Mmm, that looks delicious." She picked up a pitted black olive from Margot's salad and popped it into her mouth. "And the outfit won't be wasted on Nonie. I wouldn't get past her front door, let alone be considered for the job of decorating her guest house, if I were to show up for lunch dressed in mommy gear. Even with my hair bushed, lipstick applied, and my blouse free of baby drool, it'll be a minor miracle if she gives me the commission."

Margot picked up a knife and sliced the thick sandwich in half. "Why wouldn't Nonie pick you? It'll probably take all of ten minutes of listening to your ideas to recognize how good you are. If she doesn't hire you, it won't be because you can't do the job. It'll be because she's jealous that you're beautiful and talented."

Jordan laughed. "That's sweet of you. But we're talking about *me*. Let's remember who's the successful model here."

Her sister stopped crumbling goat cheese on top of the salad to glare fiercely at her. "You of all people shouldn't buy into that hooey, Jordan. I'm not any more beautiful than you—or millions of other women. The reason I'm successful as a model has nothing to do with my being especially beautiful and far more to do with the fact that the distance between my earlobe and my jawline is just so and my eyes happen to be spaced exactly thus far apart." She held out a cheese-coated thumb and index finger to indicate the width before picking up the crumbled mound and scattering it over the dark greens. Salad finished, she took the thick sandwich she'd made for Travis and transferred it onto a plate. "I'm paid ridiculously good money because of a lucky roll of the genetic dice and because my face happens to photograph well. Oh, and also because I haven't let even a crumb of one of your 'death by chocolate' brownies pass my lips no matter how much I've craved a bite. Big whoop," she said with a bored sniff.

Grabbing a bag of potato chips and dumping a small mountain of them next to Travis's sandwich, she continued. "What I do doesn't take any talent. I only wish I could be like you—you've always been able to make things beautiful. Remember when we were little? How on rainy days you'd go upstairs and rearrange all the rooms in that Victorian dollhouse Mama gave you? Remember the wallpaper and the slipcovers you made for those teeny sofas and chairs?"

"Margot, that was child's play."

"What you did for Travis and my bedroom certainly wasn't. I *hated* what Nicole had done to that room. But you made it wonderful for us, hanging the photographs Charlie Ayer took of Travis and me with Nocturne, and choosing exactly the right colors and furniture for the room—and for us. Travis loves hanging out there."

She raised a skeptical brow. "Somehow I think he enjoys your bedroom for an entirely different reason than my decorating taste."

A happy smile lit Margot's face. "Well, maybe, but you picked out the linens and the bed, too. That sleigh bed is *so* great. And what about the amazing job you did on the third floor?"

"I didn't—"

"Yes, you did," she said firmly. "It was drab and beyond sad up there before. You transformed all those rooms, turned them into these special havens for you and the kids.

That ability is so much a part of you, Jordan, you don't even realize how good you are. Other people have to pay through the nose for what you do instinctively. They may read about what antiques are all the rage and what kind of floral arrangements are must-haves for their foyers, but they still need a decorator to tell them where to put the darned things or what kind of a vase to use. It's not just decorating you're good at, either. Think of how you and Patrick have planned a new flower bed for the garden. It's already looking beautiful. Or the cookies and breads you bake that have everyone running to the kitchen as soon as they come out of the oven. That's real talent, Jordan."

It was sweet of Margot to try and boost her ego before her first sales pitch as a decorator, but Jordan knew she was far from special. "Stop. You're making me sound like Wonderwoman."

"You are in my book."

Right. Did Wonderwoman's husband leave her for a size 36D, streaked-blond associate with an appetite for adulterous, lunch-hour couplings? She didn't think so.

Her thoughts must have shown on her face, for Margot's own expression tightened. She stepped forward and wrapped her arms about her, saying fiercely, "Don't you dare let what Richard's done make you sell yourself short."

Jordan hugged her back. "I'll try not to."

"Good."

The back door opened, and Travis came into the mudroom. He bent down and unlaced his paddock boots, leaving them next to the pair Margot had shed earlier. Ellie Banner had a thing about barn dirt in the house.

Walking over to Margot, he looped an arm about her waist and kissed her.

Jordan quickly averted her eyes, fixing them on the salad Margot had prepared. Spying two more olives buried under the crumbled cheese, she plucked them out. So what if her breath smelled like olives rather than toothpaste by the time she arrived at Nonie's?

Their kiss finished, Travis grabbed one of the carrot sticks Margot had been slicing and bit off a piece. "Hi, Jordan."

She swallowed the olives and returned his smile. "Hello, Travis."

"You ready for the big lunch with Mrs. Harrison?"

"I guess. Margot's been giving me a pep talk."

"Not a pep talk. Just the facts. Doesn't Jordan look beautiful?"

"She always looks beautiful. That's a fact, too," he grinned.

Admittedly, it was wonderful to be told you were beautiful by a man as handsome and sexy as Travis Maher, but she knew his words were generated more by kindness than anything else.

"You two are becoming regular walking encyclopedias, just bursting with nifty facts," she said wryly. "Have you and Miriam banded together to form a PR club dedicated to me?"

"No surprise that Miriam thinks you're amazing when she sees firsthand how you're raising the kids. The girl's sharp," Travis said.

"I think Andy wants to ask her out," Margot told them. Andy was one of the stable hands who worked for Rosewood.

"He should go for it. Miriam's wonderful. Loads of fun. The kids simply adore her. I'm so grateful Ellie suggested she work for us part-time while she gets her degree." Jordan checked her watch. She still had a few more minutes before she had to leave. Arriving too early would be interpreted as being overeager, which in Nonie Harrison's world would smack of desperation. "So you're okay with my borrowing the Rover?"

"Absolutely. We've got loads to do this afternoon. And

since Jade drove to school, I don't have to worry about picking her up, I only have to worry that she'll take a detour and stop at Screaming Susie's." Margot had nearly fainted from shock the afternoon Jade came home with kelly green hair, the outrageous color acquired at a punk barbershop located in a strip mall on Route 50. Two weeks later Jade switched to fire-engine red and, as if that weren't enough, allowed the "butchers"—as Margot called them— to hack her long hair into a ragged mop around her ears.

"She'll run out of color options soon." Travis leaned a jeans-clad hip against the counter and took a sip of the coffee he'd poured himself. "She's gone through practically every color in the rainbow."

"I wouldn't put it past Jade to go toxic Day-Glo," Margot said. "Most girls would kill to have hair like hers."

"After what she's been dealing with at school, with the girls still freezing her out and the guys all trailing after her with their tongues hanging to the floor, I'm surprised she's *only* waging a chemical attack on her hair," Jordan said.

Margot shuddered. "Man, I am so glad I'm not seventeen. Of course Jade has it worse than your average obstinate, know-it-all, reckless teen."

That was sadly true. Jade possessed all the complications and contradictions of a bright, beautiful teen on the cusp of womanhood, plus a couple hundred more.

Their half-sister had been through hell in the last eighteen months, her world shattered when their father, RJ, and her mother, Nicole, died after the plane their father was piloting crashed into the Chesapeake. Merely days afterward, Jade was dealt another blow when the lawyer for the estate informed her that her parents had neglected to provide her with a guardian. Margot had immediately stepped up and offered to assume responsibility for Jade, but their relationship had been far from easy during the first few months. And Jade's troubles certainly hadn't ended there.

In jaw-droppingly short order, she'd intentionally gotten

herself expelled from her elite boarding school in Massachusetts, forcing Margot to move back home to Rosewood with her. Jade had doubtless believed that being back at home and attending high school in Warburg would make her happier. Things didn't quite work out that way. At Warburg High, a clique of girls turned against her and began posting on the Internet vicious stories not only about Jade but about her mother, too.

It was horrible enough to be labeled a whore and have pornographic images of oneself Photoshopped on the Web, but to have one's dead mother called a cheating slut, to know that stories were being widely circulated about her affairs was more than anyone should bear.

Wounded, Jade struck back. Unfortunately, her method of retaliation—stealing the boyfriend of Blair Hood, the ringleader of the clique, and making out with him at a wild house party in plain sight of everybody—only landed her in more hot water when the Warburg police arrived, responding to a call from a neighbor who complained about the noise.

Passed out from drinking shots of Jägermeister, Jade was brought home in the back of a police patrol car, the backseat of which was covered with vomit by the time the cruiser reached Rosewood. It was only the next morning when Margot confronted her that Jade, hungover and scared about her run-in with the police, confided to her about the bullying she was being subjected to at school. With the fierceness of a lioness defending her cub, Margot saw to it that the vile pages on the Web were removed, and that the girls responsible for the sleaze were disciplined by the school.

All this had happened last year. But even now, judging from the closed expression on their half-sister's face when she came home from school, Jordan could only assume that the clique of girls behind the Internet bullying had simply switched tactics, tormenting Jade in more devious ways.

So why should it surprise any of them that Jade's answer was to try and make herself so unattractive to the boys that the girls would stop seeing her as a threat?

But her plan hadn't worked as intended. From the constant buzzing of her cell, the boys were still after her. Not even her bored replies when she bothered to take their calls deterred them.

If the boys were this crazy for her, then the girls must be puce with jealousy. Navigating a social scene like that had to be a waking nightmare. Jordan only prayed that Jade would manage to keep her cool and not get provoked into doing anything more serious than driving Margot nuts with her polychromatic 'dos.

Having finished slicing the carrots, Margot arranged the sticks in a neat pile next to Travis's sandwich and passed him the nearly overflowing plate. "Here you go, honey."

"Thanks. This looks great," he said, a smile spreading across his lightly tanned face. Travis was a very good-looking man. When he smiled at Margot like that, he made movie stars look homely.

"You want anything else to go with that?" The breathlessness in Margot's voice showed just how susceptible she was to her husband's slow smile.

"Maybe later," he said softly.

They stared into each other's eyes, lost to the rest of the world.

She was not going to be jealous of Margot and Travis's happiness, but right now three was most definitely a crowd.

"Bye, guys," she said, her voice extra chipper.

"Oh!" Margot gave a start at the sound of her voice but recovered admirably. "You're leaving?"

She nodded. "Miriam will chew me out if she finds I'm still on the premises."

"Good luck, sweetie."

"Yeah, break a leg, Jordan."

"Thanks." She smiled. "I should be back around three."

"I'll stick a bottle of the champagne Damien gave us as a wedding present in the fridge—we can toast Rosewood Design's first commission and your taming of Warburg's scariest dragon lady."

"Sounds lovely." Jordan only hoped she would have something for them to celebrate.

The Harrison house, formally known as Overlea, was located a mile outside of Warburg. As Jordan drove along the winding country roads that led toward town, she steeled herself for what was bound to be a less than relaxing lunch. Nonie Harrison handily captured the title of Warburg's most domineering woman, which was probably why her husband, Eugene, extended his winters in Palm Beach through early June.

Nonie belonged to Jordan's father's generation, and Jordan had always wondered whether she'd married Eugene Harrison because she'd been unable to catch the dashing RJ Radcliffe—the dashing and recklessly foolish RJ Radcliffe, she quickly amended. While Eugene might possess all the excitement of a pet rock, at least the Harrison fortune was intact, whereas their spendthrift father had been afflicted with horrendously poor judgment when it came to investments.

Thank God for Margot and her perfect jawline and photogenic proportions. Her success as a fashion model had saved Rosewood, which had been in the family since the 1840s, from bankruptcy. Without her generosity and determination to preserve their heritage, they would have been left with no alternative but to sell the beautiful mansion and the horse farm.

Of the multitude of Richard's selfish acts during the last year of their marriage, Jordan was most ashamed by his dishonesty in refusing to help Margot with the debts. He had claimed that they needed to put aside money for their own three children. As it turned out, his pious excuse was just one in a long string of lies. The real reason he hadn't wanted to lend Margot any money was that he'd siphoned a lot of his and Jordan's savings to buy a fancy D.C. love nest for Cynthia Delaroux and himself.

What Jordan hated most was her own sense of blame. She should have insisted to Richard that they chip in to pay off the debts her father had left. Instead, she'd been a pushover, a docile, smiling dupe.

But no longer.

Months had passed since the divorce, since she'd up-rooted her children and moved back home. Thanks to her family and everyone else at Rosewood, Kate and Max were happily settled and far more secure than one could hope for children experiencing the breakup of their family and the absence of a father. Luckily, Olivia was too young to be anything other than a sunny toddler who adored everyone.

Jordan's relief once she knew her children weren't going to be collateral damage in the wreck of the marriage had allowed her to regain her bearings and take stock of her own situation. She'd quickly realized that it was past time she proved that she, too, could contribute to keeping Rosewood afloat—not just by helping with the horses at the farm, but with her own outside work.

Today represented day one of Jordan's plan. She was dusting off the career as an interior designer that she'd set aside six years ago with the birth of Kate. She'd named her fledgling business Rosewood Designs and hoped to target the well-heeled of Warburg and the neighboring towns in Loudon County, offering decorating advice to those with more money than taste.

Nonie fit the bill perfectly.

With the death of Nicole, Jordan's stepmother, Nonie had attained the rank of Warburg's premier social hostess. As such, she wielded a terrific influence on the rest of Warburg's "ladies." If Jordan could get Nonie to hire her as a decorator, others would eagerly follow suit.

In celebration of her rise to the pinnacle of Warburg society, Nonie had undertaken a renovation project of her guest cottage. In its final stages of completion, she was looking for an interior designer to decorate the cottage from top to bottom.

As it happened in most small communities, the news had traveled via Warburg's gossip grapevine. Lottie Mulhouse told Jordan about Nonie's plans at the grocery store checkout line. Jordan had decided to grab the bull by the horns, or, as Margot might say, the dragon lady by the tail. She called Nonie and told her she was starting an interior design company. Might Nonie be interested in having her come over and take a look at the cottage?

And now here she was, at the gate that marked the entrance to Overlea. As she drove slowly up the graded drive, the pale yellow stucco and white trim of the Italianate mansion rose before her. With the cherry trees planted at each corner of the house in riotous bloom, and rows upon rows of hot pink tulips in between, the mansion reminded Jordan of a tiered wedding cake decorated by a frosting-mad pastry chef.

Not exactly her style.

Still, the house represented an important example of Warburg's rich architectural history. Jordan loved the eclectic character of her hometown, and, without question, the over-the-top showiness definitely appealed to some.

Jordan pulled the Rover up next to a silver Mercedes, killed the engine, and checked her reflection in the rearview mirror. She quickly retouched her lipstick and smoothed a stray lock away from her face. Drawing a deep breath, she climbed out of the car. It was time to charm the dragon lady.

Chapter

TWO

A MAID in a gray, white-aproned uniform opened the door and led Jordan to the living room. Nonie Harrison, seated on a raspberry-and-gold-striped sofa, rose when Jordan was announced and came around the sofa to press her too-taut cheek fleetingly against Jordan's—Warburg's interpretation of a welcoming kiss.

"Jordan, dear, how good of you to come. It's been ages since we've seen each other."

"How well you look, Nonie. That color blue is wonderful on you."

"Thank you. I picked it up at Worth when I was in New York last week." She fingered the raw silk tunic that she'd paired with dark gold palazzo pants. Addressing the maid she said, "Sonia, please bring us some champagne."

The maid nodded. "Yes, Mrs. Harrison." And she left the room.

"Come sit by me so I can take a look at you." She patted the sofa with a manicured hand, then turned toward her as Jordan obliged. "Well, who wouldn't have a few extra lines after the horrors you've been through this year? But you really must try and take better care of yourself. The seaweed masque at True Beauty works wonders. And ask for Trina. She's marvelous."

"Thank you." Jordan managed to keep her smile in place, knowing that this was only the first of many such digs she would receive during the course of their lunch. Nonie was never one to worry about others' feelings, and no subject was off-limits to Nonie, no matter how private or painful.

"And how are the children holding up? Are they very miserable, the poor darlings?"

Case in point. "How kind of you to ask. They're doing very well. Olivia's getting bigger every day, and Kate and Max are very happy at their preschool. All three adore their aunts Margot and Jade. And like all Radcliffes, they've become horse mad. Jade is teaching Max and Kate to ride. And now Olivia's starting to get rides, too."

"You are *so* good to trust Jade with your precious angels. It shocks me how wild and unpredictable teens are these days. And Jade with that hair! It must be such a trial for you, wondering what she'll do next."

Had she not needed this decorating commission, she would have thoroughly enjoyed giving Nonie a piece of her mind. But starting a business in this economy was no easy task. At this stage she couldn't pick her clients, and alienating Nonie would be tantamount to professional suicide. While she might not be able to retaliate, she didn't intend to roll over for her, either.

"You're absolutely right. Jade is always surprising us— and with more than her hair color. Margot and I were bowled over when Mr. Farkas, the high school principal, told us that she'd scored so high on her achievement tests that she'd qualified for a National Merit Scholarship. With that and her riding, I think she'll have a nice pick of colleges to choose from next year."

Nonie's lips pursed ever so slightly.

Jordan had only a moment to savor her successful parry, for Sonia entered the living room, balancing a tray laden with a bottle of champagne and cut-crystal champagne flutes. Then she noticed the tall, dark-haired man who'd followed Sonia into the living room and the fact that there were three glasses set on the tray.

Had someone else been invited? She'd been led to believe that this lunch—champagne notwithstanding—would be very much an interview for the job.

Nonie, too, had spied the newcomer. She stood with an exclamation of delight. "Owen, darling! You made it! How good of you to make room for me in your busy day."

Trotting over to him, she gave this Owen person an enthusiastic smooch, laughing coquettishly at the geranium-red smudge she left on his lean cheek. Nonie was more than happy to dispense with arid cheek presses when a handsome man was involved.

And handsome he was, even when wiping lipstick traces off his face with a pocket handkerchief, she conceded. Well-dressed, too, in dark gray flannels and a blue blazer that were both impeccably tailored; the dark brown leather shoes that peeked from beneath his trouser cuffs were polished and buffed. It took only a second more for her to catalog his thick, closely cropped hair, the strong line of his profile, and the confidence of his bearing to understand why Nonie was gushing over him.

"Jordan, do come here and meet my darling Owen."

With an inward sigh, Jordan stood and approached Nonie and her "darling" Owen, aware that with every step she advanced, the man's chiseled good looks came into sharper relief. It occurred to her that with the exception of Travis, her brother-in-law, she hadn't been exposed to a really handsome man in months. No great loss, however. Thanks to Richard, Jordan was immune to men.

"Owen, this is Jordan Ste—"

"Radcliffe," she corrected automatically.

"Yes, of course," she said with a tiny smile. "This is Jordan *Radcliffe*. She's starting her very own interior design company and is here to give me some ideas for the cottage. Jordan, this is Owen Gage."

The name threw her. Owen Gage? Surely not—oh, Lord, it must be. Hadn't the buzz a while back been that Nonie had hired Gage & Associates to do the renovations on the guest house? Of course Jordan had heard of him. She made a point of buying *Antique House* and *Architectural Digest* whenever his restoration and design projects were featured.

But why had Nonie invited him today? Dumb question. Although Owen Gage must be twenty years her junior, Nonie had always been a fool for good-looking men.

"Hello, Miss Radcliffe." His tenor had a gravelly rumble to it, as textured as his gold-flecked brown eyes.

"How do you do?" She must have put her hand out for him to shake, for suddenly it was wrapped in his own. An unwelcome jolt of surprise coursed through her at the feel of his warm skin pressed against hers. For what should be a strictly formal gesture, the sensation struck her as far too intimate. She tensed, only just managing to stifle the urge to snatch her hand away.

At the flash of amusement in his deep-set eyes, she knew he'd felt her instinctive reaction to his touch. His firm lips curled and a dimple appeared by the corner of his mouth. "I'm very well, thank you," he replied, only then freeing her hand.

Owen Gage might be an excellent architect and builder, capable of exceptionally fine restorations, but he was a shade too cocky for her taste. He obviously believed he was God's gift to women. She returned his smile with a cool, unimpressed look before fixing her attention on her hostess.

"When Owen mentioned he'd be in town today, I couldn't resist asking him to lunch," Nonie told her brightly. "He did such a marvelous job on the guest cottage. You have heard of Owen, haven't you, Jordan?"

"Of course." As if she could claim to be a decorator and *not* know that his restoration projects had won awards from preservation societies in the D.C. and Virginia areas. "I'm a great admirer of your work, Mr. Gage."

"Thank you. It's always good to know my neighbors appreciate my firm's work."

Neighbor? What was he talking about?

At her frown of confusion, he clarified, "I recently bought Hawk Hill. I'm hoping to bring the house back to its original glory."

"You personally bought the house?" Nonie asked.

"Yes, whenever I happen upon a house that's on the market and interests me in terms of the period or design, I buy it, restore it, and then sell it. It's something I do on the side. A hobby."

"Quite a profitable one I'm sure," Nonie cooed.

Owen Gage shrugged. "It's a chance to do the restoration work exactly as I choose."

Jordan was silent, busy absorbing the fact that she was looking at her new, albeit temporary, neighbor. She hadn't realized the Barrons had managed to sell Hawk Hill. Not that her ignorance was a big surprise, considering how preoccupied she'd been making sure Kate and Max were adjusting to their new lives at Rosewood, as well as coming to terms with the idea that the man she'd loved for nine years had been willing to destroy their marriage.

Hawk Hill must be in a rather sad state. The house had been sitting empty for more than a year now, the Barrons having been forced to move into an assisted-living community after John was paralyzed by a severe stroke. Though it would have been nice to hear from their closest neighbors that they'd sold their property, Jordan could hardly blame Nancy Barron, a quiet and reclusive woman, for not telephoning. If they were ever forced to sell Rosewood, Jordan couldn't imagine being eager to share the painful news with others. And Hawk Hill was just as old and fine a property as Rosewood.

"I can't wait to see it when you're finished. I know you'll do a superb job, Owen," Nonie said.

"I hope Miss Radcliffe will think so, too."

"I'm sure the renovation will be very impressive, Mr. Gage," she returned politely.

"Do let's dispense with this stuffy 'Mr.' and 'Miss,' which Jordan isn't any longer. Though I hope you're not calling yourself 'Ms.' now. I've always considered that beyond hideous-sounding! Besides, if we're drinking champagne, we should all be on a first-name basis. It's so much more deliciously intimate. *N'est-ce pas,* Owen?"

Jordan suppressed a gag at Nonie's overt flirting.

If Owen Gage was bothered by their hostess's manner, he didn't show it. He merely inclined his dark head and said, "Absolutely, Nonie."

But when he turned to her with a smile, she once again detected an unholy spark of amusement in his brown eyes. "Since we're now officially on a first-name basis, Jordan, may I coax an invitation from you to visit Rosewood?"

"Oh, yes, Jordan, you simply must have Owen over! He's a treasure trove of information when it comes to these old houses."

Jordan managed an anemic smile. As proud as she was of Rosewood, it was completely illogical of her to wish that she could ban Owen Gage from stepping foot inside her beautiful home. But right now she couldn't care less that he was widely praised for the meticulous attention he gave to restoring historic homes. The man made her hackles rise. Just knowing that he'd occasionally have to be at Hawk Hill in order to supervise the restoration work was irksome. Hawk Hill, a mere trail ride through the woods from Rosewood, was far too close.

"My family and I would be pleased to have you visit Rosewood, Mr. Gage." Dear Lord, how many lies would she utter for the sake of politeness before this lunch was over? And how infuriating that he seemed to see through her dissembling, as if he'd known her forever instead of five minutes.

"Owen," he reminded her with that dimpled, too charming smile. "I'll hold you to that invitation, Jordan."

Terrific.

Just then Sonia returned to announce that lunch was served, and she once again found herself having to ignore the warmth of his touch when he wrapped his hand about her elbow to escort her and Nonie into the dining room.

She could thank him for one thing. Whereas previously she had been nervous about having to pitch her ideas to Nonie, now she couldn't wait to get through lunch and begin discussing how best to decorate the guest cottage. Then at least she'd have the satisfaction of saying good-bye to him.

The lunch verged on inedible. The poached salmon was rubbery, the asparagus drastically overcooked, and one bite of the cloyingly sweet key lime pie that Nonie served for dessert had made Owen's teeth ache. Just as syrupy and distasteful had been Nonie's "dear" and "darling" every time she addressed him.

Yet surprisingly Owen was enjoying himself. The chance to sit across the china-and-silver-laden table from Jordan Radcliffe more than made up for the meal's deficiencies.

Owen studied the woman seated across from him. A man who appreciated contrasts, he could not help finding her fascinating. Such a curious mix of social poise and palpable hostility. And for a woman with more prickle than a cactus, she had the smoothest, silkiest skin imaginable. She also happened to live in one of the finest houses in Virginia. This fact alone made Ms. Jordan Radcliffe extremely worthy of his attention.

Guessing what a lunch at Nonie Harrison's would be like, he'd made every attempt to avoid it. But then she dangled the promise of Jordan Radcliffe's presence. He would dutifully eat an entire platter of overboiled asparagus for the chance to step inside Rosewood. The house was rumored to be a near-pristine example of Greek Revival architecture in Virginia, passed down through generations of Radcliffes. The family had apparently never deemed it necessary to alter the home built by their ancestor, the storied

Francis Radcliffe. To the architectural historian in Owen, visiting a house like Rosewood was like mining the mother lode.

He'd seen a few tantalizing glimpses of the house in a *Vogue* photo spread that an assistant had brought into his Alexandria office to show him. One of the Radcliffe sisters was a fashion model and had agreed to a photo shoot in the ancestral home. Now he remembered seeing in the spread a picture of Jordan, as well. That he should have noticed her at all was nothing less than remarkable. He'd been scouring the photographs for details of her ancestral home, not for images of its owners.

Indeed, if someone had asked Owen a mere hour ago which would hold greater interest, meeting a direct descendant of Francis Radcliffe, who'd commissioned Rosewood in 1840, or getting a chance to explore the mansion inside and out, his answer would have been immediate. I'll take door number two.

But that was before he'd met Jordan. To say he found her intriguing was an understatement. When he'd shaken her hand earlier, he'd felt the slight trembling of her fingers clasped in his and caught the flash of feminine awareness in her wide blue eyes. Yet rather than acknowledge that they were two individuals who recognized a spark of attraction between them—he was always more than happy to admit any interest in a beautiful woman—she had abruptly gone all prickly on him.

Her dislike seemed a bit too determined when all they'd done was shake hands, and so to Owen she was that much more interesting. From Nonie's pointed comment, he'd already figured out that she was divorced, so what was the big deal?

Owen didn't consider himself particularly conceited, but he was rather accustomed to being liked by the opposite sex. He was decent-looking. He took care of his teeth and trimmed his nails. It wasn't hard to keep in shape by supplementing the manual labor he put in on his renovation projects with visits to the gym. But most likely the reason women seemed to gravitate toward him was because he'd always been comfortable around them. It was a trait developed early, fostered by the long string of au pairs and nannies his parents hired to care for him as they traveled the world.

By the age of six, Owen had already tapped into the winning combination of using the right words and a few disarming grins to convince almost any woman to do his bidding. Back then, he'd basically been aiming for another slice of cake and an extra half-hour of playtime in the park. At thirty-six, his tastes had evolved, but he still greatly enjoyed playtime.

The women he dated did, too.

Jordan Radcliffe, of the flawless skin, fathomless blue eyes, auburn hair, and willowy figure, was doing everything she could to let him know she wasn't remotely interested in engaging with him in any kind of activity, recreational or otherwise. Indeed, from the conspicuous lack of interest she displayed, she was letting him know that she considered him about as interesting as dry rot . . . actually, probably less.

Perhaps it was for the best. He made it a point to avoid women who fairly screamed complicated, no matter how petal-soft their skin. He preferred his affairs to be straightforward, mutually enjoyable, and brief. Brevity was key. Let a relationship continue too long and the woman developed an unfortunate tendency to make plans.

And the only plans that interested him were architectural. He'd worked his hide off to make Owen Gage & Associates one of the best architectural preservation firms in the area. While he liked contrasts and depth in art and architecture, he had no intention of making room in his life for a woman who had "complexity" written all over her.

A shame, because Jordan Radcliffe smelled really good. Owen was still trying to identify the beguiling scent he'd breathed in as he'd escorted her to the dining room and then held her chair for her. The fragrance was light and fresh and, well, he couldn't pinpoint exactly what made it so different from the perfumes women generally favored, but he liked it.

He told himself he should be grateful that she'd made it abundantly clear she didn't want him anywhere near her sweet-smelling self. Otherwise he might be tempted to ignore his established rules of engagement.

"Are you sure you wouldn't like another cup of coffee, Jordan?"

"No, thank you, Nonie. Lunch was absolutely delicious."

Nonie immediately switched her attention back to him, and as he was seated opposite Jordan, he caught the sneak peek she gave her wristwatch. The tiny slip in manners made him grin. She'd been the epitome of politeness throughout the meal—a careful, formal etiquette that he suspected she used as a shield. The possibility that Jordan might be as bored as he by Nonie's monopoly of the conversation made Owen wonder what else went on behind that perfect front.

"And you, Owen, darling? More coffee?" Nonie asked.

"Not for me either, thanks. I should be going—"

"Oh, but you *must* stay. I planned to take Jordan to the cottage and hear her ideas for how I might decorate it. I want you to come, too."

The stunned look on Jordan's face must have mirrored his own. He'd gotten to know Nonie Harrison fairly well over the months his team had worked on restoring her guest cottage, but she continued to amaze him. Was she really that ignorant of the basic notions of professional courtesy? Probably not, he concluded. A spoiled rich woman, she simply wanted what she wanted and never saw any reason why she shouldn't have it.

"I'm sure Jordan would rather share her ideas without—" he began as Jordan said, "Perhaps tomorrow would be a better time for us to discuss—"

"Nonsense." Nonie silenced them both with a wave of her diamond-ringed hand. "Why ever would she mind having you accompany us? You did such a fabulous job on the cottage. I want to be certain the finishing touches will be just as wonderful. You understand, Jordan, don't you?"

Yes, she did understand. Nonie had set up the lunch and the so-called interview as an elaborate cat-and-mouse game. Her insistence that Owen listen while she presented her decorating ideas was one more way of toying with her. Nonie had obviously decided it would be amusing to see whether she would fall apart at the prospect.

Although it was like being a first-year art student and having her paintings examined by Michelangelo, Jordan wasn't going to back down. She hadn't sat through this awful lunch, doing her darnedest to ignore the hundred little things about Owen Gage that she really did *not* want to notice about him—such as the tantalizing contrast of the dark hair sprinkling the back of his long-fingered hands and the snowy white cuff of his shirt sleeve, or how the lines that fanned out from the corners of his eyes and bracketed his mouth deepened whenever he smiled—to give up on the commission now.

"Of course I have no objection to Owen hearing my ideas," she said, bringing the tally of today's lies into the double digits.

"There, you see, Owen? She doesn't mind at all. Let's go over to the cottage right now, shall we? Oh, this will be so much fun!"

A mini replica of the main house, the intimate scale of the guest cottage made it resemble a pastel petit four pastry. As they walked up the flagstone path that led to the cottage, Jordan took in the freshly refurbished wood-and-stucco exterior, noting the meticulous repair. Owen Gage & Associates had done a superb job, she admitted to herself, and she fully expected the interior to reveal the same level of craftsmanship.

Owen opened the front door for them. Nonie entered first, chattering away as she did. Jordan, who'd been examining the carved doorframe, followed more slowly. As she stepped over the threshold, she was stopped by his hand.

Her brows drew together in a questioning frown as she instinctively pulled her arm away from the warmth of his fingers. With an effort, she resisted the urge to rub the spot on her arm that still tingled from the momentary contact. She really wished he'd stop with all this casual touching. "Yes?" she asked.

"I just wanted to say that I'm sorry about the awkwardness of the situation. I don't think Nonie realizes—"

That shows how little you know her. "Please don't apologize. Your presence makes absolutely no difference to me." A part of her couldn't believe how rude she had just been. She wasn't usually churlish. But few people succeeded in irritating her with so little effort. Indeed, he was so irritating that she decided she wasn't going to apologize for the remark. Her chin rose defiantly.

If he was offended, he didn't show it. "Well, I won't worry then," he said.

She caught the thread of amusement in the low rumble of his voice. What could he possibly find so entertaining, she wondered, before stifling a gasp as he suddenly leaned forward.

His strong-boned face was far too close. For some reason, though, she stood rooted to the spot, watching as his angled head came even nearer. *My God, was he going to kiss her?*

Mere inches away from her trembling lips, he halted his progress and simply inhaled. Deeply.

Jordan nearly jumped out of her skin. Had he just *sniffed* her?

"What . . . what are you doing?" The words came out in a panicked rush that matched the speed of her pulse.

His smile was as innocent as a choir boy's. "Nothing. I was trying to identify your perfume."

"I . . . I'm not . . . I'm not wearing perfume."

His face was still far too close. The gold chips glittered in his dark eyes, brilliant and mesmerizing. They made her system go haywire. She couldn't move, not even to take half a step backward.

"Are you sure?" He frowned. "How strange, because you smell wonderful." That he sounded abstracted, as if he weren't intentionally trying to fluster her, only rattled her more.

"I—" She had no idea what to say.

She was saved by Nonie, who called out, demanding to know what was holding them up.

Owen straightened, a smile playing over his lips. "I guess it's time to show us what you've got, Jordan."

Okay, now she was truly convinced he was playing some kind of mind game to throw her off balance. Perhaps he was exacting revenge for her earlier comment. Her dislike ratcheted up a notch. And, no, her antipathy had nothing to do with the fact that this man had been able to make her heart stop and then pound like a kettledrum just by bringing his classically carved face a warm, coffee-laced breath from hers.

With a parting glare she turned and strode in the direction of Nonie's voice, determined to ignore Owen Gage and to dazzle Nonie Harrison. The former now seemed the greater challenge.

Afternoon sunlight poured in through the living room's twin Palladian windows, illuminating the space and highlighting the restored plaster moldings and decorative columns. Beneath Jordan's feet the parquet floor was freshly sanded and finished. Its warm honey tones gleamed. She stopped in the center of the room, taking in the airy proportions and the vertical rhythms created by the windows and columns and the large marble fireplace on the opposite wall.

If this were her home, Jordan thought, she'd do as little decorating as possible, letting the architectural details speak for themselves.

But Nonie's aesthetic was best described as "more and more is more," so the trick to satisfying her tastes would be to suggest just the right number of knickknacks and patterned silks, without burying the elegance of the interior space under a mountain of visual clutter.

The feat would have been challenging enough without Owen listening in. Stationed by one of the windows, he was peering intently out at the garden as if fascinated by the reddish-green leaves on the still bloomless rosebushes. She supposed she should be grateful that he was attempting to be as unobtrusive as possible, yet somehow she couldn't muster even a smidge of gratitude. His silent presence was too distracting. And she was furious with herself for continuing to notice him at all—he was the last person she should be thinking about at a time like this.

The time had come to act like the professional she was supposed to be. If that weren't enough inducement, she reminded herself that the sooner she finished talking to Nonie about design ideas for the cottage, the sooner she could say good-bye to Owen Gage. With luck she'd never see him again.

She took a moment to fish a notepad and fountain pen from her large leather tote. Fixing a bright smile on her face, she said, "The restoration work is simply wonderful, Nonie. I can't wait to see the other rooms. Let me give you an idea to consider. When I started thinking about the décor for the cottage, I realized it might be neat if we could create a pretty, carefree echo of the style you've achieved in the larger house."

"How interesting. Tell me what that would look like."

"Well, as the cottage is a smaller version of the main

house, I'd like to connect the spirit of the two houses so that when your guests and family are here in this space, it'll be like an extension, a riff on Overlea."

Nonie's brow furrowed, a feat considering the number of botox sessions she'd had. "But I don't want just a repeat of what I have."

"Of course not," Jordan agreed lightly. "The purpose of the guest cottage is very different—you don't want, for example, to worry about things being broken or damaged here, so we should select pieces and fabrics that are a bit more playful, carefree, and above all *maintenance* free."

"And what about colors?"

"Well, I know how much you like lavenders and blues. I think that palette would go especially well in this room. We could work those colors into the fabrics and keep the walls an off-white with an accent trim for the woodwork. The whites will keep your blues and lavenders purer and also enhance the wonderful sense of light and air in the room."

"I like that. And what about over here by the fireplace?"

"Bookshelves."

"Bookshelves?" Nonie repeated vaguely.

She nodded. "One of the joys of staying in someone's home is discovering the library, a wonderful mix of classics and all different kinds of genres, and then curling up with a book in front of the fireplace. We can place two wing chairs and ottomans on either side of the fireplace and have the sofa over there. Your guests will have lots of room to curl up with a book in the afternoon between lunchtime and cocktails—those hours when, as a hostess, you really value your privacy. Remember, the mission of the cottage is that it's as much for *you* as it is for your guests."

Nonie laughed in delight. "You're so wonderfully clever, Jordan. Isn't she clever, Owen?"

He turned from the window and his gaze settled on her. "Yes, she is."

Why did her cheeks have to warm like a schoolgirl's simply because he hadn't said her ideas were garbage?

"This is tremendous fun! Now, tell me what you envision for the other rooms, Jordan. And in case I forget, when we get to the bedrooms, I'd want one of them to have a younger look."

Jordan nodded easily. "Jane Churchill has some exquisite papers and fabrics for children's rooms. They're so beautiful and classic an adult would love falling asleep surrounded by them, too. That sort of flexibility is important when you're decorating a guest house. I brought a sample book of her papers and fabrics to show you as well as some other designers I thought you might like."

"You are a marvel, Jordan. Truly."

An hour and a half later, the three of them were back outside the cottage. Nonie, if anything, seemed even more bubbly and vivacious than before. She spun about on her heels to clasp Jordan's hands in hers and squeeze them enthusiastically. "What a darling you've been to come and share all your ideas for the cottage. I'm quite impressed. I have a feeling it's going to look so wonderful I'll want to move in myself," and she gave a trill of laughter.

Although Jordan mustered a smile, her brain felt too much like a wrung-out sponge to formulate an intelligent reply. It wasn't so much Nonie's endless quizzing over the past ninety minutes that had worn her out but rather the constant tension of knowing that Owen was listening to her every answer. She had tried to tell herself that it didn't matter what he thought of her ideas. To no avail. Even now she was fighting the urge to turn and face him so she might gauge his reaction. Of course, doing that would involve looking at him directly, and after the way he'd managed to rattle her in the foyer, she thought that would be a really bad move. After doing her best to impress Nonie, she wasn't going to blow it by losing even an ounce of her composure.

Besides, she didn't need validation from him. She'd done a great job, and she was sure she'd sold Nonie on her ideas. The excitement of landing her first commission was enough to boost her flagging energy.

"I should be thanking you, Nonie, for the chance to work with such a lovely space. I think I've gotten a pretty good idea of what you want for the cottage. Would you like me to come by later this week so we can get started? With summer coming, I'm sure you'll want the cottage ready sooner rather than later."

"You are so right. But I'll have to consult my calendar to see when I have a free moment. My schedule is craziness itself. Why don't you call me tomorrow? Perhaps I'll have a better idea then."

"Of course."

Nonie's smile widened. "You are so understanding."

Stowing her notepad and fountain pen in her tote, she hitched the thin leather strap of her purse over her shoulder and picked up the tote. "I should really be going."

"So soon? We'll walk you to your car," Nonie said, before linking her arm through Owen's in order to walk beside him up the narrow flagstone path and begin an animated discussion about the color schemes and patterns Jordan had proposed for the bedrooms.

Forced to follow in their steps, Jordan told herself to overlook Nonie's rudeness and to concentrate instead on how great it felt to have earned her first decorating commission all on her own. Besides, the last thing she wanted was to walk next to Owen and have the sleeve of his jacket brush her arm. No, indeed, she was quite happy where she was.

At the front of the house, next to where she had parked the Range Rover, sat a silver Audi TT coupe. Of course that would be the car he drove, she thought. Sleek, powerful, and dynamic, it was an amazing driving machine. How galling that whenever she was behind the wheel of her minivan and an Audi TT zipped by, she'd be filled by a wild, secret car lust. She'd even flirted with the idea of asking Richard to trade in his Lexus for one. Thank God she hadn't—the money was better used for the child support Richard had agreed to pay.

Nonie unlatched herself from his side to offer her another air kiss.

"Thank you for the delicious lunch, Nonie," she said. Pinning a polite smile on her face, she extended a hand to Owen. "Good-bye."

"A pleasure to meet you, Jordan. I hope to take you up on the offer of a tour of Rosewood very soon."

When pigs have wings. He was sorely mistaken if he believed she was going to invite him into her home. Confident that this was the last time she'd be troubled by the likes of Owen Gage, she hardly even stiffened at the tingle of awareness that coursed through her when his strong hand engulfed hers.

Owen watched Jordan Radcliffe climb into the Range Rover, appreciating the way her silk skirt rose up her leg. Not only did she smell good, she had excellent legs. He'd even go so far as to pronounce the entire package very fine. The fact that she'd remained pointedly noncommittal when he'd again brought up the subject of visiting Rosewood didn't prevent him from wondering what it would feel like to run his hands up the length of those shapely legs. Would they be as silky soft as the skin he'd already touched? Would the back of her knees and the gentle slope of her calves carry the same beguiling scent he'd inhaled earlier?

His thoughts were interrupted by the sound of the car engine turning over. The Rover's window lowered, and she stuck her arm out to wave good-bye. "Thanks again!"

"I'll be expecting your call tomorrow, don't forget now!" Nonie said.

"I won't," she promised with a cheerful smile before driving off.

He'd lay odds that her expression wouldn't be nearly so

sunny when he showed up on her doorstep. The knowledge didn't bother him in the least. He decided he liked seeing Jordan Radcliffe with her back up. Thank God the lunch was over. He turned to Nonie. "Many thanks for the lunch," he said with an easy smile.

"You can't possibly leave yet. We need to discuss how soon you can start decorating the cottage for me."

Surely he'd misheard her. "But you're giving the commission to Jordan Radcliffe."

Nonie gave a delighted laugh. "Why, Owen, whatever made you think that? How utterly silly. Now, come back inside and we'll talk."

Chapter *3*
THREE

"LISTEN, NONIE, I don't— No, thanks," he said, declining the offer of a scotch from the crystal decanter Nonie held aloft. "What you're doing makes no sense at all. Jordan Radcliffe's ideas for the cottage were excellent."

"Hmm, yes," she murmured as she sat down on the sofa next to him. "They were good, weren't they? But your decorating department would have access to all the same designs and fabrics, isn't that so?"

His shoulder brushed the sofa's silk upholstery as he shrugged uncomfortably. "Yes, but—"

"Then there's no problem. All you need to do is tell your decorator to use Jordan's ideas for the rooms."

She must be joking. He shifted to look at her fully. "I'm afraid I can't do that. It's not especially ethical, you see."

"Not ethical? Don't be ridiculous," she scoffed. "Why shouldn't I use her ideas? It's not as if I signed a contract or said I'd actually *hire* her."

He frowned. If Nonie wanted to be sneaky and underhanded, that was her business, but he didn't appreciate being drafted into playing her game.

"I don't understand what's going on here. Why would you want to hire my firm? Jordan Radcliffe just spent close to two hours going over every square foot of the cottage with you. It's clear she's got taste and that she's detail-oriented and is enthusiastic about the project. Plus her fee will be significantly less than my firm's," he said, certain this last would sway her as no other argument could. While

Nonie demanded top-of-the-line workmanship, she did her utmost to avoid paying for it.

The irony of the situation didn't escape him. For the first time since starting his company he was advising a client to hire the competition—the competition being a woman who didn't even want to give him the time of day. But his conscience balked at taking what by all rights should be someone else's commission.

From Nonie's silence he thought he'd succeeded in convincing her, but then she shook her head.

"I suppose it's true that I'll have to pay more for your work, but then again I'm hiring a *name* when I choose Gage and Associates. Jordan's a dear thing, and I do feel wretched about the sordid melodrama enveloping her family, but really, how far should one take sympathy?"

Apparently not far enough to give a friend a job, he thought and glanced pointedly at his watch.

She didn't take the hint. "You're aware of what happened to the Radcliffes?"

"Yes, I heard about the parents dying in a plane crash last year," he said with thinly veiled impatience. The tragedy had been enough to make him decide against imposing upon the family with a request to visit Rosewood. And he'd been incredibly busy. In addition to renovating Nonie's cottage, he'd been juggling three other restoration projects and designing a Georgian colonial for a couple who'd bought some land over in Warren County. Signing the purchase agreement for Hawk Hill, and knowing that Rosewood was just up the road, had reawakened his interest in seeing whether the storied mansion lived up to its reputation.

"My dear, where *have* you been? The airplane crash was just the tip of the iceberg. As their new and closest neighbor, you simply must hear how very low the high and mighty Radcliffes have fallen."

While he was curious as to what made Jordan Radcliffe

tick, Owen wasn't interested in listening to Nonie's gossip. But before he could stop her, Nonie began dishing up the dirt, making sure to add a hefty helping of spite. Her satisfaction over the Radcliffe family's misfortunes was nothing less than stunning. Unfortunately Nonie interpreted his silence for interest.

"Even before RJ's plane crashed into the Chesapeake, there'd been whispers about him and Nicole. It's why most of us don't believe the crash *was* a simple matter of instrument malfunction, no matter what the girls would like to think. You see, RJ was the quintessential he-man adventurer and as proud as the day is long. Word has it that he finally figured out what the rest of us already knew—that Nicole was carrying on behind his back. He was not the sort of man to meekly accept that kind of blow to his pride."

"Come on, Nonie. Are you saying that people here think Jordan's father *intentionally* crashed his plane because his wife was having an affair? A little drastic, don't you think?" Christ, was this ever an argument against small-town life, he thought. The ties that bound also strangled as tight as a noose.

She shrugged, unfazed by his patent disbelief. "People do crazy things all the time, even crazier things in the grip of jealousy. And RJ was an utter fool for Nicole. But their deaths were only the beginning of the family drama. It turned out that RJ had run through the family fortune, right down to the last penny. The estate was riddled with debt."

"But they've managed to keep Rosewood. An amazing feat, if what you say is true," he pointed out.

"Margot, the middle daughter, is a model," she said as if that explained everything. "She's got that look which appeals to some." Her moue of distaste indicated she wasn't among them. "One of my dear friends, Edward Crandall, was the lawyer for the estate. He did his best to advise the girls to sell the property, but Margot refused. She was determined to 'save' her home." Her fingers formed little quotation marks. "Such an amusing notion, really, considering that RJ and Nicole had banished her from Rosewood."

"Banished?" Surely Nonie was exaggerating. "Sounds rather draconian."

"No, just very much like RJ. Of course, he was egged on by Nicole, who positively loathed Margot. They refused any contact with her for years. Seeing her flounce about in fashion magazines only fueled their anger. But RJ would have disinherited Margot entirely if he could have foreseen that she'd come home and marry Rosewood's *barn manager*. Now, I'm not hypocritical. I'm not going to pretend I either miss or mourn Nicole at all, but how I would have loved to see her maintain her queen-of-the-realm attitude after Margot tied the knot with Travis Maher. Not only is he a glorified stable hand, he's also the son of Warburg's most notorious drunk!" Smiling, she reached for the bowl of cheese sticks that the maid had silently brought in and offered it to Owen. "Have one, darling, they're just yummy."

He shook his head, not even bothering with a "No, thanks."

She gave a little pout, selected one for herself, took a bite, and sank back against the sofa cushions. "What were we talking about? Oh, yes, Margot's marrying Travis. Scandalous. Well, she's always been headstrong. To think she ended up being Jade's guardian—that's the younger half-sister. Edward Crandall made a terrible mistake there. As lawyer for the estate, he should have appointed somebody else. Anybody would have been a better pick to act as a decent role model for a teenager than a fashion model! I can't say it's any surprise that Jade's turned into a troublemaker. Last year she was nearly arrested by the police for underage drinking. It'd be one thing if Jade was just out to self-destruct, but she's the kind who brings others down along with her. Because of her, three perfectly innocent girls were suspended from the high school. One of them was my niece, Blair."

Ahh, Owen thought. Was this the motive behind Nonie's hostility? "What happened?" he asked.

"It was some silliness on the Internet. Total nonsense, nothing more than an adolescent prank. But the principal took Jade's side. No doubt he was dazzled by Margot's celebrity status when she went in and pleaded for her sister. So Jade got off scot-free while the other girls were suspended. As I said, she's a real troublemaker. Jordan's making a terrible mistake letting Jade around her children—" She paused to pop the last of her cheese stick into her mouth. "But that's the problem with Jordan. Too trusting by half."

At the mention of Jordan, Owen, who'd been doing his best to tune Nonie out, focused. "She didn't strike me as the overly trusting type."

"Terribly gullible, the poor thing. It took her until she was halfway through her pregnancy with her third child to realize that her husband, Richard Stevens, was carrying on a very steamy affair with a junior associate in his office. A friend of a friend who works in Richard's firm told me all about it. Truly torrid stuff."

Owen was still digesting the first bit of information. Jordan Radcliffe was the mother of three? Impossible. Three kids? he repeated silently. Jesus H. Christ. Owen had sensed she was complicated, but obviously he hadn't guessed the half of it. It wasn't enough for a woman like Jordan Radcliffe to have "emotional commitment required" written all over her, the sign should be accompanied by flashing lights and alarm bells. To get involved with someone like her—a divorced, cheated-on mother of three—would be pure folly, and Owen didn't consider himself a foolish man. It was definitely time he nipped his fascination in the bud.

Thankfully Nonie had moved on, too, her spite once more directed toward the youngest sister, Jade. "The girl's an absolute hellion, and Margot and Jordan do nothing to keep her in check. After the ruckus she caused at Warburg High, instead of punishing Jade as she deserved, do you know what Margot did? She organized a photo spread in *Vogue* for the three of them to appear in, like they were the princesses of the county. Typical Radcliffe ploy," she sniffed.

So that explained why Jordan had been in the pages of *Vogue*. He wondered whether he still had the issue filed away somewhere.

"Well, I can't imagine there'll be many more photo shoots for them to parade about like royalty. Travis is bound to put a bun in her oven pretty soon. Without Margot's contracts, no one believes they'll be able to hang on to Rosewood. The horses would be their only means of income, and horse breeding is such a risky business. I very much doubt Jordan will have the kind of success she needs to make a go of it as a decorator. Standards are so high here. A shame, but what can you do?"

With friends like these, who needed enemies? He decided then and there that if Nonie wanted to stick it to her dear friend Jordan, she'd do it without his help. He rose from the sofa. "I really have to hit the road. Thank you for lunch, Nonie."

She walked him to the front door. "So you'll tell your decorator what I want done with the cottage?"

"I'm afraid there's a slight problem with this plan. Emily Carlson, the interior decorator at our firm, is booked solid for the next six months."

"Six months?" Her voice rose in disbelief. "I can't possibly wait that long. I have guests coming in mid-July. Surely you can arrange to schedule me sooner, as I'm such a good client—"

She was positively deluded if she thought that. "We value all our clients equally. And we base our reputation on keeping our promises to them. Now, seeing that Emily won't be able to satisfy your needs, perhaps you should reconsider your reservations about hiring Jordan Radcliffe. Bye, Nonie."

Chapter ❧
FOUR

THE CHAMPAGNE they opened at dinner was delicious, the sense of accomplishment at having gone out and presented her ideas well to none other than Nonie Harrison and under such intimidating conditions, even more so. Jordan had done a good job, and she'd done it all by herself. She smiled into her champagne glass and took another sip.

"So the Barrons sold Hawk Hill," Travis said. "That's a nice piece of land. I hope this guy—what's his name again, Jordan?"

Her smile faltered. "Owen Gage."

"Right. Gage. I hope he's open to the idea of our riding on his property."

"I doubt he'll care very much," she answered. "It's not as if he'll be living at Hawk Hill or even keep the property for very long. Once the construction crew has finished the renovations, he'll put it on the market. It'll doubtless sell quickly."

"I remember going to Hawk Hill for the Barrons' Christmas caroling party," Margot said, spearing a halved strawberry with her fork. "The house was so pretty. It'll be a real shame if it loses its character for the sake of keeping up with the twenty-first century."

Jordan gave a quick shake of her head. "That's not how he works. He's scrupulous when it comes to preserving architectural styles. Nonie's cottage looks wonderful." No matter what she thought of him as a person, Owen Gage's talent for restoring old homes was beyond reproach.

"Well, if Jordan likes him, that's good enough for me," Travis said.

"I didn't say I *liked* him—"

Luckily Jade spoke up, relieving Jordan from having to define how she felt about their new neighbor. "Since you guys are too uptight to let me have any champagne, I'd like another slice of Jordan's angel food cake. And a big spoonful of the whipped cream, too," Jade held her plate out to Travis, who obligingly cut her a thick slice before passing her the bowl of whipped cream. "Cheers, Jordan," she said, lifting a large forkful in the air. "Here's to getting Mrs. Harrison, the Witch of Warburg, to hire you. She gives me the evil eye every time she sees me. The last time she did it, though, I stuck my tongue out at her." Opening her mouth wide to accommodate the whipped-cream-topped slice, she chewed with a happy grin on her face.

"That's extremely mature, Jade," Margot said. "Speaking of mature, I ran into Officer Cooper at the gas station. It seems somebody's signed him up for a Doughnut of the Month club. You happen to know anything about that?"

Jade turned a shade of pink that exactly matched her hair. Instead of answering, she forked up another enormous bite of cake and chewed busily.

Margot pursed her lips. "Brilliant. It's always a good idea to antagonize the local police."

"Maybe if he's eating doughnuts, he'll stop writing totally undeserved parking tickets," she muttered thickly.

"Totally undeserved parking tickets, did you say?"

Jade speared another piece of cake. "Totally," she insisted.

"Well, I sincerely hope you aren't blowing all the money you earn on designer doughnuts and god-awful dye jobs." Jade received a salary for helping to train and exercise the green horses at Rosewood, and Jordan paid her a weekly fee for the riding lessons she gave Kate and Max. "Because if you don't pay your parking fines, you can bet Officer Cooper will be very happy to stick a boot on your car."

"I paid them. Now if only Robocop would quit driving around town looking to ticket me."

"Oh, please! Warburg may be small, but I'm going to guess that *Officer* Cooper has a couple more pressing matters than targeting your mom's Porsche."

"Yeah, like scarfing down doughnuts."

Margot rolled her eyes in exasperation. "Jade—"

Travis cleared his throat, but when he spoke his voice carried more than a hint of laughter in it. "So, Jordan, when do you think you'll start on the cottage at Overlea?" he asked in an obvious attempt to steer her sisters away from what had become a hot-button issue: Jade's willingness to rile Rob Cooper, the officer who'd busted the underage drinking party last year and brought her home in the back of his police cruiser.

Jordan followed Travis's lead. "With summer coming I assume Nonie will want me to order fabrics and papers as quickly as possible and get the work crew assembled. I'm calling her tomorrow to set up our next appointment."

"We're all thrilled for you," Margot said, mercifully dropping the subject of Jade and Rob Cooper. "To celebrate, Jade and I will do the dishes, while you check on the kids."

"I don't think I have to worry about them sleeping. Thanks to Miriam playing tag with them most of the afternoon and then Jade giving them a super-hard riding lesson, they were zonked by bath time. Olivia was asleep before her head hit the pillow."

"Then maybe you'd like to come down to the broodmares' barn and check on the mares and foals?" Travis suggested.

Jordan smiled. The night check on the broodmares was one of her favorite chores. "I'd love to."

Seated beside Travis, Margot leaned over and touched her lips to his. "I'll do my Pilates mat while you're doing the barn check." As it was spring, the fashion magazines were gearing up for the coming fall fashions, and Margot was already getting bookings for shoots. The discipline Margot demonstrated to keep her figure as lithe as a gazelle's was amazing. But in Jordan's opinion, even more than maintaining her lean physique, it was the glow of unalloyed happiness Margot radiated since she and Travis married that enhanced her beauty and fueled her modeling career.

When Travis reached up to stroke the side of Margot's face and then twined his fingers in her hair to draw her closer and offer a kiss of his own, Jordan and Jade exchanged looks. Silently they rose from the long kitchen table.

"Jeesh," Jade said in an undertone as she turned the faucet on and began rinsing one of the pans before placing it in the dishwasher. "One minute they're fairly normal and then *wham*. Do you think they're ever going to get tired of all that stuff?"

"Not if they're lucky." At moments like this she really felt for Travis and Margot. It couldn't be easy to have her, Jade, and the kids around all the time. If her sister and brother-in-law were alone right now, she seriously doubted they'd be limiting themselves to a few kisses. Fortunately, the house was big and their bedroom suite offered them a private haven. She thought back to Margot's comment about how she and Travis loved the bed she'd selected for them when she'd redecorated their room. An image sprang to life in her mind's eye, of herself wrapped in a man's arms—a man who bore a startlingly uncomfortable resemblance to Owen Gage. Her cheeks grew hot with acute embarrassment.

It was hours since the lunch at Nonie's and Owen was still bothering her. Her cheeks burned even hotter as her wayward imagination offered yet another scenario: his strong body covering hers, pressing her into the soft mattress.

"Jade, tell Travis I've slipped outside to get some fresh air." Please God, let the cool evening air clear the very graphic fantasy that had formed in her mind—not that there was anything wrong with fantasizing, just as long as Owen Gage didn't play a starring role.

"Sure," she said, glancing up from the pot she was scouring. "Hey, you look funny. You're not sick or anything?"

"I'm fine. It was probably that second glass of champagne," she said, seizing the most obvious excuse.

"A real lightweight, huh?"

"Something like that," she replied.

The broodmares' barn, with its spacious double stalls, was softly lit and comfortably snug from the heat of the horses' bodies. It was especially peaceful at this hour, the mares' snorts and whickerings, the rustling of the straw bedding muted and occasional. Like Jordan's own children, the new foals, some barely a month old, were almost all asleep, worn out from their day romping in the fields under their dams' watchful eyes.

Jordan and Travis were standing in front of Allure's stall, watching the mare and her new foal, who was lying quietly in the straw, inches from her hooves. A protective mother, Allure didn't leave her colt's side. And having already foaled five offspring, she was used to the routine of the evening barn check, aware that the humans would depart shortly.

Although the foal's fuzzy ears twitched, it continued to lie quietly on its side, its spindly legs folded neatly against its belly, its ribs rising and falling with each breath. Jordan wasn't surprised to see the three-week-old colt dozing so soundly. This morning he'd been tearing around the pasture with all the spirit of his sire.

They had named the colt Grayson. His sire, Stoneleigh, had been a magnificent dapple gray Thoroughbred, their father's favorite stallion and Rosewood's top stud for the past twenty-two years. Last spring he'd covered Allure but now he was enjoying a well-earned retirement. They had high hopes for this last of Stoneleigh's get, and equally high expectations for the foals sired by their new stallion, Nocturne.

They shut and latched the stall door and then moved on

to the next stall, where Margot's own mare, Mystique, and her foal, Cascade, were both on their feet. More curious than Allure, Mystique ambled over to them. Cascade followed, his chestnut ears swiveling back and forth like a radar.

"He's going to be a real beauty," she said. "And so big. He's the largest of the foals, isn't he?"

"Yeah, he should reach seventeen hands easily. We've already had some interest in him—Tim Mitchell came by this afternoon."

Tim Mitchell . . . *TM.*

No, she was not going to indulge her private obsession and wonder whether Tim Mitchell was the mystery man who starred in her stepmother's diary, the TM who, according to the pages Jordan had read over and over, had changed Nicole's life. The question of whether Nicole had betrayed their father was always in the back of Jordan's mind, troubling her to the point where any man between the ages of twenty and sixty-five with the initials TM was a possible suspect.

The only exception was the man standing beside her. Travis Maher belonged to that rare breed of good, honorable men. But the mystery of who TM could have been nagged at Jordan. For some reason she couldn't let go of her compulsive need to figure out who might have been involved with Nicole. And when in its grip, she would pull out Nicole's diary from its hiding place in her closet and read it, searching for clues. The diary was loathsome, its existence a dark ugly secret shared among Margot and Travis and her, one none of them wanted revealed to Jade. At times she wanted to throw it away or burn it, but it didn't feel right to throw away her stepmother's private writings. And so the bright pink journal with its equally shocking prose sat on a shelf in her closet, buried under a pile of clothes.

"Tim's a good rider," she said. Tim Mitchell wouldn't

have been Nicole's type. Compared to RJ, her father, Tim had the charisma of a doormat.

"Yeah, he's got a good seat and light hands. And he likes our horses. Cascade might be a good match for him. An additional plus is that Tim would let us train Cascade. But before we draw up a bill of sale, we'll have to see whether Margot can bear to let this guy go. Colchester and Gulliver were hard enough for her." He reached out his hand, letting the colt catch his scent before scratching the underside of the foal's jaw.

She smiled. "It's funny how Margot's so disciplined and focused—even driven in some respects, and such a softie."

"Saying good-bye to any horse you've cared for is hard. Gulliver was tough because he was the first horse she met when she came home after your dad died. And Colchester, well, he was so fine, even I had a lump in my throat when we loaded him into the van. All of us will understand if she decides she can't sell Mystique's first foal."

Jordan loved Travis for being sensitive enough to cherish what made Margot special. "She's going to make a great mother."

"Margot? Yeah, she will." There was such love and pride in his voice.

"I hope you two are getting serious about baby-making. My kids need some cousins to play with."

She never would have thought to see Travis blush, but there it was, two bright flags coloring his lean cheeks, visible even in the subdued light. "We're working at it," he said.

"I hope so. As they say, practice makes perfect."

A slow grin split his face. "I don't think we can get much more perfect, but I'm always happy to try." More seriously he continued, "But I don't want to rush Margot before she's ready. She's got her career to think of. The contract for the Dior campaign's almost up, so she and Damien are booking as many shoots as she can fit into her schedule to create a financial cushion for Rosewood."

"We're doing okay with the farm, aren't we?"

"Better than I'd have thought, given the size of the hole we were in. But every year in the horse business is different. I've been mulling over a couple of ideas about how to add to our revenue. A number of horse owners—some die-hard fox hunters and a few who like to compete in local shows—have approached me about the possibility of buying our horses and boarding them here, so I could offer training sessions, perhaps even lessons. I know RJ would never have considered opening up Rosewood this way—"

"But we're not Dad," she said firmly. And she was as determined as Margot not to repeat the ruinous mistakes he'd made. "Times change. Rosewood Farm will have to change, as well. So we should definitely consider all the options available to us. But, Travis, won't offering lessons and training sessions add to your responsibilities tenfold?"

"We'd have to start small, increasing the number of boarders and lessons only once we're sure they aren't causing a negative impact on the breeding and training program. But as to the extra work, I wouldn't mind it. I love what I do. For now, though, this is simply a fallback idea in case we find we can't get the farm's finances into the black, or if Margot decides to take a break or even say good-bye to modeling."

"Well, you can count on my support." Whatever decision was reached, she knew Travis would never sacrifice the quality of care and training of any horse. "And if I get this interior decorating business running, that'll bring in money, too—not the kind Margot makes, but at least it will be something to add to the kitty."

"Speaking of taking on too much, I have a hunch that working for Nonie Harrison won't be any picnic. She's got a reputation for putting people who work for her through the wringer."

"I'm sure she won't be that bad, though I confess to feeling unusually warm and fuzzy toward her right now," she said with a smile as she stepped out of the box stall. Travis gave the colt a final scratch on the neck and drew the latch behind them.

"I hope you're right," he said, as they walked toward the barn door. As Travis hit the lights, shutting off all but the center row, she stepped outside.

Only a few errant clouds marred the night sky. Tomorrow would probably be as fair as today. When she talked to Nonie in the morning, she'd ask whether she could drop by the cottage with some paint chips so she could look at the colors with the light pouring in through the windows. She was eager to start work. It wasn't everyone whose first commission entailed putting the finishing touches on such a great renovation project.

The sound of Travis's boots on the gravel courtyard roused her from her introspection. "The weather's getting so lovely," she said, still looking up at the night sky. "I'm going to start serving dinner out on the back porch. Better yet, maybe I should serve dinner for you and Margot out there. You two don't get enough time to yourselves."

"Jordan, if there's anyone who needs private time, it's you. You do everything for the kids, you run the house for the rest of us, and now you're starting this business. Don't you think you need to do something for you alone? Not all guys are like Richard—"

"Don't worry about me. I'm fine, Travis. Really. With a few exceptions—you and Ned and the rest of the guys at Rosewood—I've decided the male species is vastly overrated. Thanks to Nonie, I now have something far more interesting to think about."

Jordan lowered her tea mug to the kitchen counter with a loud clank. "You're saying you've changed your mind? You want Owen Gage's firm to decorate the cottage?" There was no way she could suppress the reed-thin note of disappointment in her voice.

Nonie didn't seem to notice, answering breezily, "It makes such better sense, Jordan. Owen and I talked after you left and the longer we discussed the pros and cons, the more I realized I'd really rather have Owen's firm do the interior. With Owen I won't have to worry about anything going wrong, and everything will come out just as I want. I'm sure you understand how it is. Listen, dear, I must fly, I have a hair appointment. Let's lunch again soon. And you must come and see the cottage when it's finished."

Like hell I will, Jordan retorted. The words went unspoken, though, for the phone clicked on the other end of the line and she was left with dead air.

Anger welled inside her as she slammed the receiver onto its cradle. She could just imagine what Owen Gage had said to change Nonie's mind. He'd probably shot down every one of her ideas within minutes of her departure. Damn Nonie, too, for being so easily persuaded. Given her penchant for gossip, she bet Nonie would be sharing the results of her decision with everyone she met at the hair salon, the local market, and every single party she attended in the coming weeks. It galled that her best chance to get her business off to a flying start had just crashed to the ground.

Shoving her stool away from the counter, she stood, grabbed her tea mug, and went over to the sink to dump its tepid contents before putting it in the dishwasher. Her movements jerky, she closed the dishwasher with barely controlled violence.

Damn, damn, damn, she thought. Why couldn't things go her way for once? Hadn't Richard done enough damage? Why did her first attempt to make something of herself professionally have to be snatched away, and by the likes of Owen Gage, too? He had everything: good looks, charm, success . . . and greed galore. How embarrassing to think that while her heart had been fluttering madly in her chest simply because he'd lowered his face to hers, he'd been plotting to steal the decorating commission from her. Men were such cheating, underhanded bastards—

"Hey, have you seen my car keys?" Jade asked, hurrying into the kitchen, a bulging bike messenger bag slung across her shoulder. "I swear they were in my bag but I can't find them anywhere and I'm going to be late for class if I don't leave in, like, thirty seconds. Mr. Jawolski is a headcase about coming late to class."

"Try Olivia's Sesame Street Playhouse. Or Max's fire truck. Olivia was playing with them earlier in the library."

Jade dropped the heavy book bag at her feet, spun around, and dashed out of the kitchen. Less than a minute later she was back, keys clutched in her hand. "They were in the truck. I gotta tell ya, Jordan, your kid is deeply weird and possibly a klepto. What's with taking my stuff all the time?"

"Because it's yours, Jade. She thinks you hang the moon in the sky."

"Well, you should tell her she's risking any chance to ride Doc if she keeps making off with my wallet and keys." She stopped, her gaze narrowing on Jordan's face. "Is something wrong?"

"No, nothing."

"Come on, you can't fool me with that super-calm look. What's the matter?"

"Don't you have to go to school? Have you forgotten Mr. Jawolski?"

"For God's sake, Jawolski can suck an egg. What's up?"

"It's nothing, really. I'm just a little disappointed. Nonie Harrison decided not to hire me."

"What!"

"She's decided to give the job to Owen Gage's firm."

"That fat witch. I can't believe it— No, I take that back. I can totally believe it, and it's my fault. She's getting back at you because I got Blair suspended last year."

"Don't be silly, Jade. Nonie made it perfectly clear it was because she preferred Owen Gage's ideas to mine, which is completely within her rights."

"There's no way he could have better ideas than you."

Jordan smiled. "It's nice of you to say that, but I'm afraid you don't know how good he is."

"Here's what I know," she countered. "One, Mrs. Harrison's a vindictive cow. Two, I should never have turned Blair and Courtney in last year. It's not like anything good came of it."

"Doing the right thing isn't like winning the lottery. Often it's hard and difficult and scary. But that doesn't make it any less important. And do you really think that things at school would be easier if you'd let Blair and her friends continue to bully you?"

"But now it's not just hurting me, it's affecting you, too."

The last thing she wanted was for Jade to feel guilty because Nonie Harrison happened to be selfish and status-obsessed.

"Nonsense," she said briskly. "I'm a big girl and more than able to take care of myself. There'll be other interior decorating jobs—and until then there's loads to do at the farm helping Margot and Travis. You better get going or you'll be late for Mr. Jawolski's class. This is the spring semester of your junior year. Grades are crucial." She didn't know why she was saying this when her little sister never brought home a grade lower than an A and she'd scored above the ninety-fifth percentile in all her standardized tests.

Clearly of the same opinion, Jade rolled her eyes. "Thanks for the newsflash. You and Margot should give the college thing a rest. I'm not even sure I want to go. It's ridiculously expensive, and as far as I can tell we're about fourteen vet bills away from being broke. Besides, everything I want to learn about is inside our three barns."

Jordan suppressed a sigh. "Thanks to Margot, we're a whole lot better off financially than last year. We both realize how important Rosewood is to you, but the farm will always be here for you. College offers experiences far beyond the classroom and course books. And who knows, you might discover some interests other than horses."

"Yeah, sure." Jade's laugh was a rich mix of amusement and patent disbelief.

"Your mom would have wanted you to go to college."

Jade's mirth vanished, replaced by a stony expression that made Jordan's heart ache. It didn't matter how often or in what context one brought up Nicole, Jade's reaction was unchanging: shuttered and unyielding.

Suddenly absorbed with adjusting the strap of her messenger bag, Jade said, "It's time I split." She reached out and plucked an apple from the bowl.

"Please don't tell me that's your breakfast."

"Nope, haven't had it. This is for Aspen. He needs a special treat since Travis and Ned are giving him his shots this morning. See ya. Oh, and remember to tell Olivia not to swipe my keys or I'm gonna ground her big time. Seriously." With that she loped out the kitchen door, car keys in one hand, a bright green Granny Smith in the other.

What a funny kid. One minute Jade was the quintessential teenager—nonstop drama—the next she revealed an altogether different and surprisingly mature side to herself. Her patient yet firm manner with the children showed real insight into their characters, especially Olivia's. Those car keys wouldn't go wandering again once Olivia heard that Aunt Jade would bar her from Doc's back if she took them to Ernie and Bert and Cookie Monster's house.

Jade was similarly gifted when it came to handling the young horses she rode. Admittedly she'd been taught by the best in the business, Ned Connolly and Travis, but they wouldn't have assigned her more youngsters to work with if she hadn't possessed a knack for "reading" a horse so well. The early experiences of a green horse were too important to risk with careless or heavy-handed training.

But what impressed Jordan most was her little sister's fierce loyalty and protectiveness. Ever since that horrific morning last year, when they'd listened to Richard's philandering voice over the kitchen answering machine's amplified speaker, Jade was always ready to leap to her defense, shield her from every hurt. Though she'd tried to convince her that she was okay, that she could handle things now, Jordan realized that when Jade looked at her, she probably saw her as she'd been that morning, curled in a ball on the kitchen floor, screaming in pain as her heart was sliced to shreds by her husband's words.

Jordan flinched at the memory. No, she told herself, shaking her head as if she might dislodge the disturbing image, she wasn't going to revisit that awful time. She wasn't going to think about Richard and what he'd done or how much she hated him for destroying her faith and love.

That he and Cynthia had gotten married three weeks ago actually helped, effectively killing any screwy, masochistic reconciliation fantasies she might have harbored in moments of weakness. He was out of her life now. Even his role in their children's lives was limited . . . thanks to Jade.

Jade had been canny enough to save the damning recorded message with Richard and Cynthia's sexual banter turning to heavy breathing and guttural groans, silenced only when the tape finished with an audible click. The presence of the tape had been Jordan's ace in the hole. Richard's lawyer had murmured not a single word of protest when her lawyer requested full custody of the children in the separation agreement. In the months since their move to Rosewood, Richard had driven to Rosewood on weekends to take the kids out for an ice cream and perhaps listen to the story hour down at the Corner Bookstore, but because of Jade's quick thinking, her biggest fear, that Richard might fight her for custody of the children, never materialized.

The only way Richard could continue to hurt her now was if she allowed the cut of his betrayal to fester. The same principle applied to being passed over by Nonie. It was stupid to brood over the fact that Owen Gage had snatched the job away from her. She had plenty of things to do and ways to contribute to the farm. Indeed, even now she was wasting her precious free time while Kate and Max were at school and Olivia was bonding with her fellow tots at the toddler center's water table and sand box. She should be down at the barns helping Ned rather than wallowing in self-pity.

Grabbing a quilted vest off the row of hooks along the mudroom wall, she took her cellphone from her purse and dropped it into the vest's side pocket, then hurried out the back door into the spring morning.

With the mild weather, the foals were already in the pastures with their dams, but Jordan also worked with the yearlings and two-year-olds, helping Ned accustom them to a variety of stimuli and situations so they developed the confidence needed to be steady and dependable horses. Rosewood Farm's reputation was built on breeding and training horses that were beautiful, sound, and sane. Fostering a willing and easy temperament in a horse was something everyone at the farm worked on, starting a few short hours after a foal's birth until the day that horse was sold to a grateful new owner. Ned and Travis's method of starting and training young horses was a time-consuming process that took infinite care and patience. But having a horse load calmly into a van, canter smoothly past a rumbling tractor or a barking dog, and soar fearlessly over a brightly painted jump was a deeply satisfying reward, a goal they all strove for and worth every minute of effort.

Ned was in the main barn with Solstice, a colt with a deep chestnut coat. Ned was brushing the yearling while Tito, one of the barn's assistants, held him by a lead rope attached to his halter.

Walking up to them, she held out her hand for the colt to catch her scent. "Sorry I'm late, Ned. Hi, Tito."

"Not a problem, Miss Jordan. We only just started. Travis and I were giving the three-year-olds their booster shots."

"Did you catch Jade slipping Aspen an apple on the sly?"

Ned gave a laugh. "I'd have been surprised if she didn't. Aspen's the first horse she's ever trained. That's special."

"She's doing a real nice job with him. A little extra loving won't do him any harm," Tito added.

Jordan pressed her lips together to hide her smile. Tito was a burly man, with a close-shaven head and bulging muscles covered by extensive tattoo work. But though he came to work on a souped-up Kawasaki motorcycle, he was one of the gentlest souls she knew, always the first to volunteer for the night shift when the mares were due to foal.

"So what do you need done today, Ned?"

"How about taking Turner down to the ring? Miss Margot and Andy are riding Saxon and Mistral." He glanced at his wristwatch. "They'll be just about starting their workouts."

"Okay," she replied, nodding. They'd been teaching Turner, another of their yearlings, to stand quietly in the center of the outdoor ring while the other horses circled him at a trot and canter. This was a fundamental lesson for a herd animal, whose natural instinct was to join the group, and essential for a horse destined for the show ring or the hunt course. "Should I take him down to the pasture afterward?"

"Yeah. We'll probably be done with Solstice by then. They can play outside together."

"What are you doing with him today?"

"He's going to get a mid-morning snack on a plastic tarp," Tito said.

"Sounds like fun."

Ned moved the cloth he'd been rubbing over Solstice's back to his neck and shoulders. "If you have time before you pick up the children, I'd appreciate your giving Sava a workout. You could take her for a trail ride, get out and enjoy the spring sunshine."

Sava was one of their broodmares. She'd come into heat

last week and had been covered twice by Nocturne. To keep her in condition throughout her pregnancy, she would be ridden several days a week on the flat. "I'd love to ride out-doors today."

Ned nodded pleased. "Thought so. I heard you met the new owner of Hawk Hill."

"Uh, yes, I did."

"Travis said you were sure he'd let us continue to ride on the property. Next time you meet him, you might want to let him know we had an understanding with the Barrons. Hey, maybe you could ride over there today, see if there's any sign of life. You don't happen to have any idea if he's a rider himself?" he ended hopefully.

"I wouldn't know, but I doubt it." And after learning how conniving Owen Gage could be, she'd rather walk over hot coals than set eyes on him again. "In any case, I think I'll take Sava out toward the Gilchrists'. I haven't been there in months." Deciding it would be better to end the conversation now than answer any more of Ned's questions about Owen Gage, she said, "I should get Turner down to the ring. Have fun with Solstice, gentlemen."

Chapter
FIVE

JORDAN THREADED the lead shank through Turner's leather halter before leading the colt out of his stall and down the barn's spacious aisle. The stalls had been mucked and the aisle's concrete floor swept clean of debris, everything as neat and orderly as when her father was alive. As she walked the bay colt down the wide aisle, Jordan wondered what he would think if he could see Rosewood now, his three daughters running the horse farm that, in his day, had been an exclusively all-male domain. Would he be pleased that they'd taken on responsibility for the business that had been in their family for generations and were even making a success of it?

Their father had been such a frustrating mix of arrogance and inflexibility, viewing the world solely on his terms, understanding very little about his daughters. His rigid conservatism had been especially hard for Margot, who, though craving his approval, rivaled him for stubbornness. Time and again they'd clashed as he tried to mold her to fit his notion of what she should be and do, she resisting his every attempt.

Sadly, predictably, the inevitable showdown came. Ironically, the battle began because Margot wanted to work at Rosewood with him, learning to train and breed their hunters and jumpers. He refused to consider the possibility, insisting she go to college. Doubtless he expected Margot to follow the path Jordan had just taken: college graduation and, a short month later, a lovely antique lace wedding.

Had her father been remotely in tune with Margot, he would have known that she was already in love with Travis, at the time Rosewood Farm's trainer, and an excellent horseman, though not exactly the husband RJ Radcliffe would pick for one of his daughters. The showdown culminated with Margot threatening to run away to New York and—horror of horrors—take up modeling rather than being packed off to college.

His response had been that of an enraged king bent on subjugation. He swore that if she left to pursue her harebrained scheme, she'd never be welcomed back at Rosewood. It wasn't until eight years later, when their father was lying near death in a hospital's critical care unit, that Margot saw him again. He had just a few brief minutes to gaze upon his adult daughter before his badly damaged heart failed.

It had been so much easier for her, Jordan reflected, to satisfy her father's expectations. She often wondered whether, as the eldest child, she'd internalized cues from her parents, noting how her father adored her mother and thus adopting her gentle ways. But perhaps she was simply more like Mama, her desire to please others an inherited trait, just as Margot and Jade's steely determination and even their devil-may-care attitudes pointed straight to their father. The question couldn't but fascinate Jordan as a mother, as co-owner of a breeding farm.

Whatever the reason, she'd done her best to embody their father's conception of what a proper Radcliffe woman should be. She'd always been domestically inclined, happy baking cakes and tarts with Ellie to surprise Mama with a treat when she was weak from the medications the doctors prescribed to fight the cancer. Unlike Margot, she never complained when the rain drove down in silvery sheets, making it impossible to ride outside. Those were sweet, quiet days when she could curl up next to Mama on her bed, sewing clothes for her dolls, asking her what colors

she should choose for the rooms in her dollhouse, listening
to her tell stories about Rosewood.

Her mother had loved the old house and knew the history of the Radcliffe family probably even better than Dad,
though he could recite the lineage of each of Rosewood
Farm's foals back to the first stud Francis Radcliffe brought
to Virginia from England.

After Mama died, it seemed more important than ever to
please her father by emulating her. So on that bright Sep-
tember morning of her senior year in college, when Richard
showed up at her dorm with a box of fresh-from-the-oven
pecan rolls with their tantalizing scent of cinnamon, brown
sugar, and butter, and the news that James Saller, a senior
partner at the lobbying firm of Hudson & White, had offered him a position as an associate, she'd felt a gush of
pride that her handsome, clever boyfriend was going to
make his mark on the world of business and politics. Pride
blossomed into stunned elation when he pulled a square
burgundy velvet box from his jacket pocket and set it on top
of the bakery carton. "The salary's good, too, babe. How
about we call the folks after we eat these so they can start
making wedding plans?" With that lopsided grin of his,
which never failed to turn her insides to mush, Richard
whispered huskily, "Say you'll marry me, Jordan, or these
sticky buns will go cold while I do my very best convincing."

It had never occurred to her to suggest that they should
perhaps wait to be sure of each other—or of themselves
and their dreams—that perhaps they should grow up a little
before taking such a big step. She was in love. And after all,
her mother had married young; she'd been loved and cher-
ished.

As Jordan cried with joy, kissing Richard over and over
again while he fed her bites of sweet, buttery bun, she knew
she could make a beautiful home with Richard, too, one
that would be filled with love.

And like her mother, she'd been happy, blessedly so,

married to the man of her heart, until the day came when she was no longer what Richard wanted. And nothing—not her love, not three wonderful children, not nine years of marriage—could keep him by her side.

The sight of the exercise ring's wooden rails jarred her thoughts. Enough with the navel-gazing. She had work to do. It was a beautiful morning and she needed to concentrate on something besides herself and her failed marriage. She was darned lucky Turner was such an easygoing fellow. She'd walked the yearling down the gravel path without his causing a moment's fuss.

"Whoa, Turner." She brought the colt to a halt and lifted the latch but waited to open the gate until Andy had trotted past on Mistral. Margot, astride Saxon, a big dapple gray, spotted her and circled at the far end of the ring to give her plenty of time to lead Turner into the ring. Even though Turner was a mild-mannered colt, he still needed to have his learning situations carefully controlled so that nothing came at him too fast. Once a young horse was overexcited, its ability to learn effectively went right out the window. If the horse became rattled or spooked, it might then have negative associations with the experience, making the lesson wind up like the game of Chutes and Ladders, sending the youngster backward rather than forward in its development.

Jordan had already practiced opening and shutting the gate with Turner, and he was used to it from the daily trips to the pasture as well, so she met no resistance when she opened the gate wide enough to lead him through it, turned him in a half circle, and then brought him back slowly to the gate, again using her voice as an aid to halt him before she closed it.

The big difference between Turner's experience in the pastures and in the riding ring was that in the ring he was being taught to understand that he would be working with humans, and still under their control. As yearlings were deeply inquisitive creatures, Jordan took her time walking him, letting him see the other two horses and the wooden jumps positioned at various angles and distances in the center of the ring. Both Margot and Andy had slowed their mounts to a walk, and would resume trotting and cantering once Turner was comfortable with the goings-on.

The colt held his head high, pricking his ears forward as he gazed around, his gait over the raked sand quick and lively. Walking on his left side, careful to stay in his line of vision, Jordan kept her stride deliberate and the tension on the lead rope light.

"That's a boy. Nothing new here. You've seen this all before. Soon you're going to be like Saxon here, getting ready for the show season, making sure those flying changes are as smooth as silk. The judges are going to love you, you're such a clever, handsome fella. It'll be nothing but blue ribbons for you." She prattled on, her voice as confident as her steady stride, letting her body language communicate to the young horse that there was nothing to fear. After another tour of the ring she angled their path toward the center and again brought him to a halt. Casually she delved into her pocket, brought out a dried carrot treat, and let him swipe it from her open palm as she patted his neck.

"All set?" Margot asked, as she and Saxon passed near them.

"Yeah, he's doing great." She stroked his neck just beneath his halter's leather strap.

"He's always good for you," Andy remarked. "He's not nearly as happy when Felix takes him out."

"Jordan, hon, I saw Jade as she was leaving for school. I'm so sorry—"

She shrugged and continued scratching Turner's neck. "Don't be. It's Nonie's loss. I had some good ideas, but she obviously preferred Owen Gage's. That's the name of the game."

"I am sick to death of Nonie and her spiteful ways. What

is it with the women around here, behaving as if they're still in junior high? I'd understand if she wanted to stab *me* in the back, but you didn't have anything to do with getting Blair suspended. And now Jade's upset, convinced she's cost you your first job—"

Knowing Jade and Margot were blaming themselves made it all the worse. "Margot, this really doesn't have anything to do with what happened between Jade and Blair at school—as I already told Jade. You two are far more upset about this than I am."

"Because we love you."

"Which I'd have to be dense not to know. But even so let's keep a sense of proportion, okay? Nonie is not the only woman who has a house in need of redecorating in Warburg. I'll get in touch with Marla Hamilton next week. Her youngest is going off to college in the fall, so I'm sure she's got it in the back of her mind to do a major renovation project. And Marla would be fun to work with. So you see, all is not lost."

"No thanks to Nonie," Margot muttered.

"Again, this is not a big deal. I've got other things to focus on right now. Like this colt here. Ned won't let me go near Turner again if I don't do a good job with him."

"As if you'd ever do a bad job with any of the youngsters or mares. They go all mellow when you handle them. You're soothing."

"Or so boring I put them to sleep."

Andy, walking Mistral on the rail, shook his head. "Not so, Jordan. A bored horse isn't a happy horse. Just look at Turner. He's paying attention to everything that's going on but he's relaxed. A happy horse," he added deliberately.

"Let's see whether I can keep him this way while you guys are cantering. Oh, and did you know that Miriam's a big fan of the band Airborne Toxic Event? They're playing in D.C. next month. I think she mentioned that tickets go on sale this Saturday."

He was such a sweet guy, trying to fight back the grin that spread over his face. Surrendering, he beamed. "Good to know. Thanks, Jordan. You're all right."

She smiled. "And don't you forget it."

Jordan hadn't intended to ride Sava in this direction. It was doubtless because of the conversations she'd had with her sisters about Nonie Harrison and of being forced to extol Owen Gage's skills and his firm's excellence that she found it so difficult to get the dratted man out of her head or to squelch her curiosity about Hawk Hill.

She realized that it had been ages since she'd ridden out this way, what with her pregnancy with Olivia, and then with the turmoil of the divorce and settling into a new life at Rosewood. And from what she could see as she slowed Sava down to a walk and emerged from the wooded trail into the clearing around Hawk Hill's open fields, it had been an equally long time since anyone had done the most basic maintenance on the Barrons' old house.

Drawing the mare to a halt, she loosened her grip on the reins, letting Sava rub the side of her head against her foreleg. While the mare stood docilely, Jordan took in the sorry state of the Federal-style home. Its wood shutters hung askew, some torn off their hinges entirely, giving the façade a dilapidated look. The twin chimneys were in dire need of attention. From her perch on Sava, she could see daylight streaming through large chinks where the bricks were missing. That either chimney was still standing was a miracle, and Jordan had a sudden vision of Olivia's red sneakered toe shooting out, connecting, and sending the remaining weathered bricks flying through the air as easily as one of her cardboard towers.

The roof was hardly in better shape, with shingles missing or warped, curled like the dried leaves that spilled out of the damaged gutters that, wrenched by winds and dislodged by ice, listed drunkenly. The elements had taken their toll on the paint and siding, too. Near the damaged gutters she saw ugly black patches, the discoloration a telltale sign of rot. Many of the clapboards were badly split or warped. They, too, would have to be replaced.

Nudging the mare forward with her boot heels, she said, "Come on, Sava, let's take a closer peek at the old lady."

She knew she was being fanciful to anthropomorphize the house, but she couldn't help it, any more than talking to horses. Sava had listened to her thoughts these past twenty minutes, twitching her chestnut ears in silent, sisterly sympathy, and she seemed more than willing to listen to Jordan discuss the house as they approached it.

And the house did resemble an old lady's careworn face, a sad and lonely old lady with no one to love her. Those shutters hanging crookedly looked like mascara streaked by tears. Jordan felt a shiver of sympathy course through her. If the interior was in as sorry shape as the outside, it was going to take a lot of money and even more hard work to restore the house to its former beauty. However much she resented Owen Gage right now, as someone who loved architecture she had to be grateful that he was making the effort.

As they approached the broad lawn ringing Hawk Hill, her eyes roamed over the façade's details, taking in the double-hung windows with six-over-six muntins. The front of the house had an elliptical fanlight and sidelights bracketing the center door. On the second floor was a large Palladian window. Despite its neglected condition, it had a lovely symmetry, with graceful proportions. "Like Mama used to say about Rosewood, Sava, this house has really good bones."

"I couldn't agree with you more. Hawk Hill's going to take a lot of work, but I'm optimistic we can give the old house new life."

Jordan started in surprise, her abrupt movement causing Sava to sidestep and toss her head.

She concentrated on her horse first, settling her weight more solidly in the saddle and gathering the braided reins that had slipped through her fingers. "Easy, Sava, atta girl," she said, giving her horse a quick pat just below the neck strap of the martingale before acknowledging the man who'd approached them. "I didn't notice you were here. There's no car." Oh, God, she couldn't believe she'd been caught talking to her horse by *him*.

No, Owen thought, she'd been too busy studying the dilapidated house he'd bought. He had noted that about Jordan yesterday: how still and intense she got when she looked at something, focusing on it as if she were absorbing its essence. "I parked my car over by the barn," he said by way of explanation. He hadn't been especially visible, crouched behind one of the evergreen shrubs, inspecting one of the corner pilasters for rot. Hearing the snap of twigs and then the snort of an animal, he'd risen slowly so as not to startle the animal.

Even with her hunt cap strapped on, he'd recognized Jordan. It was something about her posture. Some part of his brain had already committed to memory the way she held herself. She possessed the same graceful posture in the saddle as she did standing. While he probably could have continued his scrutiny undetected for another few minutes, he'd stepped out from behind the bushes in order to look at the horse she was riding. He wasn't ashamed to admit that he'd also been happy to take a closer look at those long legs of hers, encased in rust-colored breeches and knee-high black riding boots. He'd be a fool to pass up such a fine sight.

"Good morning," he said with an easy nod. "Now I really know I'm in horse country. Do you visit all your neighbors on horseback?"

"No . . . no, this isn't a visit. I had no idea you'd be here." Her cheeks coloring, she continued hurriedly, "I was just out for a ride and happened to pass this way. We had an understanding with John and Nancy Barron. They allowed us to ride on their fields and through their half of the woods. In return we maintain the trails, clearing the brush and undergrowth, and mow and hay their fields free of charge. You don't mind if we continue—"

"Ride over any time you want, though it won't be quite as tranquil around here starting tomorrow when my crew arrives. So this is one of the famed Rosewood Farm horses," he said as he reached out his hand, smiling at the blast of moist warm air on his skin as the mare sniffed him. "She's a beauty."

The delicate line of Jordan's neck extended as her chin lifted proudly. "Yes, this is Sava, one of our broodmares. She's given us five great foals."

Abruptly he remembered Nonie telling him that Jordan was the mother of three. Incredible. He still couldn't believe it. Three kids *and* a messy divorce . . . he definitely should not be checking out the way her slender thighs gripped the saddle so securely.

"She looks really fit." He hoped to God that Jordan hadn't noticed he'd been eyeing her shape and not the horse's. Deliberately he focused on the chestnut mare standing quietly before him. Solidly built, she looked strong enough to travel over the Virginia countryside for hours at a time. He touched his palm to the mare's velvety muzzle and smiled at the sound of her teeth grinding against the steel bit. "What is she, a warmblood?"

"Yes, she's a Hanoverian, a German warmblood."

There'd been surprise in Jordan's voice when she answered him. She clearly hadn't expected him to know anything about horses. He could have told her that his father had been posted in Vienna for four years. On days when school was out, his mother, busy with her writing or engaged in one of the endless rounds of Foreign Service socializing, would arrange for his nanny to take him to watch the Lipizzaners perform at the Spanish Riding School. Then there were the holidays when, invited by his parents' wealthy friends, he would be buttoned into a blazer and pressed flannels, his hair slicked and combed so that he could pass muster sitting in a box at Longchamps or Ascot. His father would reward an afternoon's good behavior by letting Owen pick a horse in each race. So, yes, he could distinguish between the high-energy, hot-blooded legginess of a Thoroughbred and the characteristics of other breeds. But he didn't enjoy recounting tales of his childhood years with his capital-hopping, peripatetic parents. He'd rather store up whatever bits of knowledge he possessed and use them to keep Jordan slightly off balance.

"Do you breed warmbloods exclusively?"

"No, about fifty percent of our breeding stock are warmbloods, the remaining broodmares are Thoroughbreds. But following the tradition established by my ancestor, Francis Radcliffe, we stand only Thoroughbred studs. He started Rosewood Farm with his first stallion, Tallis."

"This is the Francis Radcliffe who oversaw the construction of the house for his bride, Georgiana? A talented man."

"Yes, he was."

"And there are riding trails connecting the two properties? I'm going to have to take a walk through the woods one day soon and return this neighborly visit—"

He'd brought up his wish to see Rosewood yesterday, too, Jordan remembered. Then he'd waited until she'd left to convince Nonie to have his firm decorate the cottage. Boy, he was really a smooth operator.

It irked her, too, to realize that those dark, rugged looks had succeeded in distracting her again. While they'd been talking she'd kept stealing peeks at him, noting how well he looked in olive green trousers and a crisp white shirt, the sleeves rolled up to expose the solid strength of his forearms and the liberal sprinkling of dark hair—why she was so obsessed with this man's body hair was beyond her. He'd snuck past her defenses, too, with his questions about

Sava and Rosewood Farm, making her forget about the cottage and the reasons for her dislike.

"I'm sure you'll be far too busy for any rambles through the woods. I spoke to Nonie this morning by the way. Congratulations."

Her abruptly cool tone alerted Owen to the fact that he'd made some gross misstep. "Thank you. May I ask what you're congratulating me for?"

"Why, the commission, of course. Nonie told me she's decided to have you do the interior for the cottage. She said you made a very compelling argument for choosing your firm."

He cursed silently. "She did, did she?" So much for his attempt to stay out of Nonie's game of petty revenge. She either hadn't listened to a word he'd said or had decided to drag him into her lies. What irritated him even more, however, was that Jordan seemed all too eager to brand him as the villain in all of this.

"Yes, she did." Jordan's very nice chin rose in the air once again. "Which is interesting, since I distinctly remember you agreeing with Nonie that my ideas for the cottage were excellent."

"I did think they were good. I told Nonie that repeatedly. Listen, I didn't try to—"

Clearly on a roll, she cut him off. "You obviously said something to dissuade Nonie from giving me the commission."

"I didn't say anything against you or your ideas." His clipped tone betrayed his growing impatience. "I *encouraged* her to go with you. Though I've got to tell you, if you intend to stick around in this business, you might want to develop somewhat thicker skin. The majority of designers routinely pan their competitors' work."

"I'm perfectly able to take criticism, but in this case there wasn't any. Nonie liked my suggestions."

Annoyed that he'd been drawn into an argument when he'd done his best to encourage Nonie to hire Jordan Radcliffe, he shrugged. "Why Nonie ended up choosing Gage and Associates is her business. I don't spend my time analyzing my clients' motives. If I had to guess, I'd say she chose us because she knows the quality of our work. I even told her that our decorator's booked solid. But I guess she decided to wait until Emily was free."

"I just don't understand it. I was so sure she liked my ideas."

And because the confused look on her face made him feel even more damnably awkward, he let his mouth run. "Maybe she was worried that the demands of the project would be too much, after all you've been through." He shut his mouth with a snap and felt like grinding his teeth as loudly as the mare was playing with that steel bit. *Damn it all,* that was about the worst thing he could have said.

He continued cursing himself as he watched her expression change from confused to blank with hurt.

"With all I've been through?" she echoed.

"Look, I'm sorry. I have no idea what Nonie's reasons could have been—" he backpedaled quickly, then stopped. She wasn't listening to his lame explanation. She'd gathered her reins and backed Sava up a few paces, putting distance between them. Realizing she was just going to ride away made him try again. "Jordan, will you please wait a second—"

Talking to him for another minute was more than she could bear. If she tried to speak, her voice would crack, and she'd been humiliated enough for one morning.

Oh God, she wailed silently. Was this never going to end? Didn't it matter that she was still haunted by the death of her father and stepmother, and by whether their marriage had been just as much of a lie as hers and Richard's? Did the events of the past year and a half have to be kept fresh by the likes of Nonie Harrison's vicious tongue?

It mortified her to know that Nonie had gossiped about her and her family to Owen. Had he been repulsed or entertained by the Radcliffe family's sordid trials? A shudder gripped her as she imagined him, for all intents and purposes a stranger, listening to the details of her failed marriage. And now he was a front-row spectator to her first professional disappointment.

She had to get away from here. Refusing to spare him even a parting glance, she nudged Sava behind the girth, turning the mare in a half circle, then urged her into a collected canter over the bright green fields, not slowing down until she was deep in the shelter of the woods and far from the man she was coming to despise.

Chapter
SIX

TWO WEEKS had passed since Jordan's ride to Hawk Hill. Thanks to the children, she hadn't been able to stew over Owen Gage. Kate had caught a bug in her class, which then hopscotched from one child to the next. With the three of them home all day, her hours had been defined by deft positionings of Kleenex and promptings of "One, two, three, and there you go with a big blow!" She'd baked cookies with M&M faces, each sporting a red nose, had spooned as much chicken soup into their tummies as they'd been willing to swallow, and pillaged the linen closet for old sheets so they could build a tent fit for a sultan in the double parlor downstairs. There they'd camped, organizing and reorganizing all the stuffed animals they'd brought down from the third floor and munching on Goldfish. When their fevers peaked and they were too miserable and fretful to nap, she would crawl into the plush animal–crowded tent and read their favorite stories until they'd quieted.

Max and Kate had returned to school, and Olivia was pretty much Kleenex-free. But too many restless nights in a row had left the toddler atypically cranky; little nothings set her crying and she refused even her favorite foods. Though she was fever-free and Jordan knew her daughter wasn't in any real discomfort or likely to starve if she didn't eat her shepherd's pie or chocolate pudding, it tore at her heart to see her sunny angel teary-eyed and woebegone. Despite the house being full of people whom Jordan loved, and Miriam coming daily to help lift the kids' spirits, it was on days like these that she felt the loss of Richard as a partner and parent acutely. She might justifiably condemn him as a husband, but he'd always shown his better self with the kids.

To pacify her unhappy toddler, she'd had Miriam play a *Sesame Street* DVD—Olivia's absolute favorite—while she ran some errands for Margot and Travis and did the grocery shopping before picking up Kate and Max from preschool.

Her first stop was Steadman's Saddle Shop, the town's tack shop, which stocked five-thousand-dollar Hermès Steinkraus saddles for the horse show set and wool hunt coats in the Warburg Hunt colors for the avid fox hunters—as well as every other item a horse or rider might want.

The brass bell attached to the door rang as she entered. There were a few customers in the store, some browsing through the racks of breeches, others checking out the boots that were on sale. Sara Steadman was over by the bridles with Freddy Banks, discussing the different types of bits displayed on a wall. They broke off to call out a hello.

"How's that new stud of yours doing?" Freddy asked.

"Great. Nocturne's a real gentleman. We're having him cover Mystique today—you might recall she's the mare Margot did so well with in the Hunt Cup." She didn't need to say more. Two years later, people were still talking about how Margot, Travis, and Jade had blown away the competition the year RJ Radcliffe died. "She's just given us a fine colt, too, one of Stoneleigh's get. We're hoping she and Nocturne will give us an equally stunning foal."

"I'll have to drop by someday soon. I'm in the market for a new hunter."

"You should, Freddy. We've got some nice horses we're bringing along that would make excellent fox hunters. Just give Travis a call," she said lightly, careful not to reveal how thrilled she was by his comment. It was a sign that in spite of the many changes that had come to Rosewood

Farm in the past two years, local riders and horse owners
continued to view it as a source for their future mounts.

Turning to Sara Steadman, she said, "Is Adam around,
Sara? I've got some pieces in need of his expert care," and
she opened a canvas tote full of leather.

"He just went to put a pair of paddock boots away in the
stock room—oh, here he is. Adam, Jordan has some leather
that needs to be repaired."

"Good to see you, Jordan," Adam said, stepping out
from behind the counter. "All that for me?" he asked, eyeing the bag. "Come on over here where the light's better."

She followed him over to the counter and laid two girths,
a bridle, two stirrup leathers, and Jade's pair of chaps on
the glass countertop. "Ned was wondering how soon you
might be able to repair these."

"Let me take a look."

She waited while Adam Steadman, who'd owned the
store with his wife, Sara, since Jordan wore jodhpurs with
garters and short pigtails, picked up the pieces and examined where the stitching had worn away.

"This lot's not too bad. I think I can get it back to you by
next week."

"And the chaps? They're Jade's. She wears them almost
every weekday. It's so much quicker than changing into her
breeches."

Adam ran his finger along the zipper lining the inside of
her sister's worn suede chaps. "Looks like I'll have to replace the zipper. See how the teeth are missing? And the
other leg looks like it's going, too. But on account of their
being Jade's, I'll get to work on them right away. How she
doing? She still teaching your little ones?"

"Yes, and doing an excellent job with them. I think you'll
be seeing Kate in the walk-trot classes this summer."

"Can't wait to see the next generation of Radcliffes in the
hunter ring. By the way, we've got a sale on children's saddles
coming up in two weeks. There's usually a run on them, as

parents get ready for the show season and pony clubs. With Max following in his sister's footsteps I thought you might be interested, too."

If she'd gotten the commission from Nonie, she could have easily splurged on a new saddle for the children. "Will you have trade-ins for sale, too?" She wondered if her question had shocked him. Surely this must be a first for him, to have a Radcliffe inquire about used equipment. But as she'd said to Travis the other night, times had changed. She couldn't continue her father and stepmother's spendthrift ways and burn through money. Especially if she didn't have a job.

But Adam, who over the years had sold thousands upon thousands of dollars in merchandise to her family, merely nodded. "Good thinking. I'll look over the used ones we get in and set a couple aside for you."

"Thanks, Adam, I really appreciate it. I'll send their instructor down to look them over. She's very particular."

"Don't I know it. Jade made Brian earn his wages when she came in to buy a running martingale for that gelding, Aspen."

Brian was Adam's nephew and a year ahead of Jade in the high school. Like his older cousins and siblings before him, he worked for Adam and Sara in the shop after school and on weekends. "I hope she didn't give him too hard a time."

"Learning how to do his job is good for him. Jade's a smart one. She had him detailing the relative merits of the Pessoa, Showmark, and our own martingale, which is made for us in England. He might not have gotten his nerve up to ask her out on a date, which I know he's real keen to do, but at least he got her to buy our model."

"If it'll make him feel better, tell him I don't think anyone else has worked up the courage to ask her out, either. He shouldn't give up hope." Jordan wasn't sure it was wise to offer false encouragement, but Brian was a nice kid. And

since he knew about horses, maybe Jade would relax her
antiboy stance.

Adam smiled. "I'll definitely tell him, but only at the end
of his shift. Don't want the boy mooning about. Tell Jade
I'll have the chaps repaired by tomorrow afternoon."

Back in the minivan, Jordan made her way to West Elm,
where the supermarket was located, passing the small shops
and establishments that were the lifeblood of the downtown
area. Warburg's small size had allowed it to retain its horsey
country roots; its proximity to Washington, D.C., gave it a
certain patina of sophistication. It was a town that sup-
ported three churches and an equally well-patronized liquor
store that stocked Dom Perignon and single-malt whiskeys.
There were four restaurants and a bagel shop that also
served thick, hearty deli sandwiches and soups for the lunch
crowd. Three or four days a week, Felix, one of the farm's
hands, would stop at Braverman's Bagels to pick up bagels
and smears for the hands' mid-morning break. But today
Jordan was doing a sandwich run for Margot and the guys
after she'd done the shopping.

Many of the stores in town were independently owned—
the Corner Bookstore had managed to survive in the era of
Barnes & Noble and Amazon by joining forces with the
small cafe next door and smashing through the adjoining
wall so that patrons could wander from one space to the
next and even buy a book to enjoy with their mocha latte.
In the mid-morning the place was a meeting spot for mothers and their preschoolers. After three, teenagers invaded to
sprawl on the sofas and armchairs and slurp their frappes
and munch on chocolate chip muffins. In the evenings the
bookstore ran several different book clubs, and on weekends the staff offered reading events for children.

Two doors down was True Beauty, a beauty salon with a
crème de la crème day spa on the second floor, offering hot
stone massages and aromatherapy body wraps for the likes

of Nonie Harrison and her sister, Pamela Hood. The florist, Fleur de Lys, did a bustling business creating lush arrangements and exquisite posies for the steady stream of dinners and parties thrown by the social set. One of the bigger shops, J.T. Ross, was a women's clothing store that carried Lily Pulitzer and Ralph Lauren. When Margot did a shoot for Ralph Lauren, the store blew up posters of her and hung them in the store's windows. Afterward, the manager wrote a letter thanking Margot for what had been the best run on their inventory ever, hinting, too, that they couldn't wait for her next shoot with Ralph.

Another boutique, Annabelle's, bravely ventured beyond Scotch plaid and flamingo prints, but it, too, had gotten a publicity boost when word got out that Margot shopped there. With a life full-to-bursting with her new marriage, running the farm, and flying to New York for shoots brokered by her agent, Damien Barnes, she was less aware of the surreal celebrity status she'd attained. But as the mother of two school-aged children, and thus more involved in town life, Jordan was often made aware of Margot's star power—and how a number of women resented her for it.

With Jordan it was a different story. They were either kind—too kind, regarding her with that odious light of pity in their eyes—or they kept her at a distance as if her divorce, like the nasty little cold Kate had brought home, was infectious. Both attitudes galled, and there were times Jordan dreamed of doing something that would shatter their notions with the force of a megaton bomb.

She never did, though, for despite her impatience with some of Warburg's inhabitants, she had a deep-rooted affection for the town. Moving back had made her aware of how much she prized the sense of connection that came with living in a place where she knew almost everybody by name. And not everyone was petty or idiotic. She had friends here, other parents and many of Warburg's merchants, like Sara and Adam Steadman, or Edie Morse, who owned

Annabelle's. But it had taken the divorce for her to realize that many of the couples in Georgetown with whom she and Richard had shared dinners and gone to parties had been Richard's friends rather than hers. With the split had come the shift in allegiance, everyone moving into the "his" column.

She turned into the Safeway. The parking lot was crowded, as many of the townspeople preferred to park here, in the large lot, while they did other business, rather than waste time circling for a spot in the street. In this respect Jordan was no different. Parking by the low split-rail fence that wrapped around the lot's perimeter, she checked her errand list and glanced at her watch, calculating. Yes, she could get the shopping done, go to the post office, pop into Braverman's to pick up the sandwich order, and still make it to the preschool on time. If the sandwiches were ready and waiting, she might even be able to dash into the Corner Bookstore and buy a new Maisie book for Olivia. The adventures of the little girl mouse never failed to bring a smile to her daughter's face.

Half an hour later, Jordan wheeled a shopping cart filled with groceries across the parking lot and stowed the bags in the back of the minivan. Feeling like a contestant in the game show *Beat the Clock*, she dashed around to the front passenger seat, gathered up the bills and letters to be mailed, and hurried down the street.

At the post office her errands race was hampered by a customer sending packages to Japan. By the time she reached Braverman's Bagels, a line had already formed leading to where George Rollins manned the cash register.

"Hi, George," she said when she reached him. "It's busy today."

"Hey, Jordan. Insane is more like it. Spring fever has struck. Everyone wants picnic sandwiches."

"Is the order Margot called in ready yet?"

"Let me go ask Roger." He stepped away from the register and went over to the back counter where five of the staff stood elbow to elbow building sandwiches, while those at the front counter sliced bagels and ladled homemade soup into cartons. George patted the deli owner's shoulder and then pointed to her. She raised a hand in greeting.

"The order'll be ready in five, Jordan," Roger called.

"Thanks."

George came back to the cash register. "Want something to drink while you wait for your order?"

"Actually, yes, can I have a large peach iced tea?" The tea here was delicious. Lightly sweetened, it came garnished with slices of peaches and sprigs of mint.

Sipping her iced tea, she made her way to the back of the deli to wait for her order to be completed. She entertained herself by reading the deli's menu that was on an enormous blackboard suspended over the front counter. The board was filled with colored-chalk descriptions of equally color-ful, and delicious, sandwich combinations and daily soup offerings.

"Jordan! Hi!"

Jordan turned. "Oh, Marla, how great to see you!" she said as she exchanged a quick hug with Marla Hamilton.

"How have you been? I haven't seen you around town."

"The kids came down with a bug. Max and Kate only just went back to school today. Olivia's still under the weather, but with half of Max's class still out, I feel pretty lucky. And how are you? I've been meaning to call you."

"Absolutely famished. I've been with Nonie Harrison all morning. She was showing me her guest cottage and telling me what she and Owen Gage have decided to do with the interior."

"Really?" A cold weight settled in her stomach. So Owen had his design team at work on the cottage. So much for the huge delay. She wondered what else Owen Gage had mis-led her about. Though it was like picking at a scab, somehow she couldn't prevent herself from asking. "So what did he recommend to Nonie?"

"Well, lots of really good, practical ideas for the rooms, like putting in bookshelves in the living room so that her guests can curl up with a novel by the fire, and installing glass-faced wood cabinets in the kitchen to make it easier to find the dishes, especially useful for guests who don't know the space. And they're going to install this green marble for the countertops that's called Verde Italia that Nonie could use with majolica pieces to add splashes of color and pattern. The colors they chose are just wonderful, Jordan. The master bathroom's going to be done in ocean hues with a glass and stone mosaic for the walk-in shower, called Pacific Blue. The rest of the bathroom will have marble and ceramic tiles in a deeper hue. And the decorator had this idea for installing a double-ended claw-foot bathtub that is so romantic! I would love to have one to soak in alone. Or," she paused, her eyes twinkling merrily, "now that Bruce and I are going to have the house to ourselves, I might invite him into the tub, too. We haven't done that sort of thing in years.

"And if the tub hadn't sold me, the decorator picked out the sweetest wallpaper by Jane Churchill for one of the smaller bedrooms. It has these Indian elephants. It was so whimsical yet tasteful. I simply adored it. I've made Nonie promise to put a word in for me so I can get bumped ahead on their waiting list. You must get her to invite you over the second the cottage is finished. I know you're going to love how it looks."

That wouldn't be hard, Jordan thought, furious. From what Marla told her, Owen Gage had ripped off her every idea, right down to her suggestion of using majolica pieces to enliven the kitchen space. She'd known Nonie would go for that, because she loved to collect Victorian majolica. And now, piggybacking on her insights and creativity, he was going to get Marla's business. Damn him.

Did the man have any principles? Dumb question. What really angered her was that there was no way to set Marla straight. It wasn't only Owen who was being underhanded. Nonie was lying through her teeth by giving him credit for her ideas. Soon half the town would be discussing Owen Gage's *brilliant* ideas.

"Marla, I haven't told you but I'm opening my own des—"

Her overture was cut off by a shout of "Order's all ready, Jordan."

She turned. George was holding a large shopping bag aloft. Giving him a nod of acknowledgment, she opened her mouth to finish telling Marla about her new interior design business, but then Marla began speaking.

"My God, look at this crowd. I better jump in line and place my order before I faint from hunger. I've decided on the curried chicken salad on sourdough with a side of the purple coleslaw and extra pickles. And I think I'll get the pastrami on rye with red onion chutney, too. It's Bruce's favorite. I'm going to drop by his office and surprise him with lunch—what better way to butter him up for when I tell him I want to hire Gage and Associates to redecorate?" she said with a conspiratorial grin.

Jordan walked out of the deli in a daze, barely registering the faces of the people strolling along the street, completely oblivious to the cars rolling past. She didn't even notice the silver Audi TT that slowed to a crawl, its driver's side window descending.

"Jordan."

She spun about, the weighted paper bag she was carrying bumping into her leg. She gripped the cup of iced tea in her other hand, its surface cold and slick with condensation.

Owen Gage had braked to a complete stop. He shifted in the driver's seat and gave her that easy, confident smile.

Without warning, something inside her cracked, and the anger she'd buried exploded.

"You jerk." With a snap of her wrist, she dashed her iced tea into his too handsome face. Just as quickly she turned and marched down the street, ignoring his enraged cry of, "What the hell!"

He deserved it, every last stinking drop, she thought. That was a small price to pay for going and lifting her ideas for Nonie's cottage and then effectively stealing Marla, a client she'd been hoping to land. What an arrogant so-and-so, to believe he could hail her with impunity as he drove by. As if his underhanded dealings didn't matter.

Fury propelled her for the next block and a half. Then suddenly her feet stalled as out of the corner of her eye she caught sight of Fleur de Lys's window display. She turned to stare at the pale ivory arrangement of peonies, tulips, and white roses suspended in the center of the window, creamy silk ribbons hanging from it in gently curling streamers.

Her bridal bouquet had been made of peonies, too, entwined with the palest green viburnum and wild hibiscus.

Jordan's anger died as abruptly as it had erupted. Its flames extinguished, she was left with nothing but an aching hole.

Yes, she'd been infuriated to learn of Owen's sneaky business tactics, but her anger was ultimately superficial compared to the despair she had experienced listening to Marla Hamilton. Her friend's happy chatter about how she was planning to surprise Bruce with one of his favorite sandwiches in order to sweet-talk him into agreeing to a redecorating project, her pleasure at the prospect of recapturing sensual thrills with him, of loving him enough to want to rekindle the excitement and passion in their marriage of many years, had reminded Jordan of how very much she had lost. So many things were gone from her life and who knew when—or if—she would ever be so lucky as to experience them again?

And then Owen had materialized, a man who, with a single inquiring lift of his dark brows, probably had women jumping into his bathtub for a splash-filled romp. In her anger and despair she'd lashed out at an obvious target.

Oh, God, she wailed silently as tears began to slip down

her cheeks. She was an emotional wreck. How could she have behaved so badly, with such an appalling lack of self-control? How could she have called a man she'd only met twice a jerk and then hurled iced tea at him? Even if she could somehow justify her behavior, she was *not* the type of person who flew off the handle in public—or private.

She stared at the lush flowers that shimmered like sunlit silk through the wash of her tears. She couldn't remember when she had last received a bouquet from a man. Impossible to calculate as her tears had now become choking sobs.

God, when will it stop hurting? Pressing a fist to her trembling lips, she abruptly became aware of the bag weighing down her other hand, and with it the pressing weight of her other responsibilities.

She had to pull herself together, she thought, wiping her tears. Resolutely turning away from the flower shop, she hurried down the street toward the Safeway parking lot so she could perform an emergency makeup application in the seclusion of the minivan. Even if it took all the lessons Kristin had taught her to hide the evidence of her crying jag, she couldn't let Kate and Max see her sad. And, by the time she pulled into Rosewood Farm's drive, she would have her cool and unruffled mask firmly in place.

Her family had enough to worry about without her adding to the list.

The woman was certifiable. A dangerous virago. What in hell had possessed Jordan Radcliffe to chuck her tea at him? He hadn't even *seen* her in two weeks.

Dripping wet and boiling mad, Owen pulled into the nearest space and jumped out of his car, intent on catching her and demanding what in the blazes she'd thought she was doing. But by the time he reached the spot where he'd seen her, she was already halfway down the block, beating a fast retreat. He followed her with his eyes boring twin holes into her slender back, and even called her name, but she'd obviously decided to pretend she was as deaf as she was crazy.

Although he walked fast, he didn't manage to close the distance between them. Those long legs of hers, which he'd so foolishly admired, were eating up the sidewalk.

But then as if she'd run into an invisible wall, she stopped, turning to stare, as if entranced, into one of the store windows.

For some reason—perhaps on account of the strange stillness that had stolen over her—Owen found himself hanging back.

He glanced at the store's sign, surprised to find that it was a flower shop and not a jeweler hawking Cartier. Yet Jordan was looking at the window display with the fixed intensity and longing most women—certainly the women he knew—reserved for the most radiant of diamonds.

Suddenly he noticed her shoulders were shaking. She was crying. Something inside him twisted into a tight knot of helplessness at the thought of this beautiful woman weeping openly.

He was still standing in the same spot when abruptly she dried her tears. He watched her visible effort to compose herself, draw a deep breath, and throw back her shoulders as she quickly walked away.

Unwilling to disturb a woman who only seconds ago had been weeping as if her heart was broken, Owen remained where he was. But his gaze followed Jordan until she was lost from sight.

He'd made the right decision, he told himself. Strangely shaken by what he'd witnessed, he wasn't sure whether he'd end up chewing her out or pulling her into his arms to make her hurt go away if he actually confronted her.

Even considering such a move was colossally stupid.

If he had been too dense to read the signs before, today's encounter removed all doubts. This woman had enough emotional baggage to scare off any man who possessed an ounce of self-preservation. While he might be really good at bringing old houses back to life, tackling a divorcee's battered emotions wasn't his thing. The job was too messy and involved, calling for a commitment he wasn't willing to make for anyone.

So why in hell, an inner voice mocked, was he stepping up to the florist's window to try and figure out what could have caused those tears?

Because he hadn't been able to stop thinking about Jordan these past couple of weeks, that's why. And whenever those thoughts popped into his head, he couldn't help feeling an uncomfortable twinge of guilt for the way he'd handled things when she'd quizzed him about why Nonie hadn't given her the job of decorating the cottage. Although he'd have liked to blame Nonie Harrison for the whole sorry business, he knew he was partly responsible. Busy with other projects and lining up the crew to start work on Hawk Hill, he'd neglected to tell Emily Carlson, the head of his interior design department, to stonewall Nonie if she called about having her cottage decorated. As a result, Nonie had run roughshod over Emily, insisting that as she already knew exactly what she wanted done to the cottage, all Emily would have to do was order the materials. And that being the case, there should be absolutely no problem fitting her into the spring schedule.

Why people who behaved as badly as Nonie should be rewarded by strokes of good luck was one of life's great mysteries, but as it happened, one of their clients had been forced to postpone a remodeling project due to an unanticipated surgery. With a newly open spot on the schedule, Emily acquiesced.

"As great a pain in the butt as Nonie Harrison is, Owen, she's good for business. Having redone her cottage inside and out will boost interest in Hawk Hill," Emily had pointed out reasonably when he'd belatedly phoned her. "And as busy as I am with my other jobs, it's kind of nice to have one that's a no-brainer. She really does seem to know what she wants, even down to the tiles in the master bath."

He'd understood the wonder in his decorator's voice. As a general rule, clients dithered, changing their minds about paint colors and cabinet styles and fixtures about as often as they blinked.

"Yeah, well, as they're not our ideas, I'd like you to come up with some alternatives for her to consider."

"I'd be happy to. But as you've reminded us in meetings so frequently, the client is always right."

"Very funny, Em."

Never having interfered in Emily's artistic decisions before, and unwilling to jeopardize a very good working relationship, Owen decided to let her deal with the walking talking headache that was Nonie Harrison in her own fashion. He only hoped Emily was going to be able to convince Nonie to use her ideas rather than Jordan Radcliffe's.

And when he thought of how ham-fisted he'd been in revealing to Jordan that he'd heard some of the stories circulating about her and her family, he had to acknowledge the uncomfortable truth: Jordan hadn't been too off the mark in calling him a jerk. Perhaps that was a sufficient reason to be standing like this in front of the florist window, critically examining the cream-colored bouquet in the center of the display.

It was nicely done but too cool in its hues and too uniform in its palette for a woman as subtly complex and emotional as Jordan Radcliffe. She deserved flowers that exploded with lush color, whose blossoms carried a fragrance as alluring as the scent of her soft skin.

Chapter ✸
SEVEN

JORDAN SAT CROSS-LEGGED, flashlight in hand, reading from *No Fighting, No Biting* while Kate, Max, and Olivia lay flat on their tummies, their bodies like spokes on a wheel, a bowl of Goldfish the hub. They listened to the story, munching happily, pausing in their plundering of the bowl every now and again to flip over onto their backs and shine their own flashlights onto the roof. In the darkened interior, which Jordan had created by placing a light blanket over the sheets so that the kids could pretend they were having an overnight camping trip, the beams crossed and dueled to muffled giggles.

" 'Willy, you are squeezing me,' " Jordan read, her voice pitched in a childish whine.

The chime of the doorbell interrupted her next sentence. "Okay, guys," she said, closing the book. "You sit tight while I answer the door. I'll be right back."

"Who is it, Mommy?" Kate asked, scooting onto her knees to accompany her to the door.

"Probably the DHL man with an envelope for Aunt Margot."

Her answer had Kate flopping back down onto the stuffed animal–littered floor. The kids were more than used to the comings and goings of the DHL man delivering envelopes and picking up signed contracts.

"Will he have pictures of her?"

"I imagine so." Earlier in the week, Margot had flown to New York for two whirlwind days of photo shoots for Marc

Jacobs. "But we'll have to wait until later to look at them, when we're all done riding and Aunt Margot's finished with her work at the barn."

The doorbell rang again.

"Back in a sec," she promised. Crawling through the tent's flaps, she got to her feet and hurried to the door.

Opening it, she was greeted by a riot of lush pinks and lavenders with bright spots of yellow.

"Oh!" she gasped at the enormous bouquet, which arced in a profusion of pink peonies, purple lilacs, tuberoses, sweet pea, and brilliant yellow freesia. "How beautiful." Her gaze swept down to note black-trousered legs and polished loafers. She looked up again to find Owen Gage gazing back at her.

Every muscle in Jordan's face tightened.

"Oh." The exclamation was toneless this time. After what she'd done earlier today, he was the last man she had thought or hoped to see again.

"Here, a peace offering."

When she made no move to take the flowers, he extended them a fraction more, and she caught a hint of their heady fragrance. She inhaled again.

"Come on, show a little mercy. I really am sorry." The corner of his mouth lifted in the beginning of one of those compelling smiles that for some reason never failed to make her insides do a little flip-flop.

She narrowed her eyes. "What *exactly* are you apologizing for?"

"I'm not sure," he admitted, unabashed. "Though I'm assuming it has something to do with Nonie Harrison and her blasted cottage."

"You took my ideas for the interior and are using them on the cottage," she accused flatly.

The slight tightening of his lips was the only outward sign that her comment stung. His voice remained calm. "My interior designer has been offering her own suggestions for the cottage, but Nonie's apparently quite taken with your ideas. So far she seems bent on following through with your every recommendation. Believe me, I'm not happy about the situation, and obviously I'd like her to be more receptive to Emily's ideas because she's got a terrific eye. But there's not a lot we can do when a client's mind is set. For what it's worth, I am truly sorry about the entire business."

Jordan refused to be mollified. "Nonie's going around telling people that you're the one who came up with the design ideas."

"Ahh. Well, I can promise you that while we may be doing the work on the cottage's interior, no one at Gage and Associates is claiming credit for the interior design. Emily has plenty of other projects that demonstrate her talent. So you'll have to go and pour iced tea on Nonie if you want to avenge yourself for that particular wrong."

Color rushed to her cheeks. She knew it was her turn now to apologize for having dumped her drink on him. She wished she didn't have to. She wished, too, that his explanation of the events wasn't so reasonable. Of course Owen wasn't going around claiming her ideas for himself. He didn't need to. Any interior designer who worked for Gage & Associates would be top-notch. It would be churlish to hold this situation with Nonie Harrison against him, when it was clear who the guilty party was. The thought of marching up to Nonie and tossing iced tea into her botoxed face made the corners of Jordan's mouth lift in a reluctant smile.

Taking a breath, she straightened her shoulders. "I apologize for losing my, um, temper. I don't usually do that sort of thing. I'd be happy to pay the dry-cleaning bill if I stained your shirt."

He inclined his head. "Apology accepted," he said simply. "And I pay for my own dry cleaning. Now, are you going to accept my humble peace offering?" He took a step forward so that the blooms of the massive bouquet were tantalizingly close.

The man was dangerously clever. He knew that the flowers were too beautiful to resist. A bouquet like this must have cost him a tidy bundle. If this was his idea of a humble peace offering, she wondered what he did when he really screwed up.

When she made no immediate move to take it, he added cajolingly, "I had the florist cut the stems. They'll need to be put in water very soon."

Right. If she wasn't going to get a commission any time soon, she might as well console herself with a truly gorgeous floral arrangement. Meeting his gaze defiantly, she reached out to relieve him of the flowers only to realize she was still holding on to the flashlight and book.

"Here, take these," she said, handing them to him in exchange for the cellophane and raffia–wrapped bouquet. His startled expression gave her a sweet sense of satisfaction. How nice to see the smooth Owen Gage caught off balance.

"Come on inside," she said, stepping back into the foyer. "Feel free to take a look around while I go find a vase—I know that seeing Rosewood's a principal reason why you're here."

Jordan sorely underestimated her own appeal if she believed that, Owen thought. She'd been on his mind far too often these past two weeks, and somehow every encounter with her left him more intrigued. This despite the warning signs that with any other woman would have had him staying very much away.

He told himself that he kept ignoring all his well-honed instincts because she was uncommonly beautiful.

That was true. Even now he found his eyes fixed on her retreating form. She was barefoot of all things, with her long legs encased in black breeches that ended mid-calf. She looked as fine walking away from him as she had staring up at him with her wide blue eyes. He could now add the fact that she possessed a very lovely ass to the growing list of attractions he'd compiled about her. With her hair pulled into a casual ponytail and her torso hugged by a snug-fitting top, she looked far too young to be the mother of three . . . far too sexy as well.

He eyed the book in his hand. Charming title. Had she been reading it as a sermon? The book obviously meant the kids must be lurking somewhere in the house. But what the hell was the flashlight for? he wondered as he stepped across the threshold into the foyer.

But then he beheld the majestic circular staircase with the stained-glass oculus centered above it, and the architect in Owen took over, crowding out the specter of fighting and biting rugrats and the puzzle of what one used flashlights for in the middle of the day.

One didn't have to be an architect to get lost in the beauty of the house. Its exquisite details hearkened back to a golden age of craftsmanship and design. The examples were everywhere—from the inlaid star pattern in the center of the foyer's parquet floor to the intricate carving of the door surrounds—and as he looked about he couldn't help but feel awed. Stepping into the rooms was like stepping back in time.

To his right was the double parlor, its length divided by a screen of slender Corinthian columns, and in the center of each space hung matching crystal chandeliers. Sheer white curtains covered the windows, and where the windows had been thrown open to let in the fresh air, they billowed and shifted like ghosts coming home. Though he wasn't into whimsy or Ouija boards, he found Rosewood the type of place to inspire thoughts of ancestors who roamed the rooms. The ghosts would be happy here, their spirits at rest in a place so lovingly preserved.

To be honest, he hadn't really expected the interior to be as fine as the exterior, with its soaring columns and wide porches and magnificent presence. So many generations had lived in the house, it was reasonable to assume that some kind of architectural butchery would have been committed along the way. It was rather amazing that the family had had the sense not to destroy the place in the name of modernization, and that where they had updated—installing central heating, for instance—the alterations were as discreet as possible.

It was impossible not to get lost in the beauty of the space as he moved about this first room, soaking up the details of cornices and flutes. He only wished that instead of shoving a flashlight into his hand, Jordan had handed him a measuring tape and notepad so he could jot down proportions, sketch a detail of the ceiling's moldings.

And, God, the antiques. He knew people at Christie's and Sotheby's who would cheerfully commit murder to get their hands on some of these pieces. That the furniture was being used daily by Jordan's family, rather than cordoned off or stuck inside a glass case, would probably kill *them*, though. Auction house people got uptight about original Duncan Phyfes. Owen, however, liked seeing the fuchsia iPod resting on the marble-topped side table and the open laptop on a tall, clawfoot secretary. He even liked the kitschier details of the décor: the lamps whose bases were made from what looked like trophies—horse trophies, he assumed—and the porcelain statuettes of hunting dogs pointing at an unseen quarry. All these prevented the room from feeling like a museum, or worse, a mausoleum.

And though the room had a lived-in feel to it, the Radcliffes were obviously taking pains to care for the antique furniture. Every piece gleamed softly, polished and dust-free. The pieces in the second parlor must require special care; they'd been covered with sheets for extra protection.

He crossed the center of the room, admiring the carved capitals of the columns. A low whistle of appreciation escaped him when he saw the grand piano tucked into the corner of the second parlor. He had a sudden vision of women in white and men in cutaways, cognac snifters in hand, as the notes of the piano floated through, as clear as the crystal teardrops of the chandeliers. Okay, this place was really something, but it was time to cut out the ghostly fantasies, he told himself.

The muffled giggle behind him had the hair on the back of his neck standing straight up.

He spun around and saw no one—no Jordan, vastly entertained by his architect's awestruck expression for what to her was simply her family home. So who the hell had made the noise?

The laughter came again, this time followed by an equally loud "Shhhh!" and his eyes zeroed in on the sheet-draped furniture.

They were in there. The kids. Damn. He'd have preferred a few moldy ghosts.

He really didn't do kids. Perhaps if he was quiet they'd leave him alone.

No such luck. The sheet twitched like a live thing. Three little faces appeared in the vee where two sheets, draped over the backs of chairs, met.

They were staring at him. Six round eyes unblinking. The two older ones had on jodhpurs, long-sleeved polo shirts, and socks. The littlest one, about two feet tall, wore elastic-waisted blue jeans and a pink shirt.

"Uh, hi."

"Who are you?" The largest one, a girl, asked.

"I'm Owen."

There was a silence as they digested that piece of information.

One of them was a boy, with hair Jordan's deep russet color. His eyes, however, were a greenish brown. Across his nose and cheeks there was a liberal smattering of freckles, which Owen knew many would find the height of adorableness. But he was too preoccupied by the weird, bright orange smear across the kid's face to feel any softening of the heart.

It looked like the boy had been drawing on his face with a marker. Then he opened his mouth and Owen saw the stuff crusted on his teeth.

"Are you here to weed?" the boy demanded.

Did he look like a gardener? "No."

"That's my sister's book." His stubby index finger pointed accusingly. "Are you going to weed to us?"

"Oh, right, *read,* not weed—no," he said hastily. "I'm not here to read. I came to see Jord—uh, your mom."

"Are you a friend of Mommy's?"

He hesitated. That was a tough one. How to answer? "I guess so."

"Do you want to sit in our tent?"

He didn't know which was more unnerving, the questions the boy kept firing at him or the steady blue stare of the other two kids.

"I think I'm too big." There was no way he was getting in there with them.

With no warning, the littlest one started to lurch toward him. This set off the others: they advanced in single file behind her. As they neared, he took a step backward and bumped into the piano bench with his calf.

"You know, I wonder where your mom is. Maybe you guys should go find her—*ooof!*" The littlest one, moving in that downright frightening half-walk, half-lurch, had collided into his legs with surprising force.

Dropping the book and flashlight onto the piano bench, he reached down to steady her—Christ, the last thing he wanted was for the kid to get hurt and start to cry—and that seemed to be some kind of signal for her to climb into his arms. Agile as a blond-haired monkey, she hung about his neck and somehow he just knew she wasn't going to release him without a hell of a good reason.

Then she started talking, a rush of gibberish of which he couldn't understand a syllable. Whatever it was she was saying, though, she seemed really happy about it, pumping her legs up and down against his gut in ecstatic punctuation.

"Can either of you translate? Does she need to go to the bathroom?"

The question prompted peals of laughter from the little boy, while his older sister continued to stare at him with her deep blue eyes. Meanwhile the babbling and leg-pumping continued unabated. He was getting seriously worried; he'd already gotten drenched with iced tea today. No way was he going to tolerate leaking tots. "Really," he said with a touch of desperation. "What is she saying?"

"Olivia's telling you that she's going riding with her aunt Jade after Kate and Max have their lessons."

Damn, but he was happy to see Jordan. The arrival of her mother had the blond monkey scrambling out of his arms with a finally intelligible cry of, "Mommy!"

Her other two children switched their focus, as well.

"Those are really pretty flowers, Mommy," said the older girl—Kate, that was her name.

Jordan put down the flowers, which she'd arranged in a large blue and white Chinese vase. "Yes, they are. Mr. Gage gave them to me."

"Is that Mr. Gage?" The boy pointed to him.

"No pointing, Max. And yes, that's Mr. Gage. Now—"

"Owen," he interjected. "You can call me Owen." Being addressed as "Mr. Gage" by someone less than three feet tall made him feel about ninety years old.

Jordan paused fractionally, the only sign that she'd heard him. "You guys better run to the bathroom before Aunt Jade gets home or you'll be late for your lesson."

"Is Owen going to watch us wide?" piped up the boy again, and while Owen was remembering to translate "wide" into "ride," the tot began babbling wildly again.

Even the older girl, the quiet, watchful one, spoke up. "I'm going to be trotting on the rail all by myself today."

"And that's a huge accomplishment, sweetie, but I'm not sure Mr. Gage—Owen," she corrected at his pointed cough, "will be able to stay long enough to watch."

So she wanted him gone already, and his five minutes' exposure had definitely exceeded his tolerance limit to kids. But her answer had the perverse effect of making him actually consider sticking around.

"I'd be delighted to watch you—" He was going to say her name but damned if he hadn't forgotten it. Jordan didn't look any too pleased by the news, but the little girl gave him a shy smile. At least he could win over some females.

"You'd best get ready then, Kate. Max, your face needs a good wash. No way will Aunt Jade let you ride looking like that. And please take Olivia with you so she can clean her hands."

Olivia, however, didn't seem inclined to follow the program. Wrapping her arms about Jordan's legs, she buried her face against her knees and began stomping her feet with surprising force.

Certain she was going to blow, he tensed. Maybe he *should* get out of here. Toddler tantrums were definitely outside his comfort zone. Taking a cautious step sideways, he caught the flash of what looked like a smile on Jordan's face. But then she was bending over and scooping up her child and planting a quick kiss just beneath her ear. Setting her back down on the ground, she dropped to one knee. "Go on, Olivia, so you'll be all ready for Aunt Jade. If you're a very good girl, she might let you help groom Doc."

The kid blurted out a long response. Owen felt as if he were watching a foreign movie with no subtitles, straining to catch an intelligible word.

But Jordan merely nodded and said, "Yes, I'm sure he'd love to meet Cookie Monster someday."

"Come on, 'Livia." The older girl walked up and took one of the toddler's hands.

"Yeah, come on, Wiv," Max said, grabbing hold of the other.

Orderly as soldiers, the three of them marched from the room.

He looked at Jordan with renewed admiration. She obviously had untold gifts, able to interpret sounds that had, at best, only a tenuous connection to language, able to quell impending riots with a simple kiss. Although now that he thought about it, he wasn't so astonished by the latter. He was beginning to suspect that he might do a hell of a lot for one of her kisses.

The million-dollar question was, what exactly would it take for him to convince Jordan to kiss him back?

He realized how novel the question was, one that he'd never had to ask. The women he dated all knew the rules of the game and were expert players. He liked that, looked for it in a woman, so why was he even entertaining these thoughts about the highly inappropriate Jordan?

The problem was that he'd been working too hard lately. His fixation was his body's way of telling him that he needed to get back to Alexandria this weekend.

He would ring Fiona Rorty, a lawyer he'd been dating for the past couple of months, and invite her out to dinner. Bright, sexy, and more committed to making partner in her corporate law firm than ensnaring him as a partner, Fiona was just to his taste. A night with her would be the perfect antidote to Jordan. Back to normal, he'd be able to look at Jordan without wanting to grab her and drag her like some caveman into her kids' tent.

She was standing by the table where she'd placed the vase of flowers, adjusting the arrangement. She lingered at the task, fiddling with the stems, adjusting the arrangement, and then stepping back to study the effect.

"That was extremely impressive, the way you talked the little one down."

She glanced over her shoulder at him. "Pretty routine stuff, actually. I'm sure if you cast your memory back you'll remember your mom doing much the same."

His mother? Not likely. She had things to do: articles to write, important people to meet, parties to attend. In all probability the nannies his parents hired had possessed those skills. Honestly, though, he couldn't remember ever even contemplating a temper tantrum. His parents would have made sure to spoon-feed him instructions about the proper protocol for a career diplomat's offspring with his baby cereal. "I was an only child. My mother's job description didn't call for the same level of involvement or finesse."

"An only child?" She turned to face him. For a moment she was silent, as if pondering that fact, though why that would be an important piece of information was beyond him. "I've always thought being an only child was kind of sad."

He shrugged. "It might have had its drawbacks but it had advantages, too."

She looked unconvinced. "I know my childhood would have been a lot harder without my sisters. Even now, I don't know what I would do without them." A door slammed and she checked her watch. "Speaking of which—"

"Hey, everybody, I've been released from the salt mines," a voice rang out. "Jordan?"

"In here," she called out before explaining, "It's my youngest sister, Jade, back from school."

Ah, yes, this was the one Nonie wanted locked up in a juvenile detention center.

The younger sister strode into the room with the snap and crackle of a fast-approaching storm. It wasn't due, however, to her I-don't-give-a-crap deep pink hair color, shocking though it was. It was the raw sexuality she exuded that made one think of a night filled with lightning strikes. A sexuality made all the more potent for her obliviousness.

No wonder Nonie despised the teen. The older woman would give her eyeteeth to possess a tenth of the kid's high-octane sex appeal.

Owen thanked his lucky star that he wasn't the type of guy who lusted after jailbait, like Nabokov's character Humbert Humbert. He had definite age requirements for his bed partners. They needed to be old enough to have actually seen an LP record and have voted in at least two presidential elections. He liked women, not girls.

Besides, Nonie was right: Jade Radcliffe definitely looked like trouble—that is, for the guy who fell for her. He had no doubt she was the sort who would put a man through the wringer.

None of this meant that Owen was blind or that he couldn't appreciate the sensuality of Jade's lithe figure or the intensity of her jewel-like gaze as it swept over him with open curiosity even as she began speaking to Jordan.

"So are Thing One, Two, and Three ready to go? The clock's ticking." She tapped a huge, ugly watch strapped to her delicate wrist.

"I sent them off to the bathroom to wash up after their snack. They just need to put on their boots and they'll be ready to go. And I talked to Olivia. She's very sorry about taking your keys. I don't think she'll be playing with them again."

"She better realize this is strike two. One more time and I'm going to have to get seriously tough with her."

Owen wondered exactly what getting tough with a chubby-cheeked linguistically challenged tot entailed.

"Wow, those are really nice flowers you picked up. Are we planning a party, or did Margot score a mega contract?"

"No party plans, no new contract," Jordan replied. "Owen brought these. Jade, this is Owen Gage. Owen, this is my sister Jade."

"Hi there, Owen Gage," she said, friendly enough as they shook hands. But then her eyes narrowed in suspicion.

"Whoa, wait a minute. Aren't you the architect who stole the decorating job Jordan wanted with Witch Harrison? That's, like, so lame."

It was a toss up as to who was more embarrassed by the question, Jordan or him. "Nonie was already my client—" he began as Jordan simultaneously answered, "Jade, I told you it's not that big a deal."

She shot them both down with a derisive snort. "What total BS. Mrs. Harrison should have given you the job, Jordan. He must know it, too," and she gave a toss of her magenta head in his direction. "Or he wouldn't have brought you half a freakin' garden."

"I bought her the flowers because—"

Once more Jordan's answer edged him out. She was obviously accustomed to the teen's rapid-fire delivery. "He only brought me the flowers because I flung my iced tea in his face and called him a jer—" she stopped, the word hanging unfinished in the air, a bright flush stealing over her face, clearly appalled at her admission.

Not so her sister. "You called him a jerk? Good one, sis," she said approvingly. "That was really ballsy of you. But FYI, guys don't give you flowers after you dump a drink on them. It's far more likely he gave you the flowers because he's suffering from a major guilt trip. Or else it's because he likes you. So which is it, dude?" she asked, pinning him with her green gaze.

He opened his mouth but nothing came out.

"Wow, such eloquence." She snorted again. "Cripes, are men losers."

Jordan pinched the bridge of her nose. "Jade—" she began in a weary tone.

"What? You're a great decorator and the local talent. It's not right for him to get away with muscling the little guy out of the marketplace." Shifting her attention back to him, she said, "You should see what Jordan's done to the third floor. Take him upstairs, Jor—"

"No! That's really not—" and there Jordan stalled.

This time it was Owen who won the "who could respond to Jade faster" contest.

"I'd be happy to see what your sister's done on the third floor, though I'm already well aware of how talented she is. Actually, that's one of the reasons I'm here—to ask Jordan if she'd be willing to decorate Hawk Hill for me." It wasn't even a lie. With Emily booked through the fall, he'd been wondering what to do about the interior. It had occurred to him that he could contract the job out. And why not take advantage of the "local talent," as Jade had so charmingly put it?

It was immensely satisfying to have rendered both sisters speechless with one simple announcement. Score one point for the male gender, Owen thought.

Jade recovered first. "You're going to hire my big sis to do the interior of Hawk Hill?"

"If Jordan wants the job."

"Cool."

"The project is a bit more involved than Nonie Harrison's cottage."

"Jordan can handle it, *no hay problema.* You should do it, sis."

"I . . . uh . . ." Jordan's voice was faint.

"Maybe you're not a total loser after all," Jade informed him. Then, with the speed of a ricocheting bullet, she switched topics. "God, I'm starving. The burgers they served today looked like shoe leather. Hope there's something to raid in the cookie jar. What are we having for dinner?"

"Baked red snapper with spinach and cherry tomatoes, and parsleyed baby potatoes," Jordan replied.

"A Margot meal," she pronounced with revulsion. "Can't imagine anyone will be having seconds, which means there'll be enough food to invite your new boss to dinner."

"I don't— He's not—"

"'Cause not only is he your new boss, he's our new neighbor and good-looking in an older guy kind of way. You know who Owen here reminds me of? Clive Owen, the actor you liked so much in that Queen Elizabeth flick you made me watch over and over again."

"Jade, I don't really think—"

"You don't see the resemblance? Well, maybe not." Jade gave a careless shrug. "Sorry, Owen. I guess my big sister doesn't think you're that studly after all. But no matter, as the most important reason to invite him, Jordan, is it's the right thing to do. Neighborly. And you and Margot are all about doing the right thing, aren'tcha?" She paused, letting this last sink in, perhaps just waiting until Jordan's lips tightened in exasperation. She wasn't disappointed.

The kid was masterful, playing her sister expertly. And Owen sensed she wasn't finished.

"You'd be doing Travis a favor, too. He'd probably dig having a guy other than Max to talk to—and could you tell me where in Toledo those brats of yours are?" she demanded.

Just then the pounding of feet on the parquet floor reached them. "At last. Any longer and I would've had to charge you overtime."

Jade, obviously savvy about her wrecking ball of a niece, prevented Olivia from barreling straight into her by catching her under the arms. Holding her wriggling frame firmly in place, she glanced over at Jordan. "Diaper?"

"Dry." Jordan answered with the voice of someone who'd just stepped off one of those gigantic roller coasters.

"All rightie then." With a practiced motion she hoisted the toddler onto her hip. "You guys ready to rock and ride?"

The two older children nodded vigorously, while Olivia squirmed and squawked with terrifying glee.

"I guess we're outta here then. You coming down to the ring?" At Jordan's dazed nod, she said, "Good, 'cause Travis and Margot will want to meet Owen before dinner. And don't forget to show off the third floor. It might help you negotiate a higher fee. You're going to have to start shopping for another pony pretty soon, you know."

Ignoring the excited cries her comment generated, she turned to him. "Nice to meet you, Owen."

He answered her impish grin with a broad smile. "A pleasure, Jade."

Chapter
EIGHT

A STRANGE AND EERIE QUIET, like the aftermath of a tornado, descended over the parlor after Jade left with the children.

Jordan got no further than a shaky, "Well . . ." Her mind reeled, her thoughts in too great a disarray for coherent speech.

Had Owen really come to Rosewood to offer her a job when he had an undoubtedly top-notch in-house interior designer at his disposal? The notion staggered. She remembered him saying something about how his decorator was booked through the summer, but still, he must know scores of other decorators. Why would he offer the job to her, an untested, unknown entity? Finding a reasonable explanation for his motives was too difficult after Jade had so thoroughly muddied the waters.

What had prompted her normally hypercritical little sister's about-face with regard to Owen? Jade couldn't really believe that simply because Owen claimed he was here to give her a decorating project, that made him one of the good guys and that he should be rewarded with an invitation to dinner? And wasn't it too cute of her to spout that line, "It's the right thing to do," to justify her meddling.

The prospect of having Owen stay for dinner didn't alarm Jordan nearly as much as the idea of taking him on a tour of the third floor. Violence of any kind was abhorrent to her, but right now she could cheerfully throttle Jade for her nifty suggestion.

And she was definitely going to have to find a way to even the score with Jade for having pointed out how much Owen Gage resembled Clive Owen.

Darn her for being right on the money. The two men did share the same dark, rugged good-looks. The last thing in the world Jordan needed was to be thinking of Owen in movie star terms, especially as he had already assumed a leading role in a few of her sexual fantasies.

Hawk Hill might represent a terrific career opportunity, but she was not showing him the third floor. A sudden vision popped into her mind of Owen crossing the threshold of her bedroom, entering it, filling that intimate space with his masculine presence. No, a hundred times no.

Absorbed in her thoughts, she started at the sound of his voice.

"It sounds as if you've done quite an impressive job with the third floor."

"Jade was exaggerating. A teen thing."

When he simply smiled, she added a bit desperately, "Really, it's basic stuff up there. I was on a very tight budget and had to do a rush job on the rooms because I wanted the children to be comfortable as quickly as possible after the divorce." Oh, good one, Jordan. First denigrate your work and then bring your personal sob story into the mix to guarantee you sound as unprofessional as possible.

"That's all to the good. It'll be interesting to see the choices you made under less than perfect circumstances. I'd also like to see what you've done to create a family-oriented space since it'll likely be a family that buys Hawk Hill."

She didn't budge. "It's really messy up there. The kids have been home sick."

At this he cocked a dark brow. "Are you going to tell me next that the CDC quarantined the entire floor? You *are* interested in decorating Hawk Hill for me, aren't you?"

"Oh, all right. Come this way."

Her aggrieved tone made her sound far more like her sister

Jade than the coolly elegant and poised Jordan Radcliffe he'd come to know. Magnanimous in victory, he gestured politely for her to precede him.

"After you," he said, careful to hide his smile as she strode from the room.

Even though Owen was retracing his steps, the grandeur of the double parlor still impressed. "I haven't had a chance to tell you how much I like your home. It's incredible."

He saw her shoulders relax a bit. So he was right: the prospect of acting as tour guide to the rooms she and her children shared unnerved her. Well, he was more than happy to distract her by discussing Rosewood, though he found it rather sweet that she was in such a twist about showing him the upstairs quarters.

"I'd like very much to come back and study these rooms more carefully, perhaps make some sketches. The interior details are remarkable."

She hesitated, perhaps torn between her pride in the house and her reluctance to have him in it. "I'll have to ask Margot and Jade how they feel about that."

"Of course." He was pretty sure he'd get a yes vote from Jade. Now, after meeting the teenager, he was extremely curious to make the acquaintance of the fashion model. If Nonie's antipathy was any gauge, she must be something. He wondered why Nonie wasn't openly hostile toward Jordan, who was beautiful, talented, and smart; then he remembered the cheating husband. Pitying Jordan would be even more satisfying to someone like Nonie. He was suddenly damn glad that he'd asked Jordan to decorate Hawk Hill.

His steps slowed to admire the ornate molding over the doorframe.

Noting his interest, Jordan looked up. "Nice, huh?"

"Yeah."

"Some of the details, like the acanthus molding and such, were designed by John Butler in consultation with Francis and Georgiana. He sent them drawings in his letters and then modified them according to their suggestions. My mother, who loved this house and knew practically everything about it, used to show them to me."

"The letters?" he asked, following her into the foyer. "Are you saying you actually have letters written by John Butler to your—what was he, your great-great-great-grandfather?"

"Tack on a couple more greats, I think, and you'll have it. Yes, we've got his letters. His pattern book, too."

He paused with his hand on the bottom of the carved banister to stare at her in astonishment. "You have his pattern book?" A book like this, with the architect's drawings for a gamut of details from cornices, to windowsills and aprons, to mantels, was usually to be found only in a rare-book room of a great public library or a university collection.

"Yes. One of his descendants visited Rosewood and presented it to my great-grandfather as a gift. He thought it only right for us to have it as, according to family lore, even at the end of his career, Butler considered Rosewood his greatest artistic achievement. The pattern book's in the library. I could show it to you now if you want to look at it," she offered casually.

He very nearly took the bait. Jordan was too smart not to understand exactly what leafing through John Butler's architectural designs would mean to him. So although on any given day he'd be willing to sell his soul to spend an hour poring over those pages, suddenly, bizarrely, doing so came in second to another wish: to go up to the third floor, with Jordan Radcliffe leading every step of the way.

Her reluctance, neither coy nor feigned, only made him more determined.

"Perhaps some other time," he said, matching her studied casualness.

The smile she gave was more like a grimace.

What did she think he was going to do once they were up there? he wondered. Jump her bones? Come on, she should credit him with having a little more finesse than that.

Or maybe not.

There was nothing sexy about her clothes. Nevertheless, the sight of those long legs encased in black stretchy breeches, her trim calf muscles flexing and relaxing as she climbed the stairs, her rounded buttocks rising and falling—hell, even the curved arch of her bare feet as she pushed off the treads struck him as impossibly erotic. Now and again he caught that elusive scent which seemed to be Jordan's alone. By the time they reached the second-floor landing, his heart was thudding heavily in his chest, desire coursing through his veins. Okay, so perhaps Jordan was right to worry about whether he could keep his hands to himself.

He followed her down a carpeted hallway to the back stairs, what would originally have been the servants' stairs, which led to the top floor. Normally he would have been peering into every nook and cranny and slowing his steps past every open door. Hypnotized as he was by the subtle sway of Jordan's hips, the only bedroom he wanted to spend time in was hers.

An hour or so with her naked beneath him would do nicely for the present. Even as the thought registered, a question blared in his mind: what in God's name was he thinking, indulging in seduction scenes with this, of all women? But with arousal thrumming through him, a reasoned answer seemed unnecessary.

The servants' stairs were narrower. In the confined space the sound of their breathing was as heavy as the pounding of their feet. He could feel the heat of her body. The light fresh scent of her filled his head.

She pushed open the narrow door at the top of the stairs and then turned with her palm flat on the edge of the door as if she might slam it in his face.

Smart of her.

A part of him was surprised by the strength of his attraction and how much he wanted to know what she would feel like in his arms. And he really wanted to see her naked. Unfortunately, rather than looking as if she might be interested in peeling off those breeches for him, she looked ready to jump out of her skin.

She quickly moved away, into the center of the room, and was gesturing with sweeping strokes of her arms. He suspected she'd fell him with a roundhouse punch should he venture too near. It was time to show her he was a civilized man. He drew a deep breath to clear his head of the way she smelled, the way she looked, and made himself focus on the room.

"So here it is. I decided to make this space into an informal living room and play area for the kids," she said brightly, her cheerleader peppiness doing little to hide her nervousness.

"It's nice. Very nice." A sweeping glance was all he needed to recognize the skill she'd put into decorating the space. She'd made it a comfortable nest of colors and patterns, a room that charmed and invited.

He remembered Jordan saying that she'd been on a tight budget. She'd chosen where to spend wisely—on wallpaper with playful motifs and on beautiful fabrics for the window treatments—and where she'd saved by choosing simple furniture that could withstand the wear and tear of little people. A sofa was rendered that much cozier by a hodgepodge of throw pillows.

His imagination revved into sixth gear as he pictured just how cozy the sofa might be if he could figure how to get Jordan on it. But the sight of the toys put the brakes on that idea.

An easel in the corner had a chaotic scribbled crayon drawing on it; wooden train tracks were laid in loops and figure eights on the carpet; a stack of multicolored building blocks was piled against the wall. In another corner, three rocking horses stood in a neat row, waiting for a good gallop.

The forcible reminder of her three very real children, and

the whole messy package of domestic commitment and responsibility they represented, should not just have dampened his libido, it should have annihilated it. That Jordan
still tempted him showed the power of the attraction he was
fighting.

Christ, what was it about her?

There were plenty of beautiful, talented, and beguiling
women in the world. No need to get involved with this one.

When Jordan began talking, he was filled with relief. The
running debate going on in his head was growing tiresome.

"As I warned you, the room's pretty basic. I'm sure you'll
want to present a more sophisticated look at Hawk Hill.
Am I right to assume that the decorating will be on spec?
Or do you have a buyer lined up already?"

"No one yet," he replied. "But over the years I've learned
that potential buyers have an easier time envisioning themselves in a furnished home, so now I always get a decorator
to put the finishing touches on the houses. Bare walls, like
a blank canvas, can intimidate the hell out of people. Sometimes the buyers like what we've done so much they want
to move into the house exactly as it is, lock, stock, and bar-
rel."

He watched her slender throat work as she swallowed.
"So no pressure on me at all."

And he remembered exactly how she had smelled just below the line of her jaw when he'd brought his face close.
How her breath had caught . . .

"Not a bit," he replied, managing to hide his distraction.
"You just have to dazzle an imaginary customer. Think
Nonie Harrison to the power of ten. That'll do."

"Thanks. Now I'll never get any sleep."

He could suggest lots of things that would help her sleep
like a baby. Will you get a damned grip, he told himself
sternly.

"Uh, the kids' rooms are just down here if you want to
take a look."

"Sure." Was it possible she was unaware that her reluctance to show her own room only increased his curiosity?

The first bedroom she showed him was the little boy's. "How long have you been here?"

"It'll be a year next month. Why?"

He shrugged, looking at the pictures and photographs that she'd affixed to one of the cork-backed walls to create a visual archive for her son. He thought of the frequent moves of his own childhood as his nomadic parents traveled from one foreign post to the next. Photographs were certainly taken, to be then stuck inside albums, which in turn were stored on bookshelves, or boxed in a storeroom if the rented apartment was too small. City after city, his bedroom walls remained invariably blank and indifferent. "Tommy's a lucky kid."

"Max, you mean?" she asked with a smile in her voice.

"Right, Max. Sorry." He'd have expected her to be insulted rather than amused that he couldn't recall her kid's name. "So what about your room?"

"My room?"

"Yes, I'd like to see what you do with a grown-up bedroom," he said, determined to get back on familiar footing. Quaint childhood memories and warm, fuzzy family interiors were not it. Although his parents were fine people, they simply hadn't been parenting material. Unfortunately, they only realized their complete lack of interest and talent after he came along.

As they crossed the hallway, he assured himself that he was focusing on business. But the anticipation building inside him belied the notion. Jordan, clearly dreading what was coming, walked beside him with the boardlike stiffness of an aristocrat heading toward the guillotine.

Whereas in the other rooms she had employed an artful blend of patterns, textures, and colors, Jordan's bedroom was a different kind of experience. His immediate thought was that they'd stepped into the soothing white of a cloud on a hot summer's day. And like a cloud, the whiteness of her room was actually a nuanced symphony of many shades, ranging from bluish violets to grays. The flashes of pale gold mimicked piercing rays of sunlight.

The pieces here—a vanity table topped by an oval mirror and a bench with gently flared legs, an armchair with a matching damask upholstered ottoman—were deeply feminine without being girly-frilly. But it was the bed that captured Jordan's character perfectly.

Sensuous yet restrained. That was how to describe the four-poster bed with roped carving. He pictured her lying there against the snow white matelasse coverlet, her hair a cinnamon red, her naked body pale as poured cream, smooth and delicious.

His heart had begun pounding like a sledgehammer against a stone wall. Christ, why was he fighting his attraction anyway? There was no law against what he was feeling, a healthy dose of I-really-want-to-fuck-this-woman. They were both adults . . .

This was worse than she had imagined, Jordan conceded. Far, far worse. For all his smooth, worldly polish, Owen Gage was pure male, and being forced to watch him prowling around her room, her private haven, put her on high alert. When he passed her vanity table and casually picked her atomizer of Chanel's Cristalle, she almost shrieked, *Don't touch that!*

The command died in her throat as he lifted the bottle, sniffed it experimentally, and then replaced it with a frown.

Okay, so he was obviously something of a scent freak. What really worried her, though, was that she found his preoccupation—heck, obsession—arousing.

Or was it the barely leashed energy she sensed in him that was causing her nerves to vibrate to the point where she could all but hear them hum? When he abruptly pivoted, approaching her with all the dangerous grace of a leopard, Jordan fought to suppress the whimper that threatened to tumble from her lips.

It was a miracle she could make any sound at all when she was this close to hyperventilating.

She edged toward the door. "Well, that's it for the grand tour. Jade will have finished tacking Doc. I should head down to the ring." She took a hasty step backward that didn't do any good in maintaining distance between them.

He was way, way too close. "What . . . what are you doing?" she said breathlessly. She couldn't remember being this nervous or this aware of another person.

"I'd think that would be fairly obvious."

His voice was as warm as the hand he'd slipped around the nape of her neck. How had he managed to do that? she wondered stupidly, her brain struggling to process what was happening. His fingers lightly stroked her skin, his touch simultaneously thrilling and yet disconcertingly foreign. A fine trembling seized her, want warring with bone-deep uncertainty.

His face, already so close she could count the gold chips in his eyes, came nearer still as he angled his head. As if hypnotized by the sensual spell he'd cast, her lids grew heavy, her body strangely languorous. Still, some part of her resisted, tried to prevent what she feared, what she hoped was coming. "I think—"

"Bad idea to think. Especially when we can do this," he whispered, bringing his lips to hers.

The touch of his lips was a slow and easy graze. Its very lightness sparked her desire. A millisecond that could have been an eternity elapsed while everything in her went still and waiting, just waiting, for his lips to meet, to taste hers again.

She lifted weighted lids to find his eyes focused on her. Lord, he was so beautiful, his face the sculpted perfection of a Renaissance statue, his eyes a rich, burnt umber lit with gold. Trapped in her chest, her breath escaped in a soft moan.

At the hushed sound, a signal of her acquiescence, his

gaze burned brighter. Again his mouth claimed hers, this time boldly, his lips clinging, learning. Sensations rushed through her like a storm breaking and her heart thundered. She trembled, buffeted by the force of her response.

Solid and strong, he pressed closer, his mouth command-ing, silently urging her to open for him. Instinctively she obeyed, inviting the bold sweep of his tongue. She regis-tered the taste of him—warm, exotic, slightly salty and de-liciously male and then their tongues were tangling, rubbing in a sleek erotic slide that unleashed a flood of heat inside her. She breathed in citrus and sandalwood on his warm skin, the scent intoxicating enough to make her head spin, her toes curl into the rug, and her hands fist against the hard wall of his chest as everything inside her went fluid and soft, melting with desire.

Oh, oh, oh, she chanted in a silent litany, rendered mind-less by his kiss, by the touch of his hands on her fevered skin. Knowing only need and want, she opened her mouth wider, kissing him back hungrily.

Her response earned her a rumbled groan of approval and more, as he deepened the kiss, plundering ever more boldly, as the fingers of one hand tangled in the base of her ponytail, his other hand wrapped around her waist and then slipped beneath her cotton shirt, drawing her flush against his hard length . . . his very hard length.

The dual, high-voltage shock of his warm hand splayed over the small of her bared back and the unmistakable bulge of his erection had her jumping back as if scorched.

"No." The word was an alarmed yelp.

Owen's hooded eyes closed for a second and then opened. "No?"

"No." Dear God, what she would give to make her voice sound steadier right now.

"No," he repeated, watching her carefully. "And no means no."

"Yes—no. Definitely no. I don't do that. This," she corrected with a wild wave of her arm as if it would clarify her inane babbling.

She couldn't believe what she'd just done. She'd kissed him and it had been thrilling and hot and . . . she refused to consider what else.

"I'm not quite sure what you're saying. You don't kiss? It was just a kiss, Jordan."

Just a kiss? That's how he perceived what was nothing less than earth-shattering to her, the first kiss she'd shared with a man after Richard? Then again, why should this be in any way, shape, or form significant to someone like him? Owen probably had a revolving door installed in his house or apartment, the better to facilitate the comings and go-ings of the females in his life. It abruptly occurred to her that she'd just kissed a man and she didn't even know where he lived. However banal this kiss might have been to Owen, for her own peace of mind she had to make sure it never happened again.

"Even so, I would rather you didn't do it again. Ever."

His dark brows rose in astonishment. "Never?"

"Definitely never to be repeated." Because who knew how far things might go or whether she'd be able to resist him if he kissed her a second time.

" 'Never' strikes me as a little excessive. You seemed to be enjoying the kiss as much as I did. Men and women do kiss, you know. But if you insist—"

"I do. Especially if you want me to work for you," she added. There, she sounded calm and professional, very adultlike. An utter sham, as she wasn't feeling any of those things. Thankfully he seemed to buy it.

Christ, he thought, irritation mixed with a good deal of frustration. Who in the world stopped a kiss that was as mind-blowingly good as the one they'd just shared and then went on to decree it should never be repeated?

But Owen rarely stooped to begging and never to forcing himself on a lady. So he offered a careless shrug instead.

"That's fine, I got the message. For your information, though, I'm well able to keep business separate from pleasure. And since you'll be working for me as a freelance decorator, the operating rules are a little more flexible. So, if you ever happen to change your mind and decide to lift your embargo on kissing, let me know. I might be willing to oblige."

Chapter %
NINE

THEY HAD ONLY just started on dessert and Jordan was finding it hard to pretend that Owen Gage wasn't irritating the hell out of her. But to allow her family the tiniest glimpse of how thoroughly annoyed she was would surely give rise to some very uncomfortable questions, ones she definitely wished to avoid.

He certainly wasn't laboring under any such difficulty. She could have been a dust mote for all the attention he paid her. He hadn't seemed to think she was so uninteresting or uninspiring, so totally invisible, when they'd been in her room. The man obviously had the memory of a gnat, while hers unfortunately functioned all too well. She could still recall the warm weight, the exquisite pressure of his lips moving over hers, and, when their bodies met, the heart-stopping solidity of his erection. Try as she might to be blasé, it was impossible to get past the fact that a short while ago she'd kissed this man and he'd had an erection for her.

The nerve of him to claim that it was *only* a kiss they'd shared. Or that if she wanted to do it again, he might be willing to oblige? An arrogant oaf, that's what he was—

"Yo, Jordan, earth to Jordan," Jade's voice broke into her thoughts.

"Sorry, what did you say?"

"Maybe you've tossed the berries enough now, sweetie," Margot said, looking at her curiously.

She stared down at the ceramic bowl in front of her,

realizing belatedly that she was holding the serving spoons in a death grip and that the fruit salad of blackberries, blueberries, and kiwis that she'd prepared were indeed looking a little worse for wear. "I drizzled a pomegranate and citrus sauce over the fruit. It needs to be well mixed," she said, so Owen wouldn't think she was abusing blueberries over him.

Margot offered a plate of lemon squares that Jordan had baked to Owen. "So how long do you think it will take to restore Hawk Hill?"

"A few months at most. Luckily the house isn't in too terrible shape structurally, and I have an excellent crew, and the electrician and plumber I use are set to go. Kitchens and baths always take the longest in a renovation, so the sooner I can get Jordan's ideas on cabinets, counters, appliances, bathtubs, fixtures, etcetera, the better. The key to keeping on schedule is to avoid lag time for the construction crew."

It was good the kids had fallen asleep so quickly tonight, she thought. She was going to have to start scouring design sites.

"And what about the barn in back of the house? Is that in decent condition?" Margot asked.

"I haven't really bothered to check it out too closely, but I assume it won't be difficult to convert into a garage."

An appalled silence met his casual answer. Jordan told herself that she was pleased her family was at long last taking a more critical view of their dinner guest. Until now they had struck her as far too accepting: after riding Mistral, Travis had taken Owen on a tour of the barns to show him the horses, introducing him to Ned, Tito, and the other guys. And while she'd been feeding and bathing the children, Margot had shown him the other rooms in the house. It was all a little too chummy for Jordan's taste.

The silence around the table lengthened, stretching uncomfortably. Owen broke it with a cough that to Jordan's ears sounded more like a strangled laugh. "Then again, maybe I won't be turning the barn into a garage."

"Good call. You nearly risked getting tossed out of here on your ear," Jade said. "Turn a horse barn into a garage? Are you totally nuts?"

"Jade, if you could avoid being rude to a guest—"

"I'd say we have an obligation to inform Owen he's totally gonzo if he thinks he can sell Hawk Hill without its barn being restored as a horse barn and not some stupid shack for a BMW." Turning to Travis who was seated next to her, she said, "Aren't I right, Travis? And could you snag me another lemon square while you're at it?"

"I think I'm supposed to offer them to our guest first. Here, Owen. Better take a second one now, before the kid inhales the whole plateful. With respect to Hawk Hill, I have to agree with Jade. I can't imagine anyone being serious about purchasing a property like Hawk Hill if it didn't have the added value of a modernized barn."

"Yeah, 'cause in case you hadn't noticed this is *horse* country, dude," Jade pronounced triumphantly as she took a huge bite of her lemon square.

"Thanks for the news flash," Owen replied.

To his credit, he didn't seem terribly taken aback by Jade's attitude. Jordan guessed it was only little children who scared the daylights out of him.

"I did notice that Rosewood's barns are almost as impressive as this house," he continued mildly. "Could it be possible I'm hearing from a biased constituency?"

"Guilty as charged," Travis said. "So you should ask Jordan. She doesn't have a biased bone in her body, does she, Margot?"

"Jordan's definitely the fairest of us all."

"Yeah, she only tosses her iced tea at people who really deserve it," Jade chimed in, snorting with amusement.

Jordan's face flamed as all eyes turned to her. She even felt the weight of Owen's gaze on her. Of course it would be *now* that he'd decide to look at her. And she was pretty sure she'd caught him smiling into his dessert plate when

Margot said that nonsense about her being the fairest. She supposed she should be grateful he hadn't fallen out of his chair laughing. Fairest was not the word that came to mind when in the presence of Margot and Jade. Try plain as vanilla ice cream (which she happened to love), boring. Those terms fit to a T. If only everyone would hurry up and finish dessert, she would have an excuse to clear the plates and stay in the kitchen until her flaming cheeks cooled.

"So what's the verdict, Jordan? Barn or dumb garage for city folk?"

There were times when she was sorely tempted to suggest Jade put a sock in it. "You and Travis are right. If Hawk Hill were closer to town, like the Harrisons' Overlea, the lack of a barn wouldn't matter. But someone buying out here will presumably be interested in what the open country offers, and in Warburg that means either fox hunting or hacking over fields and trails. The horse barn should be renovated."

Owen inclined his dark head as if her opinion alone was enough to convince him. "There's only one hitch. I don't know anything about barn design."

"That's easily solved," Margot said. "Come and look at ours. Travis and Ned can give you tips on the best designs, too, can't you, hon?"

For a woman who valued her privacy more than most, Margot was being unusually friendly. Jordan could only conclude that Owen must have been at his most charming while Margot was showing him the house, except that Margot wasn't the type to be easily snowed, and Jade even less so. The teen had an ultra-sensitive BS meter. Even more baffling, though, was that Travis seemed to like him, and Owen didn't even ride.

It occurred to Jordan that perhaps the three of them were being gracious to him because of her, that they believed something might be brewing between them. Or, worse still, that they *wanted* something to develop.

If so, how embarrassing to be the object of their matchmaking. Couldn't they see that Owen was all wrong for her? A pretty big clue was that he was a womanizer. On top of that, he seemed positively allergic to children.

"I might just take you up on that offer," Owen said to Margot. "Coming over here and studying the layout of your barns would be a nice way to finish off a day's work at Hawk Hill."

Her fingers suddenly nerveless, Jordan's fork landed on her plate with a loud clatter. "*You're* going to be working at Hawk Hill? As in a physical presence there?" she asked, feeling all the self-consciousness of a teenager at pronouncing the word *physical*. The man had the worst effect on her. Surely by now she should have been able to shake the memory of his body pressed against hers.

Wasn't this interesting, Owen thought. A good three hours and change had elapsed since Jordan had addressed more than four words to him. Since the deceptively simple kiss they'd shared, one that packed enough heat to fry one's mind, she had been doing her best to ignore him.

To be honest, he'd been relieved to step back and distance himself, at least until he was satisfied he was completely over the kiss. But hours had passed and he had yet to forget a single second of it, or the way she'd felt in his arms. So he took a certain satisfaction in letting Jordan know that he was very much going to be around Hawk Hill.

"I've developed a habit of living in the houses I'm restoring. It allows me to get a real feel for period details so that the restoration work is as authentic as possible. It's more convenient, too. I can work on the house at pretty much any time I want, day or night. I like that kind of flexibility."

Jordan seemed to have lost the capability of speech. Not so her sisters.

"Isn't that rather unusual?" Margot asked. "What happens when they're working on the kitchen and baths?"

"Like, don't you make enough to afford a house of your own? Sis, you'd better make sure he doesn't stiff you."

"Living in a house while I'm restoring it may be a bit un-orthodox, but it works for me. That's the bonus of being the head of your own firm. I get to do what I want."

As he answered Margot and Jade's questions, he was aware of Jordan's continued silence. He'd really thrown her for a loop this time. Good. What in hell was wrong with her that she would decree a ban on any future kisses? A pleasure of that magnitude deserved to be explored to its very limits. But not according to Ms. Jordan Radcliffe . . .

A prude, that's what she was.

She didn't kiss like a prude, a niggling voice reminded Owen.

No, damn it, she didn't. She kissed with a sweet sinful-ness that had made him go hard and aching the instant her lips parted for him. He hadn't been that turned on by a kiss since he was . . . that he couldn't remember that far back was one more reason to be aggravated by her irrational dic-tates. And if she kissed like that, he could only imagine how responsive she would be when she made love. He took a long sip of ice water to cool his thoughts.

"So where do you live, when you're not working on a house?"

"I have an apartment over the firm's office in Alexan-dria."

"And your family's from Virginia originally?"

Careful as he was to avoid entanglements, being sub-jected to the third degree was for him as novel an experi-ence as meeting the family of one of his lovers. Since he wasn't even involved with Jordan, Margot's grilling both amused and exasperated.

Her sisters and her brother-in-law had clearly appointed themselves Jordan's protectors. Even the old gent, Ned Con-nolly, who Owen gathered was Rosewood Farm's second-in-command, had given him the distinct impression that he would come after him with a pitchfork if he gave Jordan a second's distress.

It was interesting that none of them seemed to realize that Jordan was very much a grown woman. But while Owen's parents might have been better at raising dachshunds or growing orchids, they hadn't produced a total fool. He wasn't going to rile the Rosewood clan or mess with any of them individually. Travis Maher looked more than capable of going at it hammer and tongs; Jade would probably slash his tires. He couldn't guess how Margot would retaliate, but something warned him to underestimate her at his peril. If she wanted to do a background check, he'd provide a few answers.

"I don't really have a family home. My father's a career diplomat in the Foreign Service, so my parents are what you'd call permanent ex-pat nomads."

"Oh. Where are they now?"

"Warsaw."

"Wow. Cool."

Owen smiled at Jade. "They like the life."

"So you must've traveled around a lot growing up."

"Yeah, quite a bit."

"That would definitely be cool," Jade repeated. "I'd be totally into saying 'sayonara' to my fellow inmates at Warburg High right now. They're all either loser dweebs or evil, vicious, and malicious bit—"

Jordan seemed to have recovered from the shock of hearing he'd be at Hawk Hill on a daily basis and jumped into the conversation before her kid sister could finish that particular declaration. "So, Jade, I was at Steadman's today. I gave Adam your chaps. He's going to have Brian call you tomorrow as soon as they're ready so you can pick them up. I wouldn't call Brian a loser dweeb—"

"Definitely not," Margot chimed in. "And he's a good rider, isn't he, Travis?"

Owen had already witnessed how seriously they took anything related to horses and riding. Leaning against the rail of the outdoor riding ring, he'd watched a scene that might be nothing more than routine to this family, but that possessed the marvel of an equestrian circus fused with the disciplined movements of the cavalry. At Owen's end of the ring, Jordan's little boy bounced around and around on a shiny dark bay pony that was attached to a long longe line, a beatific expression illuminating his freckled face as he followed Jade's instructions. The girl, Kate, stood beside her, a pigtailed version of her aunt's utter seriousness. Her little face was a study in concentration, as if she were memorizing her aunt's every instruction to her brother in preparation for her own lesson. It stunned him that for the half hour of Max's lesson, Kate never fidgeted or whined that it was her turn to ride.

When Max's jouncing grew too painful to watch, Owen let his gaze stray to the others. Here was a lesson to be learned: if you started bouncing in the saddle at about Max's age and somehow survived irreparable damage, you might, if you were very lucky, end up being able to sit a horse like Margot Radcliffe or Travis Maher.

Of course, the real trick would be to ride beautifully and fluidly with a maniac toddler clasped in front of you. The incumbrance daunted neither Margot nor her husband. They took turns passing Olivia between them whenever they slowed their horses to a walk. The maneuver was done with the ease of long-standing habit, this equestrian method of babysitting clearly as natural to them as cantering over the brightly painted jumps positioned around the center of the ring. Owen bet they'd have been equally able to make a circus act out of it, tossing Olivia from one rider's lap to the next, the toddler chortling with fearless glee as she flew through the air.

Travis nodded in response to Margot's question. "Brian's got serious talent. He did really well at the horse trails at Crestview last month. He and Castlerock won the cross-country and came in third overall."

"Yeah, and guess who has the major hots for him? My

BFF, Blair Hood." Jade's voice dripped with sarcasm. "So thanks but no thanks—not that I'd want to go out on a date with him anyway. I've got better ways to waste my time, like going bowling with God." At this she glanced at the clunky watch strapped to her wrist and jumped out of her seat. "Speaking of which, I gotta fly. The Rev had to bring his car into the shop so I'm driving. Think Robocop will give me a ticket if he catches me speeding with the Lord's main man as my copilot?"

"You could have the whole heavenly host crammed into that car and Rob Cooper would still nail you, so don't even think about it," Margot fired back. "Really, Jade, I am serious. You do not want to mess with him."

"Jeesh, you need to chill. After all, Robo would have to catch me first." With a grin that probably struck terror in the hearts of her two older sisters, she snagged another lemon square and sauntered out of the dining room. Seconds later, the sound of her feet hammering the wooden steps as she raced up the stairs reached them.

"Dear God, why did she have to inherit Nicole's Porsche?" Margot asked to no one in particular.

Travis reached out and placed his hand over hers. "She's just razzing you. Didn't you see how much she wanted to avoid talking about Brian Steadman? Bringing up Robo— uh, Rob was a guaranteed diversion. Anyway, getting pulled over for a speeding ticket is way too tame for Jade. When she screws up, it's on a grand scale."

Margot frowned at her husband. "Thanks. I find that so reassuring."

Owen cleared his throat. "Excuse me, I know this is none of my business, but I just have to ask. What is bowling with God?"

Owen earned a rare smile from Jordan for having steered the conversation away from Jade's penchant for trouble. "Jade and our minister, Reverend Wilde, have struck up an odd friendship. After the plane crash we arranged to have

Jade talk to him, hoping it would help her with her grief. The reverend's an unusual man. Once Jade got comfortable with him, he suggested they go bowling together. He thinks it's a healthy and safe way for her to release some of the anger inside her."

Owen considered the idea, taking into account Jade's character. "Whatever works. I remember I had a drawing teacher at boarding school who counseled going into the school woods, taking a big stick, and whacking the day-lights out of the rocky outcrops. Knocking down pins might be even better."

Margot nodded. "The competitive aspect works for Jade. She and Stuart Wilde have a standing rule that whoever loses buys the pizza for the week. I hope the man doesn't go broke. So, you went to a boarding school?"

"Yes."

Jordan noticed the look in Margot's eye and realized her sister was all set for another round of cross-examining Owen. This was really getting to be too much. "Would anyone like more coffee?" she asked.

Margot would not be diverted. "Was your school in Europe?"

"No, here."

"So you went back to wherever your parents were posted during the school vacations?"

Owen shook his head. "No, I was on a scholarship and airline tickets were pretty steep back then. But I had room-mates who invited me to their homes over the breaks. It was interesting to see how other families lived."

Jordan found Owen's casual answers, and the picture they painted of what must have been a lonely childhood, disturbing. As Margot looked ready to continue peppering him with questions, Jordan decided it was past time she cut her off. She stood and began to clear the dessert plates and coffee cups. Margot and Travis immediately rose to help.

Owen followed suit, brushing away objections. "I usually

have to pay to enjoy a meal this delicious, so let me at least help with the dishes."

That was nice of him, Jordan thought, though she rather wished he wouldn't be so gallant. Then she wouldn't feel conflicted in the least. But knowing he was going to be staying at Hawk Hill, and how appealing he could be, would only make it harder for her to ignore her physical attraction to him.

"If you offer to do the dishes around Jade, she'll probably pay *you* to have dinner with us," Travis said, taking two fruit-stained plates from him and putting them in the dishwasher.

Owen grinned. "I'll be sure to mention my love of a well-scrubbed pot."

"You do pots? That settles it, then," Margot said lightly. "You have a standing invitation. Right, Jordan?"

Oh, no, she thought. "Of course," she replied.

Once the kitchen was set to rights, Margot and Travis said good-bye to Owen. "Time for us to do the barn check," Margot explained. "It was nice to meet you, Owen."

"The pleasure was mine. Thanks for showing me the house. You and your sisters have done a great thing in trying to keep it in the family."

"Thanks." Margot smiled. "Come again soon."

Travis shook his hand. "Good to meet you, Owen. Ned and I will be happy to answer any questions you have about renovating the barn at Hawk Hill."

With their departure, Owen noted that Jordan's skittishness ratcheted up several degrees. She tried to hide it by vigorously wiping the pristine counters and arranging the folded dishtowels hanging over the oven door just so, but he was beginning to be able to read her.

"So, is tomorrow morning a good time for you to come over to Hawk Hill?" he asked.

"Oh . . . yes, I can be there at about a quarter past nine. Olivia's sitter comes at nine o'clock."

"Sounds good. I'd like to start on the kitchens and bath-rooms to get the materials ordered as soon as possible."

"Okay," she said, nodding.

It was as he'd thought. She calmed down as soon as he brought up the job, which meant she'd been half-expecting him to make a pass. He was exceedingly sorry to disappoint, but he hadn't a clue how long a barn check took and he wasn't about to have her sister and brother-in-law barging in. "We should also discuss your fee. But I'll let you see the rooms first so you get a better sense of the work involved."

"Oh . . . I . . . well, yes, I suppose that's best."

And she was clearly uncomfortable about charging people for a talent that was obviously natural.

Remarkably, having deciphered a small part of Jordan's personality only made Owen interested in figuring out the rest of what made this incredibly beautiful woman tick. For instance, he couldn't help wondering how she'd react when he kissed her again. And whether she'd taste just as sweet.

Chapter TEN

SHE HAD TO APPLY her makeup extra carefully the next morning. Nervous about meeting Owen at Hawk Hill and providing ideas for a man whose tastes were more discriminating than any audience she'd previously faced, she had sat in front of her computer until well past midnight, surfing design sites and jotting down ideas in her notebook. Still not satisfied, she had leafed through her collection of catalogs, magazines, fabric samples, and color wheels, knowing perfectly well that any ideas she had now would most likely undergo a one-hundred-and-eighty-degree shift once she was actually in the rooms and able to take in their size and gauge the quality of the light in them. Still, it was better to have some ideas, lousy as they might be, to ground her and provide a starting point. Her biggest fear was that she'd walk into Hawk Hill and draw a mortifying blank, unable to see anything but Owen, unable to think of anything but how he'd kissed her and how strangely, perversely disappointed she was by the fact that he hadn't betrayed the slightest interest in repeating the experience.

The hours of research should have calmed her. They didn't. Exhausted, she had fallen asleep to dream of strange rooms, each one more bizarrely decorated than the previous. She'd struggled to rouse herself only to be caught in the grip of a new set of dreams that shook her to the core. They were of Owen. For some reason her unconscious had changed him into a little boy, an adorable boy of about nine or ten, his hair neatly combed, and wearing what she recognized as a school uniform. His eyes were huge in his child's face, his mouth pressed into a tight, rigid line. He was walking alone along the boulevard of a foreign city—one she couldn't identify—looking up at the adults rushing past. She knew instinctively that he was lost, exhausted, and afraid but too proud to stop one of the harried grown-ups and ask for help.

The dream shifted. Now he was the adult man she was coming to know . . . but just as alone as before. He was seated on a street bench, twilight settling around him. His profile, his posture, too, were fixed while he stared up at the row of houses across the street, their windows aglow, warm gold with life.

Unlike in the previous dream, she was sure she recognized this street, was absolutely convinced she had lived in one of those rose-brick row houses. She wanted nothing more than to approach Owen on his solitary bench, slip her hand in his, and invite him into the bright warmth of her home. A futile wish, for she knew that he would only turn away in a wordless rebuff. She was reduced to watching, part of the scene yet helpless to act, her heart weeping for the lost little boy inside the man as he was slowly enveloped by the dark of the starless evening, and her straining eyes could see him no more.

A night spent dreaming of Owen Gage would have rattled her under any circumstances, but for him to appear in the guise of a lonely little boy was especially troubling. Striving to be rational, she reminded herself that it was ridiculous to be swayed by the games her subconscious played.

Whatever his childhood may have lacked, Owen Gage had overcome the deprivation and developed the skills necessary for a successful life.

Yet no cool argument could prevent her from recalling how he'd looked in that schoolboy's uniform, struggling to hide his fear as he made his way through the unfamiliar city peopled by indifferent adults. The image was as stubbornly clear in her memory as if she were looking at a snapshot of him from twenty-odd years ago.

She cursed her psyche for having latched on to the one representation of him that was sure to pierce her heart and leave her vulnerable. That road led to folly. The worst thing she could do was to get soft and mushy-hearted around Owen.

As she wielded her makeup brush, she resolved to maintain a strict professional distance. It was too bad that attitude wasn't shared by the rest of her family.

Her own little boy couldn't stop talking about him. Max was at that age where he was intensely curious about what grown-ups did, especially men. When he learned that Owen designed and built homes, he immediately wanted to know whether Owen would be willing to come over and build a super-duper tower with him, maybe even a whole city full of super towers. She blamed her foggy brain for her ill-considered response: she told him that Mr. Gage would be too busy to come and build towers as he was working on Hawk Hill, the house just down the road. Eyes lit with excitement, he'd asked whether Owen would be hammering and sawing and everything. Max was already a tool junkie, a future Home Depot weekend warrior. Before she could figure out a way to divert his interest, he was clamoring for a trip to Hawk Hill to see Owen at work, and she knew he was already imagining hammers pounding long, shiny nails and circular saws buzzing their way through planks of wood.

Owen remained Max's principal topic of conversation all the way through his maple syrup–coated waffle and cup of juice. Margot and Travis, working their way through the pot of coffee and bowls of steaming oatmeal, didn't help matters when they agreed that he should go see Hawk Hill, especially as Mommy would be decorating the interior of the house. That got Kate into the act: she wanted to go, too, so she could help pick out colors. For Kate, so meek and careful, to ask for something, well, what could Jordan say but that she'd try to arrange an afternoon for them to go over and see the work being done on Hawk Hill.

"And did Mommy tell you Owen's going to be rebuilding Hawk Hill's barn, too, Max? Isn't that neat?"

Max managed to smear maple syrup over his face as he nodded enthusiastically.

Jordan shot Margot a look for having fanned the flames to bonfire proportions. Max really liked barns.

"What?" Margot asked, all innocence.

"We don't actually have to help Owen Gage modernize the barn, you know."

"Why not? If you and he are going to all the trouble of making over the house, the barn should be equally spiffy. The higher the selling price for the house, the more people will be talking about the work you've done. Besides, I like Owen. He obviously felt bad about how Nonie treated you, so he's provided a brilliant way for you to get back at her. And what about those flowers he brought you? They're as lovely as Jade claimed—I was sure she was exaggerating. Weren't those flowers Mommy got from Owen pretty, Katiebug?"

Kate nodded solemnly. "I like the big fluffy pink ones."

"Those are called peonies, sweetie." Jordan leaned over and kissed her daughter's brow. "Of course Owen Gage has good taste in flowers. With his background he's probably constitutionally incapable of giving an ugly bouquet."

Margot shook her head. "You're as stubborn as Jade."

"Y'all talking about me again?" Jade asked, coming into the kitchen and making a beeline for the cupboard that held her favorite sugar-loaded cereal. She sat down next to Olivia's high chair, poured herself a heaping bowlful, and then liberally sprinkled some on Olivia's plastic plate.

"I'll make sure Miriam knows who's to blame for Olivia's sugar high this morning," Jordan said dryly as she passed Jade the milk. "And no, we weren't talking about you."

"Jordan's the breakfast topic," Travis informed her.

"Lucky you," Jade said, grinning.

"Lucky me," Jordan repeated. "Here Max, let's wash your hands and face. They're a little sticky." She scooped him into her arms with an exaggerated grunt. "You, Maxwell Robert Stevens, are becoming a very heavy young man! Kate, honey, as soon as you're finished, you need to run upstairs and get those teeth brushed. Don't want to be late for school."

"Okay, Mommy."

"You want us to take Olivia down to the barn until Miriam arrives? Then you can go straight to Hawk Hill after dropping these two off at school," Margot asked.

"Not necessary, thanks. I told him I'd be there mid-morning." She wasn't going to arrive a minute earlier than that.

"Oh, so the topic really was the new dude in town and whether he has a thing for Jordan," Jade said.

Jordan gritted her teeth. "I promise you, he does not have a thing for me."

"What kinda thing does he have, Mommy?" Max asked.

"Good one, guys. Now, could you stop before certain little pitchers' ears grow even bigger? And more inquisitive?" Not to mention concerned, she added silently. Kate and Max were still grappling with the fact that their daddy had recently gotten married and was off honeymooning in a place called Hawaii with his new wife, Cynthia. She had no idea how they would react to the idea of a man coming into her life. Though Jordan was apparently the only one who could see that Owen Gage had commitment-phobe written all over him, she didn't want the kids worried needlessly.

Some might argue she didn't know Owen well enough to classify him as relationship-averse, but the signs were there. Owen was successful, extremely good-looking, knew how to kiss a woman so that she melted in his arms, yet he was still single at the age of thirtysomething. His smooth charm was doubtless handy in slipping free of ties.

Another obvious clue that the man was unwilling to commit was that though he loved architecture, he didn't even own a home. Jordan hardly needed the hours she'd spent in Abby Walsh's office having her every emotion and habit dissected to figure that one out.

Margot gave her an abashed look. "Sorry, Jordan," she said quietly. "We didn't mean to be indiscreet."

"It's not like you need to lock yourself away, though."

"So speaks the girl who won't even go on a date with Brian Steadman," Jordan said, before turning on the faucet full blast to drown out Jade's inevitable retort. Testing the water, she handed Max the bar of soap. "Okay, buddy, scrub away."

By the time Max's cheeks were free of maple syrup, she found to her immense relief that the conversation had moved on to the weekend's horse show.

"Do you want to braid Aspen after school today or should I ask Felix to do it?" Margot asked Jade as she poured more coffee into her and Travis's mugs. Jade was going to be riding Aspen in the green hunter classes.

"No, Felix will have enough to do with Gypsy Queen, Mistral, and Sweet William. I'll do Aspen's braids. If he could give him a shampoo for me, though, that would rock."

"I'll let him know," Travis said, getting up from the table to clear the oatmeal bowls.

"What time are you guys hitting the road?" Jordan asked.

"Five," Travis said. "It'll take a couple of hours to get down to Lexington. We're entered in a few afternoon classes, but if they aren't running too far behind schedule, we should be able to leave the show grounds by four P.M." He sat back down and took a sip of his coffee.

"Can we go, too, Mommy?"

"Lexington is a little too far away for us all to go, Max."

"But Jade's riding," Kate said.

"Now I know how chopped liver feels." Margot laughed. Though the kids adored Margot and Travis, Jade was the supernova.

"Don't worry, Kate," Jade said. "There'll be lots of chances to see me ride Aspen."

"And we need to stay here tomorrow and take care of the other horses with Ned and Andy. We'll be really busy."

"I can help Ned with the wheelbarrow. I'm really good at pushing it," Max said.

"He'd like that," she assured him. "So Kate, are you finished with breakfast? Then let's get upstairs and brush those teeth."

She arrived at Hawk Hill with her sixteen-foot tape measure, her notebook and pen, a brick of color chips from her favorite paint company, and a number of folders filled with kitchen and bath design ideas. Armed with these tools, she was nevertheless unsure how useful they'd be in keeping her focused if Owen elected to use his charm on her. She didn't dare contemplate how she'd react if he kissed her again.

The sight of two trucks parked alongside his Audi TT made her almost giddy. Nothing to worry about, she told herself. The work crew would provide an excellent bulwark.

Walking past a large Dumpster and sawhorses with planks of lumber neatly stacked beside them, Jordan looked up at the house. What a difference two weeks had made. New cedar shake shingles covered the roof. The shutters had been removed from the windows, and scaffolding erected alongside both chimneys. Noting the fresh yellowy-brown of new clapboard siding to replace the rotted and warped areas, she realized Owen hadn't been exaggerating about having a hardworking construction crew.

She didn't bother ringing the doorbell as the front door was propped open with a brick to let the spring air in. She

stepped onto a brown paper path that had been laid to protect the hardwood floors and followed it toward the male
voices.

Though she was sure the scrunching of her steps on the paper had been drowned out by the U2 song playing on the ra-
dio, Owen must have been listening for her. He immediately
turned his head as she entered what had been the Barrons'
living room, empty now except for two armchairs covered in
canvas. His gaze was surprisingly intense, simultaneously
sweeping and penetrating, as if he could assess her mood
with a single look.

Perhaps he could. It struck Jordan that she had acted far
more emotionally around Owen than she normally did in
public. He'd certainly seen how hurt she was by Nonie's
malicious gossip, and he'd been very much on the receiving
end of her outrage, his unsuspecting face her target. As an intelligent man, he'd most likely gathered all sorts of clues
about her yesterday at Rosewood—how easily he could
make her respond to his kisses and searing touch topping the
list. Reserved and collected around others, she'd revealed
more facets of her self to Owen in their short acquaintance
than many people had ever been permitted to see.

He wasn't the only one blessed with powers of observation, however. She was confident in her growing ability to
read him. For instance, after the look he'd aimed her way,
brief and intense as lightning, his gaze became shuttered,
his expression carefully bland. Polite but distant.

She wondered how early he had learned that particular
trick from his career-diplomat parents.

But after last night, she preferred impeccably mannered
aloofness over riotous kisses, which led to troubling dreams,
both kisses and dreams threatening to turn her carefully ordered world topsy-turvy.

"Good morning," she said, assuming her best professional manner.

"Good morning. Doug, Jesse, this is Jordan Radcliffe.

I've asked her to do the interior design for the house. Jordan, these are two of my crew. Doug Brandt's my foreman, and this is Jesse Frye, my carpenter. They'll be on site most days."

Thank God. The more people around, the better. "Hello," Jordan said with a friendly nod at the two men. Doug Brandt, with salt-and-pepper hair, looked to be in his early fifties. Jesse was a good deal younger; Jordan put him in his mid-twenties. In work boots and jeans, their cellphones stuck into leather cases that hung from their belts, they were attractive men, well built and amply muscled. What surprised Jordan was that Owen, looking his well-dressed self in a crisply ironed, blue-on-blue-striped shirt with navy blue trousers and brown loafers, was just as much of a masculine presence as the two brawnier men in their cotton T-shirts and worn jeans. She would have much preferred to find him too showy in comparison. No such luck.

"You from around here, Jordan?" Jesse asked.

"I grew up in the house just next door, right up Piper Road. So I guess I'm as local as they come, though I did live in D.C. for several years."

"Jordan and her sisters live in a terrific Greek Revival that's escaped being destroyed by a mess of modern additions. How do you suppose that happened, by the way?" Owen asked. "It's a pretty rare occurrence."

"Luck, I suppose. For the most part the Radcliffe women all loved Rosewood just as it was. Nicole, my sister Jade's mom, insisted on redoing the kitchen and the baths—and given her and Dad's scale of entertaining, she was probably right. But she, too, understood that Rosewood should stay as it was. And the men in our family have always preferred to spend money on our horses." Or on toys she added silently, remembering with pain her father's extravagance in buying his own Cessna and his insatiable love of expensive cars.

"Jordan and her sisters raise horses, the family business," Owen explained to Doug and Jesse. "I'm going to use their barns as a model for when we rebuild the barn here at Hawk Hill."

"Horse barns, huh? That's a departure for Gage and Associates."

"Expanding our repertoire, Doug. Gotta keep you and Jesse on your toes."

"I don't have a problem building a horse barn. I like horses. Though I can't say I've ever been around them much," Jesse said.

Jordan smiled. "Well, I guarantee that whoever buys Hawk Hill will really appreciate a newly renovated barn. Horses are pretty much the main reason people move to a place like Warburg."

"I did notice that the hardware store in town sells almost as much horse stuff as anything else," Doug said.

"And they also stock carrot and corn treats in the pet food section of the grocery store," she told them.

"Gotcha." Jesse grinned. "We better make that barn a showcase."

"Hey, Jesse, you almost finished replacing the clapboards?" Owen asked.

"Still have the north side to finish. Then I was going to start repairing the pilasters."

"Sounds good. Get as much done as you can today. Monday's forecast is for rain."

"Okay." He gave Jordan a friendly nod. "Nice meeting you, Jordan."

"It was nice meeting you, too."

"Hey, Jesse, will you pick me up the turkey with jalapeño jack when you do the run to Braverman's?" Doug said.

"Sure. Are you going to want anything, Owen?"

"I'll take the roast beef with mustard on pumpernickel."

"How about you, Jordan?"

"Oh, no, that's all right. I've—"

"Jordan's got to pick up her kids at school," Owen answered for her. "She's got three of them."

There was a barely perceptible pause, and then Jesse said, "So that's one turkey and jalapeño jack and one roast beef on pumpernickel with mustard."

From the way Jesse beat a path to the door, one would have thought motherhood was contagious, Jordan thought with amusement. What she found especially intriguing was that Owen had felt it necessary to announce to his workmen the fact that she had children.

But she didn't have the chance to analyze his motives, for Owen had decided the time for idle chitchat was at an end.

Turning to Doug, he said, "Now that Jordan's here, I'd like for the three of us to go through the layout for the kitchen and bathrooms so we can tell the electrician and the plumber what we need and where. And Jordan, we'll need your order for materials and equipment as soon as we can get it."

She nodded. "I understand."

"Then let's get started."

Jordan had never been in the Barrons' kitchen. From the peeling blue-and-white-checkerboard linoleum floor, metal cabinets, and Formica counters, she guessed its last renovation had been at the beginning of the Barrons' marriage. The sleek Italian espresso machine—obviously Owen's—looked positively space age in the decidedly tired kitchen. The kitchen's dimensions were more than ample, though, especially with the addition of the butler's pantry nestled between the kitchen and dining room.

Times had changed so much since the Barrons' style of kitchen. Nowadays kitchens were a much more public part of the house. They had to be aesthetically pleasing for when family and friends were gathered around, and they also had to be designed to maximize their versatility and efficiency.

She looked around, noting the position of the windows. Then, mentally blocking out the current layout, she imagined

herself preparing a variety of meals, from a family breakfast, to a dinner party for twelve, to a holiday party where
the house would be overflowing with guests.

"I'd go for an L-shaped design, with an island here,
where the children or guests could sit," she said, gesturing.
"Now, assuming the ledge of the island goes out to about
here, that leaves enough space to put a table over by that
window for casual family meals, and for extra counter space
when a large party is being thrown."

"What appliances where?" Owen asked.

"First, I'd put the stove and exhaust hood over there,"
she said, pointing.

"You don't want the range located on the island? That's
a really popular design these days," Doug said.

Jordan shook her head. "No. If it's a family with small children, you don't want little kids sitting at the island and being
near hot pots and pans or spattering oil. I'm not keen on having the range on the island for aesthetic reasons, either. Just
imagine, if you place the stove top here, the exhaust hood
hanging overhead would be ponderous visually. But if the
stove is over here," she said, walking over to the wall to her
right, "whoever's cooking is still part of the group and able to
join in the conversation. It'll also be easier to set up the exhaust vent, as this is an exterior wall."

Doug gave a slow nod. "That's a good point."

Owen had his pen out and was drawing on a sheet of
graph paper. "Okay, stove here, island here. Sink?"

"Here, centered opposite the island, with the dishwasher
on the right and a pull-out garbage on the left—though you
may want to make sure you can switch the two, in case
whoever's the principal cook is a leftie. Then we have room
for a cabinet with cutlery drawers. The refrigerator goes
next, and we end the line with a tall pantry for foodstuffs."
She paused, watching while Owen sketched her ideas onto
the graph paper with quick, sure strokes. "Above the
counter there should be a row of cabinets."

"All right. What about on the wall where the stove is located?" he asked.

"I think we should have counters and cabinets on either side of the stove. And under the island, there should be cabinets and shelves on the three sides where there isn't seating. That, along with the cupboards in the butler's pantry, should provide enough shelving and storage space for even a large family. The main gripes people have about their kitchens center on insufficient storage space, and too little counter space."

"Well, let's get some measurements to make sure this design will pan out. You got your measuring tape on you, Doug?"

Doug patted his waist and grimaced. "It's in my toolbox outside. Just a sec—"

"I've got one here," Jordan said, digging it out of her briefcase and handing it to Doug with a smile. "I also brought along some specs for stoves, dishwashers, and refrigerators. I wasn't sure how high-end you wanted to go, so I printed out a bunch of different models." She pulled out a file and laid it on the scarred Formica counter.

Owen paused to glance at the file, then resumed sketching in the elements of the layout Jordan had described. "You did this last night?" he asked.

"Yes."

"Are we going to see another file labeled 'bathroom' that has tubs, sinks, and fixtures?"

"Yes."

"How about lighting?"

She nodded. "I found some terrific energy efficient designs I thought might work."

"Of course you did," he said gravely.

She gave him a sharp look. Yes, that was a grin lifting the corners of his mouth. "Are you laughing at me?"

"No. I'm laughing at that idiot Nonie Harrison."

"Oh," she said, feeling a warm burst of happiness at his

words. Ducking her head to hide her smile, she pushed a lock of hair behind her ear and tried to focus on the plan Owen had drawn. A definite challenge when she knew he was still looking at her.

A second passed, then Owen said, "Let's start measuring, Doug, before Jordan puts us completely to shame."

She was an even better interior designer than he had thought she'd be, Owen acknowledged after they'd finished measuring the kitchen and discussing materials, makes, and models. It took a great eye and terrific instincts to be able to walk into a room and see its potential as clearly as Jordan did.

And even though this was a big project, she wasn't intimidated by him or Doug. She had a quiet confidence in her opinions that he liked . . . a lot.

When the discussion turned to countertops and cabinets, Jordan said that before she began looking into styles and materials, she wanted to see what was under their feet. Doug, perhaps in a subtle power play, initially brushed off her request, telling her that they could install any type of floor she wanted.

Curious to see how she would handle the situation, Owen remained silent.

Jordan didn't back down or lose an ounce of her poise. "It's just that I have a hunch the original flooring might be underneath this sad old linoleum," she said. "Do you have an X-Acto knife? I do."

From the depths of her leather tote, which Owen was beginning to think was like Mary Poppins's magical carpetbag, she pulled out a utility knife and passed it to him.

Her comment had successfully piqued Doug's curiosity. Minutes later he was prying off a scuffed and faded blue square of linoleum, and then, as they discovered the wide-planked wood floor underneath, cutting out another section of the checkerboard pattern while Jordan and Owen knelt beside him.

"What do you think, Doug?" she asked.

"It looks like white oak, doesn't it, Owen?"

"That'd be my guess. We'll be able to tell once we get the glue and varnish off. The planks are definitely old, though. Look at the width."

"This is great." Though Owen caught the satisfaction in Jordan's voice, she was too tactful to ruffle Doug's feathers by trumpeting her triumph. "White oak has a lovely range of tones."

"How'd you guess what was underneath?" Doug asked.

"Our kitchen at Rosewood had wide-plank flooring, too, and both houses were built within roughly the same period. Unfortunately our flooring got destroyed when my stepmother had the kitchen remodeled. She was set on having a ceramic floor—they were all the rage. Though it's a perfectly fine ceramic floor, I've always thought her decision was a shame. It's nice when you modernize to preserve something from the past, too. Historically, wide planks like these were used in the less important parts of the house, where no guests would ever set foot, but I think the contrast of the more rough-hewn look with the intricate parquet in the formal rooms is wonderful. And luckily, wide planks are back in style. You'll be able to refinish it and bring it back to life, won't you, Doug?" she asked reaching out and running her fingertips over the glue-covered wood.

Owen's gut tightened as he imagined her fingers touching him with the same exploratory caress.

"Oh, yeah, we can make it look great."

"Wonderful." She smiled. "I'll be able to work off the honey and brown tones of the floor when I pick out the cabinet finishes and counters."

After that, Doug was pretty much a goner, felled by the double whammy of Jordan's savvy and the beauty of her smile. Owen was willing to predict that over these next couple of months while they were renovating Hawk Hill,

she would have Doug and Jesse eating out of the palm of
her hand as neatly and happily as the horses she raised.

To him, the fact that she knew about antique flooring in
grand old homes was downright sexy. As sexy as the forties-
style dress she was wearing.

With the exception of Emily Carlson, his cute-as-a button
designer who was married to her equally adorable husband, David, the women Owen spent time with generally
got a glazed and vacant look in their eyes if he let the conversation veer into the nuts-and-bolts details of his restorations. They preferred to exclaim over his projects once they
were finished and prettified. Their lack of interest in the
minutiae of building trends and tastes had never especially
bothered him. His criteria for dating a female didn't involve her acing a quiz on the evolution of wainscoting or
being able to identify a hip from a mansard roof. But that
Jordan could look so lovely while she stood in the kitchen
and spoke about how she liked to preserve older elements
of a home even when updating a room for the twenty-first
century was, well, pretty damn arousing.

If Doug, their unwitting chaperone, hadn't been there,
Owen would have had a hell of a time keeping his hand
wrapped around his pen and not working the buttons that
formed a long row down the front of her dress. The thought
that with each freed button an inch more of her creamy
skin would be uncovered and the soft curves of her breasts
revealed tantalized and tormented him. As delighted as
he'd been to see the old wooden floor, right now he'd give
a hell of a lot to be able to see Jordan's breasts, cup their
luscious weight in his hands, and watch her face as he caressed them.

A terrific fantasy but a terrible idea. He was keeping his
hands and his mouth off Jordan, just as she'd said she
wanted.

So although he could have taken the measurements for
the bathrooms without Doug's help, his contractor's pres-

ence served as a much needed safety barrier. With Doug around, Owen could act like he wasn't at all affected by her, or remotely inclined to kiss her. In fact, he'd pretty much resolved the night before while tossing and turning on the mattress in the master bedroom that he wasn't going to touch Jordan again. At least, not until she asked him to.

But a resolution like that was a lot easier to keep when she wasn't in the same room. What amazed him was that she didn't even seem to be aware of her effect on him. She was just being herself. It was small consolation that he wasn't the only one falling under her spell. From the way Doug was acting, it was clear he would happily rip up any number of rooms just to make Jordan smile.

By all rights he shouldn't have had to worry about Jordan's effect on Doug. The man was on his second marriage, with kids from both wives. At least he'd warned Jesse off. As soon as Owen caught that appreciative gleam in his carpenter's eye, he'd made sure Jesse understood Jordan was in a different league from the local women he invariably became "friendly" with when he was on a job.

Never particularly territorial, Owen found it strange that he should feel possessive about a woman who not only wasn't his, but who had gone so far as to tell him point-blank that she wasn't interested in enjoying any kind of intimacy with him.

Thank God it was Friday. After work, he'd ring up Fiona and see whether she was free this weekend. There was a woman who wasn't afraid to express her interest in a man.

Finished with the kitchen, they worked their way through the butler's pantry and then started on the bathrooms, measuring and debating design ideas, with Owen sketching in the details of the layout that he would later enter into a CAD program. They were on the second of the three and a half baths when Owen caught Jordan glancing at the slim watch on her wrist.

"Time to pick up the kids?"

"Yes, in about fifteen minutes," she said, "I'm sorry I can't stay longer. My babysitter is off early today so I can have her all day tomorrow." Her explanation trailed off as if she knew how little interest the topic of babysitting schedules held for him.

"That's all right. Let's just finish laying out this bathroom. It'll only take a few minutes. No need for you to stick around, Doug. I think I heard Jesse's truck pull up a few minutes ago. Probably back from his run to Braverman's."

"Lunch sounds pretty good right now. Want me to bring your sandwich?"

"No, I'll eat after I've checked out the chimney on the east side of the house. And, Doug, remember to request liners for both chimneys."

He nodded. "I'll call Donahue. Well, it was nice meeting you, Jordan. See you next week."

Jordan shook his hand. "It was nice to meet you, too, and thanks for all your help today."

After Doug left, Jordan watched quietly as Owen, leaning over the sink's counter where he'd balanced his pad of paper, roughly sketched in the bathroom's layout. "So you think we should have the bathtub here and the walk-in shower over here?" he asked, pointing with the tip of his pen.

She moved closer. "No, I think the tub should be angled away from the window, like this," and she drew her finger across the paper. The gesture caused her hair to fall forward, the curling end of one auburn lock grazing his forearm.

The sound of his indrawn breath was magnified in the tiled bathroom. She felt Owen go stock-still beside her, and for a second everything inside her went still as well . . . except for the racing of her heart. As if abruptly finding herself on the edge of a precipice, she took a hasty step back and tucked the wayward lock of hair behind her ear.

Owen remained where he was, his gaze fixed on the graph paper. Then, in a tone that betrayed nothing, he asked, "And the sink over here?"

"Yes," she replied. She told herself she was relieved he was behaving so professionally.

She waited, this time keeping a careful distance from him, while he finished the floor plan. When he capped his pen she picked up her leather tote and said brightly, "Well, I should be going."

With a nod he stuck his notepad under his arm. "I'll walk you to your car." But as they left the bathroom, crossed the sunlit bedroom that adjoined it, and then started down the hallway to the stairs, he said, "Jordan, aren't you forgetting something?"

She stopped, patted her bag and opened it, double checking. "No." She shook her head, then said, "Oh, thank you! My folders for the kitchen are downstairs."

His mouth twitched and then that smile, which had such a devastating effect on her, appeared. "I was actually thinking of money. You haven't told me what you plan to charge me yet."

"Oh! That's right."

They descended the wide staircase and went to the kitchen where Jordan had left her files. As she gathered them into her arms, he said, "So?"

Her cheeks went warm at the amusement in his simple prompt.

She met his gaze reluctantly. "This is much harder for me than selecting bathroom hardware. I'm rotten at figuring out what I should charge for a job I love doing."

"Loving your work is immaterial. You still need to be paid for the hours you're going to spend working your fanny off, which I know you'll be doing because this place offers a great opportunity to showcase your talent. I'd just like to know what it's going to cost."

She hesitated. "Seeing that your firm already has accounts

set up with retailers and distributors, I guess a flat fee commission would be appropriate."

"That sounds reasonable. And?" he prompted.

"Right." She drew in a breath. "How about four thousand dollars?"

He gave a bark of laughter. "That's ridiculous," he said, shaking his head.

"Ridiculous? I—"

"You should be charging twice that."

"Twice that?" she gasped. "That's insane. Four thousand is already double what I was going to charge Nonie."

"Stupid of you. You'd have spent an easy thousand on aspirin alone to deal with the headache of working with Nonie."

She fought back a smile. "No, because to do that, I'd have to be popping aspirin around the clock and I don't believe in going past the recommended dosage."

"You've never worked for Nonie."

The smile won. "Nevertheless, I can't charge you eight thousand dollars."

He cocked a dark brow. "Why not?"

"It's too much."

"I promise you by the time this house is decorated you'll have earned every penny."

She shook her head. "Doubtful, but even so, it just doesn't feel right to ask that much money until my reputation as a decorator is established."

"Okay. Then consider this. Though you may be doubling your original fee, it's only a third of what we're billing Nonie."

An appalled laugh escaped her.

"You may laugh," he said, grinning himself, "but there are certain advantages to charging a higher figure, and to prove I'm a nice guy I'll share my wisdom with you, my rookie competition. First, if you charge too little, people will instinctively wonder why and assume it's because you're not good enough to charge more. They'll pass you over when they're collecting bids for a job. Second, if you don't charge enough and have the misfortune to land someone like Nonie Harrison as a client, she's going to start adding to her wish list until suddenly you find you're not just decorating the cottage, but redoing the main house, too. And you can forget about renegotiating your fee. You'll be lucky to get five hundred more dollars from her. A higher commission fee keeps shameless opportunists like Nonie in line. So while it may seem like hubris to charge a little more, it's actually a sound business principle."

"All right, you've convinced me. Eight thousand it is. Even Jade's going to be impressed with that princely sum. Thank you for being so generous." Her smile slipped for a moment. "By the way, I'm really sorry to have to cut out so soon today."

"Don't be. We got a good amount done and we can finish up the remaining bathroom and powder room on Monday. Unless you want to come by tomorrow."

Owen couldn't believe he'd just proposed they work on a Saturday, when he had every intention of going back to Alexandria for the weekend and, with any luck, never straying far from Fiona Rorty's bed. He blamed his insane suggestion on the fact that he could still feel where the ends of her hair had grazed his skin. The thought of her glossy auburn hair wrapped around his fists as he tasted her again, having it brush against his naked chest as she moved over him, was enough for him to add, "I really would like to get the bathroom layouts finished as soon as possible."

She shook her head. "I'm afraid I can't tomorrow. Margot, Travis, and Jade are taking some of our horses to a show down in Lexington, so I'm in charge of the barns with Ned and Andy."

"Oh. That's okay." He ignored the pang of disappointment.

"I could come over on Sunday, though I'd have to bring the kids with me. Max and Kate are very curious to see the house. Of course Max would be happiest if every single one of your crew was on site so he could watch them at work. He's a bit tool-obsessed."

Having her kids underfoot was *not* what he'd envisioned. Keeping in mind how much Jordan liked them, he crafted a carefully noncommittal response. "I may have to be in Alexandria on Sunday—"

But something about the amused smile that lit Jordan's face had him adding, "But feel free to bring them over another time when Max can see the crew in action." It'd be far better if there were lots of other people around to entertain them.

"Thanks. And I'll use the weekend to brainstorm tiles and stone and cabinet styles for the kitchen and the bathrooms we've already been through."

"Good," he said with a nod. "I'll have my interior design department fax me a list of the merchants and retailers with whom we have accounts and get you listed as a freelance contractor so you can place your orders directly. I'll get my assistant to fax the employee forms for you, too."

"That'd be great."

They walked through the open front door. Spotting Jesse and Doug sitting on aluminum beach chairs and eating their lunch, Jordan waved good-bye, nodding at their calls of, "See ya later, Jordan."

When they reached her car, Owen stepped forward. "Here, let me get that," he said, opening the door for her.

"Thanks."

Though he knew she had to leave in a few minutes to collect her kids, he found himself wanting to continue talking. "So your sisters and brother-in-law are competing in a horse show this weekend?"

"Yes, show season's gearing up. Margot, Travis, and Jade are going to be busy proving beyond a doubt that Rosewood horses are still the ones to beat. Once school gets out, we'll have Kate and Max entering in the short stirrup classes."

She turned to stow her bag on the passenger seat and as she leaned over, the fabric of her printed floral dress smoothed over the supple contours of her buttocks, hips, and waist.

The dress was as seductive from the back as the front, he decided, though he had a niggling suspicion that Jordan could be wearing just about anything and he'd be thinking about those lovely curves and how they'd feel beneath his hands.

As she straightened and turned back to him, he made sure to keep the conversation going so she wouldn't guess the direction of his thoughts. "And what about you?"

"Me?"

"Do you compete in horse shows, too?"

"Oh, yes, but not very often. I got out the habit of showing while I was married. Then last year things were kind of crazy."

Owen supposed "crazy" was one way to describe what she'd gone through, with two members of her family dying and discovering that her husband was unfaithful. Though he was willing to admit to a growing curiosity about Jordan's ex, he'd already blundered once by broaching the topic of her private life. Remembering Jordan's pained expression when she realized he'd heard some of the gossip surrounding her divorce made him decide to skirt the topic.

"So you don't live for the weekend horse shows the way most of Warburg does?"

She shook her head. "No, I far prefer the day-to-day routine of training the horses." More at ease now, she smiled. "At this point I only show when it's an 'all hands on deck' event, like the show at Crestview at the end of next month.

Crestview's a big draw for all the locals, so we try to have as many of our horses entered as possible. Luckily, we have some really nice green hunters who are being shown under saddle—that means on the flat—which is just about my speed these days. I'll leave the jumping classes to the rest of my family. Jade and Margot are both great competitors, and Travis is simply amazing. He makes our horses look so good."

"I got a sense of that yesterday." He also remembered that she looked like a pretty good rider herself, cantering away into the woods on Sava's back.

"Well, when they enter the show ring, they take it to a whole other level. You should go to the Crestview show." She flushed as if she'd said something wildly forward and added, "That is if you're around and if that sort of thing appeals to you—"

"I like equestrian events."

"Oh! Well then." In the silence that followed their glances met and held. "Well, I should be going," she said, a touch of breathlessness in her voice.

He nodded, still looking into the deep blue wells of her eyes.

"Good-bye."

"Good-bye."

With a quick, shy smile she slipped behind the wheel of the minivan. Owen shut her door and stepped back as she started the engine.

He stood watching as she shifted the car into reverse and backed up. Braking suddenly, she stuck her head out the window. "By the way, I forgot to give you a message from my sisters. An invitation to dinner. Feel free to come any night." Without waiting for a reply or letting him ask whether she, too, was extending the offer of a meal, Jordan turned and drove off.

Owen stood smiling with his hands shoved deep in his pockets as the criminally ugly minivan disappeared down the drive. When he considered the fact that only yesterday Jordan Radcliffe had dashed ice-cold tea in his face, having her smile at him and extend an invitation to dinner, even if it was initiated by her sisters, was definite progress. Now all he had to do was to keep his hands off her until she finally came to her senses and accepted what was clearly a case of mutual attraction.

THE ADULTS AT ROSEWOOD were up before dawn on Saturday, Jordan coming downstairs to fix Margot and Travis a thermos of coffee for the road and pack sandwiches, energy bars, and fruit for lunch. She made enough for Travis and Margot, as well as Felix and Tito, who were going as grooms for the four horses they were bringing to the Lexington show. Jade would hit the concession stand to gorge on fries, hot dogs, and cheeseburgers—her only opportunity to eat "normal" food as she liked to put it.

Jade came down last, wearing a pair of sweatpants over her breeches and a hoodie to protect her white ratcatcher. She made a beeline for the stool at the kitchen's island and plunked down on it. Freshly showered, her hot pink mop was several shades darker than usual.

"Morning," Jordan said, taking the orange juice out of the fridge and pouring a glass for her.

"Morning," Jade mumbled. "What's the weather forecast?" she asked before taking a sip.

"It's supposed to stay clear."

"Hot?"

"No, around seventy degrees."

"That's good. My sleeveless ratcatcher's got a wicked stain on the front."

Ketchup or hamburger grease, Jordan would guess, but she wisely kept her mouth shut about the probable cause. Five-thirty in the morning was not the time to enter into a discussion of Jade's eating habits. "I think they're still having a spring sale at Steadman's. You could pick up a new one next week." Jordan got Jade's favorite cereal—Lucky Charms—out of the pantry and placed it in front of her.

"Not a great idea." She grabbed the box of cereal and poured a small mountain of it into a bowl, splashed milk over it, and dug in.

"Why not?" she asked.

She munched in silence, then said, " 'Cause if I go Adam Steadman will just send Brian over to help—as if I'm so clueless I can't figure out my freakin' size. Picking up my chaps was embarrassing enough."

"What happened? Did he ask you out?"

Jade shrugged.

Which meant yes. "Brian seems like a really nice young man, Jade."

Another shrug.

"Maybe you should consider it. It's not like you wouldn't have loads to talk about. Or you could go out as a group, with a bunch of frie—" Before the word was even out, Jade's face went all tight and closed.

"Friends?" Jade finished for her sarcastically. "Newsflash, Jordan. Brian is, like, ultra popular because he's a good rider, cute, and a senior. So here's a pop quiz for you. Guess who's in his set of friends and who would not hesitate to start talking about me and Mom in a real *unfriendly* way if she thought I was going after the guy she's hot for?"

"I don't think he's the type to believe what Blair says. He'd see that they were lying about you, and just being cruelly vicious about Nicole."

"Cruelly vicious but not necessarily lying about Mom?"

Never, ever again would she engage in a serious discussion at five thirty-nine A.M. with her razor-sharp, seventeen-year-old half-sister, she promised herself.

"Yes, lying," she said, looking straight into the green eyes Jade had inherited from her mother, and wishing she'd never read a single damned page of Nicole's diary. "You

know how much your mom cared about Dad. Her life re-
volved around you and him. The airplane crash allowed
the good citizens of Warburg to engage in their favorite activity: gossipmongering. Easy as pie to do when the deceased
can't defend themselves." Realizing how bitter she sounded,
she drew a deep breath. "Jade, the last thing Margot and I
want is for you to spend your life worrying about what
people like Blair Hood are callous enough to say. Be true to
yourself."

Jade's expression was as inscrutable as a sphinx's. "Yeah,
whatever. Are any of those muffins left?"

Seizing on the change of topic like a lifeline, Jordan nodded energetically. "Yes, do you want me to heat it up while
you get your things?"

"No, that's okay. I'm going to eat it on the go."

"You're all packed and ready? Gloves? Boots? Riding
jacket?"

"Check, check, check."

"And you remembered hairnets—those new black ones
Margot bought for you?" In an effort to camouflage Jade's
wild hair color, Margot had been forced to purchase a
heavier-than-standard-weight black hairnet, as the lighter
blond ones weren't up to the task of hiding the dye job.
Hunter judges were sticklers for a rider and horse's turnout.
Shocking pink hair, like unpolished field boots, a mount's
dirty white sock, or a sloppily braided mane, could very
well detract from her and Aspen's score.

"Ugh," Jade said, rolling her eyes in disgust. "Yeah, they're
in my bag. Sunblock, too," she said, preempting Jordan's
next question.

At the sound of the kitchen door opening, both sisters
turned their heads. A second later, Ellie Banner stepped in
from the mudroom, the slippers she liked to wear when
cleaning the house in one hand, the Marc Jacobs satchel
Margot had given her for Christmas in the other. "Good
morning, girls."

"Hi, Ellie," Jordan said. "Thanks for coming in early."

"Happy to." She placed her handbag on the granite island and slipped her feet into a pair of sheepskin-lined moccasins. "Good luck today, Jade."

"Thanks, Ellie. Did you happen to see the van in the court-yard as you drove up?"

"Yes, and the ramp's down."

"Gotta grab my stuff then," Jade said. Shoving a last spoonful of cereal into her mouth, she hopped off the stool and ran up the back stairs.

"Bring down the stained ratcatcher while you're at it," Jordan called after her.

"Gotcha," Jade bellowed from the top of the stairs.

The two women listened to the sound of her sprinting down the length of the hall. "I'd have to eat twenty bowls of Jade's cereal to have that kind of energy," Jordan said as she tore off a paper towel and wrapped the blueberry muf-fin in it for Jade to eat on the road.

"Mrs. Radcliffe had that same energy. She just didn't know how to direct it in a positive way."

"That's an interesting way of looking at it, Ellie. I'm not sure I've ever thought of Nicole's, uh, energy like that." When her stepmother was alive, Jordan's main objective was to deflect her barbs and accusations, and if that wasn't possible, then at least to emerge relatively unscathed. To analyze their cause would have consumed too many pre-cious hours, hours she had no desire to give to a woman who had never shown her or Margot a drop of affection. It was enough to understand that for some reason their step-mother regarded them as adversaries, rivals for her hus-band's affection. More painful still was the knowledge that nothing they did would ever change Nicole's attitude.

"It'd be easier for someone in my position to see Mrs. Radcliffe differently, now wouldn't it?"

"Yes, I guess it would." Unfortunately, she wasn't going to avail herself of Ellie's more objective view of Nicole by asking who might be the "TM" Nicole had written about in her diary with such excessive praise. Discussing Nicole's private journal was too awkward, and felt too much like a betrayal. "How about a cup of coffee, Ellie?" she asked instead.

"That'd be lovely. Then I'll start on the laundry."

"Oh, by the way, that ratcatcher I asked Jade to bring down? She was telling me it has a stain on it. Would you mind soaking the shirt in a mild bleach solution?"

"If it's Jade's, the stain's most likely chocolate or ketchup."

Jordan smiled as she set a cup of coffee in front of their housekeeper and passed her the milk and sugar. "That'd be my guess, too."

Ellie added milk and two teaspoons of sugar to her coffee and stirred. "I'll give it a soaking but I can't promise that anything will get out a stain that's already set." She took a sip of her coffee. "So are you off to the barn now?"

"Yes. After the van leaves I'm going to help Ned and Andy muck out and give a few horses a workout."

Ellie nodded comfortably. "I'll just put in this load of wash, then go up and dust the third floor so I can hear the little one when she wakes up."

Jordan checked her watch. "You've got some time yet. Olivia is usually up by six-thirty, Kate and Max a little later. If you want, I can nip back up to the house once we've turned the horses out."

"No need for that. Patrick's going to be working in the garden. Once they've eaten and gotten dressed, they can help him pick flowers for the house and do some watering. They love that. By then Miriam should be here."

Fully aware of how much more she could get done helping Ned and Andy if she didn't have to run back up to the house, she said, "Thanks. I don't know what I'd do without you."

"It's no cakewalk raising three small children on your own. On top of that you're starting a new business *and* pitching in with the horses. I'd say you deserve all the help you can get."

Feeling self-conscious, Jordan lifted her shoulder in a light shrug. "I'm only able to do these things because I have all of you. It's the women who tackle the demands of single parenthood and work all on their own who deserve our admiration."

"True, but that doesn't change the fact that you're also doing a really hard thing. Just because you're a remarkably capable woman shouldn't mean you *have* to do it all on your own."

Jordan swallowed the painful lump in her throat as she recalled one of Richard's complaints. He'd accused her of being so self-sufficient that he felt unneeded, and that in turn had justified his affair with Cynthia—Cynthia had *needed* him. She wondered why Richard hadn't cared enough to perceive what Ellie seemed to understand so easily. The pounding of feet on the stairs saved her from replying.

Jade dropped from the last step with a thud, her boot and gear bag slung over her shoulder, the stained white rat-catcher balled in her hand.

Jordan straightened. "You set?"

"Yes, indeedy. Here you go, Ellie." She put the shirt on the counter.

Ellie flattened it and frowned at the large brown splotch. "I have a piece of advice for you at the show today, Jade."

"Count my strides on the hunt course with Gypsy Queen? Keep Aspen rounded at the canter and away from Annie Prout's mare, Tattoo, who's got a mean streak a mile wide and Annie's not strong enough to handle her?"

"Seeing how you already know all of the above, that would hardly constitute advice, now would it? This, however, might be useful. Stay away from condiments."

As Ellie had reported, the horse van was already parked at the open end of the gravel courtyard that lay in the center of the three horse barns, its loading ramp lowered in readiness.

Outside the main barn, Tito and Felix were setting down the four bulging hay nets that would go in the van once the horses had been loaded into its stalls.

Spotting them, Jade hollered, "Top of the morning to you, guys," as she veered off toward the side door of the van, where the tack and tack boxes were stored, to stow her own gear.

Jordan approached with a "Good morning" and "Looks like it'll be good weather for you today" to Tito and Felix as she passed through the barn's double doors.

The barn was filled with the sounds of oats being munched, rubber feed tubs banging against the wooden stalls, and the rustling of hay as the horses finished their breakfasts. Down the center aisle Gypsy Queen, Saxon, and Sweet William stood in a line, their fleece-covered leather halters attached to the cross ties. As she walked toward the black mare, Travis looked up from where he was kneeling beside her hind leg, his hands circling the white quilted cotton wraps with a dark blue bandage, passing the roll back and forth between his hands. Gypsy Queen's other legs were already wrapped to protect her from injury during the drive to the show grounds.

"Jade with you?" he asked.

"Yes, she's putting her gear in the van."

"Good. Aspen's probably finished his grain by now. He needs to be wrapped."

"I'll go bring him out," she volunteered. "The bandages are by his stall?"

"Yeah. His summer sheet's hanging on his door. Had to take it off to shake the shavings out."

"He lay down last night? Did he get any shavings in his braids?"

Finished wrapping the mare's leg, Travis stood. "Yup. Rubbed them pretty bad."

"Who rubbed what?" Jade asked, coming up to them. "Hey, Gypsy," she said, patting the mare.

"Your favorite boy. And that would be his braids he rubbed."

"Aspen rubbed them?" she said in a horrified tone. "Are they ruined?"

"Did his best. Don't worry, I rebraided them for you."

"Oh my God, have I told you that you're the coolest brother-in-law ever?"

The corners of Travis's mouth lifted in a grin. "Don't forget it, kid. Now go get him wrapped and ready for the road. We need to start loading in fifteen."

"Need a hand?" Jordan asked her.

"That'd be sweet."

At the next cross ties, Margot was prepping Saxon. Like Gypsy Queen, the chestnut gelding was braided from forelock to tail. Under the fluorescent lights his groomed coat gleamed like buffed copper. Margot was wrapping his tail so that the French braid wouldn't be destroyed in transit.

"Hey, Margot, that hubby of yours is one fine human being."

"Really?" Margot smiled. "I had no idea." Pressing the Velcro end of the bandage together, she patted the gelding's haunch and then reached for the light sheet he'd wear in the van.

"Gospel truth. You should be super nice to him. You know, he might meet Gisele at some photo shoot and then where would you be?"

"I think Tom Brady's got me covered there. I guess Travis will have to settle for adoring Gisele from afar."

"Who the hell's Gisele?" Travis asked.

"As in Bündchen? You don't know who Gisele Bündchen is?" Jade asked.

"Nope, and unless she knows how to wrap your horse's legs I'm not real interested in knowing her, either. Besides, there's no way can she be more beautiful than Margot."

Margot laughed. "You're right, Jade. I *am* going to have to be super nice to my very fine husband."

"That so?" Travis sounded distinctly interested.

"Definitely. As it happens I'd already planned a surprise for you this evening. It's a little something I picked up at La Perla on my way to the shoot in New York."

"What color's this little something?"

"Telling would spoil the surprise. My lips are sealed."

Travis smiled. "Looks like I'm going to have to test my powers of persuasion on the way down to Lexington."

"You're more than welcome to try," Margot said with a smile that had made her millions of dollars.

"Okay, that settles it. I'm riding in the van with Tito and Felix so I don't have to watch you guys smooch at every red light."

"You still here?" Travis grinned.

Jade rolled her eyes. "No, I'm actually a hologram."

"Ahh, so that means the corporeal you has already got Aspen out of his stall and one of his legs wrapped."

"Correctomundo."

"Glad to hear it, because the clock's ticking."

As Jordan and Jade turned to continue down the aisle, Margot said, "Oh, yeah, before I forget, Hologram Girl, you need to crack open your American history textbook on the ride down so you'll be ready for the AP test that's coming up. And I seem to remember you've got a Spanish test next week, too."

"*Dur!* That's the other reason I'm riding with *mis amigos*. I'm going to tell Tito and Felix about the New Deal and have them quiz me on my reflexive verbs. *Nos metimos en una mala situacion*," she said with a grin.

"Kid, you're going to find yourself in a whole new impossible situation if you don't start hustling to get Aspen ready. Scat!"

"*Si, si, señor,*" Jade laughed, giving Travis a mock salute before trotting the rest of the way down the aisle.

Jordan knew her smile was as wide as Travis and Margot's. "Tito and Felix will be lucky if they get a word in edgewise."

"I know. To think there was a time when getting her to talk was like pulling teeth. Although I'd rather have Jade's motor mouth any day of the week," Margot added hastily.

"Me, too," Jordan said. "I suppose a happy medium would be too dull for our sister."

"You've got that right," Travis said, laughter threading his voice.

Aspen, the least accustomed to riding in a trailer, was loaded last. Jade led the gelding up the rubber-covered ramp without incident, however, and then Travis helped her back him into the stall next to Sweet William. While Jade fed each horse a carrot, Travis and Felix made quick work of hanging the hay nets so that the horses could eat during the trip to Lexington.

Within minutes the van's ramp was up and its doors shut with Felix, Tito, and Jade settled in the cab. Behind the van, Travis drove the Range Rover with Margot beside him.

Waving good-bye and shouting, "Good luck!" and "Ride clean and clear!" Jordan waited with Ned and Andy until the van had rumbled out of sight. Then the three of them set to work.

The morning flew by as they followed the farm's daily routine. The horses that would be turned out for the first half of the day were walked down to the pastures. Then the mucking out began. Divvying up the stalls, they made their way down the barns' aisles with their pitchforks, filling the wheelbarrows with soiled shavings and droppings and then laying down a fresh layer of wood shavings. After topping off the water buckets and sweeping the concrete aisles clean, they were ready to exercise the horses.

Key to their horses' soundness and happiness was the carefully devised schedule of exercise and turnout times and days off that Travis and Ned planned for each horse. On days like today, with three riders and two stable hands traveling, Jordan was especially happy to do her part to keep the farm running smoothly. And though she couldn't say that she was *happy* to be divorced from Richard, she realized that were she still with him, the demands of her married life would have made it next to impossible to help her sisters with the horses they bred and trained.

That would have deprived her of something special. Helping Margot and Jade was much, much more than saving their family's horse breeding farm and beautiful old home. Their coming together had strengthened the bond between them in so many ways. Jordan liked, admired, *knew* them in a way that few adult siblings with their disparate lives ever enjoyed in this day and age. For that gift, she was more than willing to put in a twelve-hour day tackling any job that needed doing.

First on her docket was to school Mistral and Indigo, two of their four-year-olds, since Andy, who normally rode them, would be exercising the stallions, Faraday and Nocturne, in the indoor ring, and Ned would be riding three of the broodmares. After that, she'd give Ned a hand with the foals while Andy worked with their two- and three-year-olds. Attentive to the last detail, Travis had even allotted time for her to longe Doc Holliday and turn him out in the upper pasture so he'd be relaxed when she gave the children a lesson.

Then there were the foals and their dams to bring in from the pastures. The foals needed daily handling as part of the gentling and training process. When the remaining horses were brought in from the fields, all would be watered and fed. With the horses tended to, Jordan would clean her and the children's saddles, as well as the bridles she'd used. Only then would she go into the office and return phone calls or emails inquiring about the horses or booking fees for Faraday and Nocturne.

Andy had jumped both Mistral and Indigo the day before, so Jordan's job was to give them a good workout on the flat. Jordan groomed Mistral, a bay Thoroughbred gelding who possessed both the conformation and easy, willing attitude to make a fine hunter prospect.

After tacking Mistral, she led him down to the outdoor ring. Walking into the center of the ring, she slipped the reins over his neck, checked her girth, lowered her stirrups, and then, sticking the toe of her field boot into the stirrup, swung herself up into the saddle.

She let Mistral stretch his muscles at a loose-reined walk for ten minutes and enjoyed the noises of the spring morning: the chirping of the birds and the chattering of the squirrels punctuated by the occasional whinnies of the horses in the south pasture calling to each other. By the time she gathered the braided reins, Ned had entered the ring with Tidbit.

She was glad of Ned's company in the ring. Ned was of the old, classic school of riding, espoused by such greats as Bert de Nemethy and George Morris, and he'd taught Jordan and her sisters to ride—and Travis, too. His presence made her pay even greater attention to getting the horse beneath her moving in a collected, balanced stride. A happy, engaged horse carried himself in an unmistakable way— with a smooth forward flow of motion—and was equally supple rounding corners and circling. Achieving this fluid athleticism was the goal of every serious equitation rider.

Having Ned in the ring didn't just make her ride better; watching him was a treat in itself. Tidbit was a twelve-year-old mare who'd given them four fine foals and had already been covered by Nocturne this season. Yet Ned had the broodmare moving around the ring with her ears pricked forward, her neck slightly arched, and her hooves skimming the sandy footing, as alert and responsive as any of the horses they showed.

When they'd ridden for a half hour, they slowed to a

walk, allowing the horses to rest and stretch. Glancing over at Tidbit, Jordan said, "You should have taken her to Lexington, Ned. She'd have been in the ribbons."

"Tidbit would have come home with a blue." And he leaned over to scratch her sleek white neck fondly. "But you would have had to show her, Miss Jordan. I don't have the patience for it anymore. I can get more accomplished staying here at Rosewood. How's Mistral going for you? Looked like he did that simple change real nicely at the canter."

"Yes, he did. I know Andy's been introducing him to the flying change, but I didn't want to ask him for it in case I confused him." A flying change was aptly named, conveying the way a horse would switch leads in midair between strides at the canter—thus while "flying." It was an essential move for both show hunters and jumpers. A flying change allowed a horse to switch leads as it changed direction, and thereby approach a jump balanced on the correct lead. In the show ring, a hunter could be penalized and lose points for a poorly executed or failed lead change.

"Mistral's not easily rattled. Why don't you do a figure eight down at the end of the ring and see how he goes? Just be sure you've got his haunches engaged when you give him the command, because that's where the change is initiated. Ask him for one change in each direction and then bring him back down to a walk."

"Okay, I'll give it a try." Gathering her reins, she sat straighter in the saddle, closed her legs, moving her outside rail leg slightly behind the girth and applying a light pressure on the outside rein, and gave Mistral a "cluck," a verbal cue. When he responded, lifting his inside shoulder to pick up the gait, she urged him forward with both legs.

Moving along the rail, she kept his canter collected and concentrated on feeling the rolling movement of his hindquarters beneath her while maintaining a light pressure on the reins so that when she reached the point in her circle where they would change direction, she'd have him set up to make the flying change.

When she reached the center of the figure eight they were executing, she shifted her seat bones deeper into the saddle while moving her outside leg slightly behind the girth, as her fingers closed about her inside rein. She felt Mistral respond to the dual signals with a surge of his hindquarters as he took his next stride. When he came down on his foreleg, he'd changed leads.

Jordan's face split in a grin as relief flooded her. She continued cantering, however, reminding herself to make her circle large enough to set him up properly for this last change of lead. It wouldn't be right to screw it up for Mistral when he'd executed the first change so cleanly. She couldn't afford to be complacent, either. Horses, like humans, had a stronger and weaker side and this might well be Mistral's weaker side, although he'd picked up the lead easily enough when she'd cantered him earlier.

She focused on the rocking three-beat gait as once again they neared the spot where she would apply her aids to ask for a flying change. Mistral was a smart fellow, answering with a swish of his tail and a flick of his brown ears. Jordan felt a surge of power beneath her as he took his next stride, and then he was cantering on the other lead.

Straightening in the saddle, she closed her legs and hands to bring him to a walk, then immediately patted his neck. "Good boy, Mistral. Andy's done a terrific job with him, Ned. He didn't hesitate a bit when I asked him."

"You rode that nicely, Miss Jordan, real clear and consistent. That's why he didn't back off on the changes. Even a nonrider could see that, ain't that right, Owen?"

Jordan nearly gave herself whiplash looking around to where Owen stood, forearms propped on the top rail. His casual stance indicated he'd been watching her for some time.

"Uh, hi," she said only to fall silent as she became abruptly aware of how filthy she was after a morning spent cleaning stalls, brushing horses, and then riding under the warm spring sun.

From her perch on Mistral's back, she could tell Owen was as impeccably dressed as usual, a fact she found particularly irksome at the moment. Did he *always* have to look so good? And what was he doing here?

He didn't seem put off by her less than genial greeting. "My office assistant is alarmingly efficient. She faxed me the tax forms yesterday afternoon. I brought them over for you."

"Oh." Pricked by guilt that she'd been less than thrilled at his unexpected presence when he was actually being a considerate employer, she quickly tacked on a "Thank you."

He nodded before shifting his attention to Ned. "I think I saw them practice that maneuver at the Spanish Riding School, only in Vienna the riders did it several times in a row while crossing the ring."

"That's called a 'tempi.' It's a dressage movement, performed at the Grand Prix level," Ned told him. Jordan could tell he was thrilled that Owen had made the connection between her flying changes and the far, far more advanced dressage movement. "So you've been to the Spanish Riding School?" he asked.

"My parents lived in Vienna for a while. The performances and some of the training sessions are open to the public. One of my nannies liked horses."

"If I lived in Vienna, I'd be at the school, ticket in hand, every time they opened the doors. Do you know they accepted two women into the program in 2008, Miss Jordan?"

"No, I didn't. They must be exceptional riders."

"That's for sure. I saw the riders—all men—perform in D.C. when they were on tour. Not a sight to forget. You're lucky to have been able to see them in the Winter Riding School."

"I know. The building is almost as impressive as those Lipizzan stallions."

Smart of him to know that for Ned the beauty of a horse would always outshine any man-made marvel, Jordan thought. But when Owen added, "Jordan looked pretty darn impressive doing that flying change on this horse here," she was sure that even Ned, though proud as one could be of Rosewood's horses, would think he was going a bit far.

But no.

"You've got a good eye," he said approvingly. "Mistral's only four, but Miss Jordan had him moving as smooth as cream poured from a jug. You should stick around and watch her ride Indigo. Now there's a real talented mare. Travis and I think she's got the potential to be a three-day eventer."

"I'd like that. I don't need to be in Alexandria until later this afternoon. Actually, I was going to ask you both if I could spend some time looking at the main barn, taking measurements and getting a sense of the layout. I know you're busy today, so if it's inconvenient—"

"That won't be a bother, will it, Miss Jordan?"

It would be useless to say anything to the contrary. Ned wouldn't understand her reluctance. In Ned's world, any-one who showed a smidgeon of interest in anything equine should be encouraged until the person was certifiably horse mad. Then, too, if she made any protest, Owen might con-clude that his presence somehow affected her, which was definitely not what she wanted her brand-new employer to believe. And wasn't she being a little silly and overreacting, anyway? Owen was obviously respecting her request that their relationship be strictly professional. He was being a good employer and an affable neighbor. Maybe it was time she followed suit.

Recalling the grace with which her mother had treated their neighbors, she said, "Certainly. And if you have time, feel free to go up to the house. John Butler's pattern book is in the library. It's easy to spot. It's on the fourth shelf from the top, to the right of the writing desk. Ellie Banner or her niece, Miriam, my babysitter, can help you if you have trouble finding it."

It was just too darn bad that when he smiled, Jordan felt a delicious warmth unfurl in the pit of her stomach, a sensation she hadn't felt in ages and one that made her forget why exactly she wished to maintain a professional distance from Owen.

OWEN DID HIS BEST not to get in Ned and Jordan's way. Essentially a city slicker, he found the work at Rosewood Farm fascinating. He'd always liked watching horses, so this was hardly a surprise. What did astonish him was the breadth of Jordan's involvement in their training. He'd expected her day to involve riding a number of different horses, impressive enough, but soon he discovered her duties and abilities extended far beyond that.

Finished walking around the main barn and taking notes and measurements, he'd wandered outside to find Jordan and tell her he going to take her up on the invitation to browse through John Butler's pattern book. He'd spotted her walking with Ned, the two of them bringing a mare and her foal in from the pasture. Ned was leading the mare. The foal, wearing a tiny halter, was being walked by Jordan. At the sight of Owen, the foal tried to bolt, rising up on its hind legs in a half-rear. Holding on to the lead rope, Jordan brought its head down. Its forelegs back once more on solid ground, the foal started skipping around. Although only a tenth the size of its mother, it still had enough strength to inflict some damage. But Jordan never lost her cool. Bringing the skipping, circling young horse back under control with a "Whoa, Cosmo. Easy, boy. Walk, Cosmo," she then praised him quietly when he settled into a prancing walk.

Thinking he might have caused a dangerous situation for Jordan or the foal by approaching them, Owen tried to apologize, but Ned set him straight.

"Cosmo's got a lot of spirit. We bred his dam, Hello Again, to Nocturne, so he's full Thoroughbred. He needs a steady hand until he understands that shying and spooking won't get him anywhere," Ned said.

Jordan didn't appear angry either. "He's calmed down already. So this has been a good lesson for today." With another "whoa," she halted the colt a few steps in front of him. "Here, stretch out your hand slowly, palm up, so he can catch your scent."

The colt was amazing-looking, with long stiltlike legs and a tiny, slender body—all ribs and bones covered by a fuzzy dark brown coat. Owen took a careful step forward and extended his hand. Slowly the colt brought his muzzle close, his nostrils flaring as he sniffed tentatively, ready to spook at the slightest invitation. Determined not to offer one, Owen held himself still. The foal watched out of dark brown eyes, framed by impossibly long eyelashes that looked like they belonged on a creature in a Disney cartoon. Even longer whiskers covered the bottom of his lips. Their ends tickled his open palm as Cosmo extended his neck and nuzzled him. Owen smiled.

"How old is he?" he asked, his voice low.

"Six weeks," Jordan said.

"He's beautiful."

Ned nodded. "Ain't he though?"

While they spoke, the foal's fuzzy pointed ears swiveled back and forth. Then, stretching his neck, he curled back his upper lip, exposing six small teeth in a baby horse laugh.

"Yup, he's a card, all right," Ned said as they resumed walking toward the broodmares' barn. "You should have seen him the first time he tried to stand on those legs. Somersaulted right into the corner of the stall. Didn't like that one bit. Now he's one of the fastest of the bunch. He beat Turner the other day, who's a big, strapping fellow."

Deciding to put off leafing through Butler's architectural designs in favor of watching Jordan work with the baby colt, Owen tagged along. It didn't take long for him to be hooked. Her handling of the foal was as impressive as the fancy riding he'd seen her perform earlier. Though the session only lasted around fifteen minutes, so that Cosmo wouldn't get overwhelmed, she got him to lift each of his tiny hooves, to stand quietly while Ned used a soft brush all over his body, and to back up a few paces when she applied pressure on the noseband of his halter and his bony shoulder.

Owen didn't need to be an expert to recognize the care they took with the foal. Though they clearly had a busy day, with a lot of work to accomplish, there wasn't a single hurried or rushed movement around this delightful, excitable creature.

It intrigued him that the Jordan Radcliffe whom he'd met at Nonie Harrison's, whose poise epitomized the well-mannered, garden-club, president of the Historical Society type, turned out to be equally comfortable and competent in this far more earthy and sensual world of gently mastering these brute animals, where the smell of horses was mixed with that of wood shavings and oiled leather. She slipped into the role of foal handler as easily as she would a pair of black patent pumps.

Finished with the colt, Jordan gave him a vigorous scratch along the top of his neck where a short black mane was growing in, a scratch Cosmo obviously loved, for again he stuck out his nose, curling his lip back as if in laughter.

"Yeah, this has been fun," Jordan said as she offered him a light pat on his bony shoulder. "Now it's back to the field with you so you can play with your buddies and nap in the sunshine. You ready with Hello Again, Ned?"

Ned, who'd been applying fly spray to the mare with an atomizer and a rag, nodded and stepped back. "All set."

"We've got Miss Molly and Domino next?" she asked.

"That's right." Ned checked his watch. "Though it occurs to me that with Owen here, we could double up. Why don't you have him bring in Miss Molly with you—she's a real sweetheart, Owen—while I take Lena and Carmen? That'll give us a little more breathing room for the rest of the day's activities. Little Kate would love to extend her lesson now that she's riding Doc on the rail."

Before Jordan could respond, Owen spoke. "Uh, Ned, I don't have any experience handling horses." The last thing he'd expected was for Ned Connolly, who took the job of breeding and training these horses with the seriousness of a judge, to suggest he pitch in. Perhaps he thought that since Owen had seen the Lipizzaners in Austria, he actually knew his way around a horse.

His admission didn't seem to bother the old man. "Heck, a greenhorn's gotta learn sometime. Here, we'll do a practice run. Come over here and take Hello Again's lead and walk her out of the stall."

Bemused, Owen took hold of the lead rope. "Are you sure about this?" he asked Jordan.

Had anyone else on the farm proposed that Owen and she pair up to work with the foals, Jordan would have suspected them of matchmaking. But Ned would never risk the safety of their horses.

"I think you'll do fine," she said.

Ned gave an impatient snort. "Course he will, so let's not waste precious time gabbing."

Owen probably had no idea what a huge compliment he'd just received. In Jordan's nine years of marriage, Ned had never once invited Richard to help with the horses— not that her ex-husband showed any particular interest in the horses her family raised. He preferred playing the role of the "gentleman" at Rosewood Farm, enjoying the views of the horses grazing in the surrounding fields as picturesque backdrop. Besides, working in the barn would have meant loosening his grip on his cellphone, which toward the end of their marriage had become stuck to him as if Krazy Glued.

Ned had launched into lesson mode. "Okay, Owen, as you lead her out of the stall, you want to walk on her left side, just by her head, with about a foot and a half of distance between you. You probably know this already, but we always walk to the left of a horse, same with mounting and dismounting."

"I think I did know that, but only realized it after you pointed it out," Owen replied. "Now what? Straight out the barn?"

"Yep. You're doing fine. Just keep this pace so that Jordan and Cosmo can stay by her flank."

"So, out of curiosity, what's the reason for mounting and dismounting on the left-hand side?" Owen asked as they walked down the aisle.

"It dates back to the Middle Ages, when knights would train their destriers, doesn't it, Ned?" Jordan replied.

Now they were outside the barn, Ned had his tin of chaw out and was busy packing tobacco in between gum and lip.

"That's right," he said with a nod as he slipped the tin back into his vest pocket. "A knight was trained to fight with his right hand, so his sword was buckled to hang on his left side. That made mounting on the right-hand side of the horse impossible, because then the knight's left leg would have banged into the sword as he climbed into the saddle. And mounting on the right would have entailed lifting the sword over the cantle of the saddle. And some of those swords were long. Mounting and dismounting on the left avoided all those problems. It became standard practice for English-style riding."

"Interesting. What's a cantle?" Owen asked.

"That's the back of the saddle," Ned explained. "In those days they rose up much higher than in today's English saddles. The Western saddle is designed along those lines."

"Good to know. I'll take a closer look next time I'm in a museum." Owen's tone indicated he thought Ned was finished.

Jordan bit the inside of her lip, tamping down her mirth. Owen was about to be initiated into Ned's one-man mission to educate the world in all things equestrian.

"Nowadays, there are some folk encouraging people to train their horses to accept both the right and left sides in terms of mounting and dismounting. They think it will help a horse be more balanced and avoid straining the left shoulder. I don't buy it." He spat a thick brown stream of tobacco into the dirt for emphasis. "A good horseman knows how to settle himself lightly and quickly in the saddle. No fuss, no muss. You saw how Jordan mounted Indigo, didn't you?"

"Yes, I did."

She had to give him high marks for quick thinking. Heaven forbid he admit he hadn't paid close attention to how she'd mounted the dark gray mare.

"Well, that's the way to do it. It's not as easy as it looks. Now, consider the fact that most people are righties. If they're trying to mount from the right side of the horse, they have to swing their *left* leg over and find the stirrup with their left foot. That's an awful lot harder to do when it's not the dominant leg. To my mind, all that unnecessary shifting and fumbling ends up putting more strain on a horse's shoulder and back. For accomplished riders who devote lots of time training and perfecting their skills, this move might not be a big deal, but for the beginner or weekend rider, I don't think it's smart riding. Besides, there are plenty of exercises we do in the saddle to create as balanced a horse as possible."

"Well, you've convinced me," Owen said. "Left side it is, though right now, I'm just going to concentrate on getting this horse down to the pasture safely."

Jordan felt a surge of gratitude at Owen's easy response. Not every layman would have the patience for Ned's encyclopedic answers.

"You're getting the hang of it. You got any questions, ask

Miss Jordan. She knows as much about horses as anyone on this farm."

"And if you believe that, I have a bridge in Brooklyn to sell you."

Jordan might have brushed off Ned Connolly's compliment, but it didn't take long for Owen to see that he hadn't been exaggerating about the depth of her knowledge. All he had to do was watch her with the foals they brought in from the pasture.

"Do you and Ned work with the foals like this—having them pick up their hooves and getting them to back up for you and all the rest—every day?" he asked as they walked yet another mare, Plain Song, and her chestnut filly, Penny Lane, up to the broodmares' barn.

"Ned does far more of it than I do," she answered. "These lessons represent just the beginning of what we need to teach them so that when the day comes for Travis to climb into the saddle, they'll be conditioned to accept the presence of a human on their back, something that goes against their natural instinct."

The half door to Plain Song's stall was open. "Plain Song will probably want to drink when you go into the stall," Jordan told him.

"Should I just walk her over to the water bucket?"

She nodded. "Yes. You don't have to worry about Plain Song. She knows the ropes. Penny's her sixth foal."

They entered the large stall, and while the mare slurped from the black rubber bucket, Jordan pulled out a rag she'd tucked into the waistband of her breeches and began to rub the filly's body with it. "You can unsnap the lead from Plain Song's halter and come and stand by Penny's head. That's right, just hold her lightly," she said as he took up the lead rope attached to the filly's halter.

"So what are you doing with the rag?"

"I'm teaching Penny to stand quietly while I touch sensitive areas, like her ears. It's fly season now and we have to make sure we can apply the spray wherever it's needed. We're also getting her ready for the day when we'll use clippers on her muzzle and ears. Penny's a clever girl. She stood quietly for us even the first time, a couple of hours after her birth. But a lot of training is about reinforcing learned lessons and building on them."

"I wouldn't have thought you could teach horses this young."

Jordan gave a quick smile as she walked around to Penny's other side to repeat the gentle rubbing. "Ned's a firm believer in starting early and working with the foals every day, even if it's for really short periods of time, like these fifteen-minute sessions we're doing now. The point is for the foals to realize that just as they have to learn appropriate social behavior and their place in the hierarchy of the herd when they're out in the pasture, they also have to learn what we humans expect. Think of all the things a horse is asked to do. Not only to accept a rider on its back, carry him through all the gaits, stop and turn on a dime, and take huge and scary fences without hesitating, but hundreds and hundreds of other things, practically all of which go against its natural instincts."

"And what would those other things be?"

She concentrated on rubbing Penny's belly and along the inside of her legs before answering. "Well, a few obvious examples would be standing calmly while an electric clipper is buzzing in its ear, walking collectedly past an idling pickup truck in need of a new muffler, having someone stick a hypodermic needle into its flesh, getting steel shoes nailed into its hooves, or loading into a trailer without freaking out. This means taking an animal that weighs a ton, can run thirty miles an hour, can rear and buck, strike out with hooves, and inflict serious harm with its teeth, and get it to understand that it doesn't need to do any of those things when it's frightened or threatened."

"So you start the work early on, before they weigh a ton, run like the wind, and have a full set of teeth."

Jordan smiled. "It's only logical." She took the lead rope from him and backed Penny up a few steps. Handing the rope back to him, she said, "If I were to draw up a list of everything asked of a well-trained, well-behaved horse, the only other animal I can think of which has to perform as many tasks is a Seeing Eye or therapy dog."

"But dogs are different."

"That's right. They've been domesticated and selectively bred over the centuries to work with man. We breed selectively, too, and while we hope to pass on a good temperament and excellent conformation, our real goal is to make sure that the horses we sell have plenty of good habits. Ned's method of working with our foals allows us to establish a foundation of trust early on. The proof is in our yearlings. They're as well-mannered and confident as any you'll find—though you may have trouble believing I'm an objective judge."

"Somehow I don't see you as the boastful type." He grinned, pleased when his comment caused a blush to steal over her high cheekbones. "So Ned taught you how to do all this?" he asked as she bent and picked up Penny's hoof and cupped it in her hand, scraping it lightly with a metal hoof pick before lowering it.

"Yes, my sisters and me. He even taught Travis and Dad."

"Your father as well? And was he as involved in the running of the farm?"

Jordan nodded. "Dad was a terrific rider and an exceptional horse breeder. We'll be lucky if we can match the excellence of some of the foals he bred. But his people skills weren't quite as strong. He didn't have the patience to teach my sisters and me. Most likely he considered it a waste of his time, as he never intended for us to enter the business. When he was alive, Rosewood Farm was very much a male-run operation."

Owen caught the dry note that had entered her voice. "You three women seem to be doing a pretty damn fine job."

The smile she flashed him over her shoulder was beautiful enough to cause his heart to skip a beat.

"We're trying. Thank God it's something we all love doing." She set the filly's hoof down and straightened.

"That's easy to see." He would have said more but was unsure how to proceed.

She must have sensed his hesitation for she cocked her head. "What is it?" she asked.

"I'm curious about your decorating business. Where does it fit in with all of this? And don't think I'm implying you shouldn't be starting your own design company. I wouldn't have hired you to decorate Hawk Hill if you didn't have a great eye."

"Thanks for the compliment," she said with quiet sincerity. "As you've probably gathered, it's doubtful my own father would approve of my running a business. He certainly hated it when Margot chose to become a fashion model rather than what he envisioned for her—that is, to go to college and get her 'Mrs.' degree."

"Her what?"

"You know, marry and have babies. A 'Mrs.' degree."

"Oh, right. A little medieval in his attitude, huh?"

"Slightly," she said in a wry tone. "Dad was pretty conservative. He wanted Margot to find a nice rich husband, preferably a horsey one with a good Virginia pedigree whom Dad could groom to take over Rosewood Farm."

"And Margot said 'Thanks but no thanks'?"

A flash of humor lit her face. "Something like that. As the more tractable daughter, I did follow his wishes, though I got a degree in interior design in addition to a husband. Unfortunately my marriage was a failure, except for our three wonderful children. But since my divorce, I've realized I need to prove I can succeed at something that's all mine. Thus the idea for Rosewood Designs. Now I'll be able to throw my energy into a project and, when it's finished, say, 'There, *I* did that. It's whole and it's beautiful.'" She stopped abruptly, as if suddenly aware of how much she'd revealed. With a determinedly carefree shrug, she continued, "Besides, being an interior decorator provides me with a perfect excuse to change out of my breeches, don a dress and nice shoes, and go antiquing to my heart's content. So again, thanks for giving me my first project."

At first Owen couldn't immediately identify the emotion that filled him. Then he realized he was feeling protective of Jordan. He hated the fact that this ex of hers—this dick, who'd been bastard enough to cheat on her—had blown her confidence to smithereens. It made him fiercely glad that he'd followed his instincts and asked her to decorate Hawk Hill. For a woman as exceptional and bloody gorgeous as Jordan to be made to feel a failure was criminal.

"My pleasure," he murmured.

At the rough huskiness of his voice, her gaze flew to his. In that split second, the atmosphere in the stall became charged, awareness crackling between them.

He wanted to reach out and haul her into his arms and cover her petal-soft lips with his and drink in the taste of her. He wanted to run his hands over her supple curves and cup that sweetly rounded ass he'd been trying not to stare at, and draw her tight against him until they formed a perfect whole.

But this wasn't the time or the place. He wasn't about to risk frightening the filly she was working so hard to train. Though his body ached, he made himself settle for the satisfaction of seeing her blue eyes widen as their gazes remained locked and hearing the telltale catch in her breath, which matched his own erratic breathing.

He thanked God for his self-control when just then the sound of three squealing voices reached them, calling for their mommy. If his kiss hadn't frightened the filly, Jordan's jumping out of his arms as if zapped by a Taser the instant she registered their approach certainly would have.

An adult voice was with them. "Ned said Mommy was in Plain Songs' stall. Which one is that, Kate?"

"It's down here."

"No, Max, no running or skipping in the barn. You know better. We all walk *quietly*."

Then Owen heard the single squawk of "Mommy!" belonging to the littlest one, Olivia, and wished he'd scanned the broodmares' barn for an emergency exit.

Interestingly, he wasn't the only one who was dismayed by the Peanuts gang's impending arrival. Jordan had first paled and then turned an endearing shade of pink, a clear announcement of her flustered state—and probably not the look she was hoping for.

Unaccustomed to scouting for people three feet and under, he saw the babysitter first. A twentysomething with a coronet of blond braids and glittery, multicolored dangly earrings, she wore a tie-dyed T-shirt with the name of a rock band he'd never heard of and a pair of jeans that had likely come with all those rips the day she bought them. The jeans were rolled up to mid-calf, exposing a pair of beat-up paddock boots with no laces. An interesting look. He decided to dub it "Heidi abandons the Swiss Alps to rock out at Bonnaroo."

She was holding on to Olivia's hand, preventing the toddler from careening full tilt into her mother. But even with her arm being tugged and yanked, she sized him up. Then her gaze slid to Jordan. She'd have had to be blindfolded to miss her employer's heightened flush. Returning her attention to him, she flashed him a broad smile along with an impish wink. All that was missing from that not-so-subtle signal of approval was to give him a hearty thumbs-up.

Jordan's babysitter was one hell of a boost to his ego, he thought, hiding a grin. He hoped she didn't find out the tragic truth that nothing had happened between Jordan and him. But what were the men Jordan dated like to make her beam as if he were a special treat? Difficult to believe he could be so vastly superior.

"Hey, Jordan, hope we're not interrupting," she said.

Jordan shook her head a little too vigorously. "Owen and I had just finished." Though he wouldn't have thought it possible, her flush deepened. What would she look like if they'd actually done something? Damn if he wouldn't like to find out, and sooner rather than later. "Owen, this is Miriam Banner, my babysitter and lifesaver. Miriam, this is—"

"The architect. Yeah, Jade texted me," she said with that approving smile again. In his mind's eye, he had a sudden image of Jade and Miriam teaming up and wreaking havoc on the male population, fallen bodies littering the landscape. "You lucked out, Jordan. I took an architecture course in college and my prof had a potbelly and wore the same bow tie all semester. I think he slept in it. You don't look like the type to sleep in a bow tie," she told him.

"I'll take that as a compliment," he said gravely.

"As it was intended. Sorry if we're a couple of minutes early, Jordan. The kids couldn't wait to see you and Doc Holliday."

Kate and Max were dressed to ride. Olivia, too, he supposed, though she was wearing blue jeans with an elastic waist. Maybe they didn't make jodhpurs that small.

"Can we come in and pat Penny, Mommy?"

"Of course, Kate, but let me take Olivia first." At that, Miriam scooped Olivia up and held her out to Jordan who settled the tot on her left hip. Kind of like hanging a sword on the left side, it allowed Jordan to use her right arm to hold the filly. So Owen was surprised when she asked him to take Penny's lead.

"Uh, sure," he said.

"Has Owen been helping you, Mommy?"

"Yes, he's been a big help, Kate. Pat Penny right here, along her shoulder, Max. That's right, make nice long strokes with the flat of your hand."

"We help, too, don't we, Mommy?"

"Yes, you do," she said with a smile.

"Is Owen going to watch us ride?"

All eyes turned on him. Christ, even Penny and Plain Song seemed to be awaiting his response. "You know, I think I'm going to take a rain check and go up and look through John Butler's pattern book."

"What's a rain check, Mommy?"

"Owen is saying that he'd like to watch your lesson another day."

"Okay. We can play with him after our lesson. I want to show him my twains."

His smile felt stiff. Playing "twains" held as much appeal as a tooth extraction. The solution would be to keep an eye on his watch. Forty-five minutes with John Butler's drawings and then he'd hightail it out of Rosewood before any Lilliputians could besiege him.

Jordan seemed to read his thoughts as easily as if he'd written them on his forehead. "We'll have to see, sweetie. He may have to leave before you and Kate have finished riding."

Jordan Radcliffe was one smart woman.

The only hitch in the plan to allot forty-five minutes to John Butler's architectural designs was that the book was amazing, each drawing more detailed than the next, and far too absorbing for Owen to tear his eyes away and check the passing minutes on his wristwatch. He was studying the seashell whorl of the capitals of an Ionic column, when he realized he was no longer alone in the sun-filled library. He blamed the thick carpet for muffling the thud of their little sock-covered feet and failing to alert him. Before he could bolt, the chair where he'd been sitting peacefully and happily, not bothering a blessed soul, was surrounded.

"Hiya, Owen. Want to play with my twains now?"

"I'm afraid I can't today."

Max was undaunted. "How about Twistuh?"

Owen didn't even know if he was supposed to substitute

r's for *w*'s with that word. What was the kid talking about? And why were the two who couldn't talk the ones who were so voluble? Kate, as usual, was staring at him with solemn blue eyes so much like her mother's.

"Twistuh's weally fun," Max pronounced as if this might be the tipping point.

"I'm sure it's terrific fu—" The word became a curse that he somehow managed to swallow despite Olivia's sneak attack. While he'd been busy fending off Max, she must have been crawling beneath the desk to hurl her solid rubber body against his knees. Before he knew it she'd climbed onto his lap.

That was alarming enough. But then, with a demonic chortle, she reached a hand out toward John Butler's book.

Oh no, there was no way he was going to let those grubby mitts near the priceless book. Owen jumped to his feet, taking Olivia with him. It wasn't as if he could very well drop her. She might stumble and crack her head on the leg of the table or on the corner of the chair. Somehow he didn't think Jordan would take kindly to his giving her kid a concussion.

"Uh, where's your mom?" he asked Kate, the only one capable of providing an intelligible answer.

"She's still at the barn." He had to strain to catch her quiet response, but maybe that was because of the blood pounding in his head. Olivia had her arms clamped about his neck and was squeezing it like he was a villain in a James Bond movie. The kid was strong as hell.

"Miriam?" he asked in strangled desperation.

"She's making our lunch."

"She told us we could play until she called us," Max chimed in.

As there wasn't a single *r* in that sentence, Owen understood it just fine.

"So what d'ya wanna play, Owen?"

Oh, Christ.

*　　*　　*

Jordan wasn't sure, but if she had to bet she'd have laid money down that it was a Hoagy Carmichael tune that was being played on the grand piano in the far parlor. Only one person could be playing it, as Ellie had gone home and Miriam, though a music lover, listened to it rather than made it. Furthermore, her tastes leaned more toward Nirvana and Phish. She moved quietly, not wanting to disturb him and risk having him stop.

He played beautifully. The quicker parts of the arrangement never caused his agile fingers to trip. Not even Kate and Max sandwiching him on the piano bench or Olivia plunked down in the middle of his lap hindered him, so fixed was his concentration. Maybe that was the point. He was able to ignore their presence by focusing on the music.

Whatever his motive, he was obviously an accomplished pianist. She could have sat and listened to him for hours. She wasn't alone in her appreciation, either. Rapt, Kate and Max watched his fingers dance over the keys, their heads tracking the fleet movement of his hands. Even Olivia sat quietly, as if she, too, understood better than to join in by pounding the ivories. Incredible.

Jordan remained where she was, memorizing every detail of the scene, knowing this was a moment to preserve in her heart; too many flew by in the rush of a day to vanish before one recognized its special beauty.

The song came to an end and Owen raised his hands to hover over the keyboard. She suspected that if Olivia hadn't been planted in his lap, they'd have moved to rest there, a gesture born of childhood piano recitals. The little she knew of him was already sufficient for her to guess that his parents would have been very gung ho when it came to that particularly hellish ritual in a child's music instruction.

"That was pretty, Owen," Kate said softly.

Her daughter had excellent taste.

"Play another one," Max demanded, and Jordan frowned

slightly until he remembered to tack on "Please" to his request.

"You sure it's not lunchtime yet?"

Max shook his head. "Miriam will come and get us."

When Olivia gave a hearty bounce on his lap, Owen grimaced. "All right. But you guys have to sit still."

Her mouth fell open as even Olivia quieted. It seemed Owen's talents extended beyond the myriad ones she'd already imagined.

She recognized the tune instantly. It was Cole Porter's "You're the Top," and the choice suited him. She could easily picture him: dark and heart-trippingly handsome in a tuxedo with a coupe of champagne placed within easy reach. Instead of her three children crowding him, a bevy of beautiful women were draped seductively over the piano, each one hoping that when the time came, he'd play his clever fingers over her. She knew very well the desires those fingers could arouse.

The tableau was all too vivid. So when he struck the last note, Jordan wasn't in the least bit sorry. She stepped forward, knowing the movement would catch his attention.

He nearly leapt over the bench in his haste to transfer Olivia into her arms.

Relieved that the image of Owen as the sophisticated playboy was momentarily banished, she gave him a smile. "Thanks for entertaining them."

"I wasn't sure about 'Twistuh' so I thought this was the safer bet."

"Yes, I'd say Cole Porter is more your speed. Not that Twister doesn't have its appeal." Shifting her attention momentarily to her two older children, she said, "Lunch is ready, kids."

Max gave a whoop and tore off after Kate, while Olivia practically threw herself out of Jordan's arms in her determination to follow her siblings. Jordan and Owen watched as she thundered after them.

"Your children are rather high-energy," he observed with a studied mildness.

"Actually they're pretty typical in terms of energy. They've only destroyed a couple of antique pieces," she answered, biting back a laugh at his horrified expression. "Just kidding. They know to save their more vigorous play for outdoors."

Together they followed the children back toward the kitchen.

"So this game Max likes is called Twister," he said, stressing the "er." "What is it?"

"Twister's a great game, although somewhat difficult to describe. Not your average board game. You'll have to play sometime. Would you like some lunch? It's not much, I'm afraid. Grilled cheese sandwiches accompanied by a salad for the grown-ups."

"Thank you, but no. I should be going. There's some office work I've been neglecting. It'll probably take me right up to dinner to get everything done to my assistant's satisfaction. I can wait for you to fill out the tax form, though."

"All right. You're having dinner in town?"

"Yes. At the Grille."

"Oh." Enough said. He was having dinner with a woman. The Alexandria restaurant was expensive and delicious with a tasteful décor and soft lighting, in short too romantic to waste on another man. Although it was really none of her business whom Owen took where, a perverse impulse prompted her to add, "She's lucky—everything is delicious there."

"Yes," he replied with an easy grin, not looking the least bit discomfited that she was guessing the gender of his dinner companion when she was pretty sure he'd been contemplating kissing her in Plain Song's stall a little over an hour ago. It had taken nearly every second of those sixty minutes for Jordan to overcome her ridiculous disappointment that he hadn't.

Her own smile felt stiff. She'd already figured out that Owen was far from monkish in his habits. So that meant the annoyance freezing her features was for herself as much as it was for him. She should know better than to be attracted to a man who could even *act* like he might want to kiss her when he had a date later that evening in Alexandria.

While she was being painfully honest, she had to acknowledge that a good dose of dejection was mixed into her annoyance. Jordan couldn't stop thinking that since Owen *hadn't* attempted to kiss her, it was because she was unable to inspire anything more than a fleeting sexual interest in a man.

What would he do if she grabbed him right here and now in the parlor and plastered herself against him? Would his kiss pack the same volcanic heat she'd experienced before, when his muscular body was pressed urgently against hers? All were questions doomed to remain unanswered.

She wasn't going to try anything of the sort; she wasn't completely out of her mind. Kate and Max could easily rush in with a question or plea or simply because they were curious about Owen and already halfway to considering him *their* friend. Getting them accustomed to the fact that their daddy had a new wife was quite enough of a challenge without having to address whatever questions might arise from witnessing their new buddy Owen and Mommy locked in an embrace.

And if she'd misread that charged moment in the broodmare's stall, if Owen had lost interest in her, well, she was pretty much responsible for that, too, wasn't she? She'd been the one to lay down the parameters, insisting she was only interested in a professional or at most a friendly, neighborly, come-and-share-a-family-meal kind of relationship.

Boy, being reasonable and fair-minded really sucked, she reflected, knowing Jade would be immensely proud of her for using one of her favorite words. What really and truly sucked, Jordan continued, getting into the spirit of the thing, was that no matter how neatly she rationalized the situation, she couldn't forget Owen's kiss and how much she wanted to have his arms around her again.

Chapter ❧
THIRTEEN

FIONA RORTY was like perfectly chilled champagne. Crisp and elegant with just enough sparkle to make a man want to take long slow, savoring sips of her all through the night, right down to the last delicious drop.

He'd always enjoyed champagne. Yet tonight at the Grille, he found his tolerance surprisingly low. He was beginning to think that much more of Fiona would result in a very nasty headache.

Bizarre as it sounded, he wished he had a tall glass of iced tea in front of him.

Jordan Radcliffe made her tea surprisingly strong with lots of fresh mint, lemon, and cloves. The resulting brew was complex, a lot like the lady herself. Recalling the look on her face when she'd offered him a glass while he waited for her to fill out the employee tax form had his mouth curving in an unconscious smile.

She'd been in a snit, her blue eyes bright and sparkling with temper. Witness to her abrupt silence after he'd told her of his plans for the evening, it was easy to guess the cause. That she was peeved was, in his opinion, an excellent development. It meant that for all her gung ho professionalism, her interest in him went deeper than that. While he preferred to be discreet about his liaisons, he decided that maybe it was a good thing if Jordan realized he wasn't going to sit around and pine for her. No strings on him.

The notion of Jordan miffed over his decidedly nonprofessional activities gratified him so much that he had sat down

next to Max at the long antique kitchen table and even accepted one of the carrot sticks Max pressed on him. He'd
chomped along with the little boy and enjoyed the sweetness of the moment as Jordan moved about the kitchen radiating a delightful annoyance. Anger put a little zing in her
step, and a snap to her movements. Gone was the woman
whose every movement around the foals was perfectly controlled, as calm as a lake in summer when the wind had
died with the setting of the sun.

While he'd watched her, he wondered when he'd get over
how beautiful she was.

Retrieving a glass pitcher from the refrigerator and carrying it over to the table, she testily inquired if he'd like
some tea.

"Well, that depends. Do I get to drink it or wear it?"

Owen's smile widened as he remembered how the answering flash of humor in her eyes had dispelled the frosti-
ness in them. Her lips curving in a wry smile, she said,
"Please, I wouldn't want to be considered so dull as to repeat
myself."

"Dull is not an adjective anyone would apply to you."

He liked how pleased she was by the comment.

"For that, I won't give you the salt to sweeten your tea,"
she said.

"My stomach thanks you."

Miriam, who had been listening to their exchange as she
passed Olivia thin strips of grilled cheese to chomp on,
said, "And we all know the express route to a man's heart,
don't we?"

Jordan truly had the loveliest blush.

It occurred to Owen that he was losing count of the things
he liked about her.

"So, Owen, shall we?" Fiona's voice broke into his
thoughts. In the candlelight her smile was full of anticipated pleasure. Which was fine, except that as he hadn't
been listening to a word she'd been saying, he hadn't a clue

what she was proposing. But since they'd finished their crème brûlée and espressos and Fiona was a woman who enjoyed leisurely sex, he could hazard a guess.

"Of course," he said.

She smiled. "I'll just go freshen up."

That particular line had always made him smile inwardly, summoning as it did visions of lips lush and wet with newly applied lipstick, of perfume deftly wielded, misting the shadowed valley of an already delectable cleavage, the small hollow behind the earlobes, and even, in the hands of particularly imaginative women like Fiona, the twin points of the hips.

"Are you sure you wouldn't like another espresso before we go? Perhaps a Calvados?"

She smiled at his thoughtfulness. "No, thanks. Besides, I don't think we have time." She reached across and tugged on his forearm to peer at his watch, letting her fingers caress the inside of his wrist, as she continued. "The second set starts at ten. Caroline promised they'd arrive early to get a good table, but I'd hate to be stuck somewhere in the back if it turns out they're late."

Something clicked in his brain. They weren't going back to her apartment, but to the Blues Alley in Georgetown to listen to a Louisiana jazz quartet. They were to rendezvous with her friends Caroline and Freddy.

She stood. Automatically he rose from his chair, dizzy with something that felt absurdly like relief. Going to the nightclub was merely delaying the inevitable, but surely by the end of the jazz set he'd remember what made Fiona desirable.

The letter arrived in the afternoon mail. It was sheer chance that Jordan decided to place a large vase of irises and larkspur on the table in the foyer and so came upon the stack of bills, magazines, and catalogs, which Ellie had placed there, before her sisters returned from the Lexington

horse show. The letter was sandwiched between the electric
bill and an appeal from the Nature Conservancy. Picking
up the envelope addressed to her, she glanced at the em-
bossed name in the upper left-hand corner and dropped the
rest of the mail back onto the table with fingers that trembled. A quick prayer went through her that Ellie hadn't recognized the name Upton and Crawford as the law firm
Richard had retained to represent him during the divorce
proceedings. Margot and Jade would have.

She held the envelope warily, as if it might sprout fangs and
bite her. Whatever the letter contained, she didn't want to
deal with it. But she couldn't put it off, either. Not knowing
its contents would be even more distressing. So if she couldn't
wait until tonight when everyone was asleep, she had to take
advantage of the fact that she was alone. The kids, happy and
exhausted from "helping" Ned and Andy water and feed the
horses, were sprawled on the sitting room sofa, watching
Miss Piggy and Kermit. Andy and Ned were awaiting the
van's return, and Jordan, in an effort to help Andy secure a
date with Miriam, had sent her down to the barn with a fresh
pitcher of iced tea and a plate of sandwiches. Ellie had left
hours ago. The letter could be read in privacy.

Far too much of her divorce had played out under her
sisters' protective eyes. That the letter would contain some
sort of unpleasantness there was no doubt; Richard didn't
pay William Upton's astronomical fees to draft notes detailing his abject remorse. It would be a relief, though, to be
able to read and digest it without having Margot and Jade
race to the kitchen drawer and grab the sharpest knives
with which to carve out Richard's heart.

The tearing of the envelope sounded unnaturally loud in
the stillness of the late afternoon. Then Jordan was hurriedly unfolding the paper and scanning the three printed
paragraphs. The tone was courteous and polite, direct, and
so very reasonable. Even so, a silent cry was already being
wrung from her heart. *No!*

Clumsy fingers tried to shove the letter back into the envelope. Would that she could make the thing disappear entirely, light a match and stomp its ashes into the ground. But he'd be phoning upon his return from Hawaii this week and she would have to agree to or refuse his request.

Damn him for disrupting the children's lives just when she'd managed to create a stable routine and home for them.

Her feet had already begun moving toward the sitting room where the kids were watching the movie. Never mind that Kate was at "The cat sat on the mat" stage of reading, Jordan hastily jammed the letter into her breeches pocket.

They were lined up on the yellow silk sofa, their legs sticking out like matchsticks in front of them.

"Mommy, Kermit is so funny!" Max said.

"Is he? I'm glad," she said, swallowing the boulder-size lump in her throat that had formed at the thought of being separated from them for even a day. Would Olivia understand what was happening?

"Wanna come watch him with us?"

She nodded tightly. "There's nothing I'd like more."

Much as Jordan had learned to present a serene façade to the world, she also knew how to take advantage of any distraction at hand in order to deflect unwanted attention. Saturday night was easy.

Returning from the show, Margot, Jade, and Travis were tired. Tired and happy. The horses had come away with the ribbons in every class. But the day had belonged to Jade. Out of a large field, she and Aspen had captured the green working hunter champion.

"It'd have been majorly embarrassing if we didn't ride away with the title. Aspen knew exactly what he was supposed to do in the ring. Every stride was perfect. The judges really liked him."

Travis smiled. "Sweet William did well for Margot, too,

though we've got to school him over in and outs before the next show. He was a little flat over the second fence."

"Human error. I probably dropped my hands," Margot replied.

"Not from where I sat. It looked to me like he was rushing," Jade said with a yawn. "I'm going to chill in front of the TV. Later, y'all."

With Jade gone, there was no lingering over the kitchen table. The mood shifted quickly. All it took was the exchange of a glance between Margot and Travis for Jordan to breathe a deep sigh of relief. She could time it: within the space of five minutes, Margot and Travis would be upstairs in the haven of their room so she could model what was doubtless a very sexy surprise she'd picked up in New York.

Sunday might have proved more difficult dodging her sisters' "Jordan's an emotional wreck" radars if she hadn't had the excuse of needing to come up with stunning designs for Hawk Hill's kitchen and baths. A legitimate excuse, just not the one worrying her to distraction.

When Margot and Jade came into the front parlor later that afternoon, they caught her sitting on the sofa, the half-dozen kitchen design catalogs next to her forgotten as she stared pensively at Max and Kate, who were building a sprawling town out of colored blocks while Olivia chattered away to her plastic Cookie Monster figurine stuck inside Max's fire truck.

Jade claimed her favorite spot on the chaise longue. Olivia immediately lurched to her feet and brought the fire truck over for inspection. Pushing the catalogs aside, Margot dropped onto the sofa next to Jordan. And though she'd tried, Jordan couldn't erase the frown from her brow, for Margot said, "There's no reason to fret your way to an ulcer, sweetie. Whoever walks into the house is going to love what you've done to the interior."

"And it's not like you have to work with a horror like

Nonie Harrison. Owen's cool. He knows you'll do a good job since he's already seen the upstairs," Jade added.

A pang of guilt pierced her at keeping them in the dark about the real reason for her preoccupation. But she needed time to think about the letter. Her sisters' reactions she could predict. They would want her to fight Richard tooth and nail. All very well, were only she involved, but there were the children to consider. Their happiness was paramount.

"Yes, but what I did upstairs was easy. I knew my clients. Even with Nonie's guest cottage, I could work off her tastes—questionable as they are—in order to come up with looks and styles."

Margot picked up a catalog and leafed through it. "Did Owen give you any guidelines?"

She smiled. "He told me to think of a client like Nonie except a hundred times more finicky."

"Ugh." Jade scowled. "Do *not* ruin that house by thinking of her."

"Yeah, it would destroy the feng shui."

"But then I'm left with a big blank."

"Wait, I know! Design the interior with Margot and Travis in mind."

Margot lifted a brow in astonishment.

"Well, why not?" Jade said. "You guys tied the knot last year and probably want to give Olivia some cousins to boss around once she gets tired of making Cookie Monster toe the line. The rest works, too. You're horsey and like nice things. And Travis goes for all the guy stuff—a big-screen TV and comfortable furniture. That'll keep Jordan from making things too girlie. It's a piece of cake."

Margot looked impressed. "That's a really good plan, isn't it, Jordan? But you'll also have to decorate a room for Jade, too."

"Make sure you put my room on the other end of the house, so I can have some peace and quiet. Margot's kids'll be a lot noisier than yours."

"Just wait, Jade. We'll have to buy ear plugs when yours come into the world," Margot countered easily as her hand moved to her abdomen and rested there.

Jordan didn't think Jade noticed the gesture, but she couldn't help but suspect that maybe Margot and Travis had decided to get to work on making babies in earnest. That "surprise" Margot had given him must have been really something, she thought, smiling inwardly.

How thrilling for them. And what a huge step for Margot, fraught with consequences for her modeling. But times were changing. Pregnancy and children were no longer the career-enders they'd once been. Actually, it seemed like every other top model was pregnant these days.

"So what do you think of my idea, Jordan? Wicked brilliant, no?"

"It is kind of inspired," Margot said.

Jordan nodded. "Definitely an improvement over using Nonie as my imaginary client." What she especially liked about the idea was that Margot's and her tastes were actually very similar. She could buy things she loved for the rooms, assured that Margot would like them just as much. "Thanks, Jade."

"*De nada*. Got any more problems?"

"None that I can think of." Or at least none that she wanted to share right now. Once she had a clearer idea of her own feelings, it would be easier to face her sisters' indignation over Richard's request.

"So, Ned told us that Owen hung out here yesterday. He must think you're pretty neat." Jade grinned.

"Ned's given Owen his stamp of approval. Has he got yours, sweetie?"

It was time to set them straight before they got caught up in their matchmaking. She didn't want things to get awkward for Owen. "He was simply killing time looking over the main barn and going through John Butler's pattern book before heading back to Alexandria. He had a date later that evening. At the Grille."

The significance seemed lost on them.

"So he's got good taste." Jade shrugged. "Figures."

"He couldn't exactly invite you, sweetie, since you were holding down the fort for us."

"Of course not. That's not—" She stopped, aware she didn't want to go down that avenue. "I think he's a nice man, and I have a hunch he gets far more out of visiting Rosewood than we can imagine."

To her annoyance both burst out laughing, though in Jade's case it came out as a very loud snort.

"He played our piano," Kate said.

"That's right, Kate," Jordan said firmly. "He plays very well and our piano is probably one of the reasons he likes to come over. What a great animal hospital you've built there. Are your dogs getting checkups?"

A terrific segue to guide the conversation away from Owen. Unfortunately her children preferred to continue on what was becoming a favorite path. "Next time Owen comes over, we're gonna play Twistuh. Mommy's gonna teach him how."

Jordan managed a weak smile for her son, while her sisters indulged in a fit of giggles. "You two are ridiculously immature," she said with a shake of her head.

"Sorry," Margot said, not sounding in the least contrite. "I was just exercising my imagination." She dropped her head against the back of the sofa and, smiling widely, she closed her eyes. "Yep, I can easily picture you teaching Owen to play Twister." She opened one eye. "Something tells me he might be really good at it."

"Definitely. That's one dude who might have some smooth moves."

"Ha, ha. Sorry to cut this totally inappropriate conversation short, but it's bath time."

"Yeah, and talk is cheap in any case. Max, you make sure

Mommy brings Owen over for a game of Twister real soon. Okeydokey?"

"Okeydokey, smokie." Max grinned, bobbing his head.

Her sisters could laugh and giggle all they wanted. The notion that a man, especially one as attractive as Owen, might actually be indifferent to her was inconceivable to them. They were each so beautiful. Margot only had to smile a certain way for men to get that stunned look in their faces; Jade merely had to walk into a room. Neither had the slightest notion of what it meant to be Jordan, divorced mother of three. Whatever sex appeal she might have once possessed had passed its expiration date.

In one respect, however, she should be grateful for her sisters' ribbing. While they'd been teasing her about Owen, she'd managed to forget the existence of the letter stashed away in her dresser drawer. But with Richard and Cynthia's honeymoon coming to an end this week, she'd have to do far more than remember its presence.

Something was wrong with Jordan, Owen realized at eleven thirty-seven A.M. the following Monday. The realization might have struck him earlier—two hours and thirty-five minutes earlier—when she walked through the door, but Hawk Hill had been hopping. The masons were swarming the chimneys in a race to install the liners and tuckpoint as many bricks as possible before the clouds overhead let loose. As if in anticipation of the coming storm, a dull *boom, boom* was reverberating through the house while Jesse and Doug slammed away at the walls of one of the upstairs baths with their sledgehammers.

Given the foulness of his mood, Owen would have been happy to pick up a sledgehammer himself and go at the faded and cracked ceramic tiles until his shoulders screamed and the synapses in his brain were fried, but the electrician had surprised them all by actually arriving on time.

As Owen and Doug took him through the rooms, their

path crossed Jordan's, but Owen had resisted the urge to look at her too closely. This morning it was imperative he prove his ability to focus on anything else, no matter how pedestrian, such as where an electrical outlet or light switch should be positioned, than on her and how he liked the curve of her bare neck as she studied the blocks of granite and soapstone samples she'd brought with her. Allotting only five seconds to imagine his mouth traveling over that soft pale flesh demonstrated his supreme self-control. And it eased the fear gnawing at him that no matter how many deficiencies he'd discovered in Fiona Rorty, the real reason he'd chosen to spend the night alone on Saturday was the woman standing in his kitchen.

Not that Fiona hadn't brought some of this on herself. It was she who'd tipped her hand with the idea of a double date at the jazz club. Double dates implied permanency. Clearly Fiona had begun to consider Owen hers, that they were an item. Her assumption tripped his internal alarm, signaling that immediate evasive action was required.

So he'd cut the evening short with a lame story about his head feeling as if it were suddenly about to explode, saying that maybe he should call it a night. Fiona, no idiot, was less than happy to be left chaperoning Caroline and Freddy at the Blues Alley.

Confident of his ability to please a woman, he wasn't so cocksure as to believe Fiona's irritation was rooted in thwarted desire. She was simply mad that he wasn't falling in line with her plans.

He told himself that ditching Fiona had everything to do with the fact that she suddenly wanted to take the relationship to a new level and nothing to do with the admittedly unsettling realization that he'd had more fun listening to Jordan explain horse-training techniques in a straw-filled stall than he'd had sitting opposite Fiona at the Grille as she talked about God knows what.

In Owen's experience, that was an insane reason to go to

bed alone on a Saturday night—or Sunday night, for that matter. And now, having forgone some seriously therapeutic sex, he had yet to shake this strange fixation with Jordan.

Thus the reason for his foul mood this morning and his decision to compensate for his fixation by doing his level best to ignore Jordan.

Except that the last time he'd gone into the kitchen, she'd been worrying her lower lip. And the time before that, he'd noticed her absently massaging the pressure point at the end of her winged brow. Though he'd known her less than a week, he could read the signs: something was troubling her.

The specs for upgrading Hawk Hill's wiring for the twenty-first century jotted down on his clipboard, the electrician left. Doug left, too, rejoining Jesse for another half-hour's brute pleasure in demo work before lunch. But just when Owen thought he might hunt down Jordan and see how she was progressing and perhaps get a sense of what was bothering her, his cell began ringing.

Sitting down on the front stoop, away from the pounding noise, he had to hold the phone away from his ear or else risk permanent damage to his eardrum. His designer, the normally bubbly Emily Carlson, was not a happy camper.

"I swear to God, Owen, if Nonie Harrison whines one more time, asking why *you* aren't here supervising the crew, I'm going to rip her a new—"

"Steady there, Em. I don't want to have to bail you out. Just treat Nonie like an atmospheric disturbance. A lot of hot air."

"She's certainly hot for—"

"Please don't finish that thought, either. Thinking about Nonie in a lather over anyone is enough to put me off my feed for weeks. The next time she asks why I'm not checking on the color blue you're using, just tell her I'm color blind."

Emily wasn't mollified. "I don't think she cares if you're

blind, deaf, or dumb. Honestly, Owen, she acts like you're much cuter than you really are."

He laughed. "Thanks. You're excellent for my ego. In return, I promise I'll pop over and shake my head dolefully at whatever shade of white you've picked out."

"Don't you dare. This job was supposed to be a no-brainer, not a migraine to end all migraines."

"Take two aspirin and call me in the afternoon."

"How about I take four aspirin and have Nonie call?"

"You're becoming evil in your old age."

"Don't you forget it, Gramps."

Disconnecting, Owen became aware of the quiet. Jesse and Doug must have gone out the back to make their lunch run to Braverman's. Compared to the earlier din, the scratch of cement being scraped and applied by the masons was hardly louder than the chattering of the squirrels. The rain had held off. It was just possible they'd be able to finish the chimney repairs. He pocketed his phone and wandered back inside.

Jordan was in the kitchen, her tools of the trade spread out over the linoleum counter. Amid the catalogs of cabinet styles and finishes and blocks of granite was a sandwich and a clear plastic bag filled with quartered carrots and celery sticks.

"You're not picking up the kids at school? May I?" he asked, his hand hovering over a carrot stick.

"Go ahead," she replied, without looking up from the catalog that was open to a page with wood cabinets in a white bisque. "Margot had some errands to run in town so she's picking them up. She has to leave later tonight for a two-day shoot in New York. I wanted to give the kids a treat and let them spend some time alone with her. It's good for them to be away from me." From the way she was frowning at the specs for the options and sizes of the cabinets, one would have thought she was trying to decipher the Rosetta stone.

He leaned a hip against the countertop. "Okay. Here's the deal. You give me half your sandwich and I listen to what's bugging you."

She looked up in surprise. "Nothing's bugging me. Take the whole sandwich. I'm not very hungry." Pen in hand she pushed it toward him.

"Are you dieting? Because that would be a mistake."

"What? No. I just don't feel like eating."

His hunch had been right. Something was bothering her. Because the dieting comment would have made the Jordan he knew go as frosty as the inside of a freezer. And he'd plunk down a hundred on a bet that when Jordan was upset she couldn't eat.

He plucked the pen out of her hand.

That got her attention. "Hey," she exclaimed.

"Sorry, but you've got to eat. I don't want to deal with worker's comp when you faint from inanition and crack your head on the floor. Plus I don't like to eat alone and I'm starving." He picked up half the sandwich and held it out to her. "So eat."

She took it with a shake of her head. "I really—"

"It's something to do with the kids, right?"

Her eyes widened. "How did you guess that?"

"My parents were repeatedly assured that their son was a genius," he said dryly. "Actually, my deduction process was fairly straightforward. If one of the horses were sick, you'd have mentioned it. What clinched it was the odd expression on your face when you talked about the kids going out on the town with Margot. So spill it."

Instead, Jordan took a halfhearted bite of the sandwich and chewed, as she considered Owen's offer. She'd gotten exactly nowhere in coming to a decision with respect to Richard's request. Her thinking was distressingly like one of those wave-simulator machines that tip back and forth: wishy-washy. It would be such a relief to talk to someone who had no stake in the outcome. "You're right," she confessed with a small sigh. "It is about the kids."

"My parents would be so gratified to know those predictions about my being a genius came true."

She tried to smile back.

Owen took a big bite of the sandwich because he knew it would be good. Swallowing, he said, "I take it this is more than a runny nose?"

"I got a letter from my ex-husband's lawyer asking me to consider giving Richard visiting rights. He'd like us to devise a schedule that would allow him to have the kids with him a weekend or two every month and for a part of their school vacations." She swallowed forcibly against the choking sensation that threatened. "I don't have to agree to his request, but maybe it would be good for the children . . ."

"You have full custody?"

She didn't know why, but having Owen immediately take another energetic bite of the chicken salad sandwich made his question somehow less pointed and intrusive. They might have been discussing whether to have a walk-in shower installed in the master bath rather than the personal details of her divorce.

"Yes. There was a tape of Richard and his mistress."

His eyebrows shot up. "A tape?"

"Audio only, thankfully."

"I know you lived in D.C., but please don't tell me you guys were wiretapping each other."

It was nothing less than amazing that he'd managed to make her laugh. "No, nothing more high tech than our answering machine at Rosewood did him in. He was supposed to join us for the weekend but he called saying he had too much work to drive out. We'd made some progress with the marriage counselor, and he'd assured me that the affair he was having with his colleague was over, so I believed him. The only hitch with his truly brilliant performance, in which he promised he'd be at Rosewood bright and early the next day, was that when he hung up, he accidentally pressed the redial button. An understandable mistake, as he was very distracted at the time. Well, to make a long and distasteful story short, our answering machine recorded an extremely explicit exchange between him and Cynthia, one that if played before the court would have been awkward for Richard professionally—so awkward that he didn't contest any of my lawyer's requests."

Owen made himself take another bite and chew vigorously. He didn't want her to see how affected he was by the story. Not prone to violence, he knew that if given the chance, he would happily pound the shit out of the son of a bitch for having hurt Jordan. Satisfying though it would have been to act the hero for the pain Jordan suffered still, that wasn't what she needed right now. She needed a rational listener to provide counsel, not a rage-propelled avenger to rain blows on her worthless scumbag of an ex.

Unfortunately, she probably needed that even more than Owen's preferred impulse: to haul her into his arms and kiss her until she couldn't even remember her ex-husband's name.

First things first. He swallowed and took a moment to school his voice so that it betrayed nothing he was feeling. "Right. I got the picture. Smart of you to keep the tape."

"That was Jade. It certainly made things easier with the proceedings. I was kind of a mess emotionally, and as Richard and Cynthia weren't married, I didn't want the children more confused by spending weekends with them. But now they *are* married, and the house they bought is large enough for all of them."

"And so your ex wants to be able to spend a little more time with the kids. Common enough desire. Here's the first question: was he as lousy a father as he was a husband?" Damn. There went any pretense at objectivity.

Her small smile told him he hadn't messed up. Given how private she was, it occurred to Owen that she didn't talk about the collapse of her marriage to many people. Maybe hearing someone say her husband was a prick was music to her ears.

"Actually, Richard was a good father. Even when he came home tired from the office, he always made the effort to play with them or read them a story. He liked being an involved dad, being part of their lives. I think Kate and Max miss that. Going out for an ice cream on Sundays isn't enough. I worry, though, that it will be hard on them—unsettling and confusing."

With a sigh, she picked up a carrot stick and nibbled on it. "To tell you the truth, Richard wasn't even a lousy husband," she said, surprising him. "At least, not at first. But whatever he felt for me died at some point, and I didn't see it. And because I didn't see it, maybe I didn't do the things that could have saved our marriage. What was weak of him was to have an affair rather than let me know he'd fallen in love with someone else."

Weak? Owen should have guessed Jordan was the kind of person who'd be generous even to those who behaved abominably. But he wasn't going to screw things up by wading into those murky waters. Sticking to the kids was a far safer.

"I've heard that kids are pretty resilient. And Kate and Max appear pretty normal." Damned if he was going to perjure himself by calling Olivia, who seemed like a cross between Frankenstein and Tarzan, *normal*. "My hunch is they'll take their cues from you and your ex."

She nodded. "Yes, I suppose they will. I know Richard would hate to hurt them any more by engaging in a tug-of-war over them."

"It seems to me that if you're confident he's going to approach the question of sharing the kids with their best interests in mind, then you already know what you're going to do. Because if you weren't sure he'd do his utmost to make their time with him as positive an experience as possible, I suspect you'd fight him with everything you've got. A sight to behold, but not necessarily kiddie-friendly." With a last bite, he polished off the sandwich. "Of course, you could decide that denying your ex the chance to be with the kids is the perfect revenge for having cheated on you."

She looked sickened at the suggestion.

"You wouldn't be the first, Jordan."

That chin, which by now he'd come to regard as her emotional bellwether, rose in proud defiance. "I'd never do that. They've been hurt quite enough."

"And you and your sisters have done everything in your power to compensate for the fact that their dad doesn't live with them. As these things go, your kids have a pretty idyllic setup."

"They don't have a father to tuck them in at night or ask them how their day went."

"A complete set of parents under the same roof isn't a guaranteed formula for happy, well-adjusted children, so quit feeling terrible about what yours are supposedly missing out on. It's pointless."

He saw that his words had taken her aback. For a second he wondered if he'd been too harsh, but then the corners of her mouth lifted in a wry smile. "Okay, no undue pity fest for having failed my kids."

"Good. Would that more parents failed as miserably as you."

"Let's not exaggerate," she said, her voice tinged with something close to laughter. "But thanks for the excellent advice. And for listening. I really needed a chance to air my thoughts. Where Richard is concerned, I've lost all confidence in my judgment. And my sisters aren't exactly the best sounding board when it comes to him."

That was a surprise. The sisters seemed close, friends as well as siblings. "You haven't spoken to them about this?"

"No. When I discovered Richard was still carrying on with

Cynthia, I kind of fell apart. Jade, Margot, and Travis kept things going, provided a stable environment and routine for the kids and me until I could pull myself together. While they were willing for my sake to forgive him the first time he cheated, the second time, well . . ." her voice trailed off.

As he'd been entertaining fantasies of bloodying the guy, Owen could only imagine what her sisters would like to do to him.

"Anyway," she continued with a little shrug. "I thought it best to sort out my own feelings first. Though all I really accomplished was to vacillate all weekend." She was staring at the counter, her finger tracing random patterns on the discolored Formica. When she spoke again, he had to strain to hear her. "The thing is— God, I hate myself for being so petty and selfish in feeling this way."

Petty and selfish were about the last adjectives he'd pick to describe Jordan. "For feeling what way?" he asked, bewildered.

"Talking with you has made me recognize why I was hesitating to let Richard have the children for visits. It wasn't just because I was worried about how they'll adjust to the arrangement. It's that I don't want them to love her— Cynthia. Not in the way they love *me*. I couldn't bear it if I lost that, too." Her words died away on an agonized whisper.

His gut wrenched tight at her confession and the knowledge of what it must have cost to voice it. *Fuck it all.* Without another thought, he drew her into his arms.

The front of his shirt soon grew damp with her tears, but still he held her loosely, doing nothing more than rubbing her back in slow circles while he wondered how in God's name he'd ended up in a situation like this. He liked her, that was it. He'd do the same for Emily Carson if she'd come to him with some sob story. Except he'd never thought about lying between Em's legs, which pretty much topped his list of things he'd like to do with Jordan.

Her bout of tears didn't last long. Nonetheless he offered

silent thanks when, with a moist sniff, she straightened her shoulders. She looked up, her spiky-lashed azure gaze briefly meeting his before dropping away to stare fixedly at the base of his throat.

"I've wet your shirt," she said to his clavicle.

"It'll dry." Providing solace had a definite upside. She was in his arms. Owen wondered whether she'd even noticed that his hands had quit their platonic, comfort-in-need rub to settle at her waist. He spanned her slender strength, the tips of his fingers meeting at the hollow of her spine. He could feel the warmth of her skin through the thin cotton of her shirt. His fingers played with the fabric, gathering it so it rode up her waist. His heart drummed with anticipation at touching that silky soft skin.

Though the kitchen was at the back of the house, the sound of the front door slamming was unmistakable, and as impossible to ignore as Jesse's ringing yell. "Owen, man, where are you? We've got your lunch."

Owen dropped his hands, balling them into fists while in his head he let loose with every single curse he'd picked up in every country he'd ever lived. He was gripped by a sudden vicious urge to fire Jesse on the spot for having the worst damned timing in the world. At the very least dock his pay.

All he'd needed was three more minutes, and he could have tasted the sweetness of Jordan's mouth and the poignant saltiness of her still damp cheeks.

Jordan had jumped back. She met his gaze with palpable reluctance. "I really am sorry about your shirt."

"Not a problem. At least it's not tea." It could have been indelible ink for all he cared. Christ, he wanted her in his arms.

Her tear-splotched cheeks turned even redder. "I'd forgotten about that. I'm s—"

"Don't apologize again. Anyone in your position would feel like crying." His brows slammed together in a scowl as

Jesse shouted again. "For Christ's sake. All right already, I'm coming!" he hollered back. "If you need anything, I'll be upstairs," he said, letting himself have one last look at her as need roiled inside him. After tearing out a piece of Jesse's hide, he was going to tackle one of the bathrooms. Some serious demo work might put a dent in his frustration.

Too swamped with conflicting emotions to speak, Jordan merely nodded. Part of her was relieved at his departure. Now she couldn't make more of a fool out of herself. If there were a reality show for the biggest idiot, she'd win it hands down. How could she have gone and spilled not only her heart but her tears with Owen?

Divorced and living in a sexual desert, she might be. But even Jordan knew the basics. Turning on the waterworks was the quickest way to turn a man off.

If Owen had once been interested in her, she had done everything, by spilling the details of how fully she'd played the role of the pathetically deceived wife and then revealing how selfish she was as a mother, to squash any atom of desire he might have felt.

What utterly brilliant timing she had: just when she was starting to walk back, albeit with bumbling baby steps, from the idea that a physical relationship with Owen would be something to avoid at all costs, she'd gone and painted herself as a loser with a capital L.

Owen could attract any woman he fancied. Sad, insecure divorcées need not apply.

But it had been such a relief to unburden herself that Jordan couldn't regret her inability to edit her words or paint a more flattering representation of herself. Embarrassed as she was now, being able to talk had been immensely helpful. That it had also made Owen even more attractive in her eyes was only natural.

But the last thing she needed was for Owen to become any better-looking. He'd been so kind, not only listening to her but also offering his opinion on a subject that had no interest whatsoever for him. When he'd held her so she could weep out her misery, a part of her had ached to have him enfold her in the muscled strength of his embrace as he thrilled her with the hot passion of his kiss.

An unlikely event. She was beginning to accept that she was a rank failure when it came to sustaining a man's sexual interest.

Owen had rubbed her back as if she were a nun.

But while he may have decided she wasn't worth pursuing, he had offered her something that in certain respects satisfied an equally deep yearning, something that Jordan hadn't experienced in years: a friendship with a man. Looking back at her marriage, she realized that in many ways she *had* effectively lived the existence of a cloistered nun. An invisible barrier had separated her from most married men and practically all single men. Were she still with Richard, she would never have been friends with someone as attractive as Owen.

Proof that he could be a very good friend had been given right here in this tired old kitchen. The knowledge brought a burst of happiness, a feeling very likely not so different from the excitement that bubbled inside Max when he talked about Owen coming over to play trains with him.

As Jordan and Max had discussed during his first week of nursery school, when Max told her about Will Mahoney, who liked Shrek and playing with trucks in the sandbox, it was very nice to make new friends.

Indeed it was. Thanks to her new friend, Jordan was going to do the right thing for her three wonderful children when Richard called.

AN ADVANTAGE of having been married for close to ten years was that Jordan could calculate to the hour when Richard would call. The lobbyist in him would want to pitch his case in addition to the letter his lawyers had drafted; the father in him would want to talk to the children and hear how they'd been faring while he was honeymooning in Hawaii; the ex-husband in him would want to choose an hour when it was most likely his former in-laws would be out of the house.

When the phone rang within ten minutes of the predicted hour—four hours after his plane touched down—she glanced at the caller ID and couldn't help but wonder whether Cynthia had already acquired this kind of knowledge and, if not, how many years it would take before she understood her husband as well as Jordan did.

The children, Miriam, and she were in the double parlor, gathered around a puppet theater she'd fashioned out of a cardboard wardrobe-size moving box with maroon hand towels serving as curtains. Kate had drawn the backdrop's scenery. It was filled with masses of flowers and a smiling sun surrounded by puffy clouds. Jordan had helped write out and cut admission tickets for the performance Kate and Max had decided to put on that evening to surprise Margot, who'd bought the puppets during their trip into town. This was the dress rehearsal. If one were to gauge the show by Olivia's reaction, it was a smash hit. She kept clapping her hands and talking to the puppet animals. Luckily the

audience's enthusiastic participation didn't rattle the per-
formers, nor did anyone notice when Jordan slipped into
the adjoining parlor to answer the phone on the second
ring.

"Hello, Richard."

"Jordan, hi. I'm glad I caught you. I'm not interrupting
anything?"

"No, the kids are playing. Miriam's with them."

"That's great, just great." He fell silent. It struck her then
that he was nervous, perhaps for the first time unsure of his
power to persuade. He was actually scared of saying the
wrong thing. His hesitation showed her more than any of
his facile words how important spending time with the
children was to him.

Taking pity on him, she said, "I got the letter from your
lawyer."

"Oh, right! Yeah, that's one of the reasons I was calling."
There was another pause, then his words came out in a
rush. "The thing is, Jordan, now that the work's finished
on our new place and Cynthia and I are back from our, um,
trip to Hawaii, and summer is coming with the kids on vacation from school, I thought it would be a really good
time to . . . to kind of reintroduce myself into their lives."

"Yes."

For some reason, nervousness probably, Jordan's reply
didn't register. As soon as he'd drawn a breath, Richard
plunged back into justifying his request. "The house has
plenty of room. We've set up two bedrooms right next to
each other. I'm going to contact Susannah and pay her
whatever she asks to come and sit for them again. Cynthia
and I agree it'll be good to have another familiar face on
hand so they won't be too overwhelmed . . . God, Jordan, I
can't begin to tell you how much I miss them."

It would serve no purpose to point out that if he'd only
honored his wedding vows, he wouldn't be missing them at
all. And as she'd told Owen, while Richard had failed her

as a husband, he loved his children. Antagonizing Richard would be a terrible way to start this next phase of doing their best as parents. "Richard, I think it's a good idea for the children to spend time with you and Cynthia."

"You do!" His breath came out in a long whoosh of relief. "Ahh, Jordan, thanks. Really, thanks a million. I knew you'd do what was right."

Yes, she could be counted on to do the right thing, she thought, a touch cynically. But if Richard believed he could use that to steamroll over her, he was sorely mistaken. "I'm willing to work out times for you to spend with the kids, but I want you to understand from the outset that you'll need to be flexible about their visits. I don't want them to miss out on things they might want to do here—weekend birthday parties and sleepovers, horse shows, and the like—that are bound to increase in number as the kids get older. In return, I'll do my part to make sure you and Cynthia have as much advance warning to adjust your own schedules. The weekend and vacation visits can't become a tug-of-war between us. Even more important, they can't become a source of tension for the kids. If you can't agree to that kind of flexibility—"

"I can. I do. I want this to work amicably and I want the kids to enjoy their time with Cynthia and me. They won't if they're missing out on stuff."

"Okay then."

"Okay then," he repeated happily. "God, this is great, Jordan. You've made my day. So, when do you think I can have them?"

Owen walked through the woods to Rosewood. The trees were beautiful, their leaves a bright green canopy overhead. The deeper into the trail he went, the cooler the air became, relieving his simmering temper. Damn Nonie Harrison for going behind Emily's back to complain about the "exorbitant charges" for wallpaper and curtains and how long the job was taking and how really, when all was said and done, Emily Carson wasn't quite at the level of the quality she'd come to expect from Owen's firm.

Yeah, right. Nonie was sexist, plain and simple. She was bitching because a woman was working for her. It would serve Nonie right if he left her high and dry and pulled Emily off the job. Except that Gage & Associates was his baby and he wasn't going to let anyone sully its reputation. And Nonie had a hell of a big mouth. She'd exercised it for a good hour when, forced to shelve his own work, he'd gone to Overlea to calm her down.

Not even the hour he spent explaining how even rush orders took time and getting her to acknowledge that the work which had been accomplished looked smashing placated Nonie. She wanted more from him and in her supreme egotism expected him to kowtow to her whim. "Well, I expect the cottage to be ready for my spring fête next week."

"I'm sure Emily will do everything she can to be finished by then."

No sooner had the issue of Emily's ability been settled, than Nonie informed him of a cocktail party being thrown by Mitch and Karen Langdon. Mitch, like Nonie, sat on the board of the Warburg Historical Society. "You'll come with me, won't you, Owen dear? Mitch is quite impressed with the work you've done on the cottage. I'd so like you to meet him before we vote on the annual preservation award." With that heavy-handed hint, she'd obviously assumed he was her captive.

The high point of Owen's visit was setting her straight. "As pleasurable as that sounds, I actually think it's better not to have contact with people who are casting votes on my work."

"How very idealistic of you," she said. "But in Warburg success is so much a question of who you know."

"Nevertheless," he replied easily, "I'm afraid I have a

prior commitment. I'm expected at Rosewood later." Jordan had invited him to a family dinner. The kids were putting on some kind of show and insisted he be included in the festivities.

Her smile turned as hard as the stone patio on which they sat. "Unlike your employee, Ms. Carson, you obviously know how to work fast. Jordan must be so gratified by the attention."

He hadn't risen to the bait, merely stood and thanked her for the iced tea, which, like so many things Nonie served, was tasteless.

"Give my regards to your neighbor," she said as he climbed into his car. "By the way, how is Hawk Hill coming?"

"We're only at the preliminary stages."

"I can't wait to see it. You know, Owen, darling, I might be able to steer some prospective buyers your way."

"I'll be sure to keep that in mind."

"I assume the ever-so-talented Emily Carson will be doing the interior work?"

Enjoyable as it might have been to rouse Nonie to indignation by telling her that Jordan was decorating the house for him, he decided against it. Why provide her with material to twist into her own nasty version? Pretending not to hear her question, he started the Audi's engine with a satisfying roar and got the hell out of there.

If anything could serve as an antidote to the horror that was Nonie Harrison, it was Jordan. Hell, he'd rather be locked up in a room with Jordan's kids than suffer . . .

Owen didn't finish the thought, for the trees had thinned, opening onto a hilly meadow. It was a terrific view from up there. He could see Rosewood's sloping roof line, the layout of the pastures, the three horse barns, and the lush green of the majestic chestnut trees lining Rosewood's long drive.

As he looked around, he noticed a split-rail enclosure off to his right. The fence was too low to be used as a pasture. Curious, he moved toward it.

The stone markers rising from the mowed field explained everything. The enclosure's wooden gate, left open, seemed to invite him in.

The headstones placed near the entrance to the cemetery, along the perimeter of the fence, puzzled him at first. Comprehension dawned and he smiled. Of course the Radcliffes would wish to rest for all eternity as they had lived: in the company of their horses.

He came upon the oldest graves. The moss growing over the age-pitted stones made the letters that much harder to decipher, but from the *F* and the *G* he knew that he standing before Francis and his beloved Georgiana. She'd died first, he saw, with Francis following a few weeks later. They'd left behind sons, though. He tracked their lives and those of their offspring with measured steps.

Too brief, he thought, reading the shockingly short span of years some Radcliffes were given on earth. The tragic death of RJ Radcliffe, Jordan and her sisters' father, had already been foreshadowed in his ancestors' untimely ends.

The stones were newer at the far end of the plot, the last row enhanced by a glorious rosebush. In this open setting, where the sun shone unobstructed, the roses were already in full riotous bloom, their lush shade an almost exact match for the head of the other visitor.

She came to her feet, turned, and noticed him just as he spoke. "Sorry, Jade. I didn't mean to intrude. I must have taken the wrong fork when I was walking through the woods. The trail gave out here."

Not meeting his eye, she nodded. "It's okay. I was leaving in any case."

Behind her lay a mass of flowers, nestled at the base of the third stone. "Your mother?" he asked.

She nodded again.

"Nice flowers."

"It was her birthday last Saturday. I missed it because of the show. I had to bring her something." She shrugged.

"Not that I would have if she was alive. Mom was totally weird about her birthday. She loved throwing parties, but when I was around twelve, she suddenly put the kibosh on celebrating her own b'day. She didn't even want a card. But as she can't get any older, I figure it won't freak her out to have some flowers."

Not knowing what to reply to that statement, he opted for, "I imagine you miss her a lot."

She shot him a look. "I'd be pretty freakin' unnatural if I didn't. She was my mom, after all. And just in case you're wondering, I miss Dad, too. The difference is, Mom only has me to miss her."

She began walking toward the gate. Owen fell into step beside her. "I'm sure she's missed by her friends."

"Nice thought, but no. Mom had frenemies, not friends. I think Ellie, our housekeeper, liked her, though I bet she preferred Dad's first wife, Katherine. So besides me, there ain't a big Nicole Warren Radcliffe fan club. Except the Rev. He's always bringing her up when we go bowling. Of course, he's *supposed* to be kind and forgive everyone's sins. He suggested I come up here today. Thought it would be good for me. Cathartic. I knew he'd get all sad-eyed and quiet and throw nothing but dead balls all night if I didn't, so I went and cut some flowers from the garden when Patrick, our groundskeeper, wasn't around. No biggie, really. But—" She paused as if suddenly needing to choose her words with care. "But if you could keep it to yourself that I was up here and not tell Margot and Jordan, I'd be seriously grateful."

"No problem."

Her quick sideways glance betrayed her surprise. "Margot and Jordan really didn't get along with Mom, so they'll just get all weird, wanting to *talk*. They'll twist themselves into knots trying to pretend they liked her."

Having just enough brains to keep his mouth shut, he nodded.

"Watching them do that is too awkward for words. After all, Mom never had a nice thing to say about them. She and Margot used to go at it tooth and claw and she was pretty harsh with Jordan after Margot left Rosewood to model."

"My guess would be your sisters understand now that being a stepmother might not have been an easy role for your mother."

"Maybe, but there's other stuff she did, too. Stuff that can't be explained away with an 'Oh, I'm older now, I understand what Nicole was going through' line. And if there's the remotest chance Mom was, well, no one, especially not Jordan, would ever forgive her." In a violent punctuation to her thoughts, she gave a well-aimed kick to a dandelion that had the misfortune to be growing in her path. Its yellow head sailed through the early-evening air.

Though Jade's sentence was jumbled, with tantalizing skips, Owen knew just enough of everyone's story that he thought he could piece it together. Having herself suffered the pain of a spouse's infidelity, Jordan shouldn't be able to forgive Jade's mother for cheating on their father.

"Anger's not a very productive emotion."

"Yes, it leads to the dark side, Obi-Wan."

Ouch. Well, he'd deserved that. At least she hadn't compared him to Yoda. "What I meant was that Jordan strikes me as someone who knows that it's better to focus on what you can change."

"Yeah, well, she's a way better person than I am. You do get how terrific she is, don't you, Owen?"

A vision came to him of Jade's leg whipping out and dealing him the same lethal blow that she'd given to the dandelion if he didn't answer correctly—or convincingly enough. "Absolutely."

"Good, 'cause I promise you, you hurt her and I'll make you sorry. Unlike Jordan, I'm into vengeance."

He decided not to deflate her by telling her he'd already

figured out that when it came to protecting Jordan, Jade would be joined by every able-bodied person at Rosewood. A veritable private army. Instead he gave her an easy smile. "I think you're getting ahead of yourself. I was only invited for dinner. And some sort of show."

The teen blasted him with another withering look. "For a smart guy, you're pretty clueless, aren'tcha?"

Okay, so maybe Jade had a point, Owen thought, several hours later. Dinner at Rosewood was a whole lot more involved an affair than elsewhere. A participatory experience from the moment he walked into the house with Jade helpfully bellowing, "Yo, Jordan, I've got Owen with me."

Her voice triggered an earthquake, the old wood floors shaking, an ominous rumbling echoing from the back hallway, and then her nephew and nieces erupting forth as they rushed to greet her . . . and him, too. Their ongoing enthusiasm mystified Owen. It wasn't as if he encouraged it.

"We're putting on our puppet show after dinner, Jade. Mommy and I made tickets for everyone," Kate said, slipping her hand in Jade's.

"Yeah, and we get to stay up late as a treat," Max informed him, jumping up and down from the excitement that announcement engendered.

The news of the day kept coming, spilling out of their mouths like a leaking faucet as they made their way toward the kitchen.

"Not Olivia, though, she's too little. She has to go to bed when the show is over."

Owen thanked God for small favors. Maybe when summoned to bed, the toddler would let go of his leg. She'd latched on like a ball and chain.

As if reading his thoughts, Jade leveled one of her green-eyed gazes at him. "Dude, you know we might actually reach the kitchen before the next millennium if you'd just *pick* 'Liv up."

Feeling strangely embarrassed, he hoisted Olivia into his arms and resigned himself to a slow strangulation.

Never in his wildest imaginings would he have predicted that he'd be grateful to have Olivia's solid bulk hanging from his neck. But it turned out the kid made a damn good shield to duck behind when Max dropped the bomb.

They'd made it into the kitchen where Margot was helping Jordan prepare dinner and Travis was setting the long table for a family dinner that would include the children—why that was desirable, Owen had no idea—and Max was still talking about the great stuff going on in his life: the all-school picnic, a playdate with someone named Will, his elation over the fact that his mom had baked a cake that they were going to get to eat with ice cream and so on and so on.

Owen listened with a quarter of an ear, doing a pretty fine job of faking the appropriate noises as he tracked Jordan's movements around the kitchen. He liked watching her move, liked thinking of his hands running along the curve of her hip and then slipping around to cup her ass, liked imagining lifting her up onto the counter and stepping into the vee of her slender thighs.

"And you know what, Owen?"

"No, what?" He kept his eyes on Jordan, who'd opened the fridge and was bending over to pull something out of the lower shelf. He'd very much like to see her naked, just like that.

He nearly jumped a mile at the impatient tug on his trouser leg. He looked down at the reddish brown head that didn't even reach the counter Owen was leaning against. Christ, he could probably be arrested for thinking about Jordan this way with her kids present.

"And you know what else, Owen?"

He shook his head. "No, I really don't, Max."

"Me, Kate, and Wiv are going to see my daddy and stay at his house!"

It was difficult to say for sure if Max had actually shouted the news or if the momentary lull in the grown-up conversation just made it seem that way, but the sentence resounded with the force of a major explosion.

Stunned silence filled the room as Jordan's sisters stared at her. Even Travis, whom Owen considered a master of unshakeable calm when dealing with his wife and sisters-in-law, frowned with dark concern.

Olivia was still clinging to his neck. Owen decided this would be the perfect time to make himself invisible. He ducked his head, bringing it closer to her blond curls. She rewarded him by mashing her open palm against his nose.

"She wants you to say *beep*!" Max was a real font of information tonight.

He was saved the embarrassment of having to honk into Olivia's palm by Margot.

"You're going to visit your dad, Max?" she asked, still looking at Jordan.

Oblivious to the adults' tension, Max nodded happily. "Uh-huh. When are we going, Mommy?"

"Next Friday," she replied, setting the blue and white ceramic bowl filled with pasta salad on the counter.

Annoyed the horn was malfunctioning, Olivia slammed her palm into his nose again, making him jerk his head back. The movement caught Jordan's attention. "Olivia, let go of Owen's nose, please."

Olivia freed his nose only to begin thwacking his chest, perhaps expecting he'd go "moo." But with no hand planted in the middle of his face, he was at least able to give Jordan a smile in silent support.

Her answering smile eased the fine tension about her eyes. "Kate, can you and Max please take Olivia to the bathroom? You all need to wash your hands before dinner."

The second the kids had trooped out of the kitchen, Jade pounced. "And why is this visit happening exactly?" she demanded.

"Because I think it's a good idea. Richard and I have

talked it over and we've agreed to share the kids on the weekends and for part of the school holidays."

Owen was proud of Jordan's calm reply.

"So he just called and bullied you into agreeing? How typical."

"No, he sent a letter through his lawyer, a very polite and correct letter." Jordan plunged two long-handled spoons into the pasta salad and tossed it. "He simply wants to see his children, Margot."

"He's simply a selfish jerk is all."

Jordan could extol the virtues of having siblings all she wanted, Owen thought, listening to their exchange. He liked Margot. She was strong and smart and, for a successful fashion model, refreshingly indifferent to her knock-you-on-your-ass beauty. And Jade was like fireworks on a summer night. Thrilling and crackling and unpredictable.

But like them as he may, he'd had enough of them jumping on Jordan. "I think Jordan's doing the right thing." The surprise mirrored in their faces at his comment reinforced his determination to get them off her back. "You saw Max. The kid's over the moon at the prospect of spending a weekend with his dad. Do you honestly think Jordan would deny her kids that happiness?"

They had the grace to look embarrassed.

"Here's something else you might want to consider. These kids will have a much easier time adapting to the new situation if you don't make it quite so obvious you'd like to hunt their father down like a rabid fox. They're not totally stupid." They weren't. He was sure even Olivia would learn to read and write one day. But having said his piece, this was as far as he would wade into the Radcliffe family waters.

"Owen's right," Travis said. "What we think of Richard has nothing to do with his merits as a father. So they're going to D.C. next Friday?"

Owen was pleased Travis had spoken up. His added

support would cool Margot and Jade's tempers far more effectively than anything he could do.

Jordan nodded, giving her brother-in-law a frankly dazzling smile. "Yes, they'll stay with him through Sunday. Richard's coming to pick them up. He's even arranged for Susannah to come over and lend a hand."

"Smart of him," Travis said easily, ignoring Jade and Margot's less-than-happy silence. Walking over to the fridge and opening it, he glanced over his shoulder. "Can I get you a beer, Owen, before Olivia begins playing with your face again?"

"Please. Though maybe since I didn't honk, moo, or tweet, she'll give up."

Travis laughed. "Not our Olivia."

Owen decided that as puppet shows went, this one took the prize for surreal. The play was about a hippo and alligator taking a walk through a sunny, flower-filled meadow. It was difficult to tell if there was more to the plot. But one thing was certain, the principals' lines were so off-beat, they could have passed for the edgiest avant-garde theater in Berlin.

The show pushed the envelope in terms of audience interaction, too, with Olivia bounding from her seat to rush the stage, touch the plush actors, and up the level of the dialogue's incoherency. The puppeteers weren't shy about shouting questions to Jordan for tips with the scene.

It was a sign of how much he'd acclimated to the Rosewood environment that he wasn't at all surprised at the rousing applause the two stars, Henry the alligator and Lucinda the hippo, received when the dark red curtain went down. The standing ovation would have done Broadway proud. And he had to admit, the show had been pretty darned entertaining.

Once the play and the accolades were over, Owen was sure the children would be trundled off to bed. Naïve of him.

With Henry the alligator still jammed on his arm, Max, high on the success of his opening night, was ready to party.

"Mommy, Mommy, can we play Twistuh now?" and when Jordan hesitated, he cannily added, "Pwease." Then Owen knew, sure as bees made honey, that he was finally going to see what this game Twister was all about.

"All right. But not for long. Why don't you run upstairs and bring it down? It's on the lower shelf. You can play in the front parlor, where there'll be more room. But I'm going to have to put Olivia to bed."

Resistance came from an unexpected source. "No, let Olivia stay up. She loves to play, too," Margot said.

"She needs to go to sleep."

"Jordan, you know Twister is just not the same without her," Margot laughed.

"That's for sure," Jade said, joining forces with Margot. "Owen should experience the game at its finest." Rising from the sofa where she'd been lounging, she turned to Margot. "I gotta split. The Rev and I are bowling against a new team."

"Okay. Drive safely." Margot stood, too. "Are you ready to do the barn check, honey?"

Before Travis could even nod, Jordan said, "You and Travis aren't going to play?"

"Nope," Margot said with a little smile. "We might spoil your fun."

"So very considerate of you," Jordan replied, sounding distinctly sarcastic.

"That's what sisters are all about. Right, Jade?"

"Absofreakinlutely," she pronounced with her own broad smile. "*Hasta la vista,* y'all."

Listening to the sisters' conversation, Owen knew something was going on. But he attributed the testiness and Jordan's out-of-character exasperation as the lingering effect of their earlier spat in the kitchen. There was no reason to get this hopped up about a children's game.

* * *

This was a children's game?

Its premise had sounded so simple, banal: at the turn of the dial one had to place one's left or right foot or hand on one of the red, blue, yellow, or green colored dots lining the plastic sheet. But then the play had commenced . . .

No prude, Owen decided Twister should come with a warning label: dangerous when sexually starved. Who in hell had invented this diabolical game? It had him literally contorted with lust.

With each spin of the dial—Max and Kate taking turns because spinning was apparently just too much fun to miss out on—little bodies raced across the plastic rectangle to land on a colored spot, the frantic dash inevitably sending Jordan's body into his.

By spin number three, he no longer knew left from right, nor could he distinguish his foot from his hand. Colors? Red, blue? Forget about it.

All he could think of, focus on, was Jordan and the next careful twist and flex of her body. Because no matter how much she or he tried to avoid it, some miniature dervish was going to plow into them and there was going to be contact. Each jostle and bump, every tangle of limbs the spin of the dial produced was an electric zap of desire shooting through him.

That Jordan was trying to resist the push and shove as much as he was intensified the awareness between them as their bodies moved with excruciating care around each other. Each graze and accidental press amplified the sudden hitches in their breathing.

It was hell struggling not to respond when with each breath, he caught Jordan's unique scent. It was heaven feeling the fine quiver of her limbs when they touched and seeing her pulse hammer wildly beneath the delicate skin of her throat. Impossible not to think of touching that point with his tongue while he was deep inside her and she tight and hot around him. Weak-kneed, he went down like one of Jade's bowling pins when Olivia barreled into him. With a groan, he took them—Jordan and the kids—with him. A squirming human heap, they hit the mat.

He landed on Jordan. A second stretched into eternity as his body learned the gentle slopes of hers.

A high-pitched giggle, as effective as a stun gun, shocked them both into violent recoil. He jumped to his feet.

Christ, forget a simple advisory, the game should be outlawed, he thought, rubbing the crick in his neck that was as stiff as the rest of him but at least was a G-rated part of his anatomy. For God's sakes, this was nuts. Unless he got a handle on his attraction for Jordan, he was going to get arrested for indecent acts in the presence of minors.

"Let's play again!"

Jordan's sharp "No!" would have been funny except for the sad fact that part of him wanted to override her with a "Sure thing, Max. I'll play this game right through dawn if it means having your mom's body against mine." How was that for pathetic?

Jesus Christ, he was becoming desperate and he didn't like the feeling one little bit. What the hell was wrong with Jordan that she couldn't just give in to what was a perfectly natural urge and take him into her bed?

But no, she was only interested in children's bedtimes, he thought sourly, as she said with truly obnoxious calmness, "No, Max, it's time for bed now. Remember, you have a playdate and a riding lesson tomorrow. You don't want to be tired on such a big day. Come on, we'll walk Owen to his car. He needs to get home, too."

Yeah, so he could stand under an ice cold shower until he forgot how Jordan had felt lying beneath him.

Chapter
FIFTEEN

OVER THE NEXT WEEK Jordan hardly recognized herself. From Margot, Jade, and Travis's reactions, it was clear that the careful, composed façade she'd created over the past year had developed some very visible cracks. With everyone except the children, with whom she managed to exert a modicum of self-control and behave like the mother they knew and not some monstrous impostor, she was cross, impatient, irritable . . . a truly nasty piece of work.

Her newfound meanness followed her like a shadow, making Margot and Travis skirt her warily and prompting Jade to pronounce with astonishment on Thursday morning, "Wow, Jordan, you're really tapping into your inner witch."

"Flattery will get you nowhere, Jade. And I still won't go to Steadman's to pick up a ratcatcher for you. I've got Max's picnic, the kids' stuff to pack, and I have to get the orders in for all the bathrooms because Owen's moved ahead of schedule in the demo work." Owen, suddenly obsessed with getting the renovation completed in record time, was pushing everyone hard, including himself. She suspected that the only reason the master bathroom was still intact was because he used it.

"Fine. Whatever. I guess I'll find time between school, teaching your kids to ride, and helping Travis and Andy out while Margot's in New York doing the shoot for W with Charlie Ayer. Oh, and did I forget that AP exams are coming up? Guess I'll manage to squeeze in a couple of hours reviewing for them."

"I'm sure you will. And don't forget your appointment with the college counselor. You might want to crack open the college guide Margot bought for you."

For that reminder Jordan received a look that, had she been on the receiving end of it a week earlier, would have sent her running to Steadman's and buying every sleeveless ratcatcher Adam had in stock. Today she didn't back down an inch, merely raised a mocking brow in return.

An irate Jade had stomped out of the kitchen, slamming the back door to the mudroom with enough force to rattle the windows. That she didn't flinch was additional proof that Jade was right: Jordan *had* discovered her inner witch. Not only that, she could point to its cause. Men.

Two in particular were to blame. For when Jordan wasn't giving Jade serious competition in aiming knife-sharp comments at nearly anyone within range, she was indulging in truly bitchy thoughts about Richard and Owen.

With each passing hour, she resented Richard's plea to begin taking the children for the weekends more and more. Anticipating the pain of being without them was bad enough. She knew that when Friday afternoon came and they all drove off, her heart was going to be ripped out of her chest. Her identity, her sense of self, would be torn from her, too. How was she to survive the seventy-two hours they were gone? How was she going to endure this happening repeatedly? Every time Richard telephoned, to check on food preferences for the kids, what size diapers to buy for Olivia, and their current favorite movie, she had to tamp down on the urge to snarl that nothing he did or bought could make up for destroying their family, so it hardly mattered if he and Cynthia stocked the creamy peanut butter and blueberry jam that Max loved.

As for Owen, where to begin with her list of grievances? How about the fact that whenever he came near she became as twitchy and jumpy as one of their mares coming into heat. If she disliked the condition, she positively despised its cause: her inability to stop thinking about the weight of Owen's solid length covering her. Because of him, she wasn't sure she'd ever be able to play Twister again. So damn him for that.

Owen's kiss in her bedroom—Lord, that day seemed so long ago, yet it was as fresh in her mind as if it had occurred only minutes before—had rocked her with its potency, her first sensual encounter since divorcing Richard. Jordan recalled how disconcerting it had felt to be in his arms, to have his lips touch hers, to taste him while the intoxicating strength of his body pressed into her. Owen's clever mouth and hands had thrilled her, and yet the foreignness of his embrace had been troubling, too. When she felt the unmistakable evidence of his arousal, she experienced a surge of panic at the passion flaring to life inside her for someone who was a virtual stranger. Someone she wasn't even sure she liked.

Owen was no longer that man. He was more familiar and far more attractive to her. Not physically more attractive, a near impossibility considering how much his dark chiseled features, keen gaze, and honed physique appealed to her. While he had character flaws aplenty, who didn't, it was difficult to focus on them when all she could think of was the glorious sensation of his weight on her, the heat of his body melting hers. Although he'd been sprawled over her for at most three seconds, within that brief space of time she'd felt so deliciously *alive*. So double damn Owen for making her achingly aware of how desperately untouched she felt, for forcing her to confront the dry desert her life had become, and for making her realize how much she thirsted for the delicious pleasure of making love to a man.

And triple damn him, because while she desired him, she was painfully conscious of how ill-equipped she was to go about rectifying the current situation.

It was one thing to be an unattached, vigorous, sexy, too-handsome-for-his-own-good, thirtysomething male; Owen had no worries about his desirability. But she'd had three babies and, as she'd taken to undressing to stare broodingly in her bedroom mirror before crawling under the bedsheets, had the body to prove it. Her breasts had changed size and shape so many times, it was a miracle they weren't hanging down to her belly button. In this age of silicone and surgical enhancements, they would no doubt appear to an experienced and discriminating eye as worn and used as the rest of her. Owen, damn his gold-chipped eyes, was far too discerning not to notice.

But even if by some miracle of nature she'd gone through childbirth three times and emerged a toned, bouncy-buxom, red-hot mama, she doubted that she'd be better equipped mentally to go about ending her celibate status.

What was she supposed to do? March up to Owen and demand to do it on the Oriental? Yeah, right.

Which meant her new mean-bitch attitude was here to stay.

Perhaps that wasn't such a bad thing, she thought when Friday afternoon arrived alarmingly quickly and Kate and Max had now become as off-kilter as she, rushing to the window every other minute in the hopes of catching sight of Richard's car emerging from the allée of chestnut trees. Olivia, who, of course, had no real conception of what was going on, happily joined in the tearing to and fro of her older siblings. When their twentieth trip to the window hit the jackpot, Kate and Max let loose with happy cries of "He's here! Daddy's here!" as their sneakers pounded the parquet in an ecstatic jig. It was only the foulness of her mood that kept her from bursting into tears and clutching her babies to her breast.

Richard had a new Volvo SUV that would easily hold the kids and their paraphernalia. She steeled herself for the sight of him and Cynthia exiting the upscale family car, ready to take her children away and begin their new happy shiny relationship, and expelled a relieved breath when she saw that instead of Cynthia it was Susannah, the sitter they'd had in D.C., who was accompanying him.

Nonetheless it was like having a hundred needles pierce her heart as she made herself greet her ex-husband and former babysitter.

"Hi, they're all ready as you can see." Kate and Max had dragged their small nylon bags onto the porch and down the steps. In his enthusiasm, Max had even gone back for Olivia's bag. "Susannah, it's good to see you. I love your new hair style. You look great." Richard did, too, with his Hawaiian tan, but she tried to avoid looking at him.

Bringing Susannah was actually an inspired idea, Jordan realized. She dispelled the awkwardness that threatened by rushing over to Jordan and kissing her. "It's great to see you, too," she said, beaming. "And the kids, they've gotten so big! Gosh, I've missed you guys!" she said, bending down to give Max and Kate two quick hugs. To Olivia, she gave another broad smile. "Hi, Olivia, my name's Susannah. I used to take care of you when you were a little baby."

Olivia, bless her sunny disposition, shoved her Elmo doll at Susannah and began, in her inimitable fashion, to tell her all about how much she liked Elmo and Cookie Monster.

While Susannah nodded and made the appropriate noises, Richard was busy fielding questions from his two older children, who wanted to know about Hawaii and the new house they were going to. But Jordan caught the quick glances he stole at Olivia while talking to his two older children. He hardly knew his youngest daughter.

The bitch in Jordan wondered whether he was going to follow Susannah's example and bend down and reintroduce himself to his daughter. It would serve him right to have to say the words, "Hi, remember me? I'm your daddy. I took you out to the Shake Shack for ice cream the last time I was here."

But while it would have given her a certain vindictive

pleasure to make this difficult for him, she had to do her part for the children's sake, for their happiness and ease, and ensure this crucial step in the transition went smoothly.

"Olivia, sweetie, why don't you show Daddy Elmo, too? He loves *Sesame Street*."

Always happy to expand the *Sesame Street* fan base, she toddled over to Richard, Elmo in her outstretched hand.

She was unable to do more than watch Richard's sandy brown head meet Olivia's tow-headed crown as he knelt to better examine the plush toy before she had to avert her gaze, blinking furiously to keep the tears at bay at the sight of him attempting to bond with his little daughter. Turning away, she began carrying the bags Max had dropped on the ground over to the rear of the Volvo. Following her cue, Susannah opened the rear passenger door that already had a booster seat for Kate and two car seats for Max and Olivia.

"Max, your dad placed you and Kate on either side of Olivia because he thought you might like to look out the window. Is that okay?"

Max looked into the car's interior and solemnly nodded his approval of the seating arrangements. He was so sweet and loving, Jordan thought, her throat tightening dangerously. Determined not to break down in front of them, she swallowed forcibly.

"Okay, then," she said, managing to sound fairly normal, "let me give you a kiss good-bye before you go with Daddy." Kate came running over.

"Bye, Mommy."

"Good-bye, sweetheart," she whispered fiercely. "You be good and help Daddy and—Cynthia—with Max and Olivia."

She said much the same to Max, and by the time she held Olivia to her, kissing her chubby neck that smelled of the baby powder she'd used to change her, she felt like she was about to shatter into tiny pieces. Passing Olivia into Richard's waiting hands, she met his gaze briefly before looking away.

"Jordan, both Cyn and I are really grateful for how generous you're being. Cynthia particularly wanted me to make sure you knew how much we appreciate this."

She nodded jerkily.

"We'll call as soon as we arrive," he said quietly.

The arm that waved good-bye as the car doors were shut and Richard drove away with her children was as leaden as her heart.

It was a very good thing that Margot, Travis, and Jade had tactfully decided to absent themselves, remaining down at the barns while Richard collected the children. The car finally out sight, they weren't there to witness Jordan crumpling onto the porch's bottom step and bawling like a baby.

If they noticed her swollen, red-rimmed eyelids when she entered the main barn an hour and a half later, her sisters wisely avoided any remarks. "Did the kids get off all right?" Margot asked.

"Yes, I just spoke with them. They've arrived safe and sound and are going out for ice cream after dinner."

"Huh. Well, Olivia won't sleep a wink with all that sugar messing with her system," Jade predicted darkly.

Jordan's brows rose in astonishment. But she decided it wasn't worth mentioning that this was a bit rich coming from someone who could easily lay claim to the title of Miss Sugar Consumption.

Jade's comment achieved the near impossible: Margot looked distinctly unmodel-like, her mouth hanging open in dumb shock. And Jordan caught Travis hiding a grin as he made a careful study of the toe of his field boot.

Seconds passed with no one knowing quite how to respond to a Jade from an alternate universe, one who sounded like the FDA's newest spokesperson, when Ned cleared his throat.

"Glad you came down, Miss Jordan. Andy was supposed to take Saxon out for a hack this afternoon but Night Wing's come into heat, so Travis needs him to ride Nocturne before his date with her in the breeding shed. Nocturne's a little less rattled about doing the deed when he's been worked first."

He pulled out his tin of tobacco and busied himself with scooping out a fingerful, but Jordan didn't miss the color on his cheeks. That the old man who'd been breeding horses for more than fifty years could still blush was incredibly sweet. "So do you mind taking Saxon out for a spin? It's a beautiful afternoon. He really needs a break from the exercise ring to keep him fresh during the show season."

She wondered how long it had taken Ned, Andy, and her family to come up with this idea, and while part of her longed to point out that a good gallop over hill and dale would *not* heal the pain ripping through her, she recognized that taking Saxon out for a ride would get her away from their collective and, at the moment, suffocating concern. "Of course, Ned. Anything to help Night Wing and Nocturne's afternoon fling in the shed."

"That's swell of you, Miss Jordan. I'll go get him tacked for you."

"Thank you, Ned, but I can do it. You have enough to do getting Night Wing ready," she replied. And if she were busy grooming and tacking Saxon, she wouldn't be subjected to any more of her sisters' worried looks.

It was irksome to admit that Ned's solution to life's ills—hop on a horse and go for a heart-racing gallop—could improve her mood, but the cross-country ride did help.

Saxon was a fine animal, big and powerful, with his sire Stoneleigh's speed and boldness and his dam Sava's solidity and willingness. After so much time riding the broodmares, having the young gray's energy beneath her as he carried her through the cool of the green woods and then over fields dotted with ox-eyed daisies and bluets, was pretty darn exhilarating. That Saxon was enjoying their jaunt was evident in the constant swiveling of his ears, the energetic blowing of his nostrils, the springy high step of his gait, reminding her of all the coiled energy just waiting to be released the second she softened her hands on the reins and squeezed him forward with her legs.

And when she did, the gelding was more than game. He literally bounded forward into a canter that within ten strides shifted into a glorious gallop. Bent low over his bobbing neck, the warm late-afternoon air whipped her face, stretching her smile as they galloped on.

The only problem with Ned's solution was that Rosewood, with its three hundred acres and the neighboring properties where they had permission to ride, wasn't big enough to banish her sorrow completely. But she couldn't keep Saxon out longer. They'd been out for over an hour and riding hard on hilly terrain. As strong as the gelding was, to do more would foolishly court injury.

Nevertheless, she realized there was an additional benefit to having ridden. By the time she cooled Saxon down, untacked him, washed him in the shower stall, and then walked him, letting him graze until his dried coat shone like burnished steel, she had killed nearly two and a half hours. Only sixty-six or so more to go until she saw her children again.

So she volunteered to help at feeding time, first walking the hose down the wide aisles to top off the water buckets in each stall, then joining Tito in divvying up sections of hay and dropping them into the stalls as Felix scooped and poured rations of grain pellets into rubber feed tubs. Long accustomed to the work, Tito and Felix were extraordinarily efficient. The three of them had the horses fed and watered in all three barns within an hour. Then there was nothing for it except to head up to the house and resist peering into the children's empty rooms as she went to her own room to shower.

But the baby powder she dusted on her body after toweling herself dry made her think of Olivia, and then the phone rang with Kate on the line sounding happy and so very far away.

"Olivia's and my bedroom has little purple flowers on the walls, Mommy. Olivia had strawberry ice cream and it got all over her shirt, but Daddy said that's okay. And Cynthia gave me a necklace made of little pink shells from Hawaii. And she gave Max a boat and Olivia a doll."

"I'm glad you're having such a good time."

"I wish you were here, too, Mommy."

"Well, this is Daddy and Cynthia's special time with you. You'll see me on Sunday when Daddy drives you back. So you keep having fun and helping Daddy with Olivia and Max. Okay?"

Max seemed equally content, and Olivia, perhaps on the sugar high Jade had so darkly predicted, or perhaps simply thrilled to be up past her bedtime, babbled a blue streak.

Hanging up, Jordan knew there was no way she could stay in the house a minute longer.

Where to go, what to do?

She could work, that's what. Seizing on the answer like a lifeline, she practically sprinted into the family room and gathered up the sample books lying by the foot of her desk where she'd been looking at them the night before. Hugging them to her, she hurried down the back stairs, immediately announcing to Travis and Margot, who were in the early stages of fixing dinner, "I'm off to Hawk Hill to get some work done. It'd be foolish not to take advantage of this free time."

"And dinner?" Margot asked.

"Not hungry."

"Even after that ride?" she persisted.

"Really."

"But—"

Travis laid a hand on Margot's arm. "Jordan's a big girl," he said, his mouth crooking in an answering smile to the grateful one Jordan sent him. "Say hi to Owen, and tell him if he wants to come and lend a hand with the foals this weekend, we could use the help. Bob Dillard called while you were out with Saxon. He's bringing some clients to look at Solstice and Beat the Clock."

"That's great. But I don't think we'll be getting any free labor from Owen this weekend. I'm pretty sure he said something to Doug about going to Alexandria."

"So he won't be at Hawk Hill even now?" Travis asked.

"I doubt it," she replied lightly. "But he showed me where he keeps the front-door key so I can let myself in. I'll probably work until pretty late. Call my cell if you need me."

"You be careful," Margot said, clearly unable to shake her mother-hen attitude.

"I always am."

The pounding bass beat of a rock song escaping through the open windows of Hawk Hill told Jordan how very wrong she'd been in assuming she would be alone at the house. It must be Owen. Diligent as Doug and Jesse were, they weren't crazy enough to work overtime on a Friday night.

She walked inside, not bothering to knock or ring because neither could have competed with the Rolling Stones at full throttle.

The music being blasted was a far cry from the Cole Porter Owen had played on the piano, but then so was his appearance, her feet and mind stumbling to a stunned halt as she took in his sweat-covered torso. He'd stripped to the waist to plane a door that was propped on two sawhorses.

For a man who looked as suave and cool as a woman could wish in impeccably tailored clothes, Owen Gage dirtied up darn well.

She swallowed, unable to take her eyes off the rhythmic motions of his strong body; the heavy flex of his biceps as he moved his arms along the length of the door; his back muscles, covered with a tantalizing sheen of sweat, rippled in shifting contours, the lines of his torso tapering at his waist to where his jeans sat on his lean hips, just below the twin hollows at the base of his spine.

Her gaze shifted south, lingered there, as she might in front of a beautiful sculpture, so easily could she picture the curve of his buttocks beneath the layer of denim, an ass she knew would be as deliciously muscled as the rest of him.

Just then Owen spun around and she was caught with her gaze directed right at the clustered bulge of his crotch.

Hastily she tore her eyes away—up. But that was no good.

God, he had such a . . . a *masculine* chest, she thought dazedly, everything inside her going fluttery and fluid at the dark hair matting the solid planes. She wanted to run her fingers through it, follow its path as it narrowed into an erotic arrow down his flat belly.

"Jordan. What are you doing here?" Owen asked with what struck her as a distinct lack of enthusiasm.

Going out of her mind, that much was obvious.

Belatedly remembering that she had four pattern books in her arms, she managed to say, "I'm here to check the fabrics and colors for the bedrooms. It's always good to look at them at different hours of the day, and I was free." That definitely sounded better than "I was staring at your naked torso and imagining what the rest of you looks like." Of their own volition, her eyes flicked over the flat brown circles of his nipples. Her own tightening in achy response, she squeezed the design books tighter.

Swamped with a sudden feeling of hopelessness, she nearly squeezed her eyes shut, too. Here was a half-naked man and she had no idea how to behave around him. She would have had a hard enough time knowing how to flirt with the Owen of old. But looking as he did now, a brawny, sweaty, musky male, he drove any flirting skills she might have possessed right through the open windows.

"And what are you doing here?" she asked with a touch of resentment. "I thought you were going to be in Alexandria."

As though underscoring his transformation into a he-man, Owen actually grunted. "Spring cold."

"You're sick?"

"No."

"Oh." And then she understood. Thank God she hadn't been foolish and thrown herself at him. He was only here because his date was curled up with a box of Kleenex.

He'd been watching her connect the dots with an impassive expression. "The children are with your ex?" he asked.

She nodded. "Yes." Her anxiety returned in full.

"And so you're here?"

His he-man transformation was complete in every way. Now he was posing repetitive as well as obtuse questions. That, combined with the dark slash of his frowning brows as though he couldn't believe she was so pathetic that she'd spend her Friday night working in an empty house, made her snap, "Yes, I forgot to line up all my eager lovers, so I had to settle for second best, figuring out whether I like 'Buffed' or 'Solo' better as colors for the east bedroom." An apt metaphor for the present situation: he was buffed, she was solo. Unwilling to hear another one of those grunts that emanated from deep inside his beautifully ridged abdomen, she spun around to stalk up the stairs.

"I'll need to take a shower in the master bathroom."

Owen naked in the shower. Water flattening the dark hair of his chest, his groin, and down his long legs as it raced in hot rivers over him.

She congratulated herself on not falling flat on her face.

Owen couldn't stop thinking of Jordan upstairs, that he and she were finally alone, not a carpenter, electrician, plumber, sister, or kid in sight. The knowledge was enough to make his heart thud heavily in his chest as sexual hunger pumped through his veins. But he made himself finish planing the door, carrying it over to the jamb to rehang it, checking that it would open and shut smoothly, even when covered with whatever new coat of paint Jordan chose for it.

The work allowed him to regain a measure of control. When he'd turned around to find her staring at him, he'd come damn close to throwing caution to the winds and jumping her. To hauling her up against the wall and diving his hands under that pretty dress so they could streak over those subtly fragrant curves that had been driving him mad for too long, and then wrapping his hands around her bare thighs and lifting her legs high on his hips as he ground his cock against her. With that light-as-air cotton dress she was wearing bunched up around her waist, it would be so easy to strip off her panties, three heart-trembling tugs and she'd be open and ready for him . . .

A pretty, come-fuck-me dress Jordan hadn't even put on for him.

As buckets of dripping cold reality went, the realization that she hadn't even been thinking about him was extremely effective at dousing his mind-searing lust. Somewhat more rational, he was able to figure out that Jordan was only here because she was freaked out about her kids' weekend stay with their father. It was not because she was twisted in pretzel knots of lust.

Though that wasn't quite right, he corrected silently. He'd caught the widening of her deep blue eyes as she checked him out. It was clear she'd liked what she'd seen. Being an object of feminine appreciation was fine by him. She could look all she wanted. He'd really like it if she went and did some touching, tasting, and feeling, too.

And if he didn't get to reciprocate in kind very soon, and show her how much he wanted to touch and taste and nibble—devour—every inch of her silky skin, he was going to go out of his fucking mind.

Keeping his desire for Jordan at bay had made for a brutal week of hammering and sawing, as he basically signed on as an extra carpenter working alongside Jesse and Doug. But the physical labor made the nights tolerable. Working late into the evening, he would flop exhausted onto the mattress in the master bedroom and slide into a dreamless sleep. The next morning, however, found him like Sisyphus: right back where he started. One look at Jordan, and the cycle of wanting would begin anew.

Determined to break it, he'd called Fiona that morning, telling himself it didn't matter that on their last date Fiona had displayed the beginnings of a verboten possessiveness, a sign that she had coupledom on her mind. He could handle Fiona's new agenda far better than the terrible distraction Jordan embodied. But when Fiona answered the phone and he heard her hoarse, nasal-clogged voice, his immediate reaction had been bizarre and inexplicable, especially as he'd been the one to call. He'd been relieved. That a part of him was actually happy to be denied the chance to lose himself in Fiona's perfectly lovely body had not improved his mood.

That's why he'd told Jordan about his plans for the evening having fallen through. Although she had at present this strange power over his libido, he wanted her to know that he wasn't going to sit around pining for her. Never mind that none of the women in his cellphone address book sparked the slightest interest. A day would come when they would.

And what the hell had Jordan meant by that crack about ignoring all her lovers? Did that mean there were no men currently in her life? If so, what in hell was wrong with the men of Warburg that they weren't lining up the long drive to Rosewood for a chance to be with her? Were they too stupid to live?

Who cared? Their loss was Owen's gain. Jordan was here tonight with him. And he wasn't going to let an opportunity like this go to waste. Time to get his butt in gear, shower off

the grit and sweat, scrape off the five o'clock shadow rough-
ening his cheeks, and pull on some clothes that didn't reek to
high heaven.

Then he was going to embark on all-out campaign to get
Jordan Radcliffe naked.

Chapter *❧*
SIXTEEN

JORDAN DECIDED on "Buff" for the wall. Not a big surprise. To choose another color would have been impossible when she kept thinking of Owen's glistening muscles.

Noting down the color, and selecting for the curtains a Highland Court linen in a botanical print that would look lovely against the off-white, she moved on to the next room, careful to stay far from the master bedroom. Owen had come upstairs. As she flipped through her block of color chips, she really tried not to think about him stripping off his jeans and stepping under a hot shower.

He'd lowered the volume on the music so even if she hadn't been hyperattuned to every squeak and creak in the house, it would have been difficult to miss the sound of his bedroom door opening or his steps coming down the hall to where she was working.

Everything inside Jordan tensed in anticipation. She stared at the colors spread out like a fan in her hands. They blurred into a pale sea before her. Then Owen spoke, and the rich tenor of his voice was so like the man himself—precise, bold, and dark. Infinitely compelling.

"It's past quitting time. Come on downstairs, Jordan, and I'll take a stab at returning some of your hospitality by feeding you."

She could play it safe.

She could be the perennially careful Jordan, the Miss Cautious she'd always been, and stay here, dutifully looking at variations on neutral. Or she could go downstairs with this man who appealed to her, who stirred and aroused her more than anyone had in a very long time. She could do something that definitely left the safety zone, something that was very unlike Jordan Radcliffe.

The cracks in the façade she'd created had already appeared. Perhaps it was time to break the protective shell once and for all and discover what the woman behind the mask was like.

Besides, she was famished. Whatever happened tonight, having a handsome man feed her would mark a definite improvement in her too-restricted life.

Owen was already busy in the kitchen, slicing a baguette into thick pieces and placing them on a paper plate. A slightly oozing Brie, shiny black olives, a thick Genoa salami, little cherry tomatoes, and what looked like a plum tart were set out on the counter.

Freshly showered and dressed in chinos that emphasized the strong lines of his body and a crisp white oxford that enhanced the tan he'd acquired, Owen, too, looked mouth-wateringly good.

She made herself concentrate on the food. "I see you've discovered Anderson's foods." The gourmet shop stocked imported cheeses, fresh and dried sausages, and other delicacies that didn't necessarily make the inventory at Safeway.

"Yes, I thought we could have a picnic."

A surprised smile lifted her mouth. "How lovely," she said, charmed by the notion. Practical, too, since Owen had only a few pieces of furniture in the house—a couple of chairs downstairs and a mattress that she'd studiously avoided looking at every time she entered the master bedroom—but no table.

Pulling a bottle of gin from the freezer, he set it next to a bottle of vermouth. "Can I offer you a martini?"

Another chance to deviate from the boring norm, she thought. A martini was about as far from her usual wine or celebratory champagne as she could get. Liquid steel, wasn't that what martinis were called? She could use a bit to bolster her courage.

It was one thing to give herself a pep talk upstairs about grabbing a chance to do something a little wild and reckless tonight, quite another to maintain that confidence when standing only a few feet away from the man she wanted to get reckless with. "Sure. Why not?"

"Coming up." Owen smiled and her breath caught. Although it always had the power to cause her pulse to quicken, she now detected an added something in his smile that was like pure octane to her system: sexual promise. A smile like that was a hundred times more potent than any martini.

It didn't take long to realize that she was being seduced by a master. It took her even less time to decide that she might as well enjoy every minute of it.

They'd laid their picnic on a drop cloth on the living room floor, eating with their fingers and drinking their crisp martinis from the plastic martini glasses Owen had come upon in the sale bin at the liquor store. Simple as could be, the meal was delicious.

Jordan already knew that Owen was a gifted conversationalist. Given his parents and his upbringing, he'd probably learned how to entertain and amuse at an early age. What was different was having all that attention focused exclusively on her. He knew what subjects would pique her interest, so he told her of the various restoration projects he'd worked on. He knew, too, how to draw her out by asking her what pieces she envisioned for the rooms at Hawk Hill. From there they talked easily about the horses at Rosewood and the Radcliffe family history. No mention was made of the children, however, but strangely enough that was all right. Though they were always on her mind, tonight she wanted simply to be Jordan.

If his conversation put her at ease, his body language

caused tremors of awareness to course through her. A brush of his arm, a graze of his fingers, thrilled and made her insides dance with excitement. And she loved how he watched her, his dark eyes lit with masculine appreciation, the gold chips in his irises warm and glowing. Even the way he held his head while he listened to her—angled just slightly so that were he to lean forward from where he sat, their mouths would meet seamlessly—made her lips tingle with awareness, made her long for the commanding weight of his lips settling over hers.

The main course finished, he insisted she sit while he cleared the paper plates and fetched the tart. With it he brought the martini shaker. "A little more?" he asked.

"Just a bit, please. You're not trying to get me drunk, are you?" Although she wasn't in the least concerned about that. Owen wasn't the type of man who needed to get a woman drunk to entice her into bed.

His mouth curved in a grin. "What would be the point in getting you drunk?"

"So you could have your wicked way with me." Wow. She'd actually said something kind of flirty. Way to go, Jordan.

"Well, I definitely want that," he said, nodding easily.

She laughed, liking that he was open and good-humored about his intentions. There was so much about him that she liked.

Spiced with wine and lemon and just enough sugar to enhance the taste of the plums, the tart was scrumptious. And when she scooped a drop of the thickened plum juice with the tip of her finger and brought it to her mouth, and she saw how Owen stilled, as if every atom of his being was focused on her finger being drawn into her mouth—well, that was pretty delicious, too.

How lovely that one small gesture could make the gold in his eyes flare brilliant and bright. And change the atmosphere, too, turn the air between them as hot as his gaze.

"So, Jordan, about all those lovers of yours. Why weren't you out on a date tonight?"

"This is as close as I've come to a date since my divorce."

"And what about sex?" The question was as hushed as the falling light in the room, as richly suggestive as the shadows around them.

Suddenly she was glad of her martini. Raising the glass to her lips, she let the cool liquid slide down her throat, smooth and strong, heating everything inside.

"No candidates there, either," she replied, taking another sip, this time letting it pool inside her mouth before swallowing. No wonder they called this stuff liquid steel. She was divulging to Owen something she would never before have voiced under threat of torture.

Thanks to the cocktail, she could even find humor in the situation.

Certainly Owen's dumbfounded expression was comical, and infinitely gratifying.

"You're kidding me, right?"

She gave him a level look. "Would I kid about something like this? Twelve, no, thirteen months without sex isn't exactly something one jokes about."

Thirteen months? Owen tried to shut his mouth, but shock had paralyzed his muscles. It boggled the mind. This he truly hadn't considered: a woman as beautiful and desirable as Jordan *not* having sex.

An unexpected unease pierced him. Did he want to be the first lover postdivorce? To do so would seriously violate his "no heavy emotional baggage" code. Blow it to smithereens. Then he thought of the chance to taste her again, to learn the soft curves of her body as she moved against him, and the surge of desire he felt drowned any apprehension. Hell, yes. He damn well wanted to be the man to make her moan and gasp with pleasure.

"Going without sex for so long is a tragedy." His voice was a husky rumble that made her shift slightly on the drop cloth.

"Luckily I think I'll survive."

The smile Owen gave her made Jordan instantly doubt the truth of her statement. She wanted him. So very much.

"Perhaps I can be of assistance. I'm available and, as you may have had occasion to note, I'm interested. Perhaps you'd like to use me as a way of getting back in the game, so to speak."

How kind of Owen to assume that she'd ever had anything close to resembling a game. Use him? Like a feather being trailed along the length of her spine, the idea sent shivers of delight dancing through her.

"We're talking sex." A pitcher full of martinis couldn't have strengthened the breathy quiver of her voice.

"Most definitely. Between two consenting adults. No strings attached. No expectations other than truly fine sex between two adults who are attracted to each other."

Just how tipsy was she, to be even considering his proposition? Not terribly, just loosened up enough for her to recognize she was sick of playing it safe. A memory flashed in her mind of the day she'd driven into Warburg, when she'd thought longingly of doing something that would wipe the pitying condescension off the faces of so many people in town.

A steamy affair with Owen would go a goodly way toward achieving that wish. That it would be steamy, she had no doubt. He hadn't even touched her, and she was already achy and hot and damp with need.

"This is very generous of you."

His smile was a slow flash of white in the shadowed room. "I'm a generous kind of guy. Always willing to help friends. Of course, this is not entirely selfless. I'm pretty sure I'll derive a few benefits from the situation, too."

"So that's what we'd be, friends with benefits?"

He gave an easy shrug that had her thinking of the muscles in his broad shoulders and how they'd feel beneath her fingers.

"You could put it that way," he said.

What heady pleasure to contemplate all the lovely benefits a man like Owen could offer. "Friends with benefits. It has a nice ring to it."

"It does," he agreed.

On any other night she'd have been appalled by how easily this conversation came to him. They could have been discussing the mahogany pawfeet dining table that she'd found at her favorite antique site and that she thought would go beautifully in the dining room, but tonight Owen's brand of sensual charm was irresistible.

"Of course, I suppose I could call you my boy toy."

He gave a bark of laughter. "You shock me, Jordan," he said, not sounding shocked at all. "But if you prefer that term, I'm game."

"No." She smiled. "Friends with benefits is fine." More than fine, she added silently, struggling to breathe normally with the sexual tension so thick in the air.

"So this is a yes?"

"Yes." That one soft word and already he was in motion, reaching for her.

Her raised hand stayed him.

"No, wait. I need to know something. How serious is the spring cold?"

"The spring cold?" Owen frowned in confusion. Then understanding the reference, his brow cleared. "Ahh. Her name is Fiona Rorty. She's a corporate lawyer. Very pretty and extremely ambitious. We've dated for a few months and enjoyed a number of evenings together. But it's not serious between us. And I don't intend for it ever to be. I'll call her tomorrow if you'd like."

He would, too, if Jordan wished it, Owen thought.

"Really?"

He nodded. "Really."

"Because I would find it extremely distasteful to be the other woman."

"I understand. Fiona's shared my bed but I'm not in anything close to a permanent relationship with her—or any woman. I like my freedom very much, Jordan."

He fell silent, waiting.

His frankness convinced Jordan more than any clever attempt at persuasion could have. After all, she'd already pegged Owen as someone determined to remain unattached. He'd be careful to avoid the entanglements and expectations of a serious emotional commitment. Whether she could do the same, treat whatever happened between them as a simple fling, she wasn't sure. But no longer could she resist the need to discover what being with this clever and sexy man would be like.

She signaled her decision with a little nod.

The rise and fall of that proud chin filled Owen with a fierce joy that was in direct proportion to the need that had been building inside him since he first held Jordan in his arms. These weeks had seemed a lifetime since that first taste of her.

Owen recognized, too, that this primal exultation came from understanding what it meant for a woman like Jordan to give herself to him, but he wasn't about to waste precious seconds analyzing his emotions.

He far preferred to get her naked.

He smiled and drew her to him so that their bodies were aligned on the drop cloth, this lightest of contact more than enough for his body to go taut with need.

"So, perhaps you'd like to lift that ban on kissing?"

"Maybe so," she whispered, gazing up at him as his smiling mouth descended.

The touch of their lips was volatile, pent-up need exploding, driving them with reckless abandon. Mouths wide, they drank each other in, pausing only to gasp as they tugged frenetically at each other's clothes, sending them sailing on the rippled sea of canvas cloth.

Then suddenly Owen was surging to his feet and bringing her with him, lifting her until she was cradled against his naked chest. "The floor's too hard for you. I don't want you uncomfortable," he explained, already moving toward the stairs.

"Owen, I can walk."

"And deprive me of the opportunity to show how strong and manly I am?"

"I'm already impressed. Put me down. I'm heavy."

"Hardly heavier than that solid oak door I hung earlier. And you're a hell of a lot nicer to carry. God, you smell good." And he dropped his head to nuzzle her jaw, his arms tightening as he did. Then his steps slowed and he was kissing her again. Deep, slow, wet kisses that made her quiver and thread her fingers through his thick hair, pulling him closer. Finally tearing his lips from hers, he said, in a voice rough with need, "I really need to get you upstairs. Hold on." And he bounded up them with the speed of a competitor in the Hustle Up the Hancock race.

Within seconds they were in the master bedroom and Owen had flicked on the wall sconces before he'd even lowered her to the floor. The light wasn't glaring, but after the enshrouding semidarkness, she felt a rush of self-consciousness.

And he was so magnificent. Strong and beautifully proportioned. In the face of such masculine perfection, the flaws in her own body seemed glaring.

Owen was looking at her. She had a pretty good body but it didn't come close to matching his splendid physique. Was he noticing the telltale signs she saw when she stripped in front of the mirror, the unmistakable evidence she'd borne three children? Oh God, was he disappointed? She averted her gaze, fixing it on a spot to the right of her foot.

His fingers reached out and traced the curves of her breasts. She trembled in response, her nipples tightening into hard points at this, the lightest of touches. His thumbs moved to circle and rub, and pleasure unfurled inside her in velvet-colored ribbons.

"God, you're so incredibly beautiful." His voice was hoarse.

"Please," she whispered, shaking her head. "You don't have to exaggerate."

"Exaggerate?" He caught her chin and tilted her head up. Reluctantly she met his frowning gaze. "I'm not exaggerating, Jordan."

When she remained silent it was his turn to shake his head . . . in disappointment. Releasing her chin, he reached for her hand instead and guided it to his erection jutting from his groin. "Feel this, Jordan. Does this feel like the reaction of a man who isn't absolutely dying to be inside you? Who hasn't been spending hours imagining this absolutely lovely body since the first day he met you? And now that he's seen you naked, isn't hoping some act of God will destroy every stitch of clothing you own?"

"No." Her lips twitched and then curved into a smile. It was kind of hard to argue with the proof at hand. He was so lovely and hard and big. She swallowed as her inner muscles clenched with need. "I'm sorry, I was being silly."

"Damn straight you were. So that's settled. You're beautiful. Gorgeous. And I want to fuck you every way I know how. After that, we can invent some new ways. Is that all right?"

Her shoulders shook. Bless him for striking just the right tone to banish her nervousness. "I guess so. If you insist."

He grinned. "I do. Come here, sweetheart."

Their progress across the room to the bed was accomplished in a dance of slow steps, deep kisses, and searing caresses. His hands roamed freely, leaving her loose-limbed, melting with arousal.

Entwined, they tumbled onto the bed, Owen, at the last second, demonstrating his agile grace. Like a diver executing a perfect midair twist, he turned so that his body landed first, cushioning hers. A flawless maneuver in which his hands never lost their grip, one wrapped in her hair, the other cupped about her ass, holding her as he kissed her feverishly, as the hot satin of his erection rubbed her clit.

His open mouth traveled across the line of her jaw to torment the exquisitely sensitive spot behind her ear with slow licks of his tongue that brought her to the very brink. She writhed against him, her hands moving down. "Please . . . I need you inside me."

"Condoms. In my bag by the stool. Take one," came Owen's hoarse command, his breath against her dampened flesh making her shudder.

An open toiletry kit rested on a stool that Owen was using as a bedside table. In it, she spied the shiny square packets. Abruptly, a memory came to her of the foil packets she'd found in Richard's jacket pocket, and she stiffened.

"Jordan?" The mattress shifted as he raised himself up on his elbows. She felt the weight of his gaze.

Resolutely she pushed the memory away. Richard was not going to destroy this as he'd destroyed so much else in her life.

She reached out, grabbed a handful, and let them rain down onto the stool, keeping one. Condom in hand, she turned back and looked at the breathtaking man lying in the bed, waiting for her.

"Six, huh?"

She planted her forearms on his chest, loving the feel of his chest hair against her breasts. "I have very high expectations. And you seem sufficiently cocky, Mr. Gage."

He grinned. "Indeed I am, Miss Radcliffe."

She bit her lip as her fingers went to work, tearing at the foil and withdrawing the condom. "I hope I can get this thing on you. I'm a novice at this business."

"I have every confidence in you," he murmured huskily. "Go on, give it your best shot."

Scooting back until she straddled his muscular thighs,

she wrapped her fingers about his straining cock, feeling a heady rush of feminine power at the low hiss that escaped him. Slowly she stroked him up and down, tracing patterns on the bulbous head, then down the thick shaft to fondle his balls. Each slow trip of her hand had the muscles in his abdomen flexing as his hips pumped helplessly against her.

Centering the condom on the velvety tip, she began to roll it, pushing it down slowly. Reaching the sensitive spot just beneath the head, she teased it, scoring it lightly with her nails and smiled as he let out a strangled moan.

"Jordan, I do believe you've gone straight from novice to expert."

"Really?" she said, drawing her fingers slowly around the base of his shaft.

"Yes, absolutely yes," he assured her with a low groan as he pushed against her hand. "God, do that again."

She'd forgotten what it was to feel so much, her every sense heightened.

She'd forgotten what it was like, the exquisite sensation of a man entering her, his penis filling her inch by inch, stretching her, as she turned liquid around him. Liquid and tight, pulsing and quivering, her nerve endings sparkling bright with pleasure as Owen began to move in long, sure thrusts. Entering and withdrawing, every stroke eliciting soft gasps of wonder. The pleasure redoubling as her own hips found the rhythm and matched him point to counterpoint.

She'd forgotten the heavy weight of a man's body pressing into hers, the shifting heft of muscles beneath her questing hands, the hair that tickled her tightly beaded nipples as he moved against her, arousing her unbearably until it felt like streams of hot light were radiating through her.

She'd forgotten the slick slap of body against body. The salty taste of sweat as it ran down the corded column of a throat. The scent of man mingled with soap, the hint of aftershave along a jaw, and farther down the rich loamy musk emanating from his groin. The smells, the tastes set her head to reeling, intensifying the mind-blurry whirl of their erotic dance as they grasped and stroked and sighed in mutual delight, as they explored and learned each other.

She'd forgotten the fever of hands grasping and clutching as their bodies shifted and pressed, limbs tangling and twisting. Each movement ever more urgent, driven by blinding need as they climbed higher and higher, while inside everything grew tight, until with that final glorious, near violent thrust, she shattered with pleasure, went soaring in a million light-filled pieces, while above he shuddered and bucked, surrendering to her body.

She'd forgotten all of these things.

And, as piece by piece she fluttered back down to earth, to Owen's heaving embrace, to the random kisses he scattered over her forehead, cheeks, nose, and lips, Jordan's smile as she returned them was bittersweet. For while with one act Owen had restored so much that she had lost, some of the incredible, wondrous sensations he'd summoned she'd never experienced before tonight.

Odious as the comparisons were, they were inevitable.

Even at his most ardent, Richard, her husband of nearly ten years, had never matched the exquisite intensity of Owen's lovemaking. Owen made love with an open passion that encouraged her to be equally free and uninhibited. A fierce hunger marked it, too, thrilling her. It had felt as if he simply could not get enough of her body, was consumed by a need to taste and touch her everywhere. He'd made her feel extraordinary, as if she held some unique power.

His lack of inhibition, his total focus on her body and in giving her as much pleasure as she could take, had made an act Jordan had always enjoyed something altogether different and new. With Owen it was transformed into a union that was not just deeply erotic, but one that also touched her very essence.

All this from a man who had offered to be her lover, not her love.

For that reason, when Owen's breathing had calmed and he'd rolled to his side, an arm still looped about her and a sated smile playing over his heavy-lidded, relaxed features, she slipped from the shelter of his body with a murmured excuse and escaped into the bathroom.

Once there she drew several deep breaths before looking into the medicine cabinet mirror suspended over the sink. The reflection that stared back at her showed a very different Jordan: her hair a riotous mess about her face, her cheeks still stained with the flush of passion, her lips lushly red and swollen from Owen's devouring kisses.

She looked like a woman who'd just been most thoroughly loved.

But most of all it was her eyes she didn't recognize. A wide and luminous blue, they reflected the intensity of all Owen had made her feel. All he'd given her.

And it was that which shook her to the core. His generosity. Despite his claim that they were simply using each other in a consensual relationship, his devotion to satisfying her until she shattered with pleasure proved his generous nature. How was she going to keep from falling in love with a man who pleased her both in and out of bed so very much? When she'd ventured downstairs to join Owen earlier this evening, she'd known that she was leaving the safe little world she'd made for herself since her divorce. What she hadn't properly calculated was how dangerous the journey might be.

But she wasn't going to succumb to cowardice and crawl back into her shell. She might be scared, but only a fool would decline the chance to experience the joy Owen had given her in his bed.

She would simply have to take care to protect herself as best she could. And knowing the day would come when he would leave, she only hoped he wouldn't walk away holding her heart.

Owen glanced at the alarm clock. He was going to give her eight minutes. Ten and he'd start missing her too much. Eight minutes would be ample time for her to regroup. Though after the explosive sex they'd just had, he was feeling a little offbalance himself.

It was because he'd been wanting her for so long. That explained the extraordinary sense of rightness when he was sheathed deep inside her. The feeling had been incredible. But that was because she was so incredible and so responsive. A fact that should come as no surprise. Jordan was an innately sensual woman; she just kept it under wraps. He felt strangely honored that she'd shown him what lay beneath that cool and poised persona she presented to the rest of the world. What a colossal fool her ex-husband had been to leave her for another woman.

And though his and Jordan's affair would end, at least Owen wouldn't be hurting her by offering false promises. He'd established the parameters for the liaison from the outset so that Jordan would know exactly what she was getting into.

It occurred to Owen that he was trying to justify himself. He'd never had a moment's worry with the other women he bedded. The reason had to be the odd jumble of emotions wracking him. Mind-blowing sex could do that to a man. And Jordan had definitely managed to blow his mind and body.

Her effect on him would pall. It was inevitable. But until then, he was planning on enjoying what he had with her to the fullest.

Six minutes. Definitely time to bring Jordan back to where he wanted her: in his arms.

He swung his legs out of the bed, pulling off the condom

and dropping it into the wastebasket by the closet on his way to the bathroom. He rapped lightly on the door. "Jordan?"

The door opened and he sucked in his breath. How, in the space of six minutes, could he have forgotten how exquisitely lovely she was? Bathed in light, her curves called to him, begging to be kissed and caressed. The breasts, which he'd suckled and stroked, puckered anew under the weight of his gaze, begging for his touch. His desire spiked. He wanted to fasten his mouth on those tight nipples as she arched into him, as his hands caressed the rest of her soft bounty. The urgency of his need to possess her again, to hear her cry of pleasure as she climaxed, took him by surprise.

He told himself to keep things light. It was how he operated best. They were friends. Friends with benefits. He could do friendly. And he damn sure liked the benefits. "Are you okay?" he asked.

She gave a quick nod. "Yes. I'm fine."

"Good." He smiled and looped an arm around her shoulder, all casual as he marched her back to his bed where, if he had his druthers, they'd remain for the next week or so. "Because I was getting worried."

She gave him a sidelong glance. "Worried?"

"Mmm," he replied, nodding. "You may have forgotten, but protocol dictates that you tell me how terrific it was for you. Otherwise I might feel inadequate."

"Owen, I have a feeling you know exactly how terrific it was."

"Ahh, but I need to hear it." Strangely enough it was true. This was clearly a night for utterly alien needs.

She stopped at the edge of the mattress to gaze at him. She looked so solemn standing there. Beautiful, too, with her dark red hair tumbling about her shoulders and that glorious, perfect pale ivory skin. Titian would have done her justice.

"It was wonderful, Owen. Thank you."

Something flipped and then flopped inside him at her simple pronouncement.

"Thank *you*," he returned huskily. Then, reminding himself to avoid any heavy emotions, he flashed her a grin. "I couldn't have done it without you."

Laughter burst from her. "I should say not!" With another laugh, she pushed at his chest, tipping him backward. As he fell, he grabbed her wrist so that she came, too, landing on him with a laughing *oomph*.

A quick roll reversed their positions. With a smile he settled over her. "Now I've got you right where I want you."

"And what are you going to do about it?" she asked.

"Actually, I was thinking we could play a little game."

He heard surprise mixed with a trace of wariness as she asked, "And what kind of game would this be?"

"Oh, you know it already. It's called Twister."

Her mouth quivered while she tried and failed to suppress a smile. "You want to play Twister?"

"Very much. But we'll have to come up with a few modifications as we don't have that mat thing or the spinner."

She nodded. "I can see how that might be necessary. What kind of modifications do you think we need?"

"Well, first of all, instead of feet, I think we should substitute our mouths. Hands, of course, remain."

"Naturally."

"And in the place of colors, we'll probably want to use parts of the body. So, when it's my turn to spin, I'll have to put either my hand or mouth over your . . . knee, for example."

She was silent, as if considering. "Then when it's my turn, I have to put my hands or mouth wherever the dial says?"

"I knew you'd be a quick study," he said with warm approval as he dropped a kiss on her nose. "So should we try a few practice moves just to get it right?"

"Maybe we'd better. This sounds awfully complicated."

"I bet you'll get the hang of it—if you pay close attention." He grinned. "Why don't I go first—only fair as I haven't played Twister nearly as much. Oh, one other thing. We each get to spin the dial when it's our turn to move. Though maybe the next time through, we'll switch it up and spin for each other. That could be fun, too."

Jordan couldn't help noticing that Owen's enthusiasm for Twister was as great as Max's.

"Okay, here goes. The dial says, 'Right hand left breast.' " Their eyes locked as his hand settled over her and in that moment it felt as if he held not just her breast but her beating heart. Then his fingers closed about her soft mound, squeezing it, and the sensation was warm and delicious. Her breath caught and she tried not to squirm.

"Your turn," he whispered.

She thought for a second. To copy his move would be a mistake. Owen, though kind and generous, wasn't interested in letting her anywhere near his well-guarded heart.

"Left hand to right buttock," she said instead.

And that was good, too. Owen had a very fine ass. Spreading her hand over its silk-smooth curve, his gluteus tensed beneath her. Instantly her imagination jumped ahead to her next spin of the dial, and excitement pooled inside her at the thought of that part of his anatomy hardening and lengthening beneath her touch.

The low rumble of his voice momentarily interrupted her fantasy. "Mmm, this is an interesting one. The spinner says mouth to navel."

Her lids grew heavy in anticipation. Slowly Owen lowered his dark head to her quivering stomach muscles. At the touch of his wet mouth, she moaned helplessly.

Two spins later, Jordan acknowledged that her sisters had been absolutely right: Owen had some exceptionally good moves when it came to Twister.

But then, so did she.

Chapter *%*
SEVENTEEN

OWEN HAD INSISTED on driving her home to Rosewood, telling her that a walk back to Hawk Hill through the woods at dawn would be an excellent way for him to start the day.

"Will I see you later?" he asked as he pulled Jordan's minivan up alongside the Range Rover, shifted into neutral, and cut the ignition.

"Oh, yes, I forgot. Travis said to tell you that a hand with the foals would be most welcome."

"I'd be glad to help out, though at some point in the day I have to go to Alexandria and catch up on stuff at the office. But what I really meant was, will I see *you*?"

It felt nothing short of wonderful that after all the "seeing" Owen had done last night, he still appeared interested in her. "I'd like that."

He leaned over and kissed her. "All right then. We could have an early dinner and afterward—ahh, damn, I forgot. Nonie's invited me to a cocktail party at her house. She wants me there when she shows off the cottage to her guests."

She squelched her disappointment. "I understand."

"You could go to the party, too."

The suggestion surprised a laugh out of her. "Strange as it may seem, I wasn't invited."

"You could come with me. As my date."

She blinked. The lack of sleep from their marathon of lovemaking was suddenly hitting her. Her brain was only following sluggishly, if at all. "You want me to crash

Nonie's party? Because believe me, that's how she'd see it, even if I went as your date."

"It's not as if she'd have the help toss you out on your ear, not when you're with her favorite architect, not when my firm shifted into high gear to get the interior finished in time for this blasted party of hers. You deserve a chance to see the finished look since the ideas for the cottage were ninety-nine percent yours," he said.

It *would* be fun to see how her suggestions for the color schemes and furniture had turned out, and she was curious, too, about the bathrooms and kitchen. If there was anything that didn't quite click visually, it would be good to know so she could avoid making the same mistake at Hawk Hill.

"All right, I'll go," she said. "But I warn you, in bringing me along you may be forfeiting your status as Nonie's favorite anything."

"Somehow I think I'll survive," Owen said gruffly, strangely touched that she'd bothered to voice a concern about Nonie's reaction, especially after Jordan had been treated so shabbily by Nonie. In hindsight, he wished he'd flat out refused to have anything to do with the interior work on the guest cottage. But had another design firm accepted the commission, they would never have given Jordan any of the credit for the results, which was what he planned to do at tonight's cocktail party, with Nonie's guests and Jordan present.

Yes, he was pretty sure that after tonight, the only list he was going to top would be Nonie's shit list. Hell, he might even edge out Jade, and he smiled at the thought.

He climbed out of the car and came around to Jordan's side, holding the door open for her. "So I'll be back in a few hours," he said and wondered whether he'd be able to last that long. Even now, he just had to have another taste of her. Lowering his head, he gave her a kiss that, like so many of the ones they'd shared during the night, triggered a rush of arousal that had everything in him tensing with need.

With an effort, he reined in his fierce urgency and, releasing her, stepped back. "I'll let you go." Damned if he wanted to, though, and this definitely was not a normal reaction after a long night of making love to a woman.

"Okay." She knew she was staring, her eyes drinking him in, but she couldn't help herself. She wanted to commit to memory how Owen looked standing there, so deliciously and sexily rumpled. And for the moment he was hers, she thought giddily.

But she knew he wouldn't be if she gave even a hint of how much she'd already come to care for him after a single night in his arms. Given his aversion to emotional commitment, he would doubtless interpret her confession as an attempt to box him in. As if to physically suppress the unwelcome words, she bit her lower lip.

Instantly his gaze zeroed in on her mouth. With a whispered, "Jesus, Jordan," he hauled her back against him, and brought his mouth to hers, using his teeth where hers had been just a second ago, tugging and nibbling with a greedy hunger.

Toes curling at the pleasure unfurling inside her, she clung to him, her fingers digging into his broad shoulders, returning his kiss with a matching fervor.

His hand was at her breast, fondling her nipple through the layers of dress and bra, teasing it into an aching bud, and driving her crazy with want, when the ringing of her cell had her jumping out of his arms.

She crouched to rummage through her bag, which minutes ago had slipped to the ground, and retrieved it. Choked by a sudden rush of worry at a telephone call this early, Jordan managed a hoarse, "Hello?"

"It's me." Richard didn't bother to identify himself. "Your daughter wants to speak to you. Here she is, Olivia. Here's Mommy."

There was a pause, then Olivia was on the line, crying and saying, "Mommy, Mommy!" over and over again, and breaking Jordan's heart that she couldn't reach out and comfort her baby.

"Olivia, it's okay, sweetheart. Tell me what's wrong. Don't cry, sweetheart, it'll be all right. Olivia, do you know what? Daddy told me he was going to make your favorite breakfast today. Well, I can't tell you if you're crying because you won't be able to hear. Daddy's going to make you, Kate, and Max blueberry pancakes. And if you're a very good girl, I bet you he'll let you put the blueberries in the batter. I think he has another surprise, too, with lots of animals. Oh, sweetie, you're going to have such a good day, there's no reason to cry. Really. Can you take a deep breath? That's my love. Now, don't forget to tell Daddy that you'd like to read *Maisie Goes Swimming* with him because it's your favorite. And give Daddy the phone, okay? Bye, bye, Olivia, I love you and I'll see you tomorrow." As she'd instructed Olivia, she drew a deep, steadying breath, and gave a start of surprise when Owen's hand settled on her shoulder and squeezed it in silent support. She cast him a grateful, apologetic glance, but then Richard was back on the line.

"She's been up since quarter to five and won't—" he began, but Jordan cut him off.

"I don't know how much of that you got, Richard, but if you could read the *Maisie* book I packed, it will help distract her. If it doesn't, the *Sesame Street* DVD, the one with Bert and Ernie, always makes her laugh."

"I'll go find them."

"Also, I hope you bought blueberries because she loves them."

"I think Cyn picked some up."

"Olivia's favorite thing is to pour the blueberries into the pancake batter. Make sure you don't give her the whole box, though. I also told her that you all would be going to the zoo."

"Ahh." That was the sound Richard made when he was hedging.

Well, too bad if he didn't particularly feel like going to the National Zoo. Their young daughter was crying and Jordan knew that seeing the elephants and the pandas would put a smile on Olivia's face, as well as Kate's and Max's. "It should be a perfect day for it, and Kate and Max haven't been to the zoo since, well, it would be a really great treat for all of them."

"Okay." The word was accompanied by a sigh. "We'll go before lunch."

Some of the tension left her. "Thanks. They'll love it."

"Yeah." He paused. "I probably should have thought of taking them there myself. I remember how excited Max used to get watching the meerkats. And thanks for calming Olivia down. She's been fine, but I guess when she woke up she was disoriented. Then the tears came. I figured we should—"

"It's fine. I'm glad you called."

"We didn't wake you up?"

"No, I wasn't asleep."

Richard gave a little laugh. "Jordan, you worry way too much." His voice had that condescending note he'd used so often during their counseling sessions with Abby Walsh.

She half turned, her gaze seeking Owen. He'd moved a few feet away and was staring off in the direction of the barns while he waited for her to finish her conversation. Looking at him, a warm surge of affection washed over her. Last night, he'd been kind and generous and funny. Everything Richard had stopped bothering to be with her. Moreover, Owen didn't resort to condescension to make himself feel superior.

And Owen had more sex appeal in his left pinkie than Richard had in his whole body, she thought with a smile.

"Jordan, I can tell by your silence you're getting all uptight."

"Actually, no, I'm not—"

"The kids have been fine with me. And they're warming

up to Cynthia, too. Listen, I better go and dig out that book and the *Sesame Street* DVD."

"Of course."

"I'll have Kate and Max call after breakfast."

"Okay. Good-bye."

Owen waited a second after Jordan had rung off before turning toward her. It had been weird to watch her go from lover to mother in the space of a heartbeat. One second she'd been arching into his hand with very sweet abandon. In the next, tense and distraught as she listened to Olivia cry.

He supposed it was good to have such a pointed reminder that Jordan was a woman who came with complications. Yet even as he made himself focus on all of them—the kids, the ex-husband, the sorting out of the visiting arrangement, the whole messy shebang—he had to stifle the impulse to go and wrap his arm about her waist and offer what comfort he could.

And he had to ignore his own queasiness at the idea of Olivia in a strange place missing her mommy. The toddler had always seemed so happy—in a terrifying zombie kind of way. His queasiness increased at the thought of Olivia crying, and her father not understanding a frigging word she was saying.

Just because he didn't want Jordan to get the wrong idea that he might be reevaluating the terms of their relationship didn't mean he couldn't show he cared. Her kid had been crying.

"Everything all right now?" he asked. And because he needed to touch her, he did that, too, stroking the side of her face with the tips of his fingers.

Jordan gave a tiny nod. "She'd stopped crying by the time Richard got back on the line."

"She'll probably be okay once Kate and Max are up. Kate's a lot like you. She knows just what to say and do with Olivia."

Jordan smiled. He noticed, though, that it didn't quite reach her eyes.

"I should get going," he said reluctantly. If he weren't certain the house was astir with her sisters and her brother-in-law, he would have done his best to coax Jordan upstairs to her room and make love to her until she forgot that her youngest child had woken up sad and missing her. Or if not forget, then at least soothe some of her pain.

He pressed his lips to her brow, knowing that if he let himself kiss her on the mouth, or wrap his hand around the nape of her delicate neck, the cycle of need would start anew.

"I'll be back soon," he said, already counting the hours until the evening when he could devote himself to making those blue eyes shine bright with desire.

He waited until Jordan slipped inside the house to start down the drive and then cut across the still-empty pastures that bordered the woods between Rosewood and Hawk Hill.

It was going to be a beautiful day, and the chance to spend it with Jordan while she worked with the foals struck him as a pretty fine way to pass the hours until he could make love to her.

The fields were abloom, colors dotting the green with an impressionistic brushstroke and when he entered the woods, he was greeted by a chorus of songbirds high overhead.

A ten-minute walk through the wooded trail and Owen caught a glimpse of Hawk Hill through the trees. His gaze sharpened, intent on studying the house from this approach.

It really was a fine house, he thought with satisfaction. He remembered Jordan saying it had good bones. She was right. And he couldn't wait to see it finished inside and out. The notion that through their joint efforts the old house would regain its gracious glory pleased him.

This was another aspect of being with Jordan he was

coming to appreciate. She shared his interests and understood what he spent his days working on. It felt good knowing he could talk about his renovation projects and that she wouldn't be bored if the conversation turned to antique joists and rafters.

Jordan was different.

It was why he wasn't reluctant or even resentful that one of the things he'd be doing this morning was to make the promised call to Fiona and let her know he wouldn't be seeing her again. A funny reaction, because by all rights he should be feeling that dreaded, trapped sensation. Was it because he'd already recognized that things were coming to an end between him and Fiona? Or was he deleting her from his address book because after tasting the passion that was Jordan, a night with Fiona would have all the fizzle of flat champagne? Though he was in a decidedly introspective mood, he stopped short of asking himself whether being with any woman could compare to the pleasure he'd found with Jordan.

It was only cocktails, and she wasn't some country mouse who'd never been to a party, yet Jordan couldn't calm the little nervous tremors that shook her as she plucked at the body-hugging sheath, wishing it were a little longer and two sizes bigger.

The dress, a multihued silk knit Missoni with spaghetti-straps, which Margot insisted Jordan wear, clung to her like a second skin. Since it was a far cry from her typical outfits and a huge step out of her comfort zone, Jordan had resisted the choice.

But Margot had won the argument, saying, "You simply cannot crash Nonie Harrison's party in any old thing. You have the Radcliffe reputation to uphold, Jordan. You need to make us all—from Frank and Georgie on down—proud. Besides, this is your first date post Richard. You should celebrate it by dressing to the nines. Luckily Owen is discerning enough to appreciate a dress like the Missoni. And the blues in the dress make your eyes as deep as sapphires."

Jordan gave another uncertain tug. "It's not too tight?"

"Not at all. Lord, what I'd give for your boobs. You've got an amazing body, Jordan. And judging from the hour you rolled in this morning, Owen must think so, too. So have fun and flaunt it. All you need is a touch of mascara and a slightly deeper shade of lipstick. I have a couple of different shades in my makeup case you can try."

Even after applying her makeup, Jordan remained skeptical of the dress's merits until she came downstairs and observed Owen's reaction. His gaze went from dazed to fiercely hungry in three seconds flat. She decided she liked that a lot.

"You look beautiful."

She smiled. "Thank you. The dress is Margot's. You look very fine yourself." His light wool suit was a bluish gray, which he wore combined with a white shirt and a navy-and-white-print tie. He looked positively mouthwatering, and she couldn't help wondering if her eyes reflected the same intense desire she saw in his. Probably.

"Maybe we should skip Nonie's," he said huskily.

"Don't you dare, Owen," Margot said, skipping down the stairs. "I can tell how eager you both are to get more work done on Hawk Hill and all, but it's payback time. You know the saying, 'Living well is the best revenge'? For Jordan, that translates into walking into Overlea on the arm of a handsome man and looking more beautiful than any other woman in the place. So have fun tonight, kids. And don't worry about the curfew."

"Have you forgotten that I'm older than you?"

"Only in years, sweetie."

Jordan shook her head. "I never thought I'd say this, but I'm beginning to sympathize with Jade."

"About time, but no worries: the oppressed will soon rise," Jade said, crossing the foyer with a thick slice of focaccia bread in hand. "You look very hot, Jordan. Though I don't see why Margot lends her duds to you and not to me."

"Probably because you'd much rather filch my Missonis outright," Margot replied with a sweet smile.

"Past crimes and misdemeanors," Jade replied unfazed.

"Yeah, last week is so ancient history."

"Too true. Say hi to Witch Harrison for us, sis," Jade said, taking a big bite of her bread and heading toward the sitting room where she had a date with the TV. She was going to Tivo her favorite show, *True Blood*.

"And tell her how devastated we are to be missing her party," Margot said with a broad smile.

Jordan nodded. "Oh, yes, those will be the first words from my lips."

Nonie had gone whole hog, with tikki torches lining the drive and all. The party was in full swing, and from the number of Jaguars and BMWs and Mercedes parked in the closely mown field, Jordan could tell that most of Warburg's "elite" had been invited.

"We don't have to stay long," Owen said, taking her hand as they walked toward the door.

"Just long enough to satisfy my sisters."

"Exactly what I was thinking," Owen replied, giving her hand a squeeze. And while they were there, he intended to make sure everyone saw Jordan looking like a million bucks and for them to realize that not only was she a knockout, she was also a very talented decorator.

It took them a few minutes to locate Nonie, as the party had spilled out over the stone patio and onto the back lawn. Then, too, many of the guests who spotted Jordan broke away from their clustered group to come and say hi. That Jordan Radcliffe had arrived at the party with Nonie's architect was clearly titillating news, Owen quickly realized, noting the sharp curiosity in their eyes when she introduced him.

Unlike her guests, Nonie wasn't curious, she was furious. She didn't even tack on her usual "darling" when she said, "Owen, how lovely to see you." Her glacial gaze then slid to Jordan. "Jordan. What a surprise."

"Yes, I'm afraid when Owen invited me to come as his date tonight I couldn't resist. I do so want to see how the work on the cottage turned out."

Nonie's smile widened, revealing her fangs. "But of course. The cottage looks fabulous. As I've been telling everyone, I couldn't imagine any other firm being able to do such exceptional work." Then, latching on to Owen's arm, she said, "You don't mind if I steal Owen away for a few minutes? There are some people he simply must meet."

When she made to lead him away, Owen smiled and planted his feet. "I couldn't possibly leave Jordan on her own, Nonie. My parents taught me it's bad manners to abandon one's date. I'm sure these people will be delighted to meet Jordan, too."

Confronting a woman like Nonie was so different with Owen acting as her stalwart champion, Jordan thought. Smiling, she let her fingers brush the back of his hand. "That's all right. I see several people I'd like to catch up with. Come find me when you're ready to show me the cottage."

Determined to get away from Nonie Harrison's party as soon as possible, Owen wasted no time setting the record straight about his role in decorating the cottage to the people with whom he spoke. Debunking Nonie's tales wasn't especially hard, even with Nonie clinging to his arm. Whenever he received a compliment on the cottage, he simply answered, "I wish I could take credit for the interior design, but I merely provided the framework. The ideas for the décor were all Jordan Radcliffe's." And when they expressed their inevitable surprise, he continued, "Oh, yes, she's an exceptionally talented interior designer. And even

though Gage and Associates has its own design department, I've been so impressed by Jordan's ideas and aesthetic sense that I've hired her to do the interior at Hawk
Hill, the house I'm currently renovating. We should have it
ready to put on the market in a few weeks. I hope you'll
come and see it." Then he'd snag a shrimp and cilantro
brochette or a tiny asparagus quiche or a slice of chorizo
sausage—all the hors d'oeuvres were catered and thus not
the usual inedible Overlea fare—and munch happily while
Nonie stewed.

After a while, Nonie unlatched herself from his arm and
went off, probably to start spinning more half-lies. Owen
didn't care. He was confident they were going to be listening to him rather than her when it came to Jordan's talents
as a decorator. It felt good knowing he was helping her
fledgling business take off.

On the other end of the patio he spotted Jordan talking
to a man and a woman roughly her age. He took a moment
to drink in the sight of her before joining them.

The dress she was wearing was really something. A riotous mix of purples, blues, deep reds, and shot with silvery white lines, it embraced her slender figure, accentuating
the curve of her hips and breasts. She'd worn her hair down
tonight, and its silky ends curled about her bare shoulders,
dark red on pale ivory. She held herself well, head high,
shoulders straight and proud. When he heard her laugh, he
found himself wondering what it would be like to catch her
laughter with a kiss and taste its sweet musical notes.

Dear Christ, he was becoming weirdly sentimental when
it came to Jordan. He supposed that was permissible, as
long as he remembered that in addition to wanting to drink
in her laughter, he also wanted to nibble on every deliciously scented inch of her.

Crossing the patio, he watched her mouth curve in welcome. Forget the dress, it was her smile—a smile that was
for him alone—that dazzled. Nice to know that he made

her happy, that he wasn't the only one walking on cloud nine right now. And he could make her even happier once they were alone.

"Hi."

"Hi," she replied, her smile undiminished. "Owen, I'd like you to meet my friends, Marla and Bruce Williams. This is Owen Gage, the architect who did the renovation on Nonie's cottage and who's also restoring Hawk Hill, the Barrons' old place."

"I'm pleased to meet you," Owen said. "I was just coming to ask Jordan if she wanted to go to the cottage and take a look at the interior. Would you like to accompany us?"

"Most definitely. I can't wait to see how it all looks," Marla said. "Nonie took me around the cottage before the work began, telling me all your ideas."

"Marla's very keen to have you come over to our place, too, and see what you can do to resuscitate its very tired interior now that our youngest child is about to leave the nest," Bruce said.

"I'd be happy to, but it's Jordan you want to have looking at the rooms. She's the one who came up with the design ideas for the cottage. My firm's just carrying them out."

He could tell his reply had surprised Jordan as much as it had Marla and Bruce.

"My goodness, Jordan, Nonie never mentioned having spoken to you about what to do with the interior!"

Jordan made a quick recovery. "Since Owen did such a superb renovating job, I'm sure Nonie couldn't bear the thought of having someone else work on the cottage. I'm just pleased that Nonie liked the ideas I suggested enough to use them," she said. "I see a group over there that's heading down to the cottage. Let's go and take a look while the rooms are still relatively empty."

As Marla and Bruce began walking down the narrow

flagstone path, she reached out and grazed Owen's hand with hers. "Thank you," she said simply.

Catching her fingers, he brought them to his lips. "You're welcome."

The cottage had turned out well. It would be a lovely guest house. And Marla was so excited, she again pressed Jordan and Owen to come over for drinks, pulling Jordan aside to whisper, "I'm so embarrassed about what I said that morning at Braverman's, but I had no idea you'd given her all those ideas, Jordan. Typical Nonie stunt. But I can also see why she'd want to keep Owen Gage on retainer. He's positively yummy. Lucky you," she grinned.

So far Jordan had managed to avoid crossing paths with Nonie again, but unfortunately as she and Owen were leaving the cottage, she saw Nonie coming down the walkway with some other guests. Busy talking about how he'd gone about restoring the cottage's façade with Martin Jeffries, who lived in a lovely Georgian down the road, Owen hadn't noticed their hostess's approach.

She prepared herself for round two with Nonie. She couldn't avoid talking to her in any case; she had to thank her for her hospitality, unintended though it was, and say good-bye.

Her social smile firmly in place, she said, "The cottage looks lovely, Nonie. You must be very happy with it."

"Yes, I am. Owen's brilliant at what he does."

"He's an excellent architect."

"He's excellent at many things." She paused for a moment, and Jordan wondered what tack she would take. "A propos of Owen, I do hope you take care, Jordan. I confess to being worried about you."

"*You* worried about *me*, Nonie? Surely not."

"It's just that you're so very innocent when it comes to men. It may seem all fairy-tale gallant of Owen to claim that he was merely implementing your ideas for the cottage and that he's even consulted with you on Hawk Hill, but his motives are painfully obvious."

"Are they?"

Nonie sighed. "It's as I thought. I would think that after Richard, you'd have learned not to be so trusting, Jordan. Or so blind. You and Owen are both my friends so you can see what a terrible position I'm in, but I wouldn't be able to sleep at night if I didn't say my piece. Jordan, you need to realize that Owen is simply using you and that whatever's going on between you will end the minute the final coat of paint dries at Hawk Hill. And speak of the devil."

Nonie's gaze had shifted to a spot behind Jordan. Her smile widened. "Owen, darling, can you imagine what Jordan and I were just talking about? You."

"Really?" he said as he came up beside Jordan, standing close enough for the sleeve of his jacket to brush her bare skin.

"Oh, yes." Jordan nodded. "Nonie was telling me about how you were only using me. I think she meant for sex, Owen."

Nonie's dental work was quite good, but seeing her with her jaw hanging open didn't do much for the rest of her face. "But I'm afraid you have it all wrong. You see, Owen has very nicely agreed to be my boy toy—I think the women of your generation might be more acquainted with the term *stud*—so it's really more a question of my using him. And I can happily report that he's as good as you've imagined, Nonie. Owen's very, very good."

"Why thank you, Jordan," Owen said with a small smile. "Are you ready to leave now?"

"Quite. Good-bye, Nonie. It's always so great to see you."

"Well, that was a different kind of leave-taking," Owen said when they were settled in his car.

"Yes." Jordan's anger had begun to fade, to be replaced by a strange sense of unreality. Surely she couldn't have actually said what she just did. "I apologize if you're upset at being dragged into this stupid, ongoing feud with Nonie. I don't usually let her get to me like that—"

"You should make it a habit. You were magnificent, shining with what I've come to recognize as the Radcliffe spirit."

"We are a rather reckless lot," she said dryly.

"Nonie was sorely in need of being taken down a peg or two."

"Maybe, but by the end of the night, you can be certain she will have made it known far and wide that you and I are doing more than looking at fabric swatches together. I hope that doesn't bother you."

"Why should it? She's not divulging state secrets. Anybody with eyes at that party would have guessed we're involved. And as your sisters already know, the news can't catch them off guard. So no, I don't care." He paused, then said quietly. "The real question is whether you're bothered by the prospect of whatever Nonie says."

She was silent a moment. Being linked with Owen would be a nice change from being pitied as the duped wife. "No, I don't care, either."

"Really?"

"Not a whit." She smiled. "To tell you the truth, this is all rather liberating."

He returned her smile. Shifting into first gear, he eased out onto the driveway. "Would you like to go somewhere? I could take you to dinner."

"I'm not that hungry. Are you?"

"No, the food was catered."

Her laugh told him that she'd immediately understood his comment.

"So what would you like to do? Something liberating?"

"Actually yes," she said as she crossed her knees. The movement drew Owen's eyes to the length of slim thigh mere inches away.

"What did you have in mind?" His voice was husky with desire.

"It's such a lovely night. I was thinking we could drive back to Hawk Hill and go out onto the lawn. Then you could take off my clothes and go down on me while I watch the stars. And then after that, I thought I could do the same for you. Just an idea."

His hands tightened around the steering wheel as he stepped on the gas pedal. The Audi shot forward, but its speed was no match for his heart, which had rocketed into hyperdrive.

"I think that can be arranged."

It was as exquisite as she'd imagined, watching the millions of diamond-bright stars glittering and winking overhead while Owen's mouth and tongue, hot and teasing, moved over her, licking and kissing her slowly, perfectly, until she dissolved in a streak of light, like a shooting star in the night sky above.

And she happily returned the favor, savoring the salty, slightly musky taste of him as she breathed in the scent of the sweet grass and the rich earth on which they lay. She loved the shudders and groans she wrung from him as she trailed her tongue over his rigid length, loved his fingers tangling in her hair as she took him deep in her mouth. And when he came in a hot burst, his hips bucking helplessly, a heady sense of feminine power and pleasure filled her, made her wet for him again, made her smile joyous as she kissed her way up his heaving chest, the damp column of his throat, to his parted lips. Once there, she draped herself over his warm body and gazed at the bold lines of his face. The flash of his smile was as compelling as the stars overhead.

"I think I just saw heaven," he said.

"Easy to do on a beautiful night like this. This is a lovely spot."

Cupping the back of her head, he kissed her lingeringly. "Mmm. And the company's pretty fine."

"That goes without saying. That feels fine, too." Her

murmur was a near purr at the light caresses he was trailing along the length of her spine.

"So you're comfortable?"

"Extremely." She dropped a kiss at the base of his throat
then moved to his shoulder, letting her teeth score the
rounded muscle.

He exhaled in a ragged rush. Changing their tempo, his
hands stroked her more deliberately but no less seductively,
as his open palms covered her rear and then followed its
contours down to the backs of her thighs. When the tips of
his fingers brushed her curls, she shivered.

"You're not chilled?" he asked, touching her again, delv-
ing slightly deeper, so that everything inside her tightened
in anticipation.

She arched into his hardening length. "Quite the opposite."

His right hand left her as he reached for his jacket and
dragged it closer to rummage in the pocket. He pressed the
foil square into her hand.

She didn't even flinch at the memory of Richard's pockets littered with the same packets. Silently she thanked
Owen for having eased the hurt so she could move forward
and enjoy a moment like this. Her voice husky with emotion, she whispered, "Came prepared, did you? Good for
you."

"We boy toys try harder," he said, grinning.

When she sat up and smoothed the latex slowly over him,
his grin became a groan of need. "I want you like this," he
said, his hands on her hips, pulling her forward until she was
poised over his straining cock. She took him in her hands,
guiding him into her, sinking inch by inch as he again gave a
strangled groan of pleasure. "Jordan, forgive me if this
doesn't come out right—Christ, I don't know how to say
it—but I can't help thinking that for a woman who's had
three kids, you're . . . ahh"—he sucked in a harsh breath, his
expression fierce with concentration—"tight."

Just saying the word had her inner muscles clenching, making them both gasp. Need made her nearly dizzy. "Kegels and riding in a two-point position," she managed, pushing down until she'd taken all of him, biting her lip at the exquisite sensation of him filling, stretching her.

"Kegels? What are— Never mind. Damn, woman, you're a miracle."

And if she hadn't been doing her utmost to protect her heart, she would have fallen in love with him right then and there for making her feel like one.

Chapter
EIGHTEEN

JORDAN WAS at her computer, staring at a mosaic border she'd ordered for the master bath that had a leaf design in dark emperador and crema marfill marble. She loved the colors, knew how striking they'd look against the paler beige tiles she'd chosen. And the mix of brown and gold in the emperador stone was incredible, she thought as she dragged the cursor over and zoomed in on the image.

Oh God, she was doing it again, she realized as she gazed at the enlarged detail. The marble she'd chosen was an exact match for Owen's eyes when his body was embedded deep inside her. A deep rich brown lit with gold fire.

Ten days had passed since she and Owen first made love, and since then nearly everything she saw that she deemed beautiful or pleasing was because the object made her think of him, whether it was in the clean lines of a dresser, the fine carving of a king-size Federal-style mahogany bed, or a Tabriz Garden of Paradise rug, this last item having reminded her of when Owen made love to her on one of the drop cloth–covered chairs. With the moonlight spilling into the room, she'd felt she was in paradise. As each piece she chose was classic, elegant, and bold—like him—it was a boon for Hawk Hill but not so great for her heart.

Especially because Jordan knew that just as every piece she selected was absolutely right for the house, so Owen was absolutely right for her.

With a sigh, she clicked onto another page and double-checked the order she'd placed for the kitchen cabinets and the granite countertop, pulling out from one of the files at her elbow a sheet of paper on which Owen had written the specs and measurements. She even liked his handwriting, the strong slash of letters precise and sure and easy to read.

If only his heart were as easy to read, she thought. Hers was all too easy, and she could no longer ignore what it told her: she'd fallen deeply in love with Owen Gage.

That she'd ever believed she could embark on an affair with Owen and *not* fall in love with him now struck her as patently absurd. With 20/20 hindsight she now understood that the reason she'd been able to enter into such an intimate relationship with him was because she cared for him. Already, Owen had become a part of her life.

She wasn't sure that he was aware how seamlessly he fit not just into her life but into that of the entire Rosewood clan. No one even bothered to ask him for dinner or if he felt like dropping by to handle the foals after he'd finished the day's work on Hawk Hill. His presence was assumed, expected.

No one blinked an eye to find him in the library leafing through John Butler's pattern book or immersed in his newly appointed project of preserving the architect's correspondence with her ancestor, Francis Radcliffe, slipping each sheet into an acid-free protective sleeve. Aghast to discover that they'd been content to keep the letters in a turn-of-the-century bandbox, Owen had insisted they adopt a more modern approach to protecting the documents for posterity.

Jade had been the one to say what Jordan had privately been thinking: that Owen was incredibly cute when he got all ruffled and stodgy and professorial. He'd endured Jade's teasing, merely lifting a dark brow at being called stodgy, but hadn't backed down about the need to conserve the letters. Margot had solved the problem by suggesting he consider himself Rosewood's archivist. And Jordan, the only one besides Owen inclined to take on such a project, had happily seconded the motion. Thanks to Owen's well-planted comments at Nonie's cocktail party, she now had more than enough on her plate; the phone had been ringing with people requesting design consultations.

Asking Owen to preserve the letters was actually a way to thank him for what he'd done at Nonie's. The task gave him the opportunity to pore over the correspondence and Butler's drawings to his heart's content. For Jordan it would be like being granted access to Winterthur's storage areas.

Observing her family interact with him, it was easy to see that her sisters, while nothing less than supportive of her and obviously wanting her to be happy, clearly liked Owen for his own merits. And despite their different backgrounds, Owen and Travis got along very well. When Owen invited him and Ned to Hawk Hill to look over the layout he'd de-vised for the horse barn, Jordan could tell Travis was pleased by how seriously Owen took the project. And Ned had begun talking about how Owen should really learn how to ride. Enough said.

Their acceptance of Owen, her children's affection for him, knowing that they all considered him their friend, was wonderful to see, but worrisome, too. Because no matter how much more comfortable Owen was with Kate, Max, and Olivia—he no longer sported an alarmed expression in their company and only flinched slightly when Olivia rushed him with an ecstatic banshee shriek—it didn't mean that he was interested in becoming a permanent fixture in their lives.

For all Nonie's mean-spiritedness, she hadn't been wrong in her assessment of Jordan and Owen's affair. Come the day the last piece of furniture was positioned just so at Hawk Hill, Owen might very well walk out of their lives.

Then where would Max find someone who could help him build such amazing castles, feats of fantastic architecture? And remember to construct an "Olivia tower" off to the side so that her daughter could reduce it, rather than the castle, to rubble with a gleeful kick of her sneaker? Where would Kate find someone who would really *look* at the drawing she'd made of a house, or teach her how to play "Chopsticks" when it was raining too hard for the kids to play outside?

And where would Jordan find someone who could understand how much she loved the process of transforming a house into a home, of hunting down the right furnishings to enhance the architectural space and also reflect the personality of the owner? Where would she find a man who was perfectly comfortable with her newfound need to break free of her usual reserve and proper demeanor, who was willing to indulge her without judging her? Where would she find a man who could make love to her fiercely, raunchily, and then with such exquisitely tender passion that afterward she wanted to weep for joy?

"Yo, Jordan, what are you doing?"

She jumped inches off her chair. Landing, she twisted guiltily toward Jade. "I'm, uh, checking an order for the kitchen."

"Some order. The computer screen's blank. I'm kind of surprised you didn't notice. You've been staring at it like it holds the secret to life. Or how to get rid of cellulite permanently."

"Oh!" Hurriedly she clicked the mouse and as the order page reappeared, made a show of going through the measurements and specs. "What time is it?" she asked. For all she knew she could have spent an hour thinking about Owen.

"Five-thirty. Thing One, Two, and Three had a good lesson. Kate's gonna make us proud at Crestview if she continues riding this well. Speaking of shows, can I borrow a sleeveless ratcatcher for Charlottesville?"

Jordan shot her an incredulous look. "You still haven't gone to Steadman's?"

"Been a wee bit busy. Still am. There's no way I can go before the show on Saturday, and the weekend's supposed to be a scorcher."

"Fine. You better make sure you buy one soon, though,

because I may need mine at Crestview. My riding gear's on the right-hand shelf in my closet."

"Thanks, sis. What are we eating?"

"You're welcome, and we're having sausage and broccoli rabe over pasta and a tomato and basil salad. Peaches and raspberries for dessert."

"That'd be totally yummy if we get to pull out the ice cream and brownies, too."

"Negotiate with Margot. But I warn you, she's been muttering about the evils of white death lately."

"That is so Gwyneth Paltrow. Next Margot'll be making us do those gross detoxes. I'll let Owen know you baked last night. He'll use some of that smooth persuasion to get the brownies on the table for sure. He's excellent at that."

Yes, he was, Jordan thought, trying not to smile at the computer screen. Just remembering some of his acts of smooth persuasion sent a frisson of pleasure through her. And if she didn't blow everything by letting Owen know how she truly felt about him, she might get to experience some more of that deliciously smooth persuasion this coming weekend.

Assured that she hadn't made any errors in the order, Jordan shut down the computer and hurried downstairs to the kitchen, where the kids would be eating a snack with Miriam. Perhaps Owen was already there, sipping iced tea and accepting the odd carrot stick or slice of apple from Max or Kate, and trying his best to ignore the offer of a sweaty Goldfish from Olivia.

Owen had a problem. Every time he saw Jordan she was more beautiful than before. It wasn't supposed to be this way. He was supposed to be growing inured to her, perhaps even slightly bored by her company. He should be at least mentally easing his way toward the exit sign in this relationship, cracking open the door so he could slip out and be free once again.

Instead it felt like he had a coat of Gorilla Glue on the soles of his shoes.

There was no other possible explanation for why he was sitting in the kitchen. He supposed shooting the breeze with Miriam about the Airborne Toxic Event concert she and Andy were attending tonight was okay. Watching Olivia create her own toxic event by dropping Goldfish into her cup of water was not. It troubled him that he was willing to risk nausea simply because he hadn't seen Jordan in a few hours and he knew that she'd take the back stairs down to the kitchen. From where he sat, he could see her the instant she appeared.

He wished he could reassure himself with the thought that his symptoms were caused by the fact that he still hungered for Jordan sexually. He hadn't been inside her in days. Days that seemed like centuries since he'd touched her everywhere he wanted to, tasted her, felt her heart pounding beneath his hand, against his mouth as he kissed his way over her naked body. God, he wanted her.

The unflagging strength of his desire troubled him, too. Craving her physically was at least understandable. Sex with Jordan was as damned fantastic as any Owen had ever enjoyed. But the problem was that his need for her encompassed more than astonishingly good sex. And it left Owen feeling like he was in the throes of serious withdrawal, ragged and edgy when he wasn't with her. Or when he couldn't talk to her and watch her absently tuck a silken strand of reddish brown hair behind her ear while mulling over something he'd said or flipping through furniture catalogs. Or when he couldn't see her smile . . . she had such an amazing smile.

So where was she?

He glanced at his watch. It was five thirty-three, definitely time for the kids' baths. He refused to consider what knowing the kids' routine implied, he simply focused on the fact that bath time heralded bedtime, and having them tucked in for the night was a magic moment, when he got to kiss their mommy the way he wanted to.

Her footsteps on the back stairs, quick and light, caused an answering skip to his heartbeat. The kids heard it, too, so that meant four pairs of eyes were fixed on the stairs. He was grateful for the clamor of little voices that erupted when she entered the kitchen. He didn't want Jordan to think she was becoming important, that he was actually having a hard time envisioning himself delivering his usual friendly exit line of, "I've really enjoyed our time together, but . . ."

Why worry about that when he could focus on the flash of Jordan's bare legs and the very nice wraparound sleeveless dress she was wearing, and bask in the knowledge that she'd chosen it for him?

"Hi," she said, coming over to the long table where he and the children were sitting.

"Hi," he returned happily as he rose to his feet, standing not simply because it had been drilled into him that one stood for a lady, but because if any woman inspired courtly manners, it was Jordan. A soothing sense of contentment flooded him as their gazes met. So what if indeed she'd grown more beautiful in the past three hours? As problems went, this really wasn't a big one.

"I was double-checking the order for the kitchen. Everything's fine. And I was able to use a software program to put together all the materials I've selected for the bathrooms. The marble in the master bathroom is going to look great with the slate floor. Oh, and the glass stall we decided to use for the walk-in shower in the second bathroom? Definitely a good idea. It allows you to see the river rock on the shower floor. It makes a great contrast with the other tiles we used."

"And how about the third bathroom and those glass tiles you found?" Because he knew she'd have run the program, so she could make sure every bathroom matched her original vision.

"I think you'll like the effect. I saved and forwarded all the pages to you."

While she was talking, she'd been going around the table, kissing the kids, plucking the orange watery muck out of Olivia's hands and dumping it down the disposal, and nodding as Kate and Max told her how great Doc Holliday had been. Amazing woman.

"Aunt Jade says you all are getting really good. I'm very proud of you."

"Yeah, and Aunt Jade says we need to buy a new pony, so Kate and me can have our lesson at the same time," Max announced happily.

"Kate and 'I,' Max," Jordan corrected. Deftly sidestepping the rest of Max's sentence, she asked Miriam, "So what time are you and Andy off?" as she wiped Olivia's mouth and hands and freed her from the booster seat.

Owen had learned enough to brace himself. When Olivia made a drunken beeline for his knees, he put a hand out, keeping her at arm's length so she couldn't smear his trousers with orange spittle. And when she began talking, he nodded and said, "Uh-huh," in response—a neat trick he'd picked up from Travis. "Uh-huh" worked wonders and was far less humiliating than being forced to make barnyard animal noises while his nose was smashed.

Olivia seemed quite pleased by his reply—if her happy grin was any indication. He smiled back warily while Jordan and Miriam continued their conversation.

"Andy and I are leaving at six-fifteen. We're going for Tex Mex before the concert starts."

"Which restaurant?"

"Cactus Cantina."

"That sounds delicious," Jordan pronounced. "I haven't had Mexican in months. I may have to go buy some black beans and chiles tomorrow. Will you have time to heat the pasta dish I made for the kids' supper before you leave?"

"Sure."

"Thanks. Okay guys, it's bath time."

"I want a black pony, Mommy."

"That's nice, Max." As she scooped Olivia into her arms, her fingers grazed Owen's thighs and their eyes locked. "Uh, if you're thirsty, there's white wine in the fridge and a bottle of Chianti in the wine rack."

"Thanks, I can wait." He let his eyes tell her what he was really thirsting for. Her blush told him she'd gotten the message. "If it's okay, I may come up and look at the mock-ups you made."

"Sure. I printed them out, too. They're in the Hawk Hill file to the right of my computer."

He smiled. "I think you and I need to renegotiate your fee. You're too good."

Her blush deepened. "I may have to, or accept a lot more commissions if Jade keeps bringing up the subject of a new p-o-n-y."

"That spells 'pony,' Mommy."

"Yes, it does. Good for you, Kate."

"That is great, Katiebug," Miriam chimed in. "You know, Jordan, most kids learn how to spell 'cat' and 'dog' before graduating to 'pony.'"

"Not in this family. Now, who can get upstairs fastest?"

Owen stayed in the kitchen long enough to say hi to Travis and Margot when they came in from feeding the horses before heading up to the third floor himself. He found the bathroom layouts Jordan had created and was once again impressed by her sense of style. And he couldn't help but be pleased when he remembered that quite a few of the materials she'd selected had been on sale. She not only had a good eye, but a thrifty one.

He was going through the orders she'd placed for the living room when Max and Kate appeared at his elbow, freshly scrubbed and in striped pajamas.

"You wanna come down and have dinner with us, Owen?"

"Thanks, Max, but I need to finish looking over these orders your mom has placed for the house."

"We're gonna come over to your house, right, Owen?"

"Yes, I think your mom mentioned something along those lines—"

"So we can see where your horses are going to live. Do you have a tractor? We do."

"No, I don't have a tractor." Owen wasn't about to disillusion Max by telling him he didn't have a horse, either, and that Hawk Hill wouldn't be his for long. The kid was so happy. "You know, I think I smell your dinner." He sniffed exaggeratedly. "Mmm, can you smell that?"

Both Max and Kate sniffed loudly.

"I bet it's going to be pretty tasty."

"Mommy's a really good cook," Kate said.

"Very true. And good food should be eaten."

"Come on, Kate. Let's go see if dinner's ready."

Owen smiled as they ran toward the stairs. If he did say so himself, he thought he was getting pretty good at this kid stuff.

When he heard their voices from the girls' room, the high-speed babble and the easy, patient answers, signaling that Olivia's bath was over, Owen decided he was done with waiting to see Jordan. The thought barely completed, his feet were already halfway down the carpeted hall.

Olivia was lying on the changing table, kicking one leg rhythmically while Jordan fastened the tabs to her diaper. Seeing him standing on the threshold, Olivia gave an excited shriek. Jordan quickly glanced over her shoulder and smiled. "Oh, hi. Did you look at the pages?"

He nodded. "They look great. You're right about the river pebble and the glass shower stall. Being able to see all the contrasting textures is terrific." He came into the room, stopping a few feet short of the changing table. Better to stay out of Olivia's range. Even squeaky clean she was more devil than angel.

"Okay, Olivia, a little powder on your legs and tummy and then we put on your pj's, and go down to dinner. We want to hurry so we can say bye-bye to Miriam," Jordan said, grabbing a white plastic bottle that sat atop the dresser and squeezing a small mound of powder into her palm. With a smile she rubbed the powder onto Olivia's tummy, neck, and wriggling limbs while Olivia giggled happily.

While Owen watched horrified.

It was over in seconds.

Jordan had Olivia's plump legs encased in light-green-and-navy-blue-striped leggings and her torso covered in a matching top and had lifted her daughter off the table, settling her on her hip before Owen could recover from the shock.

"All set." She smiled at him. "Are you coming down?"

With a supreme effort he tore his gaze away from the white plastic bottle. "I thought I'd double-check the order for the appliances in the kitchen first," he managed.

She gave him a slightly puzzled look but was too polite to point out that the order had already been placed and confirmed by the distributor. They'd even scheduled a delivery date. "Okay. Come on, Olivia."

He pretended to follow them, but as soon as Jordan's head disappeared down the stairs, he did an about-face and marched back into the bedroom.

He made himself pick up that seemingly innocent bottle, twist the top so the holes were open, and sniff, praying all the while.

The scent wrung a groan of despair from him as Owen realized that all his problems up until now didn't amount to a hill of beans compared to this one.

Distressing didn't begin to describe how he felt at finally learning exactly what the haunting scent he associated with

Jordan was. Baby powder. The discovery left him disoriented. Violated his very notion of self. It was like finding out that a pair of support hose really turned him on.

It gave rise to nightmarish visions of him wandering the drugstore aisle, past diapers and disposable bibs, teething rings and infant formula, to stare besottedly at that white plastic bottle with the pretty blue lettering as he summoned the memory of the way Jordan's skin smelled in the shadowed valley of her breasts, of how he loved to drag his mouth over that exquisitely smooth territory from her hip bone to the triangle of dark curls, inhaling deeply as everything in him went a little crazy with lust. Thanks so bloody much, Johnson & Johnson.

He couldn't help but feel betrayed, angry even, as if he were the butt of some awful joke. What the hell did it say about him, just how screwed up his internal wiring was to go weak-kneed whenever he caught a whiff of Jordan's "signature" scent? A scent that wasn't a special formula created exclusively for her by a master parfumeur in Grasse, but the stuff she sprinkled on her chubby baby's butt and barrel-shaped tummy? If he'd lacked sufficient motivation to end things between Jordan and him, he now had more than enough reason.

He carefully put the offensive bottle back exactly where he'd found it, determined no one should guess that he'd literally been sniffing around. As a point of pride, he refused to show how unsettled he was when he went down to the kitchen. Luckily no one noticed. Margot and Travis were supervising the kids' meal, while Jordan prepared the grown-ups' dinner.

"Tim Mitchell called, Jordan, to ask if he could come by and see Cascade on Saturday. I told him that Margot and I would be down in Charlottesville, but he seems really keen on coming."

"Ned and I can show him Cascade." Turning to look at Owen, she said, "Would you like some wine?"

"Please, but I'll get it." Better not to get close to her, he might catch her scent and lose it completely. "How about you?"

"Maybe after I've put the kids to bed."

"I'll open it and let it breathe then." Just as long as *he* didn't breathe.

"So this is what, the fourth time Tim's come out to see Cascade?" Jordan asked, picking up the thread of the conversation with Travis.

Owen stilled. This Tim Mitchell had been coming around an awful lot lately. And though Cascade was a really nice colt, Owen couldn't help but wonder if Mitchell's interest didn't extend beyond Rosewood Farm's horses to Jordan.

If so, that meant the morons of Warburg had finally caught on to the fact that she was incredible. Nonie and that wagging tongue of hers doubtless had something to do with it. Hearing that Jordan Radcliffe wasn't living in self-imposed abstinence must have been the signal these lame-brains were waiting for to get off their asses, pick up the phone, and dial Rosewood Farm. Coming to check out the horses was a perfect excuse.

While Jordan, Margot, and Travis were obviously happy at the idea that Tim Mitchell might be serious about Cascade, Owen was more interested in figuring the whole of his game plan.

"I think Tim's getting ready to make an offer. I'll call him and let him know Saturday's fine, then."

"Wow," Jordan said. "First Solstice and now Cascade. It'd be pretty neat to sell two horses in as many weeks."

"Yeah, and I have a feeling Bob may be back with another client for Beat the Clock."

"How are you with Tim buying Cascade, Margot?" Jordan asked before tacking on an explanation for Owen's benefit. "Cascade is Mystique's first foal."

"And Mystique is Margot's horse," Max told him. "She had a pony, too."

"That's right, Max. My pony's name was Suzy Q. I adored her," Margot answered as she went around the table clearing the children's dessert plates. "Travis, hon, could you wipe Olivia's mouth? She missed with the strawberries a couple of times. I guess I'm okay with Tim buying Cascade," she said, answering Jordan's question. Carrying the dishes to the kitchen sink, she maneuvered around Owen. "So, Owen, how's the house coming?"

He drew the cork out of the wine bottle with a pop. "It's going well. The electrician's finished with the wiring, and Doug and Jesse have replaced the old plumbing so the baths and kitchen will be ready when the materials arrive. We installed a new furnace two days ago. So I'd say things are proceeding even better than I hoped. Oh, by the way, Travis, I ordered those stall doors you recommended. I'll let you know when they arrive."

"And we're going to visit Hawk Hill," Max said in case anyone had forgotten.

"That's right, Max, after you see Daddy this weekend. Now, let's say good night to everyone."

"Why don't I put the kids to bed?" Margot's suggestion was met with cries of "Yes! Yes! And we can read *Clip Clop*" from Kate and Max.

"Your idea meets with unanimous approval," Jordan said lightly. "Thanks. This way I can get dinner on the table sooner. Jade was quizzing me about tonight's menu and gave it her stamp of approval. I'm actually surprised she hasn't come down for her premeal grazing."

"Homework, probably," Margot said. "Come on, kids. You want to come up and read *Clip Clop*, Travis?"

"Thanks, but I'm going to call Tim and let him know Saturday's okay with Jordan."

Travis's plan to remain downstairs was fine with Owen. His presence would make it far less obvious that Owen was maintaining a careful distance from Jordan, keeping on his side of the granite island with Jordan on the other. Once she started cooking and the smell of sautéing garlic, sausage, and broccoli rabe filled his nostrils, he might be able to relax.

It killed him, though, that she looked so lovely, with the tendrils of her hair curling from the steam rising from the pasta water. He knew if he put his lips to the underside of her jaw, her skin would be as soft as a dew-covered rose. And she would smell like baby powder. Christ.

Travis was setting the kitchen table and Owen was slicing a thick loaf of rustic Italian bread when Margot came back downstairs.

"The kids behave themselves?" Jordan asked, stirring the sausage and rabe.

Margot nodded. "Of course."

"Is Jade not ready yet?"

"She said she didn't want dinner," she replied, sounding preoccupied.

Jordan paused in the midst of stirring. "Not hungry? Pasta's her favorite."

"I know. I offered to bring her up a plate."

"Oh. I'll get one ready. She's had a bunch of end-of-the-year assignments."

But Margot was shaking her head. "She didn't even want a plate brought up. I offered, too."

"But—"

"She wouldn't let me in the room, Jordan. Said she wanted to be alone. Shades of last year."

Owen had no idea what that meant, so he concentrated on dropping the bread into the basket.

"But she was fine upstairs with me. She wanted brownies for dessert. She was going to enlist Owen to persuade you to let them make an appearance at dessert right after she'd gotten the ratcatcher from my closet— Oh my God!"

Jordan looked horror-stricken.

"Jordan, what is it?" He'd been listening to the conversation with equal parts confusion and amusement, unable to fathom why Jordan and Margot seemed so troubled by Jade's behavior. It seemed like perfectly normal irrational teen stuff to him.

Jordan didn't seem to hear him. "The closet," she repeated in the same tone. "Margot, it's where I keep the diary. I was distracted and sent her to look for a sleeveless ratcatcher for Charlottesville. You know how Jade is, incapable of finding anything. She tears through a space like a hurricane. I had the diary hidden beneath a pile of shirts— not riding shirts. Do you think . . ."

Margot was already heading toward the stairs.

"No, Margot, wait." In a flurry of activity, she turned off the pasta sauce, poured it over the bowl of steaming pasta, and rushed over to her. "Let me go. The diary was in my closet. I need to explain what it was doing there." She reached out and touched her sister's arm, "Margot, I am so sorry."

"It's not your fault, Jordan. We should have burned the damned thing last year. Do you think that's what's happened?"

She nodded tightly. "Yes, and I can't stand to think how much finding it will hurt her. Don't hold dinner. I may be a while." Offering Owen a quick, strained smile, she ran upstairs.

Jordan rapped on Jade's door. But though her mind had been racing as she hastened up the stairs to her sister's room, she had no idea what she was going to say beyond, "Jade, it's me. Let me in."

There was silence. Then, "Not interested."

"I need to speak to you."

"Nothing to say."

That flat monotone made Jordan want to weep. She grabbed the door handle and shook it. "Jade, come on, please let me in. You have to let me explain—"

The door opened with a sudden violence. Jade, her face

ravaged by tears, her fingers bony white, was clutching the bright pink leather of Nicole's diary in a death grip.

"This I gotta hear. So what do you want to explain to me first? That my mom didn't actually despise me? That she wasn't screwing around behind my dad's back? That she wasn't a total bitch to end all bitches? Yeah, explain it all to me. Make it all nice, like one of your pretty rooms with everything placed just so. Tell me some more lies, Jordan."

"I—" God, she had no idea why Nicole had written any of the tripe she had.

"Wow, such eloquence. Now I know my mom didn't mean any of the stuff she was writing. It was all fiction, wasn't it? Or maybe Mom was playing opposite day whenever she picked up her pen." Her sneer was ugly and heartbreaking.

Jordan tried to keep her voice level as she pleaded, "It was a *private* diary. No one should read another person's innermost—"

"That didn't stop you, though, did it? You read it, and Margot, too, I bet, and then you both spouted bald-face lies to me about how Mom adored Dad."

"They weren't lies, Jade."

"Bull. She didn't love anyone—not Dad, not me. She was a heartless, selfish bitch. And I was gullible enough to believe you. All those months I spent defending her and getting myself hated for it. All those months I missed her. All those stupid, pointless tears I shed for her, a mother who didn't give a crap about her only child."

"That diary doesn't reflect the true picture of who Nicole was. Who knows what—"

"You know what? I'm not interested in talking anymore." She made to close the door.

Jordan put her hand on the panel, stopping her. "Jade, I am very sorry that I've added to your hurt. I understand that you don't want to talk to me now. Maybe I can call Stuart Wilde?"

Jade gave a harsh laugh. "Oh, no," she said shaking her head. "My days of bowling with the Rev are definitely over." She gave a hard little smile. "And I think you should get Ned to start teaching your kids. I've got better ways to spend my time."

This time she shut the door firmly in Jordan's face.

None of them ended up eating Jordan's pasta. Margot was distracted and simply picked at her broccoli rabe and then set her fork back down again. Travis ate a few more bites, but the scowl on his face made Owen think he wouldn't mind going a few rounds with a punching bag. As for himself, even though he'd been presented with a golden opportunity to make his excuses and get the hell out of Rosewood, he couldn't stop picturing Jordan's face before she'd gone to Jade's room.

If Jordan had looked distraught before, he could only describe her expression when she came back downstairs as haunted.

Crossing the kitchen, she sank wearily into the chair next to his. He wanted nothing more than to draw her into his arms and make everything go away for her.

"How was she? Should I go?"

"It's bad, Margot. Really bad. Jade's convinced that every word Nicole wrote was how she really felt. And of course, Jade wasn't going through it as you and I did. I know I basically skimmed most of it—except the parts where she went on about *him*. But she's really reading it, giving every word weight and significance. She's looking at it with the eyes of a grieving daughter who lost her mother way too early. Those stupid rambling entries are convincing her that the mother she loved was actually a selfish monster. Damn that diary." She shuddered.

Unable to help himself, Owen reached out and began stroking her back, hoping to quiet the tremors wracking her.

"What can we do? Should I call Stuart?"

Jordan shook her head. "No, she refuses to have anything to do with him. That goes for the children, too."

"What?"

"She's furious with me because she thinks I was feeding her lies about Nicole. So she's hit on the best way to get back at me by stopping the lessons with the kids."

Margot stood. "I've got to go up and straighten this out with her."

"No, don't," Jordan said. "I mean, of course you should talk to her, but don't force her into teaching the kids."

"But she loves teaching them. She's so proud that Kate's beginning to check her diagonals."

"I know. But I don't want her to start resenting them. She's dealing with enough bad feelings. I can work with the kids or maybe I can ask Ned if he has the time. Neither of us will be able to match Jade in the children's eyes, but that's the way it is." She was silent a moment, her expression ineffably sad. "God, whatever prompted me to think that I could figure out the identity of Nicole's mystery man?"

"I can't understand what Nicole was doing with a journal in the first place. She wasn't exactly the reflective type," Margot muttered as she pushed her chair under the table. "Well, I guess it's my turn to go match wits with Jade. If only she weren't so smart. Damn, she was doing so well. Amazingly well, considering what she's had to go through."

Owen saw Jordan duck her head and squeeze her eyes shut. His hand slid up to her shoulder and kneaded it.

"Want me to come up, Margot?" Travis was already rising to his feet.

Margot nodded. "With you there she might actually open the door. As for getting her to talk to us, well, you know what she's like."

"Yup. As stubborn as you." He smiled gently. "But I don't think it matters if she doesn't want to talk tonight. At the moment what she needs is to know how much we love her."

"That's true. You're a wise man, Travis Maher," Margot said softly and slipped her hand in his.

"On rare occasions," he said. "Come on, babe, let's go do what we can to stop Nicole's poison from spreading."

After Margot and Travis left, Jordan's hold on her emotions slipped. Choked sobs rocked her bowed back.

Owen didn't hesitate. Lifting her off the wooden chair, he settled her in his lap and then wrapped his arms about her, cradling her as she cried.

"It's all my fault, I've made Jade so unhappy," she whispered into the column of his neck. "I was so stupid, staring at the computer and thinking about the house and you and whether you'd like a particular piece when I should have been listening to her. If I'd just focused, I would have gone and found the damned shirt myself."

"Shh, Jade will make it through this. She's a tough kid. And Travis is right. She's got a lot of people who love her. And she loves you all in return."

"You should have seen her face. She looked so lost, Owen. So hurt. And she's going to torture herself by reading her mother's diary over and over again. How will she ever be able to erase those careless words from her memory?"

"Give her time, Jordan," he said. And then because he couldn't stand to see her tears, he raised his hands to frame her face and began kissing them away.

Screw the damn baby powder, he thought. Nothing was as important as making Jordan feel better.

Though he'd kissed her tears dry and lifted her spirits enough that she managed a wan smile when he gave her a last, lingering good-night kiss and a whispered, "I'll see you tomorrow," his own worries came crashing down on him as he made the short drive back to Hawk Hill.

Disliking messy emotions, he'd always taken care to avoid serious relationships. So why, with the Jade crisis offering a perfect excuse to leave, had he remained by Jordan's side? What had happened to quash his excellent sense of self-preservation? A simple "I can see this is a family matter," or some similar line, would have gotten him out of there. Yet he'd stayed at Rosewood precisely because Jordan was upset and dealing with a messy, serious problem.

And in his need to comfort, he'd disregarded his own dismay at discovering the scent he considered possibly the most erotic in the world was nothing more than talcum powder.

The discovery that Jordan used baby powder to make her irresistible might seem silly and superficial. But what the powder represented was not: babies, commitment, roots. Everything Owen had previously made an art of avoiding. He'd recognized the warning signs flashing around Jordan from the first but arrogantly ignored them. Now he didn't know whether, in his complex and ever-expanding need for her, he was losing sight of who he was and what he'd always thought he wanted in life.

He passed the night staring wide-eyed at the ceiling in his Hawk Hill bedroom, wondering what the hell to do. Could he be everything he wanted to be when he was with Jordan and yet remain recognizable to himself?

And what of the neat plan he'd laid out for his life, a plan as finely drawn, balanced, elegant, and pleasing as one of his architectural renderings? As organized and efficient as she was, Jordan's life was as messy and complicated as one of Max's crayon drawings of Felix driving the tractor.

Owen just couldn't see himself in that kind of picture.

ONLY ABLE to shut out anguished thoughts of Jade for a few brief hours, Jordan awoke as exhausted as when sleep had finally claimed her. Luckily, the children, their tanks full of morning energy, didn't notice the long looks and mute head shakes she exchanged with Travis and Margot at breakfast.

"At least we have Charlottesville this weekend," Margot said with determined cheerfulness as she poured orange juice into everyone's glasses. "She should do really well with Sweet William. And maybe bring home a couple of blue ribbons with Aspen."

"Depending on how Gypsy Queen goes in the warm-up, I might put Jade on her for the preliminary jumper class," Travis said.

"That's an excellent idea. Now if we can just keep her busy until Saturday morning."

"I was thinking of asking her if she wanted to go shopping this afternoon," Jordan said. "Miriam can watch the kids."

"But we have our riding lesson with Jade."

"Jade might not be able to give you one today, Kate," Jordan replied. "But I'm going to see whether Ned has some time. You know Ned taught Jade, Margot, and me to ride."

"Can we come shopping with you and Jade, Mommy?"

"Some other day, Max. I'd like to spend some special time with Jade."

"Besides, Max, if you're out shopping, you'll miss a chance to ride on the tractor with Felix," Travis reminded him.

The question of what Max would be missing more—the joy of consumerism versus the visceral pleasure of bouncing atop a rumbling, massive-wheeled tractor—became moot.

Jade came down to the kitchen with her hair a ragged wet mop around her pale face and her lips pressed in a flat stubborn line as everyone around the table greeted her. When Jordan proposed picking her up after school to go shopping at Jade's favorite Georgetown boutique, she gave her a withering look for having even made the offer.

"A blast and a half for sure, but I have other plans this afternoon. And I don't want breakfast, either," she said, already shouldering her messenger bag.

Both Margot and Jordan spoke at once.

"And what plans would those be?"

"I'm sorry you don't want to go. I was really looking forward to it, Jade."

"Well, a little rain has to fall in everyone's life, don't it, Jordan? And you know what else? I really don't feel much like sharing info with any of you. I've got a life. Maybe you all should get one, too."

She stalked out, without a single flip comment or a casual ruffle of Olivia's hair as she passed, ignoring, too, Margot's cry of, "In case you've forgotten, there's a curfew on weeknights."

Collectively they sat with their ears nervously straining for the sound of the Porsche roaring to life, its wheels spinning on gravel. Jade didn't disappoint.

Sinking back in her chair, Margot picked up her coffee and stared at it glumly. "That was brilliant of me. Any hope she'll be going out with Brian Steadman?"

The next two days were just as painful. Jade would get up, leave immediately for school, come back home and ride, and then, announcing she had work to do in the town library, leave again. She'd return a minute before her curfew. The rare times she hung around, it was to treat everyone to a stony silence or, if pushed, to stinging replies before stalking upstairs to her room.

No dummies, the children quickly picked up on the fact that something was wrong with their superheroine Aunt Jade.

They were in Max's room, the three children playing with the blocks, using them as an obstacle course for Max's collection of trucks while Jordan packed Max's bag for the weekend visit with Richard, due to pick them up in a half hour.

"Why isn't Jade teaching us anymore, Mommy?"

"Yeah, she doesn't make funny jokes, either. Does she hate us, Mommy? Libby Teller said she hated me 'cause I wouldn't let her ride the scooter at outdoor playtime," Max said.

Feeling as if her heart had dropped right through the floorboards, Jordan sank to her knees beside them and enfolded Kate and Max in a hug. Olivia alone seemed untroubled, absorbed in ramming her truck into the bed's wooden leg.

"Jade doesn't hate you. She loves you guys. You know that. She's just very busy right now. When you get bigger, you get a lot more work at school. I'm sure when the school year finishes, she'll start giving you lessons on Doc again. And Libby Teller doesn't hate you, either, Max. She was just angry because she wanted you to share the scooter with her. Next time you'll remember to share, right, Maxwell Robert Stevens?"

He shrugged. "I guess so. Libby thinks she's the boss of me. She's not."

"No, she's not. But you still need to remember to share." She'd have to talk to Drew Farber, Max's teacher, Monday morning and make sure she was aware of the situation between Max and Libby.

"Is Owen gonna come to our house today? I wanna show him how I can climb a tree."

A worrisome side effect of Jade's hostility was that the children had become even more attached to Owen. Though Owen was growing increasingly at ease in their presence, that hardly meant he wanted to be their go-to source for entertainment.

"No, sweetie, Daddy's coming to pick you up soon, so you won't see Owen." She'd made sure to tell him she'd be busy with the kids until four-thirty, when Richard was coming.

"But if Owen came over, then Daddy could meet him. And then I could show them both how high I can climb," Max said excitedly.

What an awful idea. Not the tree climbing, but the prospect of Richard and Owen meeting. The thought made her head pound. "As I said, Max, Daddy will be here very soon, so I'm afraid that's not going to happen."

"You can call Owen and tell him to come."

She smiled. "Why don't we first make sure we have all your things downstairs and ready for Daddy?"

Jordan had steeled herself for what was coming, the rending of her heart while she stood and watched her children clamber into her ex-husband's car and drive off down the allée, gone from her until five o'clock on Sunday.

She was proud that she kept her tears firmly in check as she hugged and kissed the children good-bye and was able to address Richard with a calm, "Hi, how was the traffic?"

"Typical Friday chaos. So, you guys ready to have fun this weekend?" he asked, bending down to kiss the children.

"Is that Susannah? I'll just go say hi," she said moving toward the car.

Richard's reply brought her up short. "That's Cynthia. Susannah had something going on this afternoon."

She turned around. Her face felt stiff. "Thanks for the warning, Richard."

He didn't respond immediately, choosing instead to open the rear door for the kids to climb into their booster seats and then hoisting Olivia into hers. She heard Cynthia greet the children with gushing enthusiasm. Jordan couldn't help but wonder whether this was the way she always behaved around them or a special show put on exclusively for her benefit.

Finished strapping Olivia into the car seat, Richard shut the door, turned, and gave an aggrieved sigh at her expression. "You don't have to make a big deal out of this, Jordan. Cynthia and I are married. She needs to bond with the kids. In the car and out of it."

She looked at him levelly. "Nevertheless, it would have been nice if I could have known that she was coming."

"That's right, you like things to be nice and proper." There was an angry edge to his voice. "Though according to several sources, you seem to have abandoned any sense of propriety by flaunting your lovers publicly. Have you considered that it might be less embarrassing for all concerned if you'd try to be a little discreet?"

For a second she was shocked speechless, not by the distance Nonie's gossip had traveled but rather by the transparency of Richard's hypocrisy. "Discreet? That's rich, coming from you. But you don't have to make a big deal out of this, Richard. You and I are divorced."

"Very funny," he snapped. "There are children involved. I don't want them exposed—"

"Don't even think of going there." Her tone stopped him cold. "No conduct of mine could ever compare to your behavior as a married man with three small children. Just in case you've forgotten, my lawyer still has the tape revealing your and Cynthia's total lack of discretion."

It was his turn to look shocked. He stared at her for several moments. "You've changed, Jordan," he said finally.

"Yes, I have. I'm no longer the doormat I used to be."

The silence stretched between them. Then he gave a short nod. "I'll have the kids call when we get home."

"Please dial my cell. I may be out," she said, and if she hadn't been in so much pain at the prospect of seeing her children drive off, she would have taken sweet pleasure in having stood her ground.

She went down to the main barn, knowing it would be bustling with the preshow bathing and braiding of the horses heading down to Charlottesville. She saw Andy first. Standing on a low stool, he was braiding Indigo's mane. The mare was freshly bathed, the dark rosettes of her dapple gray coat glossy black with white highlights.

"Hi, I've come to lend a hand."

"Could use one. Jade's supposed to be here helping braid."

"She hasn't shown up yet?" School had ended more than an hour ago.

"Nope. Margot's a wee bit ticked off because not only is she MIA, she's turned off her phone." Finished working the black yarn into the lower half of the braid, he looped it around the end of the mane and knotted it so that the braid hung in a thin line next to the others.

"Oh, boy," Jordan said, shaking her head. "It isn't even the fourth of July."

"Yeah, we'll be having fireworks early if Jade keeps sparking everyone's temper." Grabbing the spray bottle that hung from the back pocket of his jeans, he spritzed Indigo's mane so it would braid more easily, then pulled out a metal mane comb to divide a one-inch section of the damp hair. His fingers crisscrossed the dark gray strands over each other as he spoke. "What ticks me off is the way she's been treating Miriam. They've grown pretty tight but now Jade's just freezing her out. Because of that, Miriam doesn't know if she should come and watch us at Charlottesville, even though Jade's the one who asked her."

It seemed the effects of Jordan's carelessness in letting Jade stumble upon the diary kept spreading in an ever-widening circle, like a rock cast into a lake. She hated her role in all the bad feelings brewing at Rosewood.

"Miriam should go to the show. She'd get a kick out of it, and Jade's not the only one she wants to see ride. You've been doing so well on Mistral. Call her tonight and tell her to come to Charlottesville."

He looked pleased. "Okay." He nodded.

"So who needs doing what?" she asked as Andy picked up a single piece of black yarn that was draped over Indigo's neck and worked it into the braid. The trick to a beautifully braided mane was to count the crossovers and add the yarn at the same spot for each braid. That way, when the braids were folded under and the yarn pulled through the top of the mane and then knotted around the loop, they would be uniform, each lying flat along the arched crest of a horse's neck, like a line of little Tootsie Rolls.

Andy finished knotting the braid and moved on to the next. "I've got Gypsy Queen to braid next. Tito's still washing Saxon. Travis said not to touch Aspen, though I figure both he and Margot will have Aspen looking ready for a beauty pageant by six o'clock even if Jade's a no-show. So, would you mind doing Sweet William?"

Technically Jade should be in charge of braiding Sweet William, too, since she'd be riding him in the hunter classes. But Andy, however aggravated he was, was trying to cut Jade as much slack as possible.

Like everyone else at Rosewood.

"I'd be happy to."

"Thanks. I already cut the yarn for him. It's lying in the tack room."

After grabbing her braiding tools from her tack box and

filling up a spray bottle of water mixed with a dollop of styling gel, Jordan got to work on Sweet William. She was halfway through the second stage of braiding, using a latch hook on each tied-off strand of dark brown yarn and pulling the yarn through the top of the braid to wrap it about the looped length and tie the braid tight, when Jade's voice reached her.

"So what, you think I'm such a loser I can't braid the horse I'm showing?"

Jordan glanced over her shoulder and had to grab a hold of Sweet William's mane or fall off her stool. Gone was Jade's shaggy mop of pink hair, replaced by a nearly white platinum blond crop. The hair had been cut to an inch and a half at most.

With her piercing green eyes, slashing cheekbones, and nearly white hair, she looked frighteningly beautiful. The pink shade had been outrageous and in-your-face, this was edgy and dangerous. It filled Jordan with apprehension.

"Your— You changed your hair," she said, still staring. Jade had achieved an almost impossible combination of arctic chill and red-hot sensuality. Looking like that, there was no telling what kind of trouble she would attract.

"Real observant of you."

"Has Margot seen you?"

Jade ignored her question. "I'll finish braiding Will." And she crossed her arms, making a show of waiting for Jordan to step off the stool.

She remained where she was. "You still have Aspen to bathe and braid, so why don't I—"

"I don't need help. And if I did, I wouldn't ask for yours."

Jordan tried to hide how much that hurt. "I'm sorry to hear that, Jade, because you're incredibly important to me." Without another word, she stepped off the stool, gathered up her tools, and walked away from the sister who couldn't forgive her.

*   *   *

She sped up the drive to Hawk Hill, keeping her foot on the accelerator even as gravel stones flew, hitting the minivan's undercarriage. Owen's Audi was there, and Jesse and Doug's pickups weren't.

Thank God, since she wasn't sure she'd have been able to maintain any kind of professional decorum right now. Her encounter with Jade had left her with an all-consuming need for Owen.

She jumped out of the van and ran into the house. "Owen?"

"Jordan?"

Dashing upstairs she reached the landing just as Owen came out of one of the bedrooms, scraper in hand. "Hey." He smiled. "I was just finishing removing this section of wallpaper before— Jordan?"

She'd already grabbed hold of his shirt, her fingers flying down the row of buttons. Pulling the ends of the shirt apart, she rained openmouthed kisses on his chest, letting her tongue drag over its salty, hairy warmth and her teeth score his suddenly quivering pectorals. Impatiently she tugged the shirt off his shoulders. It fell, landing on the scraper that Owen had dropped seconds after she began her assault.

She couldn't get enough of him, her desire urgent and all-consuming. Greedily her hands raced over the ridges and planes of his torso and down to the flat of his abdomen, his harsh indrawn breath making her even more feverish; desperate, they zeroed in on the waistband of his jeans.

"I really need you to make everything go away for me, Owen," she whispered, popping the metal button. "Right here. Right now."

Owen wasn't about to ask questions. The lady clearly knew what she wanted. And if she seemed a little crazy wild, well, it was infectious. The second she'd laid her hands on him, caressing him with that avid ferocity, his passion had exploded like a match to gasoline.

He hauled her close, seizing her mouth in a deep, wet kiss that became almost brutal as he felt her hand descend, slipping inside his boxers. He shuddered as her palm pressed down his hard length. When her fingers touched his balls, teasing them with her nails, he nearly went over the edge then and there.

He had to get her out of these clothes before he completely lost his mind. This would be the day she wore jeans, paddock boots, and a snug-fitting cotton T-shirt.

"Lift your arms." His command ended on a groan of agonized pleasure when, rather than following his instructions, she closed her hand around his stiff cock as if she never wanted to let it go. He squeezed his eyes shut, praying for control. "Jordan, I need you naked. I need to have your breasts filling my hands. I need to feel your skin on mine while your cunt's tight around my cock. So let's get these damn clothes off."

With a whimper she drew her hand up while he concentrated on not coming as her fingers brushed the head of his cock.

She released him, saying, "Hurry."

Frantic, they tore at each others' clothes, falling to the floor in a writhing mass as Owen wrestled with her jeans and the laces of her boots while loosing a string of curses. Then the boots were off, brown leather missiles flying down the hall.

Naked at last, their hands were only slightly less rough in their maddened need to touch and taste.

"Now, now," she moaned, curling her fingers into his shoulders, digging into his quivering muscles. She wrapped her legs about him, lifting her hips in frantic entreaty. "Owen, don't make me wait."

His fingers parted her. She was wet, wonderfully wet. He thanked God she was ready for him, because he'd lost all semblance of control. The fierceness of his desire made it seem like it had been years since he'd been deep inside her. Poised to plunge into her slick heat, he froze.

"Shit. Bloody fucking hell." Even as he cursed, he was wrapping his arms about her. Jackknifing to his knees, he surged to his feet and lurched down the hall toward his bedroom.

"Owen?"

"Condoms," he ground out.

Finesse was out of the question. Nearing the bed, he tossed her onto it, letting her bounce onto the mattress with a startled gasp of surprise while he lunged for the condoms in his toiletry bag. Under any other circumstance, his near-frenzy as he grabbed one, tore it open, and covered his throbbing length would have been comical—if every fiber of his being hadn't been pounding with near-insane lust, if Jordan, lying on the bed and staring up at him, her enormous blue eyes pleading, her nipples tight dusky buds, her long legs open in erotic invitation, hadn't been the most beautiful sight he'd ever beheld. As crazed as he was, he had a moment of clarity where he recognized that nothing was as profoundly important and vital as being inside her right now and making her his . . . of their becoming one.

And when he thrust inside her as deep as he could possibly go, and saw the look of wonder on her face, when he heard the catch in her breath as if, like him, she was stunned by the intensity of her emotions, and tasted the same sweet joy on her lips, he knew he was right.

Hours later, when they left the bed, Owen wouldn't let Jordan put on her jeans, saying that in his depleted state the most he could be expected to peel off her was one of his shirts—as long as she only did a couple of buttons. Her underwear, too, was banned until morning. Entering the spirit of the thing, Jordan decided to only allow him his boxers and another shirt but drew the line at letting him fasten a single button. She liked looking at his chest far too much.

"Well, I'm willing to be magnanimous," he said, pouring a glass of chilled Sancerre and handing it to her where she sat, perched on the counter. Claiming that it would be a sacrilege to hide legs like hers, he'd lifted her there. "Here's to a great ending to a truly lousy day," he said, clicking his plastic wineglass against hers. "So Jade's gone scary nasty platinum?"

Jordan took a sip and nodded. "Yes, she kind of made me think of Billy Idol morphed into a beautiful teenage girl."

"That is scary."

"I'm just hoping that tomorrow morning she'll be too tired to give me her perfect snarl of contempt. It's semi-dark at five o'clock. Seeing all those bared teeth is a little too much like the vampire show she likes to watch."

"You could stay here and give yourself a respite from all the turbulence. I make a mean breakfast."

Jordan saw that Owen was almost as surprised as she by his suggestion. Invitations to sleepovers didn't conform to his "no commitment, no entanglement" code. But she was probably reading too much into the invitation. After all, it was highly unlikely that they'd be doing much sleeping, and there was one kind of entanglement Owen enjoyed very much.

She'd have liked nothing better than to think that Owen was coming to care for her. Hearing him say so would have been as healing as a gentle rain to the parched terrain of her heart. But her divorce had damaged her confidence in her ability to read situations. She didn't want to strain things between them and hated the thought of losing him by pushing him where he didn't want to go.

So she shook her head. "I'd love to stay, but that would mean letting Margot and Travis have all the fun. Besides, I think Tim Mitchell's coming over mid-morning, and Ned will have a ton for me to do beforehand. Perhaps I can take a rain check?"

Owen looked at Jordan, gloriously naked beneath his white shirt. The shirt, buttoned just below her breasts, offered him tantalizing glimpses of those soft white globes. "Of course."

"Thanks."

The fabric shifted as she crossed her legs, drawing his gaze south and making his mouth go dry as he saw that the shirt-tails had opened in a vee over her slim thighs, with the apex pointing to the sweetest spot in the world. Their eyes met and Jordan gave him a siren's smile.

Damn, he thought, his own smile widening. She was such a breathtaking combination of polished and sexy. An elegant woman he could take to lunch at the Ritz, but who wasn't snooty about eating a cold meal on scarred Formica. Or prissy about fucking on it, either.

It was natural for him to wonder if she might not possibly be the only woman he would ever want around morning, noon, and night. He couldn't ignore the fact that being with her made him happy. A happiness that was the product of more than the sex between them, though that was fantastic enough to leave him smiling like someone who'd won the Lotto jackpot.

Yet while she made him feel things no one else had, he wasn't about to propose they start picking out china patterns. He liked Jordan a lot. That didn't mean he was ready to start thinking about what would happen between them after the restoration of Hawk Hill was finished. Though he'd made peace with his discovery of Jordan's scent of choice—baby powder—that was relatively easy. Seeing himself as a husband and stepfather was not.

But there was no need to get in a lather over any of this, better to enjoy the moment, and moments didn't get much better than having a nearly naked Jordan Radcliffe sitting on a kitchen counter, he told himself as he began pulling items out of the fridge, passing them to her. "Here, we need to eat these up. We're gutting the kitchen on Monday."

"Between getting to look at the barn and seeing a kitchen in mid-demolition, Max is going to be in heaven."

He was coming to understand that a lot of things made Max really happy: Twister, tractors, tree-climbing, and tools of any kind. And that was just the *T*'s. "Jesse and Doug will be, too. Nothing those guys like better than ripping out sinks and stoves."

"So what will you do when the kitchen's gone? I imagine the master bath's next."

He nodded. "The distributor said we should get the bathroom materials by the middle of the week. I'll be okay for nourishment. I've got the cooler, and I'll buy my coffee from the bookstore's cafe or Braverman's. If we time it right, we'll be starting the other bathrooms just as we're taking apart the master bath, so there should only be a few days where I'm driving in from Alexandria."

"You're welcome to stay at Rosewood. We have plenty of room. And even if Nonie has her spycam out, I can't imagine she'll be able to add much more to fuel my ex-husband's ire."

When they'd been upstairs lying sated yet still entangled in each other's limbs, Jordan had told him not only about Jade, but also about her ex-husband's remark. The news that Nonie's tattle had reached his ears and that he'd had the gall to try and paint Jordan as some kind of loose woman still infuriated Owen. While he truly didn't give a damn who knew about him and Jordan, for the husband to intimate that their liaison in any way made her a less than absolutely wonderful mother was outrageous. He only wished he could have been there to witness Jordan standing up to him. That must have been a beautiful sight.

"If I do come stay at Rosewood, first I'll drive to Overlea with a very large roll of duct tape and perform some basic repairs on Nonie's loose lips," he said, pleased when that earned him a smile that lit her eyes. "Now, how do you feel about a little heavy cream with these strawberries?"

"That sounds delicious."

Not nearly as delicious as what he planned to do with the cream once the strawberries were gone.

The following morning Jordan tried to limit her memories of the hours she'd passed with Owen. If she thought too much about how they'd made love, how he'd made her laugh, or how she could even now have been lying in his bed with his arms about her, she might have lost her patience and replied in kind to Jade's noxious comments.

But when the horse van rumbled down the drive, she breathed a deep sigh of relief. Her relief was short-lived, however. Ned, standing beside her, said, "That girl better snap out of it or she can forget about getting any color ribbon in the hunter classes. Judges don't like sourpusses."

"No, they don't." Hunter judges based their scores not only on the horse's conformation; its smooth, balanced gaits; and the correctness of the rider's form, but also on presentation. The horses needed to be braided and groomed until they shone. Riders were supposed to look equally shipshape: boots polished, clothes clean and neat. Thunderous scowls and body language that fairly screamed "go to hell" weren't what got a nice blue ribbon pinned to the bridle's cheekpiece. "But Jade's not stupid. She'll shake off her foul mood before she enters the ring."

"From your lips to God's ears," Ned said as they walked toward the broodmares' barn. "I realize she's hurting bad and is confused as all get-out, but—" He didn't finish, merely shook his head in saddened frustration.

"I know, Ned. It's hard to sympathize when she's lashing out at everyone. But she's had a terrible shock." She didn't have to say more, aware that Travis had filled Ned in on what had happened. "Margot and I are going to talk with Stuart Wilde Monday afternoon. He's spent so much time with her. We'll see what he recommends."

The barn lights were on, Tito and Felix having already watered and fed the mares. Low whickers from the mares, who stuck their heads over the Dutch doors, greeted them. Seeing the foals' heads peeking curiously over the doors was a mark of how much they'd grown over the past weeks.

Ned and she split up, Jordan heading to Mystique's stall while Ned went to Allure's stall. Cascade and Grayson were good pasture buddies, and Ned wanted to give Cascade time to romp before Tim Mitchell arrived.

"Owen planning on coming over?" Ned asked as they led the mares and foals down the gravel drive before veering off toward the pasture.

"Yes, he mentioned he was free this morning," she said as casually as possible, as though his name and the fact that he was her lover, and that she was falling deeper in love with him, didn't make everything inside her quiver like the leaves of a willow tree in the morning breeze.

"Let's save Cosmo for last then. He and Owen get on well. You know, I have a hunch that if we get Owen on Sava or Sky Light's back, he might start thinking about buying Cosmo."

Jordan bit the inside of her cheek. Ned was the only person she knew who made matches between people and horses. She wished Owen were with them, for she would have loved to watch that bemused look steal over his face and then listen to his incredibly tactful evasion. "I know Owen has a soft spot for Cosmo, but he lives in Alexandria, in an apartment, Ned. I don't think his lifestyle is geared toward horse ownership."

"He's got Hawk Hill, too. He could have a number of horses if he wanted."

"He bought Hawk Hill to sell. He buys and sells houses like we do horses." She slipped off Mystique's halter and stepped back while the mare spun around and trotted briskly away, Cascade cantering and squealing two strides behind her.

"And in our business we know some horses are keepers. For instance, we're not going to sell Grayson, because he's Stoneleigh's last get. We're also going to hold on to Night Watch." Ned and Travis were banking on Night Watch, a beautiful black yearling, having the same scope and talent as his older brother, Night Raider, whom Travis had sold last year to help pay off the mountain of debt her father had left behind. "So why would Owen go and sell a fine property like Hawk Hill, especially when it's so close?"

Ned didn't bother to say so close to what or to whom.

What had begun as an entertaining and lighthearted conversation became abruptly less so. While Jordan would have loved to indulge in Ned's fantasy that Owen would keep the house for himself, she knew that just as Owen loved different styles of old architecture and the challenges they presented in terms of restoration, he was equally wide-ranging in his appreciation of women. If she lost sight of this basic fact and deluded herself into believing he'd stay in Warburg, she would wholly deserve the inevitable heartache.

Shoving her hands in her breeches' pockets she fixed her eyes on her field boots, as if the dew coating them were a rare and fascinating sight. "I don't think Owen's interested in keeping Hawk Hill," she said, hoping he'd leave it at that.

"Maybe that's because he doesn't know his own mind or heart yet. It takes some people longer than others."

Suddenly tired of pussyfooting around the topic, she stopped and looked at him. "Ned, you can't expect Owen to fall in love with me."

"And why not, Miss Jordan? Anyone with eyes in his head can see that you care for him—excepting perhaps the only person who should be looking extra hard. So I'm thinking that since you know how you feel, don't you figure you should make him aware of it? Don't you think love is worth fighting for?"

She smiled sadly. "I already fought that battle once and lost badly, Ned. I'm honestly not sure I'm strong enough to face the pain of losing again."

Guessing that Jordan and Ned wouldn't have taken any kind of a break, Owen arrived with bagels and cream cheese from Braverman's. As the bagels were truly first-rate when still warm from the oven, they provided the perfect excuse to get to Rosewood on the early side. While a bag of warm bagels couldn't compare to the unforgettable sex Jordan had surprised him with yesterday, he figured that he was making sure she had enough fuel so that later tonight he could return the favor.

He wondered what would please her most, make her fingers lock with his and her body shudder and arch in ecstasy. What would put that dreamy smile on her face when afterward she lay curled against him, the beat of her heart matching his?

He was waxing awfully poetic, but it was a fine morning, and he was going to get to spend it, the day, and the night, with a woman he really liked.

Ned was emerging from the broodmares' barn with Miss Molly and her foal, Domino.

"Morning, Ned," he called. "Looks like it's going to be a beautiful day."

"Enjoy it. Temperatures are supposed to shoot up this week. Glad you're here. We need to bring Hello Again and Cosmo down to the pasture. How about going into the barn and getting them, and we'll walk down together? You've put Cosmo's halter on before, right?"

"Uh, yes, but only with Jordan watching me."

"Then you know how to do it correctly. Take your time with him and put Hello Again's halter on first, so Cosmo understands what's happening. The halters are hanging on the stall door. I'll wait right here. And you can give that Braverman's bag to me. They smell mighty fine. How many did you buy?"

Owen passed him the bag. "Six. You sure about this plan, Ned? Maybe we should have Jordan supervise. Where is she, anyway?"

"You're ready to handle the two of them on your own. I've been watching you with the horses. You're smart and careful. And Miss Jordan's busy with Tim Mitchell. Good thing you bought extra bagels."

"What's he doing here so early?"

His expression was inscrutable. "Eager beaver, I guess. Good thing he's a horseman. He's been helping us turn the other horses out and now he's watching her longe Nocturne."

Okay, so Ned wanted him to know that Tim Mitchell was comfortable tackling all manner of tasks around the barns. Bully for Mitchell. Owen was more interested in finding out if he was as much an "eager beaver" about Jordan as he was about the horses at Rosewood.

Five minutes later, Owen was leading Hello Again out of the barn, with Cosmo by his dam's side, and feeling pretty damned pleased. Cosmo hadn't even tossed his head when Owen fastened the halter. "I did it, Ned."

"Course you did. Knew you wouldn't have any problem. Let's get going. I want to see how Nocturne's going for Jordan. That horse is a treat to watch."

Ned could focus on the stallion all he wanted. Owen was far more interested in seeing Jordan—the hours had been too many. And he damn well intended to find out just how interested Tim Mitchell was in her.

Jordan had the gray stallion cantering in a wide circle at the end of the longe line. A man was next to her, talking as they both watched the horse's rolling gait.

Ned opened the gate and Owen followed him into the

ring. Noting their arrival, Jordan slowed the stallion to a walk.

"Nocturne's got great manners for a stallion," Ned said.

He didn't bother to acknowledge the comment. It seemed to him that Mitchell was standing awfully close to Jordan. Did he think that because the lighting in the large indoor ring was subdued that he was on a date?

Owen was not a man prone to jealousy.

Yet it took Jordan's smile of welcome at his approach, her meeting and holding his gaze long enough to let him know how happy she was to see him, for the tightness inside him to ease and for him to recognize what had caused it.

"You're here," she said.

Even her voice calmed him, making him remember her whispered entreaties that he never stop as he rocked inside her, or stroked the sensitive underside of her breasts, or drew circles around her puckered aureoles with his tongue. Those two words simply uttered allowed him to shake Tim Mitchell's hand when she introduced them and to note that Mitchell was fairly good-looking, tall, and sandy-haired with an easygoing manner.

Because while Tim Mitchell might know his way around horses, he hadn't made Jordan cry out in pleasure as she climaxed in his arms.

"Jordan's been telling me about the work you're doing at Hawk Hill. Sounds like the place is going to be darned impressive, especially with the barn renovated."

"That's the plan. It's a great house, and Jordan's doing a terrific job with the interior, keeping the aesthetic of the house but also making sure it has all the comforts and conveniences of the twenty-first century."

"I'd like to come over to take a look at it. Properties like Hawk Hill don't come on the market that often."

"Of course. We'll be holding an Open House."

"An Open House?" Mitchell's brows came together in a

quick frown before he nodded. "I guess that would bring in a lot of people, wouldn't it?"

"Yes, I'm fairly confident there'll be a lot of interest in the property, as well as in Jordan's new decorating firm."

Tim smiled at Jordan. "Your phone will be ringing off the hook with people offering you new commissions before Owen's even left town." Turning to Ned, he said, "I was pleased to have a chance to see Nocturne again. I think I see a lot of him in Cascade's gaits."

He then proceeded to quiz Ned on Nocturne and Mystique while sticking like Velcro to Jordan's side as they left the indoor ring. Owen alternated between amusement and annoyance at this not-so-subtle interloping. He knew he should have had to compete for Jordan long before now. That the dolts of Warburg were finally wising up was no big deal—as long as they also understood there was no way they were ever going to taste that mouth or caress that silky skin or breath in her delicate baby powder scent. Not if he had anything to do with it.

But what would happen when Hawk Hill was sold? a voice inside his head asked, and whatever amusement Owen had felt watching Tim Mitchell trying to impress Jordan vanished altogether.

JORDAN WASN'T SURE whether it was her conversation with Ned or Tim Mitchell's comment about Owen leaving Warburg after the renovations on Hawk Hill were complete, but she couldn't shake the melancholy that settled over her at the thought that her relationship with Owen would soon end. Stirring and passionate though their affair was, he would move on. And she would have to somehow forget how wonderful and fun he'd been and how he'd filled the emptiness in her heart . . . filled it to overflowing.

It only took listening to Tim Mitchell for her to appreciate anew how funny and smart Owen was. Though Tim knew a lot more about horses than Owen did, once they moved away from that topic, his conversation became dull enough to make her cross-eyed.

That Tim had decided he was interested in her was fairly obvious. That Jordan would ever wish to spend any length of time with him was doubtful. She didn't know whether to laugh or cry at the thought of letting him touch her the way Owen did. Impossible to imagine Tim dipping his finger into a bowl of heavy cream and painting a circle around her navel before slowly licking it off and then repeating the process on her hip bones, thighs, and everywhere in between. Owen was such a very gifted draftsman, she thought with a smile.

Owen was beside her at the pasture gate. They were waiting to open it for Ned and Tim, who were leading Mystique and Cascade up to the barn. She realized he'd been watching her when he said, "A penny for your thoughts."

"I was just thinking of how much I like heavy cream," she said simply.

"That so?" he asked huskily.

She nodded, smiling a little wider.

She would have said more but the two men were approaching, Tim already addressing her, obviously ready to monopolize the conversation once again.

But Owen only needed to brush the back of her hand with his for her heart to quicken.

After another hour and a half of looking over Cascade, Tim had finally left. But Ned's patience in answering his every question and her agreeing to be nominated for a position on the hunter trial committee for the Warburg Hunt Club, where Tim sat on the board, paid off. When he said good-bye, Tim asked Jordan to let Travis know he'd be calling in the evening.

"I'll tell Ron Hood you're interested in serving on the committee. Having a Radcliffe involved in organizing the hunter trials again will be a real boost to the hunt club, Jordan."

They waited in silence until his car disappeared down the allée. It was as if they were collectively holding their breath, fearful he might turn the car around to come back and talk some more.

Ned spoke first. "Dang, Tim must have wax in his ears. I didn't say a thing different today than I did during his first three visits, but he was acting like it was all news to him. I should've made a tape recording for him."

Though ninety-nine percent positive Tim would be buying the colt, Jordan was too superstitious to declare it a done deal. "If he buys Cascade, all your efforts will be worth it, Ned. Even sitting on a committee with Ron Hood will be worth it. And as connected as he is, the news will spread far and wide that he's got one of Nocturne's first foals and that Travis is working with him to train the colt."

"So he would have Travis train Cascade?" Owen asked.

Ned nodded. "Tim's a good rider, but training a green horse is a big challenge. The idea would be to have him board Cascade here so Travis could teach him how to bring Cascade along."

"Is that something Travis usually does? And who's this Ron Hood?"

"Travis has been thinking of expanding our business by offering training and boarding to a few horsemen," Jordan told him. "Ron Hood is Nonie's brother-in-law. He has a daughter, Blair, in Jade's grade. Let's say that his dislike for my sisters and me is perfectly matched by our distaste for his daughter. Luckily I'm sure Ron will nix Tim's nifty suggestion that I sit on the committee."

"Well, watching the two of you go the extra mile with Tim Mitchell has made me ravenous. And as I can't imagine why he wouldn't want a foal like Cascade, I think it's only right to celebrate. Lunch is on me."

"That sounds pretty fine, don't it, Miss Jordan?"

They had fun that afternoon. Jordan wasn't surprised when Ned managed to talk Owen onto Sava's back. Clever as a fox, he laid it on thick about how far they'd fallen behind because of Tim Mitchell, then mentioned that it would be a huge help if Owen would cool the mare down after Ned had finished exercising her, so that he could hop on Night Wing while Jordan rode Sky Light. Then the broodmares would be exercised and they could start on the remaining chores. With both Jordan and him in the ring, Owen would be getting two instructors for the price of one.

Owen did well for his first time in the saddle. Not a big surprise since he was athletic and coordinated. Moreover, he'd picked up enough from observing them all to understand that good riding was composed of minute adjustments of one's body. Abrupt, jerky movements that put stress on a horse's back or hurt its delicate mouth were to be avoided. His concentration as he followed their instructions showed her that already he felt the wonder of a horse listening and accepting the pressure of his legs and hands. Even walking sedately on the rail astride a docile broodmare could impart that extraordinary magic.

Ned kept him in the saddle just long enough to ensure that Owen's appetite was whetted.

"You did real well on her, Owen. Thanks for helping us out. Next time, we'll get you trotting. Sava's got one of the smoothest trots around. Kind of like sitting on a puffy cloud. You should think about getting some breeches and boots at Steadman's. Tell Adam you're a friend of ours. Now, you always want to walk your horse into the middle of the ring when you dismount . . ."

When Kate and Max telephoned they bubbled over in excitement as she told them Owen had ridden Sava. "Sava's a really big horse," Max said.

"Yes, and Owen did just fine on her."

"Maybe we can ride together. Tell Owen I want to go riding with him."

"I'll do that," she said, glancing at Owen. He was dividing the hay bales and dropping three sections into Miss Molly's stall, but she was sure he could hear Max's enthusiasm because he had a little smile on his face. "Have you been having a good time with Daddy and Cynthia?"

"We went to the park and got ice cream afterward."

"That sounds like a great day."

"Yup, and tomorrow we're going to see dinosaurs and then we're coming home. And the day after *that* we're going to Owen's house."

"That's exactly right, Max. I know Owen's looking forward to it, too." Maybe that was a bit of a stretch, but he was being an awfully good sport about having the children come and see Hawk Hill.

She'd only just slipped her cell back into her breeches pocket when the unmistakable sound of the van pulling into courtyard reached them.

Ned opened his hand on the hose's nozzle, shutting off the water. "They're back early," he said, and a frown knit his brows.

"We can finish up here, Ned. Why don't you go see what's up? Do you mind watering the remaining stalls, Owen?"

"Not at all. Here, let me take the hose, Ned."

While they were watering and feeding, they heard the heavy thud of the van's ramp being lowered, followed shortly by the stomp of hooves on the rubber footing, changing to a clatter as the horses were led across the gravel courtyard.

Jordan had yet to dispense the grain and the supplements they gave to the broodmares, so it was another fifteen minutes before she and Owen left the broodmares' barn.

Felix was alone in the courtyard, in the midst of slamming the bolts home on the van's ramp. "How'd it go today, Felix?" Jordan asked.

"Travis and Margot did real good," he said, dusting his hands off on his jeans. "Andy got reserve champion hunter on Saxon, and Mistral went well for him. And Travis was happy with how Gypsy Queen handled the jumper course."

"So Jade didn't end up riding Gypsy Queen?"

He gave a terse shake off his head.

"Not a good day for her?"

"Not a good day," he repeated. The flatness of Felix's tone let Jordan know that "not a good day" didn't begin to describe it. "She'll be okay in a day or two," he added. "She just needs to shake it off."

Her heart sank. "Did she fall off?"

Felix nodded. "She didn't have Sweet William balanced going into the rail jump. He stumbled and then slammed on the brakes. She went straight over his head."

"I can't believe Jade fell. Her reaction time is so quick."

"Yeah. But she was pretty rattled after her round with Aspen."

Jordan sighed. "You better give me all the bad news, Felix, so I don't say something unbelievably clueless to Jade."

"She went off course with him."

"Off course? Does that mean Jade missed a fence?" Owen asked.

"Yes," Jordan said. "The rider is supposed to memorize the jump course and follow the path the course designer has devised to test the horse's strength and balance on both leads. Jump courses can get fairly tricky, but not at the green hunter level. She must be so embarrassed."

"She cried."

"Oh, no." This was not the Jade they knew. "I better go see what I can do to help."

"Good luck to you," Felix said with a tired smile.

As she turned to go into the main barn, she sent Owen an apologetic look. "If you prefer to go up to the house, I understand completely."

He shrugged. "Jade might tone it down if I'm around. It's harder to be utterly obnoxious in front of non–family members."

Angry teens didn't seem to faze him the way preverbal tots did. In that respect Owen and she were very different. "Thanks," she said.

"No problem. And afterward you can go take a hot shower, and we'll go to your friend Marla's so you can tell her all the great things you're going to do to her house, and then we can go to Hawk Hill where you can tell me all the great things you want me to do to you."

She smiled at his generosity and also because he sounded so very much like Max had on the telephone. "That sounds like an excellent plan."

*   *   *

The temperature in the main barn was a good twenty degrees cooler, and it wasn't because they'd retreated from the late-afternoon heat. Jordan saw Travis, Margot, and then finally Jade in a line down the aisle. Each had a horse attached to the cross ties and was busy unwrapping the bandages in silence. Jade moved with an extra urgency, her hands flying around Aspen's hind leg.

When the loosened quilted wrap fell to the cement floor, she scooped it and the other bandages up and carried them over to the side of Aspen's stall, unsnapped the cross ties, and walked her horse into the stall.

"There. I'm done," she announced, her voice carrying in the tense silence.

"You're done?" Margot asked, from where she was kneeling beside Saxon's leg. "What about Aspen's braids?"

"I'll deal with them in the morning. Sweet William's, too," she replied, not even looking at Margot as she marched past her. Spotting Jordan and Owen, she stuck out her chin pugnaciously.

"Hi, Jade," Jordan said.

Echoing her, Owen also added, "I like your new hair."

"Thanks," she muttered. To Jordan she merely gave a long look.

"And how about your saddle bag? Your tackbox?" Margot asked, rising to her feet and coming up behind her.

Jade didn't turn around. "I don't have time."

Margot came around to Jordan's side and crossed her arms. "May I ask where you're so fired up to go?"

"The library."

As one, the adults looked at her.

"The library closes at five on Saturdays, Jade," Travis said, joining them.

Jade scowled even as an embarrassed flush crawled over her cheeks. "So I'm not going to the library. Whatever. But I'm still out of here."

"Well, I'd really appreciate knowing where."

"I don't see why I have to tell you. I'm almost eighteen."

"You won't be eighteen for another six months, Jade," Margot said, and from the evenness of her tone, Jordan knew how hard she was trying to be patient. "Until then I have to act as your guardian—"

Jade gave a snort of disbelief. "More like my prison guard. I'm tired of being locked up here with you and Jordan watching everything I do. I don't need your permission to go out."

Travis cleared his throat. "Jade, all Margot's asking is where you're going. Not an unreasonable request."

Perhaps it was because it was Travis speaking, his deep voice rumbling with authority for all the mildness of his observation. Jade pursed her lips as if tasting something bitter and then, with obvious reluctance, said, "I'm going to the movies with Blair and Courtney and some other friends."

"With Blair?" Margot blurted.

"Oh, Jade, are you sure—" Jordan began.

"I knew it. I just *knew* you'd be this way. Why do you think I didn't want to tell you? Because you and Jordan would immediately go into tragic mode."

"Because we've already seen that Blair's not a good person—"

"Compared to whom? My mom, maybe?" Jade sneered. "Compared to me? For God's sake you don't even know Blair."

"Maybe I don't know her well," Margot said, "but I know you, and you are *not* a bad person. It is important that you stay out of trouble, though. Remember what Officer Cooper said."

Jade rolled her eyes. "You're too much. What do you think he's going to do, arrest me for going to the movies with my friends? This is really boring. Why don't you just try leaving me alone for once? I can take care of myself."

"Jade—"

"No. I'm done here." Turning to Travis, she said, "I'll be back later."

They listened to the scrape of her boots against the concrete floor. Then it changed as she hit the graveled courtyard and broke into a run, making her getaway.

"If she really thinks I'm her prison guard, why can't I put a microchip in her cellphone and track her," Margot asked no one in particular. Moving to Saxon's hind leg, she bent down and began unwrapping his dark blue bandage, her hands moving with furious speed.

"Because Jade would somehow figure out what you'd done and toss the thing in the river. Or set it on fire. Or run over it with her car," Jordan said.

"Then how about one of those electronic ankle bracelets? Damn it, why can't she see what she's doing to herself?"

"That might be asking a little too much, given her current frame of mind," she replied quietly.

"It kills me that she wants to screw up her life by hanging out with those bitchy girls. They're not interested in being her friends." Still kneeling beside Saxon, she slumped her shoulders in despair.

"Come here, darling."

With a shaky breath Margot rose to her feet and walked into Travis's open arms, burying her face against his chest. Watching them, Jordan knew she'd have given anything to know Owen loved her so deeply, that he'd be there for her, forever.

OWEN WRAPPED HIS HANDS around the edges of the old stove. "Ready? On the count of three," he said as with a strong push, he and Jesse tipped it backward so that Doug could slide the dolly beneath it. Setting it back down, he and Jesse stepped back.

"So how was your weekend, Owen?" Jesse asked, wiping his forehead with the bottom of his T-shirt. As Ned had predicted, the temperature had skyrocketed, and the kitchen was as hot as the oven they were removing.

"It was good," Owen said. Damn good. Even with Jordan worried as hell about Jade, it had been near-perfect, but Owen didn't want to go overboard in his response since Doug and Jesse had picked up on the fact that he and Jordan had a thing going on. "And yours?"

"Excellent. I hit this bar on the edge of town Friday night. Different kind of scene from your typical Warburg watering hole."

"You mean you didn't have to dig out your seersucker jacket to fit in?" Doug grinned.

"Didn't have to flash my Amex gold card, either. So what surprised me was that some of the women there were extra fine, way above average. It's too bad this job will be finished soon. I wouldn't mind getting to know a few of them better."

"Something tells me you'll make the most of these last couple of weeks," Owen said. He, too, felt a regret that he'd spent so many nights working like the devil on the house. The renovation was wrapping up sooner than he wished.

"I'll do my best." Jesse grinned.

"So what time's Jordan coming over?" Doug asked as he began rolling the stove toward the back door.

"In about an hour." The jolt of anticipation that coursed through him was no less heady for being familiar. Owen had been with her practically all weekend, yet still couldn't wait to see her.

"Good," Doug grunted as they maneuvered the stove over the threshold. "We should be almost finished getting everything out of the kitchen by then and be set to pull up the flooring. Jordan'll get a kick out of seeing the old wood exposed. The kids coming, too?"

"Yeah." Owen didn't even mind that. Being here this afternoon would provide a distraction for the kids, since Jade continued to refuse to give them riding lessons. Nothing bothered him about Jade's acting out as much as this. Anything she dished out for Margot and Jordan, her primary targets, was okay. They could take it; they were grown-ups. But to drag the kids into her battle against the world was plain mean. Someone would have to give Jade a talking-to soon.

They worked steadily, dismantling the kitchen and carting the appliances and cabinets to the truck. The noise of their efforts masked that of Jordan's arrival, so it wasn't until he heard the stampede of little feet, Olivia's high-pitched squeal, and Max's signature "Hiya, Owen!" and "Hey, can I do that, too?" that he knew their peaceful grunt work was at an end.

Owen straightened and put his crowbar down. He gave Jordan a quick smile that didn't come close to expressing how glad he was to see her before answering Max. "I think this cabinet might be a little heavy for you, Max."

"I'm really strong." Max came over and wrapped his hand about Owen's crowbar and lifted it about an inch, his body wobbling with the effort. "See?"

"Yes, very impressive," he said.

"Hey, Owen." Jesse grinned, nodding at Olivia. "We didn't know you had such a fan club." Olivia had wrapped her arms about his leg as if she, well, Owen couldn't figure out why she often did what she did, but as sweaty and hot as he was, what he did know was that he wasn't going to make himself twice as hot by lifting her into his arms. But deciding that freeing his leg of Olivia was an exercise in futility, he let her be, ignoring Jesse's wide grin.

"Olivia likes Owen a lot," Jordan said. "We brought iced tea."

"And cookies. We baked them after lunch," Kate offered shyly.

Jordan was brilliant, Owen decided. After being in Jesse and Doug's company these past weeks, she knew they liked sweets even more than Max did. And right now he could easily guzzle a half gallon of her iced tea. "That's great. We'll take a break once we've gotten this cabinet into the truck."

"Can I help carry it?" Max asked, renewing his attempt to lift the crowbar.

"Wait until Owen and Jesse have gotten the cabinet onto the dolly, Max. Then maybe you can help push it outside. Olivia, you need to let go of Owen and come here. No, you're too little to help. Kate, why don't you hold the door open and then you can make sure Doug and Jesse are pushing the dolly up the truck ramp properly? Olivia and I will go get the cookies and the iced tea. And, Max, you have to listen and do what Owen says, or you won't be able to help."

"Okay, Mommy."

Her little boy was in seventh heaven, Jordan thought, as she watched Max take a place between Owen and Doug, his little hands flat against the side of the wooden cabinet, making very manly grunts as he and the men pushed it along the floor to where Kate was holding the back door before rolling it over the plywood that had been laid over the ground.

When Max reached the truck's ramp, Jordan told him to come away, which he did with the greatest reluctance. Fortunately, seeing the contents of the truck's interior was sufficiently distracting. "What's all that stuff doing in there?"

"Those are the appliances and countertops we removed from the kitchen and butler's pantry to make room for what your mom ordered," Owen said. "We don't need these parts but other people might, so after work Doug's going to drive the truck to a place near Washington where people can come and get them and install them in their own kitchens. That way these things don't go to waste." He paused and, evidently seeing that Max hadn't quite grasped his explanation, added, "It's kind of like recycling."

"Oh, yeah," Max said brightening. "We do that at school and at home. And I told my teacher, Miss Farber, that at the barn Tito puts the horse poop in a special place so that Patrick can use it for the flowers in our garden. She said that's recycling, too. We have a lot of horse poop."

"Horse poop happens," Owen replied, hiding his grin somewhat more successfully than Jesse or Doug.

"Yeah," said Max. When the cabinet was stowed in the truck's belly, he asked, "So what do we now, Owen?"

"Well, right now I think we should drink something cold and then it'll be time to pull up the flooring."

"Neato."

Owen felt another grin spread across his face. He had to hand it to Max. He definitely attacked life with gusto. There were few things didn't strike him as "neato." Even during the break they took outside, in the shade of a large copper beech, Max was a bubbling fountain of enthusiasm.

Circling its wide trunk with a cup of grape juice in one hand and a cookie in the other, he said, "That's a really big tree," thrusting his cookie at it for emphasis. "Have you climbed it, Owen?"

Owen glanced up at the tree. Max was right. The tree was big, with an impressive canopy and long limbs, the lowest about five feet off the ground. "No, I haven't."

"We could climb it."

"I think we need to deal with the kitchen floor first. That's going to be fun for your mom." And he let his gaze stray to Jordan, something he'd been trying to limit doing with the kids and Doug and Jesse around. She was sitting with Olivia plunked in the middle of her lap and was showing her daughter the purplish gold of the beech leaf. Her reddish head was bent close to Olivia's light blond one, and the sight did something strange to his heart. What was it that made her more beautiful to him than any other woman, even when she had a toddler planted in her lap?

"But after that we can climb the tree, right, Owen? I want to go really high up, okay?"

"Sure," he said, his eyes never leaving Jordan.

The old linoleum was a bitch and half to pull up. There was no easy way to do it except with a scraper and warm sudsy water to loosen the adhesive. Luckily, Kate, Max, and even Olivia were more than happy to go back and forth from the buckets filled with warm water carrying dripping wet sponges to the areas Owen had peeled back, while Doug and Jesse went at the moistened glue with scrapers. Jordan, wielding a mop, cleaned up the excess water and picked up the pieces of lino, dropping them into a garbage bag.

Within minutes everyone was soaked, but Jesse and Doug didn't seem to mind too much, probably because Jordan was so excited about the wide-planked floor that was slowly emerging.

"Gosh, it's going to look superb when it's sanded and finished," she said happily.

"Can we help with that, too, Mommy?" Kate asked.

"No, that's a messy job."

"As opposed to this," Owen grinned.

"As opposed to this," Jordan echoed, returning his grin as she swiped the side of her face with her bare arm. With her hair in a ponytail she looked impossibly young, more like Kate's older sister than her mother.

Having peeled up a long strip, Doug sat back on his haunches and took a gulp of his iced tea. "The next time we run into a lino floor, we're definitely calling you guys. Right, Owen?"

"This job's going faster than any I can remember."

"Did you hear that, kids? Owen and Doug think you're good workers."

"I like working." Max squeezed a large puddle of water onto the glue. "When we're done, Owen and I are gonna climb that tree all the way to the top."

They were tackling the remaining stretch of linoleum, near the kitchen's back door, when Kate ran over to Jordan and whispered in her ear.

"Of course, sweetie," Jordan said. "And let's bring Olivia, too. I think she could use a diaper change. Excuse us, gentlemen, we're going to use the bathroom. Max, do you need to go?"

"No." He shook his head vehemently even as he crossed his legs.

"Perhaps we better try anyway. And I want to show you the upstairs. You haven't seen those rooms yet. Owen removed the wallpaper in the bedrooms and Doug and Jesse built really nice shelves for the closets. Then you can come back downstairs." She held out her hand for Max, and the four of them went down the hall, the children chattering away.

"She's got a nice way with her kids," Doug said approvingly.

"Yes, she's a great mother." Jordan was great, period. Owen grabbed hold of a strip of saturated linoleum and pulled it back with a grunt.

"Jesus Christ, I'm soaked. I don't know whether it's from sweat because it's hotter than Hades or because Olivia kept dribbling her sponge on me instead of the floor," Jesse said.

"Olivia did pretty well for someone who's not even two." Owen was as surprised as Jesse to find himself defending her. Then, because Jesse was grinning at him as if he'd just announced that he liked postcards adorned with fuzzy kittens and koala bears, he said, "You guys both look somewhat worse for wear. Why don't I finish scraping this last section myself?"

Doug checked his watch. "If we leave now, we can make it to the Habitat ReStore before closing time. What do you think, Jesse?"

"Are you asking me if I want to quit work early and take a ride in an air-conditioned cab? I am definitely up for that." With a flourish he handed the scraper to Owen. "Have at it, boss."

"I'll see you guys tomorrow."

"Bright and early. Say good-bye to Jordan for us."

"And Olivia, too," Jesse added with a laugh.

"Will do," he replied, already bending over and beginning to scrape.

It seemed like only a minute later, Max literally jumped into his line of vision, his sneakers making a squishy landing inches from his scraper. "Hey, Owen, let's go climb that tree now. I want to go as high as I can."

"I'll be with you in a minute, Max. I just have to finish this bit of the floor first. Why don't you go find your mom?"

"Nah, she's showing Kate and Wiv the bedrooms. I want to climb the tree." His sneakers did a jig of impatience.

"We will. You just have to wait a little bit longer." He drew out the final syllable in a growl of frustration as he applied his scraper more forcefully. But this patch hadn't gotten as saturated as the rest of the floor. The lino wasn't budging. With a silent curse he reached for the sponge and squeezed some more water on it. "Hold on a few more minutes, Max," he said, not looking up from the damned flooring.

Owen had no idea how much time elapsed while he battled with the remaining adhesive. Yet when he straightened he was abruptly aware of two things. One, Max was no longer in the kitchen and, two, Jordan was coming down the stairs with just the girls—if Max had been with them Owen would definitely have heard his voice.

The hair on the back of his neck rose as he was gripped by a sudden, terrible premonition. Jumping to his feet, he dropped the scraper onto the damp floor and sprinted out the door, shouting "Max!" at the top of his lungs.

The first thing he saw was that one of the folding chairs Doug and Jesse sat on at lunch had been dragged over to the base of the tree, just beneath the lowest branch. "Jesus, no. Please no," his mind cried as again he shouted, "Max!"

Behind him Jordan's anxious voice echoed his call.

Then came Max's high-pitched voice. "Look at me, Owen! See how high I am? I'm really high!"

His heart leapt to his throat. Damn it, he couldn't see through the dense foliage. "Don't you move, Max!" he yelled hoarsely. "You wait till I get there!" The twenty feet remaining to the tree stretched like a football field before him.

Then Max's voice came again, and to Owen's panicked brain seemed to come from far too high above. "I think I wanna come down now."

Terrified Owen tried to run faster. In the unfolding of this nightmarish scene, however, his legs seemed to have turned to lead, unable to close the distance. Jordan seemed similarly afflicted for she was still behind him. He could hear her harsh, ragged panting.

"Owen! I need help! Mommy!"

"Max!" they cried in unison.

Then Owen was at the tree, ducking under its broad canopy, but keeping his eyes fixed above, scanning the pewter limbs. To his right, on the other side of the tree, a good fifteen feet above his head, he heard the yelped cry of "Help!" that turned into a shriek of, "I'm fall—"

He lunged toward Max's tumbling body. But too late.

Arms outflung, Max hit the twig and leaf-laden ground with a thud, followed by an agonized scream.

"Max!" Jordan reached him a heartbeat after Owen.

"It hurts, Mommy! Mommy, Mommy, it hurts!" he wailed, hunched in a tight ball of pain.

"Where does it hurt, Max? Tell Mommy where."

"My arm."

Crouched beside Owen, Jordan rocked forward, her hands reaching out. "Can I see—"

"No, don't touch it! Don't! It hurts so much."

"I won't touch, I promise, Max, but I need to see it."

Slowly, he lowered his right arm to reveal the left one lying across his chest.

Owen sucked in a breath. The back of Max's arm was covered in blood, but from the odd angle with which his wrist lay on his heaving tummy, Owen knew that more was wrong with his arm than a really nasty cut. "We need to get him to the hospital," he said, leaning forward to scoop him up.

"No! Don't touch him!"

Owen froze at Jordan's sharp command. She blamed him of course, but still—

"Max, do you hurt anywhere else? Your neck? Your back? Your head? Max, you've got to tell Mommy."

Jordan's words offered him an undeserved sense of relief as he realized she was trying to make sure Max wasn't injured elsewhere.

"No, but my arm really hurts and I'm *bleeding*." He began crying again, very softly.

"Yes, I know, sweetheart. But you're going to be okay. Listen to Mommy now, Max. Owen is going to pick you up and carry you to the car. It's going to hurt, but you're very brave and we need to get you to the hospital so the doctor can fix your arm." To Owen she said, "Let me get Olivia in her car seat and then you can pass him to me. I think it's best if I hold him while you drive."

He gave a tight nod.

His every muscle strained with the effort to lift Max gently off the ground. Cradling his trembling body against his chest, he moved as quickly and smoothly as he could to the car.

Despite his precaution, Max moaned. "*Ow*. It hurts, Owen."

His throat constricting, he brushed his lips against Max's sweaty forehead and said hoarsely, "I know, Max. Hang in there, okay? Once we get to the hospital the doctors are going to make the hurt go away."

"I don't like doctors." If possible Max's voice was even smaller. "Sometimes they give me shots."

It felt like he'd swallowed a lump of coal. "I don't like shots, either, but the doctors at the hospital are really good, and if they have to give you a shot, it'll only be to make the hurt go away. And your mom's going to be with you."

"You'll be there, too?"

Owen nodded. "I'll be there, too."

"Okay."

At that single bravely resigned word, Owen shuddered as something grabbed tight around his heart, squeezing it painfully.

It was a white-knuckled drive to the hospital, with Owen gripping the minivan's steering wheel so tightly his fingers ached. Behind him Olivia, who'd been crying steadily since seeing her brother hurt and bloodied, had now added writhing and bucking to her tears of fright as she tried to escape her car seat. Kate, usually so quiet, kept asking, "Is Max going to be okay, Mommy?"

How Jordan maintained her calm in all of this, especially with Max's moans of pain spiking every time the minivan's inferior suspension rolled over a damned pothole, was beyond Owen. But after calling both Richard and Margot to let them know they were heading to the emergency room, she stroked Max's forehead while holding a cold compress to his elevated arm (that she'd had the wits to grab the compress from the first-aid kit in the back of her car and a pillow for his arm showed an amazing presence of mind), her voice rock-steady as she told her children again and again that everything was going to be all right. Lots of people broke their arms. Aunt Margot had broken hers riding Suzy Q. Ned, too, when he fell off Stoneleigh.

"Why, I bet Owen broke his arm when he was little."

He would have lied to back Jordan up, but he didn't have to. "I broke my arm playing soccer. I was nine, so a bit older than you, Max, but not as brave."

"Did your mommy take you to the hospital?"

His mother and father had been hosting cocktails followed by a dinner with various diplomats and European intellectuals. A duke was to be in attendance. His nanny had gone in their place, then Owen and she had taken a taxi home. "Sure."

Jordan met his gaze briefly in the rearview mirror and actually smiled at him. How could she when he'd caused her little boy to get hurt?

"Take the next exit and you'll see signs for the hospital."

In the emergency room, they processed Max quickly. As the nurse was examining Max's arm, Jordan turned to Owen. "They're not going to allow us all into the room when the doctor comes."

No, and setting the arm would be a scary thing for kids to see, and Owen was sure a cut that bad would require stitches.

"I'll take them." He picked Olivia up and she buried her wet face in his neck.

"Thanks." Jordan then dropped to her knees. "Kate, honey, you and Olivia are going to sit with Owen in the waiting room while doctors fix Max's arm. It might take a while, but you need to be a big girl and help Owen with Olivia."

"I will, Mommy," Kate said, sounding just like Jordan, so serious and sweet.

Jordan gave her a fierce hug. Rising, she kissed Olivia's red cheek. To Owen she gave a lopsided smile. "I'm sorry about this—"

He let her child get injured and *she* was apologizing?

"He'll be all right," she said.

Owen nodded, feeling sick to his gut.

She left them, rejoining Max, who'd been lifted onto a gurney to protect his arm. She walked beside him as the nurse rolled it down the corridor and out of sight.

Not knowing what else to do, Owen took the girls over to the vending machine and bought some M&M's, then did his best to entertain Kate and Olivia in the waiting room by reading a story Jordan had remembered to grab from the back of the car and shove into the diaper bag she carried into the hospital emergency room with them. He could only thank God that Olivia's diaper was dry, though Owen bet Kate could have handled diapering her baby sister herself.

As they sat in the hideously ugly waiting room, it was painfully clear to Owen that practically anyone, even a scared six-year-old girl, was better suited to the role of care-giver than he. A fact that had already been drilled home when Kate solemnly warned him against buying the peanut M&M's because Olivia might choke on them.

It made his blood run cold how close he'd come to harming yet another of Jordan's children.

He read the words to a story about a dormouse called Dudley, who bit into a strawberry that turned out to be a dog's pink nose, surprising them both very much.

If he'd been asked to repeat what he'd just read aloud, though, he'd have flunked. His mind was focused on Jordan and Max on the other side of the peachy-gray metal doors. They'd be working on him by now; the doctors wouldn't keep a frightened little boy waiting. Had he been okay when they gave him the anesthetic?

Kate turned the page of the book for him, which was good since he hadn't realized he'd come to the bottom of it. The mouse was filling up his tree home with acorns. Then he was crawling into his snug little bed and falling asleep to dream happy acorn-filled dreams. Owen knew that tonight when he at last crawled into bed, he'd be dreaming of Max falling out of that tree, and of him rushing to catch that tumbling body before it thudded to the ground, and being too late, just like today. His dream would be no more horrific than reality.

God, it could so easily have been Max's neck that snapped instead of his forearm. The thought made Own want to vomit.

Under the glare of the banked fluorescent lights the truth couldn't be ignored any longer.

He was in love with Jordan.

Acknowledging this, Owen made himself admit that his love for her had been growing inside him for weeks, most likely since the day he spied her struggling to overcome her tears in front of the flower shop. All the conflicting emotions he'd felt toward Jordan, his attempts to maintain his distance and remain uninvolved, had been vanquished by this strange and powerfully intense need to be with her.

These the first stirrings of a man blind to love.

But now he saw, and it frightened the daylights out of him.

He'd spent so many years avoiding emotional attachments that to discover now this endless desire for Jordan, this dependence on her for the warm wave of happiness, the sense of completeness he felt when she was with him, made him question if he'd ever be the same. This beautiful, giving woman had changed him forever.

What scared him even more was how he'd come to feel about the children. He wasn't just in love with Jordan, he loved them, too. Kate for her shy earnestness; Max for his gusto; Olivia for her oddly beguiling weirdness.

They were wonderful kids. They were amazing. And this afternoon had shown Owen beyond a shadow of a doubt how disastrously bad he would be at caring for them, at keeping them safe. He was too much the product of his self-absorbed parents to be trusted with such enormous responsibility. The thought of failing Jordan, of making another mistake, one that might result in Kate or Olivia being injured, was too frightening and all too damned likely.

There was only one solution. He was going to have to do what he used to do best: disengage.

Time lost its meaning. Once Dudley the door mouse's adventures had been digested, Owen honestly didn't know how long he spent leafing through outdated magazines and talking to Kate about the pictures in them—thanks to her aunt Margot, Kate had a discerning eye when it came to fashion photos—and saying "Uh-huh" to whatever Olivia said.

After that activity grew old, they walked the wide corridor, visiting the vending machine to buy Oreos and then the water fountain to try and wash off the black smears coating Olivia's face. Then they returned to their plastic and metal seats to stare at the metal doors, willing Jordan and Max's reappearance.

When Olivia became antsy, Owen became desperate. The last thing Jordan needed was to hear her daughter's hysterical shrieks—and Olivia could shriek like nobody's business. Ripping two pages out of the oldest magazines he could find, he folded the paper into airplanes and showed Kate how to angle her toss so that the airplane floated for a few seconds before nosediving into the industrial carpeting.

Olivia was distracted by the twin planes enough to race

after them, like a two-legged golden retriever, grabbing them off the carpet and then running back to Owen with them. They often returned too mangled to fly again, but Owen was more than willing to keep folding paper airplanes as long as it kept her tears at bay for a few minutes more.

They had tossed paper planes into the air for what could have been eons or merely minutes when the metal doors swung open, and there was Jordan carrying Max on her hip. A blue sling covered his arm.

Both looked exhausted, but Jordan smiled as the girls rushed over.

The children talked at once, Kate wanting to know what the sling was for, Olivia saying "Mommy" and "Max" over and over again. Max, despite his ordeal, had regained enough of his usual brio to catalog his injuries.

"I have a broken wrist. The doctor said it was a di— What's it called, Mommy?"

"A distal radius fracture." To Owen she mouthed, "A clean break."

Owen felt something unclench in his gut.

"The doctor gave me a splint but in three days I'm going to his office so he can put a cast on my arm. When's three days, Mommy?"

"That'll be Thursday."

"Yeah. And I got fourteen stitches."

"Fourteen's a lot," Kate said, wide-eyed.

Yes, it was, Owen agreed silently, and his gut tightened all over again. Because of his negligence not only had he ruined Max's summer, he'd scarred him, too.

"And you know what? The doctor told Mommy I have to take a bath with a garbage bag!"

"A garbage bag?" Kate repeated.

"The bag's to keep his arm from getting wet, sweetie."

"Oh."

Just then a nurse approached them. "Ms. Radcliffe? These

are the instructions for taking care of Max's wound and his fracture." She handed Jordan a sheaf of papers. "You can call Dr. Barrett's office tomorrow morning to schedule an appointment for Max in three days' time. Until then, you'll want to keep the arm elevated as much as possible to prevent swelling and apply ice, too. If Max starts to feel discomfort, Dr. Barrett recommends children's Tylenol every four to six hours, but not more than four doses in a twenty-four-hour period."

Jordan nodded. "All right."

"If you have any questions or concerns, you can call Dr. Barrett's office."

"Thank you very much."

"You're welcome." She smiled and glanced at Owen. "You have a wonderful little boy."

"I'm afraid he's not mine." And never would be, he thought hollowly. Jordan deserved a man she could to turn to for everything in her life.

"Oh! I'm sorry—"

Not as sorry as he was. He should have listened to his instincts and kept far away from Jordan Radcliffe. The thought of letting her go, of never being a part of her and the children's lives was already slicing away at his insides, as painful as anything he'd ever experienced.

The nurse had shifted her attention to Max. "You be careful climbing those trees."

He nodded solemnly. "The next time Owen and I climb that tree I'm gonna be real careful."

By the time Max's cast was off, he would be gone, Owen thought. Until then, he would make sure his schedule was crammed full, not leaving himself any time to visit Rosewood. With his departure, the weeks would pass, turning into months, and Owen would become someone Max talked about only occasionally, maybe when he was building with his blocks.

It would take longer than months for Owen to forget this

little boy or the way Jordan fit in his arms when she gave herself to him, withholding nothing, her passion a perfect match.

It might take him forever.

Barely five miles from Rosewood, the children succumbed to sleep, their heads resting heavily, awkwardly on their shoulders. Jordan, too, felt wave after wave of fatigue crashing over her as the adrenaline drained out of her system. She wasn't sure she'd have been physically able to make the drive from the hospital back to Rosewood.

With Owen behind the wheel she'd been able to relax—as far as she was able—while quieting the kids enough to phone Margot to let her know they were on their way back. When she'd first called, Margot had wanted to come and join them at the hospital, but Jordan had told her that given Jade's current state, keeping the appointment with Stuart Wilde was as important. She phoned Richard, too, giving him an update and striving to remain upbeat in the face of his repeated questions about the severity of Max's injury.

"The orthopedist said Max's break was very clean and that he should have no problem recovering from it. Yes, he'll get the cast on Thursday. The splint is to make sure the swelling has a chance to come down. I'm to give him children's Tylenol. No, nothing stronger. The stitches? Fourteen. No, it's not that big, just a line above his elbow. The ER had a plastic surgeon on call, and he made the stitches really tiny so that Max's scar will be minimal. They'll be removed in ten days. No, the doctor said the cast wouldn't interfere with them. Swimming? I don't know, but I'll ask. The accident was my fault. I shouldn't have allowed Max to go downstairs without me. But he's really all right, Richard. Would you like to speak to him?"

She'd passed her cell to Max, who was happy to retell the day's adventure to his father. While he talked about

needles and shots and holding Mommy's hand, she'd studied Owen in the rearview mirror.

He was staring ahead, negotiating the highway traffic.
Twin furrows were etched between his brows as he frowned
in concentration. Or was that a frown of irritation? After the
hours they'd spent in the hospital, he'd be more than justified.

The last thing Owen would have envisioned when he offered her a no-strings-attached liaison would have been
making an emergency trip to the hospital for her son, serving not only as a porter and chauffeur but as a guardian for
her little girls. Today had been a tangled, sticky mess of
complications and unwanted responsibilities if ever there
was one. And Owen had the bloodstained, chocolate-
streaked, tear-blotted shirt to prove it. She felt bad for
having burdened him with so much, but also immensely
grateful.

She also knew that she was more in love with him than
ever.

In definite need of a shower and a shave, Owen had never
looked more handsome in her eyes. Or more wonderful.

When calamity struck after her son's disobedient solo adventure, Owen had been there for her and her three children. His steadiness had made it easier for her to stifle her
own panic and focus on the kids. She kept remembering
how Owen had carried Max to the car and then into the
hospital's emergency entrance, holding him with a care that
pierced her heart.

If she hadn't already been in love with Owen, that single
act would have clinched it.

He'd been there in her hour of need, and not once had he
leveled any criticism or blame at her for not having watched
her young son more vigilantly.

This afternoon had served as an important parental
wake-up call for Jordan. Max had reached a new stage

where his growing self-confidence and independence made him think he didn't have to heed instructions. On a horse breeding farm, far more serious things could befall Max if he continued like this. Once she was assured that Max was fine and that she had her emotions fully under control, they were going to have a talk about listening to and obeying adults.

But first she needed to let Owen know how grateful she was. "Owen," she said quietly.

"Hmm?" he asked, his eyes never leaving the road.

"I don't know how to thank you enough—"

"No problem. Glad to be of help." Still staring straight ahead, he flicked the indicator and made a left onto Piper's Road. "What time is it?"

She glanced at her watch. "Six-thirty. I'm sorry to have put you through such an afternoon. You were wonderful—"

"Six-thirty already. At least the traffic will have thinned out. I should get to Alexandria before eight."

"You're going back to Alexandria? Tonight?" she asked in surprise.

He nodded. "With the kitchen gone and the master bath being ripped out tomorrow, I've decided it'll be easier to move back into my apartment."

A strange confusion filled her. She told herself it was probably just exhaustion that was making her feel worried and apprehensive. "So you won't be staying with us? I thought you would be."

"Thanks, but no. You've got enough going on here. I don't want to get in the way."

The vague apprehension turned into something hard and cold as it snaked about her heart, pulling tight. She knew him well enough that "I don't want to get in the way" in Owen-speak meant: "I don't want to be involved in the three-ring circus of your family life." And though her mind had begun to grasp what was happening, for some reason her mouth still opened, letting the pitiable words slip out. "You wouldn't be in the way at all. Really. We'd love to have you—"

"That's nice of you, but I think we'll just be complicating things unnecessarily if I come and stay at Rosewood."

She supposed this was as gentle a way to be told a relationship was over as one could expect. Now that she understood what Owen was up to, she could even predict his next words.

But if she actually had to hear him say that it had all been great fun but it might be better if they called it quits between them, she might very well begin bawling louder than ten Olivias combined.

Unfortunately the tears were starting anyway. "Of course," she said, nodding vigorously so he wouldn't see them. "Now that we're in the homestretch of finishing work on Hawk Hill, I imagine you'll begin focusing on other projects."

Other projects, other women. The thought made Jordan want to scream in anguish, even as she reminded herself that Owen had never pretended to be interested in a long-term relationship. And he'd never lied and said he loved her.

Unfortunately she couldn't glean a speck of comfort from Owen's particular brand of honesty. The pain of knowing he actually planned to end the relationship was a hundred times worse than she'd anticipated. More tears pooled and she turned her head to stare blindly out the window.

Owen cast a sidelong glance at Jordan. God only knew he didn't want to hurt her, which was why this was necessary. To delay breaking things off would only make it worse. How much worse he couldn't imagine. It already felt as if his guts were being slowly shredded.

"Yes, I'll be very busy over the next couple of weeks leading up to the Open House," he said, forcing himself to look away from Jordan.

Yes, she echoed silently, he'd be busy running away from

four people who'd come to love him, and a flash of anger burst to life inside her, stronger even than the fear squeezing her heart.

The other day she had told Ned that after the heartbreak of her failed marriage, she didn't have it in her to fight for a man's love again. But maybe she'd been wrong.

Thanks to the infuriating man seated beside her, she was a stronger woman now. Owen had done so much for her; didn't he deserve to have her fight for him? So they could both win?

Perhaps Owen needed a taste of his own medicine. She'd learned a lot about acting this past year; she could play at being emotionally detached. Summoning every ounce of skill she possessed, she gave him a blithe smile.

"I understand. It's probably time for me to begin dating other men anyway. You wouldn't want me to get too attached to you."

"No. I mean *yes*—" he broke off.

His frown was sweetly satisfying.

"Of course you'll be a very hard act to follow," Jordan said lightly as if they were discussing his wallpaper-removing technique instead of his lovemaking. "Here's the driveway to Hawk Hill. Why don't you pull in so I can drop you off? You'll get to Alexandria that much sooner."

Owen's frown deepened. "That's all right. You'll need help getting the kids out of the car and everything."

"Oh, don't worry about us. Margot probably won't be back from Stuart Wilde's yet, but Travis will be there. We'll be fine."

Owen couldn't seem to unclench his jaw. Nor could he summon a logical excuse why he needed to make sure Max was okay when he woke up other than that he'd be worried about him the whole way back to Alexandria, so he did as Jordan suggested. Pulling up next to his Audi, he put the van in park, leaving the engine running so as not to rouse the kids. Then he and Jordan got out.

Jordan circled the van. Owen was watching her warily as if he didn't know quite what to expect from her: a slap, tears, or more seemingly cheerful indifference. A rattled Owen Gage was a good thing.

If he believed he could walk away from what they had together, shutting the door to his heart in the same way he shut the door on the houses he built and restored, simply handing over the keys and moving on, he was quite mistaken.

She loved him with her heart and soul, damn it.

Just because he was too emotionally obtuse to see how good, how special it was between them, she wasn't.

Her thoughts propelled her, brought her toe-to-toe to where he stood. She had a fleeting wish that she looked less like she'd spent the past three hours in an emergency room, but the flare in Owen's eyes, that set the flecks in them sparkling like topaz, told her he wasn't immune to her nearness, disheveled and rumpled though she was.

She leaned closer to him, loving the heat of his solid muscular body. "I really can't thank you enough for how wonderful you were today. In case you didn't know it, you've attained hero status in Max, Kate, and Olivia's eyes. They adore you. And I . . ."

Intentionally she let the sentence trail off into the stillness of the late afternoon. Sliding her hands up his shirt, she lightly caressed the stubble of his five-o'clock shadow.

At her touch, Owen had become like a sun-warmed stone. And beneath her fingers his pulse pounded heavily, telling her everything she wanted to know.

Arching into him, she tilted her head and raised her lips to his. In an achingly slow glide, she brushed her mouth against his, back and forth, stoking the passion she knew was there for her. The hammering of his pulse redoubled. Pressing closer still, she traced the seam of his mouth with her tongue.

A deep rumble, part moan, part groan escaped him. The

sound was desperate, as if he were being rent in two. He opened his mouth, drinking her in even as his tongue thrust, meeting hers.

The frantic tangle of their tongues mating sent shivers rippling through her. Trembling, she poured her love and passion for him into the kiss until they were both breathless from the desire that never failed to ignite between them. A desire made wondrous and sweet because it came from the heart. She understood this. She wanted Owen to, as well.

She allowed herself a last caress over the lean planes of his beard-roughened cheeks and one final liquid graze of their lips before stepping back. She couldn't help that her smile was tremulous. How could it not be when Owen made her feel so much? When she longed to tell him how she loved him?

But if she told him now, she was sure it would only cement his decision to end their relationship. Better to keep him off-balance while she waged her battle for his heart.

"So I guess I'll see you around. Have a good drive back to Alexandria," she said, slipping into the driver's seat before she gave into the urge to fling her arms about his neck and tell him what was in her heart—that she loved everything about him.

Only the stunned look on his face as he watched her turn the car around kept her foot steady on the accelerator. But as she drove away from Hawk Hill, her lips moved in a fervent prayer that she wasn't wrong about Owen's feelings for her. Otherwise the man who had restored her broken heart would be walking away with it.

TWENTY-TWO

IT TOOK OWEN ten days to comprehend that Jordan might actually be *trying* to drive him insane.

He should have been alerted to this when she'd dropped him off at Hawk Hill with her diabolical "And I . . ." She'd left him hanging, to be tormented by the wealth of possibilities her unfinished sentence left in his mind.

She'd played with his mind and his body, kissing him with a passion that stole his breath as it robbed him of his heart. Then, with nothing more than a "See you," she was gone, driving away, without having told him how she felt.

He'd wanted to sprint after the minivan and demand she finish her sentence. But he hadn't, because if she said what he craved to hear, that she loved him, it wouldn't have changed anything. He wasn't the kind of man Jordan needed.

Over the next week, he'd followed his tried-and-true prescription for easing his way out of a relationship. He threw himself into work. But instead of wandering over to Rosewood afterward, he drove back to his Alexandria apartment, a place he'd come to despise. Once there, Owen did his best to block Jordan from his thoughts or let himself imagine what she and the kids might be doing at that particular moment.

It would have been easier to rewire his brain than not think of her.

The realization forced him to recognize how much he'd

changed since meeting Jordan. Whereas before he'd been his own starring concern, now everything in his life seemed to come back to her.

Everything he cared about, that is.

Nights were spent in self-imposed exile in his apartment, a perfectly fine space, which he now saw to be as arid as the rest of his life. It was the apartment of someone with no roots or connections, with the impersonality of a Japanese sleeping pod.

But being at Hawk Hill was worse. Though he did his best to avoid being there when she was present, now that the house was nearing completion, every room he entered reminded him of her—her talent, her keen eye, her wonderful taste. It wasn't simply that her selections suited the architecture. It was that her choices for the décor and furniture that began filling the rooms pleased some part of him that he hadn't ever acknowledged existed.

And how could he not imagine Jordan lying naked in the master bedroom's king-size mahogany bed, or covered with scented bubbles in the sunken bathtub that was large enough to fit two? How could he not picture Jordan supine on the brown speckled granite kitchen counter, naked and trembling with arousal as he trickled sweetened cream over her and then slowly lapped it up?

To escape the house and the tormenting visions it elicited, he retreated into the barn, installing the equipment and hardware for the stalls that had arrived. Even there, though, his thoughts turned to the horses at Rosewood and how much he missed spending time with the foals and learning about them from Jordan and Ned.

And the kids. On the day Max got his cast, Owen had been in the midst of painting the wood trim of the second-floor study a sage green, when the sound of running feet reached him. Not expecting that Jordan would bring Max over, his defenses were down. And no sooner had he recognized to whom those feet belonged than Max was in the room.

Around his left forearm was a fire-engine red cast, in his right hand a Sharpie pen. "Hiya, Owen, you wanna sign my cast? Tomorrow I'm gonna have all my friends at school sign it, too."

With the exception of the red cast and the white gauze bandage, Max was so much like his usual self that it caused a thick glob of emotion to lodge in Owen's throat, making a reply impossible.

Max didn't seem bothered by his silence. He was already offering him the Sharpie. "Here, Owen. Mommy brought a really good pen."

Owen put his paintbrush in the tray.

Uncapping the pen, he caught a movement by the doorway. He knew without having to verify that Jordan was watching them.

He swallowed hard. "Where?"

"Right here," Max said, as his stubby finger pointed. "Put your name next to Mommy and Katie's. Wiv couldn't write hers because she's too little. So she made this."

Of course Olivia's "signature" would look like a jagged lightning bolt.

With the care Owen took to sign his name, he could have been drafting the elevation of a house for an architecture competition. Silently he handed the pen back to a beaming Max.

"Thanks, Owen." Spinning around he ran to Jordan. "Look, Mommy."

Jordan knelt to inspect his arm. "That's very nice, Max. Now remember what else you wanted to say to Owen?"

"Oh, yeah," he replied, nodding. A rare solemnity stole over him as he walked back to Owen's side. The big breath he took made his small shoulder rise. "I was very naughty 'cause I didn't wait to climb your tree with you, Owen. I promise I'll wait next time." Then he was racing back to Jordan.

"Did I say it right?"

"Yes, that was very good, Max. Now we need to get

home, so Tito, Felix, and Andy can sign your cast, too. Say good-bye to Owen."

"Are you gonna come over to my house later, Owen?"

He opened his mouth but Jordan was already answering for him. "No, honey, not today. Owen's very busy."

"Oh. Okay."

And then, thank God, they were gone, because this time the lump in his throat was coated with the acid of remorse.

If that had been all Owen had to deal with, the last ten days would have been hellish enough, but then there was Jordan. Nothing compared to the torture of seeing her and not touching her.

How could she be so calm?

How could she even consider going on a date with Tim Mitchell?

It threw him to discover that Jordan was ready to date while he was going home every night to an empty apartment, unwilling to pick up the phone because no other woman held the slightest interest for him. Adding insult to injury, it was only by chance that he learned of Jordan's new social life.

He'd sought her out, coming in from the horse barn to ask her a question that he could have had answered simply by picking up his cell. But he'd needed to see her. He found her with Doug in one of the bedrooms. She was standing on a ladder, holding a level while Doug installed wood brackets for the window curtains.

She turned to give him an annoyingly chipper "hi" before returning her attention to Doug.

"So Jesse and I have finished the first stall. Do you think Travis can come by after work tonight and check it out?" he asked, trying not to stare at her silhouette outlined against the morning sun, or note how her breasts lifted enticingly as she held the level to the wall. It was as if his hands were cupped beneath them to bring their lush softness to his mouth. He swallowed hard.

"Tonight? I'm not sure tonight will work out. He and Margot are babysitting."

"Babysitting? Whose baby?" He was imagining peeling her simple white T-shirt off and feasting on those breasts. They'd be warm and soft and when he lowered his face to them, they'd smell of her and baby powder. God, he missed her. It seemed like forever since he'd held her close.

"Doug, you need to raise your end just a hair. Yes, that's it. My babies." She cast him a quick smile as she finally answered him.

"Oh. I thought Richard would be taking them this weekend." Would she realize he'd memorized the kids' scheduled weekends with their father, or would she think it was a lucky guess?

The thought would never have occurred to him that she wouldn't even notice his slip.

"That's right. But Richard and Cynthia had a business dinner tonight so he's coming tomorrow. The children will have a shortened visit."

"So you're going out?" he asked, coming full circle to what was really preoccupying him.

"Yes," she said, still smiling.

Here was another distraction: her smiling good cheer. At the very least she should be aloof. He'd even understand if she went all snippy and gave him the evil eye. To be honest, he wanted her to scream and yell and call him a jerk and an SOB because then maybe he could banish the suspicion that he'd been merely a recovery fling for her.

A suspicion which mushroomed like an atomic blast when she added, "Tim Mitchell's taking me to the Coach House for dinner."

"Mitchell?"

"Uh-huh," she said nodding. "But I know Travis would love to see the stall and let you know whether anything needs correcting. Why don't I ask if he's free on Monday so you don't have to drive in from Alexandria over the weekend?"

"Fine." He forced the word out.

"The Coach House? That's the scraped brick place on Elm, with the flower boxes, right?" Doug asked.

"Yes, that's it," Jordan said, switching her attention back to Doug.

"Is it good?" Doug asked while he made a mark with his pencil for where the bracket would go. Finished, he climbed down his ladder and grabbed his power drill.

Jordan nodded. "Very nice. The rooms are lovely and the new chef does great things with local produce. Their corn bread is brought steaming hot to the table. When you bring Annie to show off the house, you should take her there, Doug."

"Maybe I will."

Owen left the bedroom. He really didn't want to hear about how great a date restaurant the Coach House was. He'd already known Tim Mitchell was out to win Jordan, but he hadn't thought he'd make a play for her this soon. Just thinking of what his next move would be had Owen searching for something to hammer.

When he saw her next he was still fuming over the wrongness of Jordan being involved with Tim. She was in the dining room hanging curtains from the rods that Doug had installed there.

She'd kicked off her sandals, and damned if her bare feet on the newly refinished parquet floor didn't make him weak-kneed with lust. The prospect of Tim Mitchell caressing those dainty toes and delicate arches was intolerable.

"I'm glad you came in, Owen. I wanted to ask your opinion. I'm thinking of putting a mahogany china cabinet against that wall." She pointed to a color photograph propped against the wall. "I wrote down the dimensions on the back."

He walked over and picked up the photograph. "A Phyfe reproduction?"

She nodded. "That's right."

"Nice piece."

"I think so, too. I found this cabinetmaker in Pennsylvania who specializes in antique reproductions. I thought the cupboard's proportions and lines would work well in here, but maybe it makes too much of a statement."

"I like it." Damn it, Tim Mitchell wouldn't know Duncan Phyfe from Dunkin' Donuts. Okay, so he might know about horses, but there was a great deal more to Jordan than breeding horses. What was she thinking?

"Good," she said, looking pleased.

"Those curtains look great."

"Don't they? I splurged big time. The fabric's by Manuel Canovas. But the pattern and color looked so wonderful in this room, I couldn't resist."

"So you're not really serious about Tim Mitchell." There, he'd said it.

Busy fiddling with the hang of the curtains, she didn't even glance at him. "Why wouldn't I be?"

"Principally because he's all wrong for you and because he's a bit of a bore to boot."

His observation didn't appear to faze her. "Mmm," she said. "That's what I thought at first, too. But Tim's been coming over a lot lately to bond with Cascade. I've discovered he's got an off-beat sense of humor that kind of sneaks up on you."

His gut churned. He hadn't realized Mitchell had been going to Rosewood over this last week and a half. And he'd obviously been bonding with more than the colt.

"I just think you can do better than Mitchell."

"That's very sweet of you," she said with an amused smile. "I confess I'm surprised you care at all who I'm dating, Owen, since you'll be leaving Warburg soon. I have to make a life for myself here. Tim's kind and successful and he's not afraid of emotional commitments." The very gentleness of her comment made him feel lower than a heel. She glanced at her watch. "I have to go. Max has his appointment at the doctor's."

"For his stitches?" Max had been so proud of the fact that he was the only kid in his class who'd had both stitches and a broken arm.

She nodded. "We're going to the Shake Shack afterward for a treat. They have pedal go-carts."

"He'll like that." He could picture Max's smile of glee behind the wheel of the kiddie cart.

"It's not a pony, which is what he's really angling for, but Tim has a lead on a nice Welsh Shetland cross so maybe I'll be able to surprise Max with one when school's out."

"But his cast won't be off." Mitchell would become Max's new hero.

"Dr. Barrett says that since Max is still riding on the longe line, it shouldn't pose a real risk. It turns out his daughter rides, too," she said as if that was explanation enough. She came over and plucked the photograph from his numb fingers, slipping her feet into her sandals as she did. "I'll phone Pierce Fowler about the china cabinet. He said he could deliver it by midweek, in plenty of time for the Open House. I'll see you Monday." And with another guileless smile, she left.

That's why he didn't call it quits after a long, hot afternoon installing the kitchen appliances and the granite counters in the butler's pantry with Doug and Jesse, staying on to paint the mudroom off the kitchen. It was also why he agreed to meet Jesse later at the bar he'd discovered. Going to a bar didn't even make the top ten of Owen's wish list, but tossing back a couple of drinks in a local dive was infinitely preferable to obsessing about Jordan and Tim's date, or imagining what they might do after their meal at the Coach House. He just bet Mitchell would try to convince her to come home with him.

It was past nine by the time he'd cleaned his brushes and rollers and made a stab at cleaning himself, too. Following Jesse's directions, he pulled into The Den half an hour later. The lot was crowded with cars, foreign makes parked alongside beat-up trucks and sport wagons; Jesse had clearly stumbled onto something.

Exactly what remained to be seen.

It was easy to see why Jesse had said The Den was not exactly in keeping with Warburg's comfortable WASPy style. The place looked like a shack. A big shack. Flashing colored-neon beer signs illuminated the windows, and the front of the building had Christmas lights nailed to it in what could only be described as a drunken manner. The music was loud and pounding. Owen was surprised the bar's siding was still attached.

It was a far cry from the hushed candlelit atmosphere of the Coach House, he thought grimly.

Owen only hoped the decibel-blasting beat would drive Jordan from his mind.

He stepped inside. Ten years ago the air in a joint like this would have been bluish-gray, the cigarette smoke thick enough to cut with a knife. The obscurity might have been preferable. On raised platforms positioned around the cavernous space, women writhed and gyrated as though every last one of them was auditioning as a pole dancer. Owen instantly understood the attraction of The Den for Jesse, who, as bad luck would have it, had seen Owen enter and was waving him over. It wouldn't do to hurt Jesse's feelings by turning around and walking out, but he slashed the number of drinks he intended to have to one before getting the hell out of there.

"Some scene, huh?" Jesse shouted happily.

"Yeah. I wouldn't have thought Warburg had a strip joint."

"Nah, it's a dance contest. But maybe if we're real enthusiastic, the ladies will lose their clothes." Jesse grinned.

He doubted the women would need much encouragement. "This round's on me. Where the hell's the bar?" he asked, looking around.

"Over there." Jesse pointed.

It was then Owen realized that what he'd at first taken

for a long catwalk platform was actually the bar. An understandable mistake since it was supporting more gyrating bodies. The crowd around the dancers was whooping and hollering.

Had he grown prematurely old? he wondered as he shouldered his way to the bar. No, he had nothing against a female doing a sizzling hot erotic grind on a countertop. He simply wanted the female to be Jordan. And he wanted a private show. For his eyes only. These women did nothing for him. They seemed ridiculously young—girls, really.

It was impossible to spot the bartender through the thicket of legs strutting up and down the length of the bar. As he came nearer, one pair of legs bent so their owner could bring her bright pink, skin-tight tank top down to eye level and the guys could ogle her push-up bra as they catcalled and whooped their appreciation. Owen's gaze was probably the only one that traveled farther north, to see vivid green eyes framed by short, bleached blond hair.

Oh, shit.

If there was a bright side to his discovery, it was that Jade seemed as horrified as he. Her face went white then bright red with embarrassment. He saw the second she decided to brazen it out. Assuming a haughty expression, she looked past him. Her gaze on the beer-drunk, lust-addled men leering up at her, she twisted and shimmied her very fine underage body to the music's beat.

Jade was deluded if she thought he'd let her get away with pretending he was invisible. He grabbed her wrist as it swung past him.

"What the fuck do you think you're doing, Jade?"

She made a futile attempt to shake him loose. "Let go. You're not supposed to touch the dancers. Go away. I'm in the quarterfinals. I have a bet with Blair that I can make it to the final round."

"What's the prize? Honorable mention in the police blotter? For Christ's sake, you're seven—"

"Pipe down, will you? Are you *trying* to get me in trouble?" She was wiggling her hips in her half-crouch as she spoke so it looked like she and Owen were doing a weird version of the Lindy Hop.

"Why try when you do such a superb job yourself? Come on, get down from there, right now."

"No way." Again Jade tried to free her arm. "Blair and the others will think I'm a total wuss if I back out now."

"Hey, bud, let the girlie dance." A guy reeking of beer suggested in a not-too-friendly tone. "She's the one I'm rooting for."

"Sorry, her dancing days are over. Great fan club you've got, kid."

Jade blushed but continued wiggling her hips. Her admirer started clapping, but was either too stupid or too drunk—probably both—to follow the beat.

Owen tried again. "Jesus, Jade, do you have any idea what you're risking?"

Beer-brain laid a meaty hand on Owen's shoulder, jerking him around. "I don't think you heard me right." His face was a deep red. "I told you to let the girlie dance. I want to see her shake those titties."

From behind, Owen heard Jade retort, "I am not a 'girlie'!"—the first bright thing she'd uttered. Unfortunately he couldn't follow up on that remark and point out that in that case maybe she should get the hell down from the bar's counter because Beer-brain's other hand was balled into a massive fist, its destination his face.

Owen ducked, then came up with a right hook into the guy's jaw, the shock of which felt like he'd tried to slug a brick wall. It had about as much effect, for the guy merely stumbled back a step and shook his head, raising both fists. Then Owen knew he was about to feel a whole lot worse.

The next punches landed. He saw stars and tasted blood and heard shrieks. But he wasn't going to let Jordan's little sister get into more trouble, so a brawl seemed the only solution—not that he had much choice. The guy obviously liked pummeling the bejesus out of people. The only advantage Owen had was that he hadn't been drinking all night or, if the size of this guy's gut was any indicator, every night for the past ten years. It allowed him to dodge a number of blows and land a couple of decent ones. When one of them made the guy stumble backward into a now-empty barstool and lose his balance, landing on his rear in a heaving sprawl, and when he didn't seem inclined to rise to his feet to resume the fight, Owen could have wept tears of joy.

Instead he hung his head, trying to catch his breath.

"Owen! What the hell?" Jesse's voice was filled astonished concern.

He straightened and winced as his body registered what a good job the guy had done hammering it. "One of the dancers is Jordan's kid sister. And I mean kid."

"Oh, shit."

"Exactly." He nodded, even that small move painful. "We've got to get her out of here before the cops come." Jade, finally showing some brains, had jumped off the bar. He spotted her standing off to the side, looking miserable and sullen.

"Uhh, too late for that."

So that was the noise: sirens. The police had responded awfully fast. Too fast, he realized. They had to get Jade out now. "There's a side exit." Then, giving Jade a hard look, he said, "Come on."

Unfortunately, a police officer was waiting on the other side of the door. Under the bright floodlight, the officer's sharp gaze zeroed in on Owen's face, which, from the feel of it, was already swollen, then on Jade's skimpy top and tight, fashionably ripped jeans.

He moved in front of them. "Evening. I'm Officer Cooper."

Beside Owen, Jade went stiff as a poker. Suddenly Owen recalled the name of the Warburg police officer Margot and Jordan mentioned so often, the one to whom Jade had sent doughnuts and pulled God knew what other pranks: Rob Cooper. Maybe this was another Cooper.

"I'd like to ask you some questions. But first, could I see some identification?"

Silently she pulled a plastic card from her rear pocket. Handing it to him, she ducked her head.

He glanced at it, then looked at Jade, his expression impassive as he studied her bowed white-blond head and hunched shoulders. "Jade Radcliffe. I didn't recognize you, though when the tip came in that there were minors at The Den, your name did cross my mind." He paused. "Did you get in using this driver's license or another ID?"

A fine trembling seized her as she went to her other pocket and withdrew a second card.

He took it and read, "Rachel Hammond, age twenty-one, and it seems that you attend the University of Tennessee. Fancy that."

Oh, hell.

Jade crossed her arms in front of her, doubtless trying to hide the fact that her trembling had redoubled.

"You been drinking, Jade—or do you prefer to be called Rachel?"

"No," she croaked with a quick shake of her head.

"We'll have to see about that."

Officer Cooper must really have it in for Jade, Owen thought. At the police station, he'd dealt with Owen straight away, sticking him with a two-hundred-dollar ticket for disorderly conduct. While it embarrassed the hell out of him to be slapped with a fine by someone at least ten years younger than himself and then tersely instructed to avoid bar fights in the future, Owen consoled himself with the thought that Beer-brain, also known as Howie Driscoll, was going to be appearing before the judge. It turned out he'd had previous run-ins with the Warburg police. From the sound of his protests, he was looking at something a lot stiffer than a ticket.

But after Cooper had meted out the respective fines and summonses and informed Owen he was free to go, he had gotten a call on his cell. Owen had seen him talking to another officer, and then he'd disappeared. And he had yet to reappear.

It was possible that this was part of Jade's punishment. Even though she'd passed the Breathalyzer test and hadn't driven to the bar, Owen figured Cooper probably wanted her to sweat it out by having her sit there, uncertain of her fate. The wait was taking its toll.

Of course he hadn't left Jade. The kid's face was leached of color, and beneath the light jacket he'd lent her, she was shaking with fear. Fear that was probably mixed with a good bit of self-loathing.

From the fact that no other teens were populating the station, it was obvious that Jade's so-called friends had ditched her at The Den. Owen had a hunch they might also have set her up, placing the anonymous tip that brought the police and Jade's favorite officer to the scene. He bet that thought was going through Jade's mind, too. But Jade was too smart not to realize that she'd brought this mess on herself by seeking out their questionable company.

A part of him felt sorry for her. But it was a pretty small part. Mostly, he was pissed and hurting from all the bruises blooming over his face and body. So as the clock ticked and they sat on plastic chairs and continued to be ignored by every official in the place, he decided to devote a few minutes giving her a long-overdue chewing out. So what if it wasn't his place. He was sick and tired of what she was doing to Jordan and the kids.

"I'm curious, have you spared a single thought to what your dogged determination to screw up your life is doing to your family?" he asked conversationally.

Her attitude was all belligerent defiance. "You don't know anything about any of this, so why don't you butt out?"

"Actually I do know something about it. You're reacting to whatever you read in your mother's diary. A lame excuse, Jade."

"I disagree, so maybe you can press the stop button now."

"Sorry, I'm out two hundred bucks and have a number of nasty bruises thanks to Howie, your number one fan, so the least you can do is listen."

She shook her head but refrained from any smart-aleck comment.

"Maybe you're right, and your mother was a lousy wife, a lousy mother, even a lousy human being. But I get the feeling you're so busy trying to hurt yourself in an effort to get back at a dead woman, you're no longer able to remember what she really was like. Because your mother must have done a couple of things right. You're as smart as a whip and a fairly cool human being—that is, when you're not intent on destroying your life and tearing apart the people who love you. You know, your sisters are really nice women, and you've got two nieces and a nephew who adore you. Do you even realize how lucky you are to be loved so much? Do you realize how stupid it is to put them through this kind of pain?"

As guilt trips went, Owen considered the one he'd just laid on Jade pretty damn fine. It had a special weight for being true.

"You're treating the people who love you like crap, Jade. While Jordan and Margot may understand the underlying reasons, while even Ned's going to forgive your spoiled-brat behavior, what do you think Kate, Max, and Olivia are making of the fact that you won't give them the time of day?"

When she seemed to shrink inside his jacket until she was about Kate's size, he figured that some of what he'd said must have resonated.

Deciding that she'd been lectured enough for one night, Owen fell silent, and so they sat in tense misery, Jade brooding over her current screw-up and he trying his best to ignore how much it hurt every time he breathed, when an officer approached. "Jade Radcliffe?"

She nodded and rose to her feet.

"Your sister's been contacted. She's coming down."

"What's going to happen to me?"

"I'll discuss that when your sister gets here."

"Where's Officer Cooper?"

"He had to leave. A family emergency."

Margot had probably broken the law herself, making her car fly down to the station. Entering the building mere minutes later, her steps faltered, then quickened when she saw him. She rushed over, squeezed his hand, and whispered "Thank you" to him, before wrapping her arms about her sister in a fierce hug.

Stepping back, she wiped her face with her hands and then dried them on her white jeans. "There, now that I know you're safe, I can say this: damn it, Jade, how could you be such an idiot?"

"I was only dancing."

"In the sketchiest bar in town. With a fake ID. Don't tell me you don't know that's identity theft. They can nail you for that. Big time. Where'd you get the ID?"

"Blair had an extra one she lent me. The picture didn't look like me, but the guy at the door who was carding barely glanced at it."

Not surprising, Owen thought. The guy was probably looking his fill at Jade.

"Oh, God. What were you *thinking*? You must have a guardian angel looking after you, Jade."

Jade couldn't mask her surprise at Margot's statement.

"Yeah, you heard me right. Because as bad as this is, do you have any idea what could have happened to you if Owen hadn't been there?"

Jade dropped her gaze. "I'm sorry."

Margot was shaking her head, her lips pressed tight in an effort to control herself, when the officer who'd spoken to Jade earlier came over. "Margot Radcliffe?"

"Yes."

"Officer Craig Lewis. Could you and your sister come with me?"

"Of course. Owen, can you . . . would you mind waiting for us?" With her 100-percent-proof beauty, Margot usually radiated the confidence and strength of an Amazon. Now her eyes were as anxious and frightened as her little sister's.

"I'll be here." He settled back down on the chair.

The dinner at The Coach had been delicious, the atmosphere pleasant and sophisticated, and Tim Mitchell was a perfectly nice man. But Jordan was wretched.

Tim was laboring under false pretenses. It was clear by the time they ate their crab cake appetizers just how serious his interest in her was. It was also plain that he expected his feelings to be reciprocated.

Unfortunately she couldn't summon an ounce of interest.

When Tim smiled, it was just a flash of teeth, when his hand brushed hers, or grazed her back, she felt nothing. No strange flutter, no electric shiver, no rocketing of her pulse. Nothing but embarrassed awkwardness.

Because he wasn't Owen.

They'd finished dessert, and Tim had signed the check, but he seemed in no hurry to leave, requesting a refill on his coffee and continuing their conversation with undiminished enthusiasm.

"So Hawk Hill's nearly finished?"

"Yes. We're just waiting for a few more pieces to be delivered. Owen's still working on the barn but that shouldn't—"

"How many stalls will it have again?"

"Six."

"That's a nice-size barn for a private home."

"Yes," she said. "I don't think Owen's going to have a problem selling Hawk Hill, even in this soft a real estate market."

He stirred more cream into his coffee, his spoon clinking against the china cup. "Do you think you could arrange to get me in to see it before the Open House?"

"Well, I'm not sure Owen—"

"In case you haven't guessed, Jordan, I'm seriously considering making a bid on the property. Living near Rosewood would offer so many advantages." He reached out and let his fingers brush hers.

With a smile she slid her hand away and picked up the now tepid cup of chamomile tea she'd ordered with her peach pie and ginger ice cream.

"Tim, you live close enough that visiting Cascade won't be any problem. And didn't I hear you tell Travis how you loved to make the drive because it took you past the hunt club's own fields?" she replied, deciding to be deliberately obtuse.

"There are more reasons to move than being nearer to the colt, and they're more important to me than making sure the club's fields and fences are in good condition," he replied, his gaze holding hers across the candlelight. "Jordan, I realize you're still figuring out what it is you want after the nightmare of your divorce. But I might as well tell you that my thoughts and hopes have taken a new direction since I've gotten to know you better. And I'm willing to do anything I can to make you part of my life."

She supposed some women might be flattered by Tim's words. But listening to him say that he wanted to buy Hawk Hill because it would place him closer to her, she could only think that either he was flattering her outrageously—and she'd had enough of disingenuous men—or he was extraordinarily confident of his chances for success.

Rather presumptuous for a man on his first dinner date. Jordan suddenly felt a lot better about being head over heels in love with Owen. He never took her for granted.

Her fingers tightened around the teacup's delicate handle, worried that if she put her hand down Tim might read the gesture as encouragement and try to touch her again. "Tim, I consider you a friend, a very good friend—" *But that's all,* she'd intended to say, however Tim cut her off.

"And that's an excellent foundation to build on. So you'll talk to Gage about Hawk Hill?"

He reminded her of a hound chasing down a fox, the aspect of the hunt she liked least. "I'll ask him, but I can't guarantee he'll agree to let you see it early."

"I have a hunch Gage might be just as happy to make a quick sale."

His opinion, delivered with such confidence, caused the ginger ice cream to curdle in her stomach. She didn't want to think about Owen leaving, especially when she wasn't sure her campaign to make him see all he would be losing if he walked away from their relationship was even working.

She raised her teacup, thinking another sip might settle her stomach, only to lower it as her clutch began vibrating on the linen tablecloth. "Excuse me," she said, reaching for the bag. "I'll just see who's calling."

"Of course, go ahead." Tim leaned back in his chair.

Jordan glanced at the number on her cellphone's screen and frowned. It was Rosewood. She flipped the phone open. "Hello?"

"Jordan, it's Travis."

"Travis? Is something wrong with the children?"

"They're fine. Jordan, it's Jade and Owen, they're at the police station. I'm still not sure what exactly happened. Margot went down. Maybe you want to—"

Owen and Jade? "I'll be there in five minutes."

Owen sat with his eyes closed, trying to ignore the increasing stiffness in his muscles and the pain that flared to life each time he shifted his weight on the plastic seat.

"Owen?" Jordan's voice had him jerking upright in the

chair and grimacing as he opened his eyes. But now the pain came from a different source. She was hurrying toward him with Tim Mitchell striding by her side, his hand at the small of her back. Owen knew Mitchell intended to keep it there.

"Owen, what happened? You look terrible."

And she looked beautiful.

She was dressed in a sleeveless silk sheath of deep purple, the color enhancing the red cast of her hair and deepening the blue of her eyes. Her slender legs were bare and made even longer by the stiletto heels of her strappy sandals. She looked gorgeous, and Owen wanted to go home with her right now. And he bloody hated Tim, who had gotten to stare across a table at her all evening long.

He rose and did his best to straighten, feeling as creaky as an eighty-year-old. "I'm all right. No need to worry."

"And Jade? Is she—"

"She's with Margot. They're talking in there." He tilted his head toward a closed door and wished he hadn't because it felt like a knife was stuck in his neck.

"But what happened?" she asked.

"It's a long story." He didn't want to say more in front of Mitchell.

"One that ended with you being taken here," Mitchell observed.

Such acuity. "Seems that way."

"So where did it start?" Mitchell asked.

He lifted his shoulders in a shrug and grunted. He saw Mitchell smile at the sound. Screw him. Even Mitchell might be a little worse for wear after working all day and then being pummeled like a punching bag. Too bad Howie Driscoll was gone. Owen would have liked to introduce him to Mitchell.

"Owen?" Jordan said, her gaze troubled.

He had to tell her something. He only hoped he had sufficient wits to edit his story so that Mitchell wouldn't hear too much about Jade. "I was at The Den."

"The Den?"

The surprise in her voice told him she knew the place. Judging from his smug expression, Mitchell did, too.

"Yeah, I went there with Jesse."

"Oh." The sad little syllable came straight from Jordan's heart. There was no need to ask Owen why they'd chosen to go to The Den. The bar was Warburg's principal pickup joint. Oh God, Owen was already looking for a new woman to warm his bed. The thought filled her with desolation.

Jordan knew she should be asking where Jade came into the story, and how Owen had gotten beat up so badly his face was swollen and bruised and bloodied, but all she could focus on was that while she was with Tim, thinking about how much she loved Owen, he'd been at The Den.

The tales of the bar were legion.

Her imagination was cruel. It battered her with images of scantily dressed women draping themselves over him.

"Oh," she repeated stupidly, weakly. Yet she was unable to tamp down a sense of betrayal at the idea of him checking out The Den's offerings. She'd been wrong. He didn't really care. The love was all on her side.

"I need to go make sure Jade's all right. Excuse me." Quickly she retreated, going over to the door Owen had indicated and knocking lightly before entering.

Owen would have followed Jordan, but he doubted Officer Lewis would admit non–family members. He certainly didn't want to sit here with Mitchell, toward whom he was beginning to have an allergic reaction, unless it was some other kind of reaction. Christ, he was so tired he couldn't think straight.

Maybe that was why he couldn't figure out what Mitchell was still doing here. Jordan hadn't asked him to stay. Belatedly he realized the other man was talking.

"I'm glad to have a minute alone with you, Owen.

There's something I wanted to ask. Jordan and I were talking over dinner and the question came up of whether you'd let me take a look at Hawk Hill before the Open House."

Owen stared at him blankly, not quite sure what he was hearing. "Wouldn't you rather see the house when Jordan's all finished with the decorating?"

"Frankly, I'd rather get a jump on the other buyers. Even though the market's softened considerably, Hawk Hill is a great property. There's going to be a number of interested parties. That's why I want to be totally open with you and lay my cards on the table. I believe it's the best way to deal with people. If you let me see Hawk Hill before the Open House, I'm confident we can come to a mutually beneficial agreement."

Owen barely heard him. He was still stuck on the idea of Jordan talking about him to Mitchell. "Was this your idea or Jordan's?"

"Both. She's as excited by the prospect of my buying Hawk Hill as I am."

It would have been so satisfying to tell Mitchell to take a hike, that even if he offered Owen cash up front, there was no way he was going to agree to sell him Hawk Hill so that he and Jordan could live there happily ever after.

But then Owen recalled Jordan saying how Tim was kind and funny and, most important, unafraid of emotional commitments.

That was the type of man Jordan deserved. He knew it, and she did, too. And it appeared she'd decided Mitchell was the one she wanted.

Is that why she'd been so quick to leave, without sparing him a backward glance or a smile?

All Jordan's smiles would be reserved for Mitchell now.

He felt a strange hollowness at the thought, as if his insides had been sucked out of him.

"So what do you say, Owen?"

He knew he must be close to losing it; he was actually contemplating decking Mitchell in a police station. An impulse too stupid for words, doubly idiotic given his body's battered state. Mitchell would probably wipe the floor with him.

He spoke through gritted teeth. "I'll think about it."

"That's great. Just great. I'll tell Jordan, she'll be so pleased. How does next week sound?"

He had to get out of there. Now, before Mitchell began sharing more of his and Jordan's nifty plans for the future.

"I've got to go."

"Of course. Forgive the pun, but you look totally beat. The Den's definitely the place to find excitement, but you obviously found more than you could handle."

Mitchell was a real wit, Owen thought. "Yeah. Say goodbye to Jordan and her sisters for me."

He hobbled out of the police station, his bruised body and aching heart protesting his every step. He ignored them both. Now he knew what love really felt like: crap.

ROSEWOOD WAS a bleak place that weekend. For her under-age, illegal-ID-toting adventures at The Den, Jade had been given a five-hundred-dollar fine and faced additional pun-ishment with a court date set in three weeks' time. Margot had yet to impose any punishment. Probably, Jordan thought, because she blamed herself for not preventing Jade's latest calamity.

She understood Margot's wracking sense of guilt. She was experiencing the same thing. She couldn't stop think-ing about Owen. If only she'd focused on *him* instead of her own fears. Now that she knew what he'd done for Jade at The Den, she longed to turn back time to the moment when she'd found him at the police station, his face dark with bruises and blood.

Cuts and bruises he'd received protecting her little sister from an aggressive drunk who'd become violent in his de-sire to see Jade "dance." Owen in a barroom brawl for Jade's sake only underscored what she knew already. He was a man who would go to any length to protect others, a man who gave more than he took. A special man.

If she'd needed further proof, it was provided by the only bright moment during the weekend, when she found Jade grooming Doc Holliday.

Having finished exercising Sava and Tidbit, Jordan had gone to the pony's stall to ready him for the children's les-son with Ned.

"What are you doing here?" she asked Jade in surprise.

Jade continued currying the pony's rounded hindquarters. "I figured the kids should have their lesson as soon as
Richard drops them off, and Doc was pretty dirty."

"Will Ned be ready so soon? He just got on Sky Light."

Jade shook her head, her eyes fixed on Doc's rump. "I
told Ned I'd take over their lessons for him. He has too
much to do."

That Ned was extremely busy had been true two weeks
ago, too. Jordan picked up a stiff brush from the carryall
and began brushing Doc's bay coat. The pony must have
found a muddy patch in the pasture. Little clouds of loosened dirt rose with each short stroke.

"Well, they'll be thrilled to have you teaching them
again. But can I ask why you're really doing it?" She half-
expected Jade to tell her it was to pay off the five-hundred-
dollar fine she'd received.

Jade exchanged the curry comb for another bristle brush.
"Owen said some stuff to me at the police station. He made
me realize that it's one thing to mess up, another to hurt
Kate, Max, and Olivia. After reading Mom's diary I pretty
much wanted to spread the crap I was feeling around as far
as I could. I'm sorry. They're nice kids."

Jade hadn't reached the end of her explanation before the
tears coated Jordan's cheeks.

Had she been alone, she would have succumbed to the
urge to cry her heart out. There were so many good reasons
to—for Jade, who, though wretched, was nonetheless attempting to do the right thing toward the children; for her
kids, who'd been unable to understand why the aunt they
adored had turned her back on them, but would now be ecstatic that she wanted to spend time with them; for Owen,
who cared enough to talk to Jade and try to help her; for
herself, because she loved him so much. Because she knew
she'd never find another man like Owen, a man she loved
for more reasons than she could count.

She wept because she was terribly afraid she'd lost him.

Though she ducked down to brush Doc's chest and beneath his neck, Jade noticed her tears nonetheless.

"Jeesh, you don't need to cry just because I'm giving them a lesson, it's not that big a deal." Her voice was a mix of exasperation, awkwardness, and guilt.

Jordan sniffed and shook her head, continuing to brush vigorously. "It's not just that, though I don't know whether you realize how happy you've made me and the kids."

"No, I do. So make sure you tell Owen I'm teaching them again. I don't feel like getting another lecture from him."

"I will." Privately she wondered how to make Owen understand the central role he'd acquired in all their lives, let alone how much she loved him.

She wanted to tell him that she missed the comforting strength of his arms around her, missed seeing the fierce pleasure stamped on his face when he was deep inside her, missed feeling his body shudder and heave its release and hear his heart racing for her. She so longed to experience all those things again . . . and only with him.

But how could she tell Owen any of this when he wouldn't answer his phone or return the messages she had left since Saturday morning?

On Monday Owen wasn't at Hawk Hill.

She found Jesse and Doug upstairs, installing the mirrored medicine cabinet she'd ordered for the third bathroom.

"Hi," she said. "I didn't see Owen's car. Is he coming soon?"

"He was here earlier, but he had a meeting with a new client," Jesse said, not quite meeting her eye.

"Oh. So he won't be back?"

"I don't think so," Doug said. "Can we do something for you, Jordan?"

From their carefully polite tones, Jordan knew Jesse had told Doug about what had happened at The Den. "No, a delivery for the living room should be here soon, but the deliverymen can carry in the pieces and set them where I want them to go. I really just wanted to thank Owen for all he did on Friday at The Den. And thank you, too, Jesse."

A flush stole over Jesse's cheeks. "I wish I could have thrown some punches at the dude who was hammering Owen. But I'd started a conversation with a couple of women and wasn't paying much attention."

"I understand." She really didn't want to hear about the engrossing women he and Owen had met.

"It wasn't until Owen knocked the guy into some stools and I heard the racket that I realized some bad stuff was going down. We tried to hustle your sister out, but the cops had already staked out the exits. When Owen and your kid sister had to go down to the station, he told me to head home, so I'm not being modest in saying I didn't do much. Your sister's okay?"

"It's possible that the judge will be lenient since Jade wasn't drinking. We're just relieved no serious harm came to her."

"Yeah, that dude was big as well as crazy-drunk-mean. Not the kind of guy whose eye a girl wants to catch."

She was glad she'd eaten breakfast a long time ago because her stomach roiled at the thought of what this man might have done to Jade if Owen hadn't been there.

"So Owen won't be back today?"

"Don't think so."

"Oh." Her life seemed to have turned into one big "O," as in "zero." "It's just that I told Travis and Ned that they should come by after work to look at the barn."

"I'll probably still be around," Jesse said.

"You'll be staying that late?"

"Touch-up painting and a list of other odds and ends," he said by way of explanation. "Owen wants this gig wrapped up."

Of course he did. And he wanted out of her life, too, so

he could move on with no strings attached. "I'll tell them to come and find you if they have any suggestions for the stalls."

Jordan went home after the furniture was delivered and arranged. The living room looked wonderful, but without Owen to share her pleasure in the mix of textures and outlines, there was no reason to linger. It was just a job, and she hoped whoever moved in would like her choices and want to keep them.

The kids were dressed for their lesson, and Miriam had already given them their afternoon snack.

"Wow, such organization," she said with a smile.

"The kids were pretty fired up knowing it was Jade who was going to be teaching them," Miriam said with a smile.

"During our lesson yesterday Jade told me we have lots of work to do before Crestview," Kate told her.

"I'm sure you're going to do very well and have lots of fun besides. That's the important thing at a show—to have fun with Doc."

As they walked down to the barn, Kate and Max skipping at her side and Olivia doing her lurching half-run, Kate said, "Mommy, can we ask Owen to come watch me ride at Crestview?"

Her step faltered. "We can certainly ask him." She made her voice sound as noncommittal as possible while her brain scrambled to redirect the conversation. And failed.

"We're making invitations with Miss Burnley for mommies and daddies to come to the concert we're having on the last day of school," Kate said. "I could make an invitation for Owen to come and watch me ride Doc."

"Me too," Max chimed in. "I want to write him one, too. I can invite him to watch Katie ride with me, can't I, Mommy?"

Her throat too tight for words, she could only nod. Now she'd have to worry about two more hearts breaking.

Kate and Max were talking about glitter and stickers and colored paper when they entered the main barn.

Ned was at the closest cross ties, tacking Mistral. Hearing their voices, he looked up. "All set for your lesson?"

"Hiya, Ned, we're going to make cards for Owen after we ride so that he comes to Crestview to watch Katie."

"That's a fine idea, Max." He bent down and slipped Mistral's girth through the martingale. "Owen's bound to have a good time at the show. He'll be right proud to watch you, Kate. So how was Owen today, Miss Jordan? Those bruises starting to fade? Miss Margot said he had a couple of nasty ones."

"I didn't see him." She reached out and lifted Olivia into her arms so that she wouldn't wander too close to Mistral's hooves. "He was meeting a client."

"But we're set for today? Can't wait to see those stalls."

"I'm not sure Owen will be there, but Jesse told me he'd be working late at the house, so you and Travis can still go down and look at the barn."

"It'll just be me. Margot was able to get an appointment with the counselor Reverend Wilde recommended. Travis is going with her and Jade. It's a shame about Owen, though. I'd have liked to—"

Tim Mitchell walked into the barn. "Hi, Jordan, hi, kids."

The children, not quite sure where he fit into the scheme of things even though they saw him often around the barn, didn't reply immediately. Olivia stared and then, with uncustomary shyness, buried her face in Jordan's neck.

"Kate, Max, please say hello to Mr. Mitchell," Jordan instructed quietly.

"Hello, Mr. Mitchell," Kate and Max said in unison.

"So what was that about Owen, Ned? He didn't run into more trouble, did he?"

Jordan wasn't the only one annoyed by the careless comment. Ned shot Tim a hard look. "No. I'm going to his place to look over the barn he's rebuilt. Travis and I gave him advice on what equipment company to order from and what the best layout for a small barn would be. Unfortunately he won't be there. A shame, because I like him. You here to see Cascade, Tim? 'Cause he's not due to come in from the fields for another forty-five minutes yet."

"That's all right. I can wait." Luckily Tim understood that at Rosewood, the horses' schedules were paramount. "That is too bad about Owen not being around, especially if it means he hasn't given you the green light to show me around Hawk Hill before the Open House," he said to Jordan.

"I'm afraid I forgot to leave a message asking him about it, Tim."

"Oh, he already knows. I talked to him on Friday night. He said he'd get back to me, but I think he understood that letting me get a look at Hawk Hill early could be a very shrewd move."

She stared at him. "You asked him on Friday night about buying Hawk Hill?" she asked with equal parts of shock and despair. How utterly tactless of Tim. She could only imagine what he'd said—and what Owen must have thought.

"You know how the old saying goes. The early bird gets the worm," he said, smiling.

Seeing that at dinner he'd basically linked Hawk Hill with her, she figured she'd just unwittingly been called a worm. And Tim, supremely absorbed in his own wants, was definitely unwitting. "If you'll excuse me, the children and I have to get Doc groomed and tacked for his lesson." She hurried off before Tim could suggest they spend the next forty-five minutes together.

Owen hadn't realized he possessed such a wide masochistic streak. That was the only explanation for why he returned to Hawk Hill later that afternoon. Being there and knowing that he could walk through the woods, or, hell, jump into his car and drive to Rosewood, with the perfectly reasonable excuse that he wanted to find out how Jade was doing, was torturously tempting.

He literally ached with the need to see Jordan, to breathe her in.

He hadn't let himself go inside the house. That much torture he couldn't stand. Seeing the rooms that she had furnished and imagining her living in them with Tim Mitchell would shred his heart to ribbons. The barn was bad enough. Would Max have his pony here, the one Tim had found for Jordan? Trying not to picture all five of them going out for Sunday-morning rides, a happy equestrian family, he picked up the power drill to fasten the galvanized steel latch to the sliding door he'd installed with Jesse.

"Hey there, Owen. I saw your car parked outside."

He turned around, his finger relaxing so that the drill's motor slowed to a soft whirr and then fell silent. "Ned, how are you?"

"I'm awful glad Miss Jordan was mistaken about you not being around, that's for sure. I haven't gotten a chance to thank you for what you did for Jade." Ned's gaze zeroed in on the bruise darkening his jaw and the cut along his cheekbone. "We owe you, Owen."

Owen felt a wave of embarrassment wash over him. "No, you don't. I only wish I'd been able to get her out of there before the police arrived."

Ned shrugged. "It might not turn out so bad for Jade. She might learn a lesson she won't soon forget. Most important thing is she wasn't hurt Friday night, and you saw to that. Travis intends to come by and thank you, too."

"No need, Ned." Determined to end the discussion of his supposed heroics, he put down the drill and slid the stall door open. "So, what do you think?"

Ned walked in, looked at the shuttered window that was designed to let the horse look outside during warm weather and then be latched at night and in winter. "This looks good. Really good. And installing sliding doors was the right decision. Maximizes the aisle space."

"We've put the tack room and feed storage on this end. Do you want to see the tack room?"

"Sure." Ned came out of the stall and walked beside him. "So what's this about you selling Hawk Hill to Tim Mitchell?"

Had Jordan told Ned? No, it would have been Tim. Owen bet he'd been at Rosewood, announcing his plans with the blessed conviction that he and Jordan were a perfect match. "He seems to want to buy it."

Ned gave a grunt. "Tim probably wants a lot of things: Hawk Hill, Jordan, the chance to have his pick of Rosewood Farm's foals so he can ride a different horse every day, and that's just to name a few. But that doesn't mean he should get them. I should think you'd care an awful lot about his plans for at least one of those things on his wish list."

"Ned, I care about Jordan—"

"Of course you do. Do you think I'd be wasting my breath otherwise?"

"But I'm not going to marry her, and that's what she deserves."

Ned came to a halt. Turning to Owen, he thrust out his chin and demanded, "Why in hell not?"

Owen dragged an impatient hand through his hair. He really did not want to talk about this, but he liked and respected the older man. And he figured, as one bachelor to another, his reasons might strike a chord.

"Not everyone's cut out for marriage. I'm just not good husband material, and that's what Jordan and the children need and deserve. I would think you, of all people, would understand my reservations. After all, you never married, did you?"

Ned gave him a long, hard stare. "No, I didn't get married." He stuck a hand in his trouser pocket and pulled out his tin of chewing tobacco. With jerky movements, he popped off the lid, dug out a fingerful, and jammed it in his mouth, working his lip vigorously. "I let Mary get away. She went and married a tax accountant. John Finley. They live in California now. Every year since she and John got hitched, Mary's sent me a Christmas card. The kind with a photograph. First it was just her and John. Then the babies and a silly-looking dog. The last few years, the photo has grown crowded with a whole passel of grandkids." He was silent for a moment, staring through the barn's wide entrance into the golden summer light of early evening. When he looked at Owen again, his pale blue eyes were bleak. "I hate those damned Christmas cards. Because they make me think about what it would have been like to have those fine children with Mary and share in both the joys and the sorrows of watching them grow up and find their own loves. Every year I have to face the fact that I was a damned coward to let her go. Don't you make the same mistake, son."

The sun had nearly set. But there was still enough light to see the spot at the edge of the lawn where he and Jordan had made love under a blanket of stars. He walked to it and stood there breathing deeply, remembering. She'd been as dizzyingly magical as the millions of stars sparkling overhead. It struck him that before Jordan he had never made love to a woman out of doors, but then there were so many firsts with her. Firsts and lasts. She was the first woman he'd fallen in love with; he knew she'd be the last one he would ever care for as deeply.

He made himself walk through the nearly finished house. Forced himself to stand in the living room with its newly arrived furniture and picture Tim and Jordan sitting on the sofa, her body curled into his while Kate and Max played with their blocks and animals and Olivia kicked a tower over with unholy glee. Upstairs, he moved from bedroom to bedroom, imagining the children's toys scattered about, the picture books lining the shelves that Doug and Jesse had built. In the master bedroom he saw Jordan curled into the warmth of another man's body, his arm wrapped about her middle, anchoring her to him as he breathed in her warm sweet scent, and he wanted to smash his fist into the freshly painted wall.

He let himself out of the house and in the gathering darkness walked toward the massive black outline of the beech tree. Staring up into the twisted branches looming above, he wondered how much courage he actually possessed.

Chapter
TWENTY-FOUR

THE FOLLOWING AFTERNOON Jordan placed the glitter-covered construction paper cards carefully across Max and Kate's laps before closing the van door on their cries of, "No, Olivia, you can't touch. These are for *Owen*!"

What with the drawings, the painstakingly scribed letters, and then the glittery bands and splotches enframing the whole, the invitations had taken hours, and with each excited exclamation of "I know what Owen would like on the card!" and "Do you think this looks all right, Mommy?" fear had wrapped about her heart, squeezing it ever tighter.

"Will Owen be there, Mommy?" Kate asked after Jordan started the car and steered into the green shade of the allée.

"I don't know, honey." She'd given up calling him. "But if he's not, we'll leave it in a place where he'll find it. Sometimes you have to do that with invitations."

"Oh. I really hope he's there."

"I do, too," Jordan managed.

"Me three! 'Cause he hasn't seen my scar yet!"

She made a left onto Piper's Road and only pressed lightly on the accelerator as she'd be making the next left into Hawk Hill.

Ahead, she caught of a flash of silver through the woods that bordered Hawk Hill's drive. She gripped the steering wheel and lifted her foot off the accelerator as she saw Owen's car brake and then turn right out of the driveway, coming toward them. She knew the instant he recognized her minivan by the sudden braking. Oh God, was he wishing he'd made a left rather than a right-hand turn?

Her heart beat painfully in her chest as the Audi neared and then rolled to a stop, the two cars idling side by side yet heading in opposite directions. Jordan prayed this wasn't some awful metaphor for their relationship.

When Owen lowered his window, her breath came out in a rush. She hadn't realized she'd been holding it.

They spoke simultaneously. "We were just coming to find you—"

"I had to see you—" They broke off awkwardly and she wondered whether she was going to start crying from frustration and tension.

Then Owen said, "Hawk Hill's closer. Go up to the house. I'll turn around."

She nodded, trying to tamp down the ridiculous joy she felt at the idea of his car following her back up the drive to Hawk Hill. She'd obviously gone mad.

"Mommy, Owen's behind us now!"

"That's right." If only he'd be *with* them . . . for always.

She'd already gotten out of the van when Owen turned off the Audi's engine. She busied herself with freeing the kids from their car seats, surreptitiously wiping her damp palms against the floral print of her sundress. Straightening, she turned, and Owen was there. For a second they stared at each other in silence.

The three days since she'd seen him felt like an eternity.

He looked wonderful in a crisp white shirt and light gray slacks. His face, with its still healing cut above his cheek so dear, she wanted to throw herself into his arms. But as she had no idea if he wanted her there, she drew a steadying breath.

"Hi. Max and Kate made you something."

The surprise in his face was echoed in his voice. "For me?"

She nodded and, swallowing the lump of emotion lodged in her throat, said to Kate. "Do you want to get down and show Owen what you made?"

Kate slid out from the van, holding the card in both her hands. Following her cue, Max and Olivia climbed down, too. All three were strangely solemn, even Olivia.

"This is for you, Owen. It's an invitation," Kate said, handing it to him.

His eyes moved over the invitation, taking in the drawing of a little girl on a pony in a riding ring, the band of pink glitter bordering the edge of the yellow construction paper, the painstakingly crafted letters saying, *To Owen, please come watch me ride at Crestview, from Kate.*

"Thank you, Kate." He had to pause to clear the hoarseness from his voice before continuing, "This is the prettiest invitation I've ever received."

"I made you one, too, Owen. Mommy's not sure I can ride in the lead-line in class 'cause of my arm, but maybe I can sit on your shoulders when Kate rides. That way I'll be able to see everything. Here, Owen." And he shoved his drawing at him. "See, I made a picture of you and me watching. Hey, you wanna see my scar? It's so long," he pronounced happily, lifting his cast above his head to show off the thin red line of flesh.

Owen bent down to look at it. "That's something all right. And I like your invitation, too."

Jordan wondered if she was the only one who noticed he hadn't accepted either of them.

"Hey, you've got a cut, too." Max pointed to his face. "Did you have to go to the hospital?"

"No, I was lucky."

He'd only had to go to the police station, she thought, feeling miserable.

"Max, why don't you get the ball from the car so the three of you can play on the lawn for a few minutes until it's time to go home?"

"You're going back?"

"It's getting late." Too late, she thought sadly.

"You don't want to come into the house? We finished all the touch-up painting. The rooms look great."

"I'm not sure Olivia and freshly painted walls are a good match." She tried to make her smile something more than sad. "Besides, they'll see it soon enough." She'd promised them that after the Open House she'd bring them over so they could go through it.

"Let's sit on the stoop. We can watch them from there."

She followed Owen over to the bluestone step and sat down beside him, aware of the space between their bodies. And though her gaze was trained on Kate and Max kicking the ball over the lawn, and on Olivia who was chasing it back and forth, her short legs pumping and curls bouncing, she knew that Owen was looking at her. She gripped the edge of the stone hard so as not to fling her arms about him and beg him to stay and love them, love her.

"Tim Mitchell asked me if he could come and look this place over. Before the Open House."

Everything in Jordan went still, except the painful beating of her heart. Quietly, carefully, she spoke. "And what have you decided? Are you willing to let him?"

"No. There's no bloody way Tim Mitchell is ever going to live in this house."

Her head whipped round. "What?"

His expression was fierce, nearly desperate. "You can't marry him, Jordan. I know I'm lousy parent material. It's a given I'll screw up—and just thinking that one day I might let Kate or Olivia get hurt the way I did Max shows what a selfish bastard I am. But I can't give you up. I don't know anything about being a husband or a father, but I know that no one will ever love you the way I do, damn it. If you'll just believe in me, Jordan, I'll prove it to you every day for the rest of our lives. Here."

He shoved his hand into his pocket and withdrew a small

black velvet box and pressed it into her hand. "Marry me, Jordan."

Her trembling fingers clutched the box without opening it. No ring could mean as much as the love shining in Owen's eyes. She threw her arms about his neck, kissing him as she whispered "Yes, yes" and "I love you" over and over again.

Their kisses lengthened and deepened as they clung to each other.

"Mommy! You and Owen are kissing!"

"Yes, that's right, Max." And she smiled because, although Owen had turned rather red, his arm was firmly anchored about her waist.

"Does that mean Owen's going to marry you, Mommy?"

"Yes, Kate. I've asked your mom to marry me."

"And I've said yes. Owen gave me a ring. Shall we look at it?" Her fingers found the seam and she lifted the lid to see a sapphire surrounded by tiny diamonds winking back at her. "It's beautiful," she breathed.

"The stone matches your eyes in the moonlight."

It was rather crowded with Max and Kate leaning in to peer at the ring, and of course Olivia had managed to climb onto Owen's lap, but somehow Owen managed to slip the ring onto her finger, saying, "I love you, Jordan."

"Does this mean we're going to have two daddies and two mommies?"

"Yes, Kate, it does. Is that okay with you?" Jordan asked.

She nodded slowly. "I'll make Owen an invitation so he can come to the school concert, too."

"Thank you, Kate," Owen managed to say in a voice thick with emotion. "I would like—" the rest of his sentence was left incomplete when Max tugged Owen's sleeve. "Yes?"

"Are we going to live here?"

Jordan looked at Owen and smiled. "Maybe. I think we'll have to discuss that as a family."

" 'Cause if we live here, Owen and I could build a tree house in that tree. A really big tree house."

Owen paled at the suggestion. Then taking a deep breath said, "Sure, we can build one, Max. And it's going to have really big, strong safety rails all around it."

"Neato! Come on, Kate, let's go see where our tree house is gonna be." And they tore off across the lawn.

Olivia stayed put, her sneakers firmly planted on Owen's now less-than-pristine trousers, her hands flattened against his cheeks as she stared into his face. Slowly, deliberately, she lifted one hand and squashed his nose.

For a second Owen hesitated. Then, with the beginnings of a grin, said, "Beep."

Olivia chortled with delight.

Her heart overflowing with love, Jordan kissed them both.

ACKNOWLEDGMENTS

I would like to take this opportunity to thank those who help ease the misery of this writer's life. I owe my family so much for their continued patience and good humor in putting up with the crabbiness and insecurity that unfortunately go hand in hand with my writing. More thanks go to my wonderful friend Marilyn Brant for her careful reading and wise comments. It's a brave soul who will wade through early drafts of my manuscripts. Finally, a huge thanks to the many readers who have written to me. Time and again, your enthusiasm and encouragement remind me what a joy it is to write.

Read on for an excerpt from

Trouble Me

Book Three of the Rosewood Trilogy

by
Laura Moore

Published by Ballantine Books

Chapter

ONE

JADE RADCLIFFE had her iPod plugged in and cranked. But while the Black Eyed Peas were doing a fine job of keeping her awake after so many hours on the road, her Porsche's windshield wipers weren't doing squat. Even set to high, they couldn't compete with the rain that was coming down in buckets. Route 95 had become a regular Slip 'N-Slide. While sliding over water-slickened surfaces was a favorite summer amusement of her nieces and nephews, Jade had been driving too many hours to be having any fun. Her initial "Wheees!" whenever the Porsche lost traction had turned into tired "Oh, shit"s.

The traffic had slowed to a crawl, making the driving marginally safer. But at this speed there was no way she was going to reach Rosewood tonight. When she'd left Ocala, Florida, before dawn, she'd been confident that she would reach Rosewood, her family's home in Virginia, by dinnertime. She'd badly wanted to see them all, Margot and Travis and their two kids—Georgiana, four, and Will, six months old now and thus starting to get interesting—-though Margot was so besotted she sent Jade daily email updates chronicling Will's achievements, with photo attachments. Just as she'd done for Georgie. Jade had probably been the only college student whose computer kept running out of storage space because she had so many e-photo albums of babies staring up at brightly colored mobiles or giving toothless grins in their high chairs.

The cute munchkins populating Rosewood didn't stop

there. Now there was also Jordan and Owen's baby boy, Edward, nicknamed Neddy, who was named after Ned Connolly. Having worked his entire life at Rosewood Farm, Ned was like family to Jade and her sisters; Owen and Jordan's gesture had made the old man nearly burst with pride and joy.

And when it came to being completely gaga over their new baby, Jordan and Owen rivaled Travis and Margot.

Earlier in the spring, Jade had gotten a video of Neddy taking his first steps, with Owen filming and narrating the clip. Owen was a pretty cool guy. Suave and sophisticated. But from the excitement in his voice, Neddy might just as well have been Neil Armstrong taking his first step for mankind rather than a baby tottering toward the outstretched arms of Olivia, his big sister half-sister, while the rest of them cheered him on.

Neddy would probably be fairly steady on his sneakers by now, she thought, and Kate, the oldest of the bunch from Jordan's first marriage, was showing in children's hunter classes and doing a really fine job on Doc Holliday.

Yeah, Jade definitely wanted to be back in the Radcliffe-Maher-Gage fold, insane though her sisters were sometimes. She'd missed everyone this summer while she was down in Ocala, but now, in addition to sporting her brand-spanking-new college dual degree in anthropology and education, she had earned from her training session in Florida the right to tout herself as a hunter/jumper trainer certified by the United States Hunter Jumper Association when she began spreading the word about the riding program she was starting at Rosewood.

Through the swish of her windshield wipers Jade saw the sudden bright flare of brake lights as the cars ahead of her went from a crawl to a stop, turning the highway into a long, thin, rain-drenched parking lot.

She sat, drumming her hands to Phoenix's "1901" and jiggling her legs against the leather bucket seat so that at least *something* was moving. Damn and double damn. The dashboard clock read 9:30 P.M. and she hadn't even reached Norfolk yet. There was no way she'd make it to Rosewood tonight. It wouldn't be right to show up on the doorstep at one A.M. and wake Margot and Travis. Moreover, if Margot heard she wanted to push on through in a storm this bad, she'd freak.

Perhaps she'd show Margot—and Jordan, as Jade knew Margot would get on the horn to her within minutes—how much she'd matured. Leagues removed from the Jade of yesteryear. And it was even all right to pick up her cell and speed dial, since the car hadn't moved an inch since she'd made her decision.

Margot answered on the second ring. "Jade? Where are you? God, it's pouring and the wind is picking up."

"It's pouring here, too. I'm stuck on 95 somewhere south of Norfolk—"

"Norfolk! That means you still have a good four hours of driving!"

More than that, Jade thought, since every car around her was going nowhere fast. A flash of lights in her rearview mirror alerted her to an ambulance coming up the breakdown lane. "There must be an accident up ahead. An ambulance just drove past. Listen, Margot, I'm going to get off at the next exit and find a place for the night. But I'll hit the road first thing, so make sure somebody does a Braverman's run. I've been dreaming of their cinnamon raisin bagels for the past two nights."

"Stopping for the night is a very good idea." Surprisingly, Margot didn't sound stunned speechless by Jade's announcement. "But, Jade, make sure it's a nice place and well lit."

"Got it. No Bates Motel for me."

"Ha. Very funny. You'll call as soon as you've checked in?"

"It might not be for a while yet."

"That's fine. And use the credit card on my account, sweetie. I want you to have a nice night."

"Norfolk Ritz, here I come."

"No need to get carried away," Margot replied with a laugh. "But you'll remember to call, right? I won't be able to sleep until I know you've found a place and are safe and sound."

"I'll call," Jade promised before hanging up.

As Jade's legal guardian, her older half-sister Margot had probably passed a lot of sleepless nights while Jade was off at college. She'd have passed a lot more of them if she'd known some of the things Jade had gotten up to on the weekends when she wasn't competing with the collegiate equestrian team. A good acre of wild oats had been sown.

But that was the old Jade, the one who sometimes felt the need to step right up to the edge and do something crazy with a wild, fiery lick of danger. But though she'd had her share of parties and experiences, it hadn't prevented her from getting straight A's, being the top scorer on her riding team, writing a very popular advice column for the school paper, and receiving highest honors on her B.A. thesis. Her topic: horse-dependent societies.

The four years of college parties and serial relationships— she liked the sex just fine, but her life was way too busy to bother with the guys afterward—were over. She was coming home with a plan she intended to execute with the precision of a military campaign. She was going to dispel her home-town's less than stellar memories of her by being the most model of model citizens. She was going to teach at War-burg's elementary school, train Rosewood Farm's horses, concentrate on building a young riders' program, and thus— with the possible exception of hiring a detective to uncover the identity of her mother's lover—live a life of complete respectability.

Obviously, the campaign to present a blemish-free image would be easier if she didn't have hiring a detective down on her to-do list. Unfortunately, discovering who the "TM" was that her mother had gushed about in her diary was an imperative. The need had sprung full-blown inside Jade the second she'd accidentally stumbled upon her mother's private journal in her half-sister Jordan's closet.

Like curious Pandora with her box, she'd opened the gaudy pink diary and, recognizing her mother's handwriting, started reading. Having entered Jordan's closet simply to borrow a sleeveless ratcatcher for an upcoming horse show, she left the closet with her perception of her mother forever altered. Damningly so.

She'd not only learned that her mother had been having an affair with someone she called "TM," she'd also learned from entry after entry the depths of her mother's resentment and dislike for her only child. According to her mother, she was endlessly spoiled and obnoxious, a drain that sucked all the energy out of her.

If Jade was the black hole in her life, this TM was her sun, the frigging life-affirming center of her universe.

It must have utterly destroyed Dad to read those words. And he had read them. Her sister Margot had been the one to stumble upon the diary first, finding it in a drawer in his office desk. Jade knew her dad well enough to realize that he'd have read the journal as obsessively as she, feeling more and more betrayed with each reading.

Jade despised whoever this TM was for getting involved with her mother. And since she now had access to the money her mother had left her, she saw no reason why she shouldn't use it to hire a private eye. Dad would approve, even if Margot and Jordan didn't. So the trick would be to make sure they never found out. . . .

Thank God, the traffic ahead had begun to move. She was actually going to get to shift into first gear and leave these dark thoughts behind.

Jade found a hotel outside of Norfolk. The place was ablaze with lights. No Bates Motel–like features about it. It occurred to her as she drove into the crammed parking lot that it might possibly be a bit *too* busy and, as she grabbed her duffel bag from the Porsche's trunk, she hoped there was a free room.

The rain was still coming down in heavy sheets. In the few minutes it took to shoulder her bag, double check that her car was locked, and sprint across the parking lot, she was soaked. Stepping into the lobby, she blinked, disoriented by the bright lights and colors after staring into silvery blackness for so long.

Several guests were huddled around the reception desk, asking questions about breakfast and airport shuttles and what might entertain the kids if it was too wet to go to the beach tomorrow, and God knows what else while she shivered slightly in the chill of the air-conditioning and left wet footprints on the plush maroon carpeting. Finally the last guest ambled happily toward the bank of elevators and she stepped up to the counter. Dropping her duffel bag and placing her ultra-sweet Prada hobo bag (a graduation present from Margot) on top of the wooden counter, she smiled at the black-jacketed man behind the counter.

"May I help you?"

The receptionist was in his mid-thirties and looked like he'd been on duty for a while, in other words, tired and harassed. He also wore a wedding ring. Deciding that he didn't look the type to hit on her, she gave him a friendly smile. "Yes, please. I'd like a room for the night."

"Do you have a reservation?"

"No, I'm afraid not."

He expelled a breath. "I'll have to check and see whether anything's available. We've had a crazy week, with two conferences going on. One ended yesterday, but we've just had a large wedding party arrive today."

"I really hope you have something. I've been on the road all day, driving up from Florida."

He looked up, his brows raised. "From Florida?"

Jade nodded. "From Ocala. I'm heading to Warburg. The rainstorm started somewhere in North Carolina, and then there was a pretty bad accident about twenty miles south of here. That's when I realized it might be smart to call it a night. I Googled hotels in the area and yours had the best reviews. I'd like to avoid getting back in the car if at all possible." Dragging her soaked hair from her face, she gave him another cheerful smile, as if she had no doubt that he'd do everything in his power to help her avoid that as well.

Margot and Jordan would never guess how much she'd picked up from them when it came to the art of sweet-talking. It definitely had its uses. Like now.

"Well, you're in luck. We do have a room. It has a king-size bed, water views."

She didn't give a fig about the view, since she'd be on her way to Rosewood at first light, but a big bed would be heaven after the lumpy twin bunk bed she'd been assigned in Ocala.

"That sounds perfect." Jade was already reaching into her bag. "Let me give you my credit card. Do you need my driver's license, too?"

"Yes, and the license plate number of your car, please."

As Jade waited for him to take down her information, the notes of a Rob Thomas song reached her. Turning her head toward the source, she saw couples wandering into a softly lit area.

"The bar looks nice."

The clerk nodded, his eyes still fixed on the computer. "It's got a dance floor, and Ray, our DJ, plays good music. On an evening like this, the guests really appreciate having a night spot they don't have to drive to. Plenty of Norfolk residents like to come here for a night of dancing. Here you go, Miss Radcliffe." He handed back her ID and credit cards. "And this is your electronic key. Your room number is 412. Take the elevator to the fourth floor and turn right down the hallway. The room will be on your right. Do you need help with your luggage?"

"No, thanks, I've got it."

He smiled. "Then have a good night."

"After nearly thirteen hours on the road, I'm going to sleep like a baby."